PRAISE FOR SEPTIMUS HEAP

Book One: MAGYK

"A quick-reading, stand-alone, deliciously spellbinding series opener."—*Kirkus Reviews* (starred review)

"Fun, mystery, and rollicking characters."—*VOYA* (starred review)

Book Two: FLYTE

"Terrifically entertaining. Fans of the first book will be delighted with this sequel to Septimus's story."—*VOYA* (starred review)

Book Three: PHYSIK

"Few fans of the bestselling Septimus Heap series will be disappointed by this excellent third adventure."—ALA *Booklist*

Book Four: QUESTE

"Vibrant storytelling and inventive flourishes."—ALA *Booklist*

Book Five: SYREN

"SYREN is Sage at her best."—*School Library Journal*

Book Six: DARKE

"As usual, the danger and the spellcasting alike seem vividly real and credible. A memorable, edge-of-the-seat escapade that will enthrall confirmed fans and newbies alike."—*Kirkus Reviews* (starred review)

"Sage proves again that she has an inventive feel for fantasy adventure."—ALA *Booklist*

"Sage has skillfully spun the most suspenseful installment yet in her series: Again she manages to combine lovable, creepy, and comic characters in a story that will leave her audience gasping in worry, then laughing at characters' antics. Sep's fans most certainly will not be disappointed with this heftiest volume yet."
—*VOYA* (starred review)

Also by Angie Sage

Septimus Heap, Book One: Magyk

Septimus Heap, Book Two: Flyte

Septimus Heap, Book Three: Physik

Septimus Heap, Book Four: Queste

Septimus Heap, Book Five: Syren

Septimus Heap, Book Six: Darke

Septimus Heap: The Magykal Papers

Araminta Spookie: My Haunted House

Araminta Spookie: The Sword in the Grotto

Araminta Spookie: Frognapped

Araminta Spookie: Vampire Brat

Araminta Spookie: Ghostsitters

SEPTIMUS HEAP

BOOK SEVEN

Fyre

ANGIE SAGE

ILLUSTRATIONS BY MARK ZUG

Katherine Tegen Books is an imprint of HarperCollins Publishers.
Septimus Heap is a registered trademark of HarperCollins Publishers.

www.harpercollinschildrens.com

Library of Congress Cataloging-in-Publication Data is available.
ISBN 978-0-06-124245-8 (trade bdg.) — ISBN 978-0-06-124246-5 (lib. bdg.)
ISBN 978-0-06-224697-4 (international edition)

Typography by Joel Tippie
18 19 CG/LSCH 10 9 8 7 6 5 4 3 2
❖
First Edition

For my father and mother,
thank you

⟴ CONTENTS ⬳

Prologue: Harbinger 1

1 • What Lies Beneath 16

2 • A White Wedding 31

3 • Puddles 44

4 • Migration 57

5 • The Great Chamber of Alchemie 73

6 • Listening 89

7 • False Trails 102

8 • Keeper's Cottage 119

9 • Triplets 135

10 • The Cloud Flask 148

11 • Dragon Fyre 159

12 • The Chamber of the Heart 175

13 • Welcome Back 190

14 • DisEnchantment 200

15 • The Last Day 215
16 • Missing 232
17 • Falling 242
18 • Transports 252
19 • What Might Have Been 264
20 • Witchery 279
21 • What Is to Be 293
22 • Relations 309
23 • The Alchemie Chimney 319
24 • Not a Good Morning 336
25 • The Stranger Chamber 345
26 • Bad Timing 355
27 • Mystery Reading 369
28 • Bait 385
29 • Doorstepping 396
30 • Port Palace 410
31 • Jenna's Journey 425
32 • Heaps versus Heaps 437
33 • Scorpion 447
34 • Smugglers' Bolt 462
35 • Sprung 475
36 • To the Castle 492

37 • Exits 503
38 • Dragons Away 519
39 • Intruders 537
40 • Keepers 544
41 • Deep Trouble 554
42 • Foryx 565
43 • Rocky Times 582
44 • Somewhere 594
45 • Flood 613
46 • Showdown 628
47 • Fyre 642
48 • A Queen 662
49 • An ExtraOrdinary Wizard 679
Endings 689

Fyre

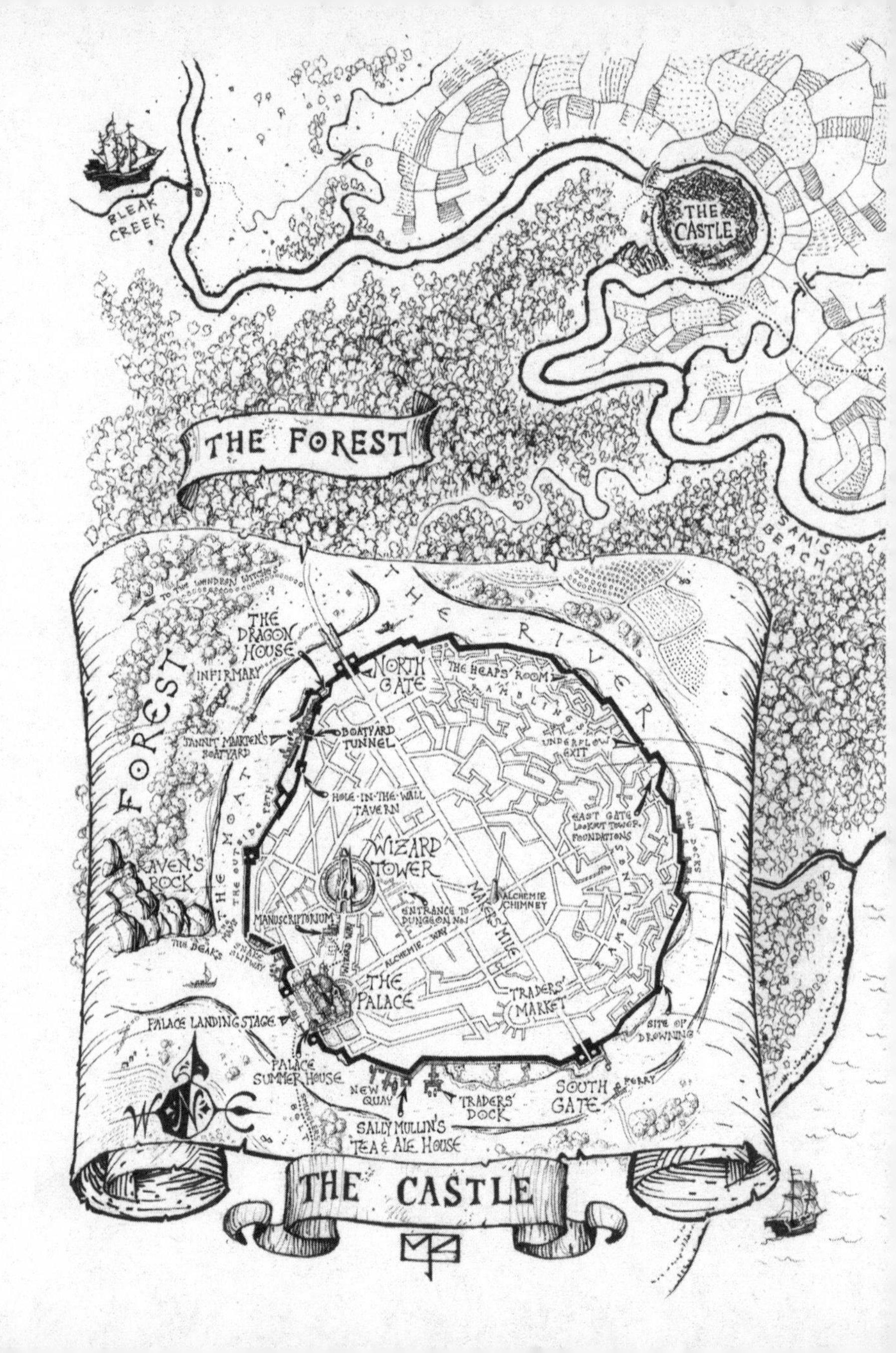
BLEAK CREEK
THE CASTLE
THE FOREST
SAM'S BEACH
THE RIVER
FOREST
TO THE WENDRON WITCHES
THE DRAGON HOUSE
INFIRMARY
NORTH GATE
THE HEAPS' ROOM
RAMBLINGS
BOATYARD TUNNEL
JANNIT MAARTEN'S BOATYARD
UNDERFLOW EXIT
HOLE-IN-THE-WALL TAVERN
THE MOAT
THE OUTSIDE PATH
EAST GATE LOOKOUT TOWER FOUNDATIONS
WIZARD TOWER
RAVEN'S ROCK
ALCHEMIE CHIMNEY
ENTRANCE TO DUNGEON No1
MAKERS' MILE
MANUSCRIPTORIUM
WIZARD WAY
ALCHEMIE WAY
RAMBLINGS
THE BEAKS
SNAKE SLIPWAY
THE PALACE
TRADERS' MARKET
SITE OF DROWNING
PALACE LANDING STAGE
PALACE SUMMER HOUSE
NEW QUAY
TRADERS' DOCK
SOUTH GATE
FERRY
SALLY MULLIN'S TEA & ALE HOUSE
THE CASTLE

TO THE BADLANDS
AND THE
BORDER MOUNTAINS
N
E
S
W
THE FARMLANDS
SMUGGLERS' BOLT
THE RIVER
SMUGGLERS REST
DEPPEN DITCH
MARRAM MARSHES
DRAGGEN ISLAND
MAD JACK'S HOVEL
THE PORT
THE DUNES
PORT PALACE

PROLOGUE: HARBINGER

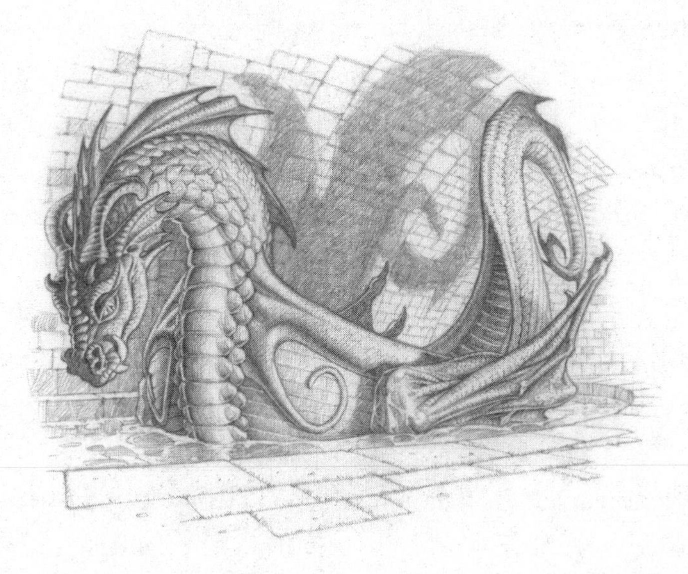

A *flame burns at midnight.* On an island in the wild Marram Marshes, a young woman holds up a lantern. Her long dark hair blows in the warm wind, salty from the sea; the lantern light glints off the gold circlet around her head and the golden edging to her long red robes—the robes of a Castle Queen.

The Queen is not alone. Beside her is an old man with long, wavy white hair held back with an ExtraOrdinary Wizard headband. He is resplendent in purple robes richly embroidered with **Magykal** symbols—this is the very first ExtraOrdinary Wizard, Hotep-Ra.

The island on which they stand is an ancient **Listening Place**, and Hotep-Ra is **Listening** carefully. As he stands statue-still, absorbed in something far away, his frown deepens. "It is as I feared," he whispers. "They have discovered me at last."

The Queen does not understand **Magyk**, but she respects it because it once saved her daughter's life. She nods sadly. She knows that this will take Hotep-Ra away from her forever.

A flame burns at half past midnight. The Queen and Hotep-Ra are underground, and the light from the lantern shows a smooth white wall covered in bright columns of hieroglyphs. The Queen is searching for a symbol. She soon finds it: a blue-and-gold circle enclosing a dragon. She places her hand on the circle and they wait. The Queen sees Hotep-Ra twist the ring on his right index finger: a delicate gold dragon with its tail in its mouth and a bright-green emerald for its eye. The ring is beautifully made, but the loveliest thing about it is the soft yellow light that comes from deep within and glows in the shadows of his hand.

And now, with a deep, slow rumble, the wall of hieroglyphs begins to move, rolling back to reveal a dark, wide space before them. The Queen smiles at Hotep-Ra. He returns her smile a little sadly and together they step forward.

The Queen holds up her lantern and its light illuminates a pair of brilliant white marble columns that rise up into the darkness. They walk between the columns, and progress slowly across the mosaic floor, bright with reds, yellows, whites and greens. And then they are there. The Queen hands her lantern to Hotep-Ra and he holds it high so that its light shines on the most beautiful creature he has ever seen: his faithful Dragon Boat.

The Dragon Boat's hull is broad and sturdy, built for the sea, and recently Hotep-Ra has gilded it. This—and the mast with its azure sail—is the inanimate part of the boat. The rest is living dragon. Tucked neatly alongside the hull are the dragon's wings, shimmering folds of green. Her head and neck are the prow and her tail is the stern. The half boat, half dragon lies in a deep sleep, alone in the darkness of an ancient underground temple, but she is awakened by the opening of the wall. Drowsily she raises her head, arching her neck upward like that of a swan. The Queen approaches the dragon quietly, careful not to alarm her. The dragon opens her eyes, she bows her head and the Queen loops her arms around the dragon's neck.

Hotep-Ra hangs back. He looks at his Dragon Boat, resting on the mosaic floor as if waiting for the water to rise and carry her away to distant lands. Indeed, that was what he had planned for her, to take her on the last journey of his old age. But now that his enemies have tracked him down, Hotep-Ra knows he must leave his Dragon Boat hidden safe below the ground, keeping her secrets from them. He sighs. The Dragon Boat must await the time when she will be needed by another Dragon Master. Hotep-Ra does not know who that will be, but he knows that one day he will meet him.

The Queen promises the Dragon Boat that she will return in a year to the day, but Hotep-Ra promises the Dragon Boat nothing. He pats the dragon's nose, then turns and walks quickly from the temple. The Queen runs after him and together they watch the wall of hieroglyphs rumble closed once more.

They walk slowly along the sandy passageway, which takes them to one of the hidden exits near the edge of the island. There, Hotep-Ra pulls off his Dragon Ring. To the Queen's amazement, he tosses the ring onto the sandy floor as if it were nothing to him. It lies on the floor, its light fading away.

"But that's *your ring*," whispers the Queen, shocked.

Hotep-Ra gives a weary smile. "Not anymore," he says.

The Queen and the ExtraOrdinary Wizard return to the Castle, but Hotep-Ra does not leave right away. He knows he is running the risk of drawing his enemies to all that he cares about, but there are things he wishes to do in order to make the Castle and its Queen as safe as he can.

Hotep-Ra **Engenders** protected Ways to allow the Queen to visit the Dragon Boat and other places that are special to her in safety. He fills his Wizard Tower with all the **Magykal** power he can spare and sets up a system of **Questes** for the brightest and best ExtraOrdinary Apprentices. That way he believes that he will still get news of the Castle and will be able to give advice if needed. He asks the Queen to visit his beloved Dragon Boat every MidSummer Day, and deep in the Castle wall he creates a Dragon House as a place for the

Dragon Boat to rest when one day it will be safe for her to come to the Castle.

But Hotep-Ra has stayed too long.

Forty-nine hours after he **Listened** to his enemies approaching, Hotep-Ra is on the Palace landing stage, saying farewell to the Queen. It is a dark and thunderous day, with a spattering of rain that mirrors the Queen's feelings about Hotep-Ra's departure.

Her barge lies ready to take him to the Port, where he has a ship waiting. As Hotep-Ra is about to step aboard there is a massive clap of thunder and the Queen screams. But she does not scream because of the thunder; she screams because of what she sees flying out from the black cloud overhead—two Masters of the **Darke** Arts, Warrior Wizards, Shamandrigger Saarn and Dramindonnor Naarn. The Wizards shoot down from the sky, a trail of darkness streaming from their robes, which spread out like ravens' wings, showing their iridescent blue-green armor beneath. Like two huge birds of prey the Wizards drop down, their piercing green eyes focused on their quarry below.

Hotep-Ra's enemies have found him.

The last time they found him, Hotep-Ra was saved by

the Dragon Boat, but now he knows he will have to face them alone. The Queen, however, has other ideas. From her belt she takes a tiny crossbow and loads it. And then, as Shamandrigger Saarn and Dramindonnor Naarn swoop in for what they think will be the kill, the Queen shoots the bolt.

It hits Dramindonnor just below the fourth rib on his left-hand side. He crashes to the ground, and the landing stage shudders with the force. But the **Darke** Wizard merely winces and as the blood gushes out, he **Seals** his heart. Meanwhile the Queen has reloaded her crossbow and is lining up the second bolt. Hotep-Ra panics; he knows the Queen has no idea what she is dealing with. He throws a **SafeShield** around the Queen—much to her disgust—but not before she has also shot Shamandrigger in the heart. The Warrior Wizard drops to the ground, but he too **Seals** the wound just in time.

The Wizards get to their feet, and the Queen is horrified to see they are huge—ten feet tall—and clasping the notorious **Volatile Wands** that Hotep-Ra has described to her. Like machines, in perfect time—*one-two, one-two*—they advance on the **SafeShield**. They speak one sentence between them.

"For this."

"We will."

"Kill you and."

"Your descendants."

"We will."

"Never."

"Forget."

Under the assault of the **Volatile Wands**, the Queen's **SafeShield** begins to fail. Hotep-Ra grasps his **Flyte Charm** and shoots up into the air, knowing that the Wizards will follow him.

And they do.

In these ancient days, the Art of **Flyte** is yet to be lost. But it is still unusual enough to bring the Castle below to a standstill, especially as it involves a fight between three powerful Wizards. But soon the spectators are racing for cover as **Thunderflashes** are thrown and the foundations of buildings begin to shake. The Castle people become anxious. Although many remember a time when there was no Wizard Tower or ExtraOrdinary Wizard, they have grown to like Hotep-Ra. He has been a good man and no problem has been too small for his **Magyk** to help. As they peer nervously from their windows, they become very worried. Two Wizards against one is not fair. And it looks like Hotep-Ra is getting the worst of it.

Hotep-Ra may be old and no longer strong, but he is still clever. He lures the **Darke** Wizards to the golden pyramid at the top of the Wizard Tower where he stands, delicately balanced on its very tip—a tiny silver square—concentrating all his **Magykal** power for one last chance.

To the **Darke** Wizards, Hotep-Ra looks like a wounded animal at bay. They sense victory and begin a favorite **Destruction**. They fly around the top of the pyramid, encircling Hotep-Ra in a blistering circle of **Fyre**. This, however, suits Hotep-Ra very well. He begins to chant a long and complex **Illusion Incantation**, the sound of which the roaring of the flames conveniently drowns.

But the circle of **Fyre** draws ever closer and the two **Darke** Wizards hover, waiting for the moment it will meet and finally **Hex** Hotep-Ra. Then they will have a little fun with their enemy—with the help of a spider or two.

Hotep-Ra is reaching the end of his **Incantation**. The heat of the **Fyre** is blistering; he can smell the wool of his robes singeing and he can wait no longer. To the shock of the **Darke** Wizards, Hotep-Ra shoots up through the circle of **Fyre**, trailing flames behind him. He shouts the last words of the **Illusion Incantation** and becomes **Invisible**.

The **Illusion** works perfectly. Shamandrigger Saarn and Dramindonnor Naarn stare at each other in horror—in place of his friend, each sees Hotep-Ra and draws the conclusion that Hotep-Ra has killed him. From within his **Invisibilty**, Hotep-Ra watches as, maddened with fury and grief, the **Darke** Wizards chase each other across the rooftops and head out from the Castle.

Hotep-Ra would like to leave them to their fate, but he knows he must make sure they do not return. As he flies off after the Wizards, Hotep-Ra hears a tremendous crash. He looks down to see the top of the golden pyramid buried point down in the Wizard Tower Courtyard below—the circle of **Fyre** has cut through it like a wire through butter.

Hotep-Ra tails the Warrior Wizards to Bleak Creek, where he watches them battle for a day and a night—so evenly matched that neither can gain any advantage. Finally, in a frenzy, they circle each other faster and faster, swooping low over the water until they create a deep, dark whirlpool just outside the mouth of the creek. The force of the whirlpool is so great that it drags the Wizards down with it, shrieking with rage as they go.

Hotep-Ra follows. Using the **Darke** Art of Suspension Under

Water (Hotep-Ra is a Master of many **Darke** arts, although he usually chooses not to use them) he dives in after the Wizards to make an end of them. But at the bottom of the whirlpool he finds that the vortex has broken through the riverbed and entered a cavern in the **Darke Halls**, which is an ancient refuge for all things evil. Hotep-Ra drags the Wizards from the entrance to the **Darke Halls**; the Wizards fight him all the way but desperation lends Hotep-Ra strength. With his last remnants of energy he hauls the Wizards up to the surface and, like a cork from a bottle, he emerges from the depths, dragging the **Darke** Wizards with him.

The Queen's barge is waiting for him. She has followed him to Bleak Creek, and now the barge's rowers are circling while the Queen stands at the prow, anxiously staring at the vortex: she knows that Hotep-Ra is somewhere beneath the water. But when he surfaces, the Queen is horrified—all she can see are the two **Darke** Wizards.

Hotep-Ra is now too weak to sustain his **Magyk**. First his **Illusion** and then his **Invisibility** slip away. Shamandrigger Saarn and Dramindonnor Naarn see each other for the first time in twenty-four hours—and then they see Hotep-Ra floundering beside them. For a few long seconds all three

Wizards stare at one another, shocked. Clutching the **Flyte Charm**, Hotep-Ra rises up from the water. Saarn and Naarn grab on to his robes and a tangle of Wizards lands on the Queen's barge.

The Queen knows that Hotep-Ra is too weak to win the fight. She takes off the **Magykal** gold ring he has given her to protect her from her enemies—a ring that may only be destroyed in pure Alchemical **Fyre**. "**Commit** them," she says, handing him the ring. "Quick!"

"It is your ring," Hotep-Ra whispers, handing the ring back to her. "You must say the **Committal**. You do remember?"

The Queen nods—of course she remembers. How could she forget something made especially for her? (It is, in fact, the only **Magyk** that the Queen does remember.)

The Queen begins to chant the **Committal**. The words roll over the **Darke** Wizards like the shadow of an eclipse; they struggle but they are too weak to fight back. Hotep-Ra listens anxiously to each word but he does not need to worry—when a Queen wishes to remember something, she remembers it. At last the Queen reaches the **Keystone** word, "Hathor." There is a blinding flash of purple light and the Queen throws the ring into it. Darkness falls. The Queen speaks the last seven words of her **Incantation** and at the last word, **"Commit,"** Time itself is suspended. For seven long seconds the world stands still.

From within the blackness come two roars of anguish, like the sound of wounded beasts. A great howl of a hurricane descends on them, the screeching of the wind drowning out the screams of the Ring Wizards, and hurls the Queen and Hotep-Ra to the deck. The wind circles three times and then it is gone, leaving the Queen's barge in tatters, the rowers prostrate with terror, and an unearthly silence, which is broken by a delicate *plink*. A gold ring with two green faces imprisoned in it tumbles to the deck and rolls into a pool of dirty water.

When Hotep-Ra returns to the Wizard Tower his old Apprentice, Talmar Ray Bell, tells him that the fallen top of the pyramid has shrunk. She does not know why.

But Hotep-Ra knows why. He knows he has narrowly escaped a most dreaded **Darke Hex**. A **Hex** that does not kill an opponent right away but reduces his size so that he becomes prey to the most terrifying creatures of all: insects. It is an ancient **Darke** pastime, to place a victim of such a **Hex** into a spider's web and watch the result through an **Enlarging Glass**. Hotep-Ra shudders. He has a fear of spiders.

The tiny top of the golden pyramid lies on the bottom of a large pyramid-shaped crater—a sparkle of gold on the red Castle earth, still shrinking. An anxious group of Wizards are guarding it. (The reputation of the Wizard Tower has spread and it now houses thirteen Ordinary Wizards.) Talmar Ray Bell clambers down into the crater, picks up the miniature golden pyramid and gives it to Hotep-Ra.

Hotep-Ra puts a **Stop** on the **Hex**. The little pyramid sits heavy in his hand, a fiery gold, glinting in the sun. Hotep-Ra smiles. "You will be the **Keye**," he tells the pyramid.

Once again Hotep-Ra is on the Palace landing stage, saying a sad farewell to the Queen. This time he is not alone. Talmar Ray Bell has insisted on coming with him—Hotep-Ra is so weakened by his fight with the **Darke** Wizards that Talmar fears he will not be able to make the journey on his own.

Hotep-Ra gives the Queen a farewell gift. It is a little book called *The Queen Rules*. It is bound in soft red leather with gold corners and an intricate clasp, and on it is embossed a drawing of the Dragon Boat. It is not his fault that a thousand or so years later the binding falls to pieces, the pages drop out and the **Committal** is lost. No bookbinder, not even a **Magykal** one, can make a book last forever. But memories will last, if they are handed down through the generations.

Hotep-Ra takes the Queen's barge to the Port. There, a ship is waiting for him and they set sail. The sea is calm and the sun shines. Hotep-Ra spends most of his time on deck, storing up memories of the open air and sea breezes to tide him over the long enclosed times ahead in his final resting place—the House of Foryx.

Night falls and the ship approaches the **Enchanted**—and much feared—Isles of Syren. Hotep-Ra sees the **Lights** shining from the four cat-shaped lighthouses that surround the Isles. He waits until the ship is safely past and all but he have gone below to sleep. Then, by the light of the full moon, Hotep-Ra drops the Two-Faced Ring into the ocean. As it tumbles down through the water, moonlight glints on the gold and an ugly cowfish snaps it up.

And there begins the long journey of the Two-Faced Ring back to the Wizard Tower. Where it now lies. Waiting.

I
What Lies Beneath

In the *Vaults of the* Manuscriptorium, *The Live Plan of What Lies Beneath* was unrolled on a large table. Lit by a bright lantern that hung above the table, the large and fragile sheet of opalescent **Magykal** paper lay weighted down by standard Manuscriptorium paperweights—squares of lead backed with blue felt. *The Live Plan of What Lies Beneath* was a map of all the Ice Tunnels that ran below the Castle—apart from the section that traveled out to the Isles of Syren. As its name suggested, the *Live Plan* was a little more than just a plan. **Magykally**, it showed what was happening in the Ice Tunnels at that very moment.

Gathered around it were the new Chief Hermetic Scribe, O. Beetle Beetle; Romilly Badger, the Inspection Clerk; and Partridge, the new Scribe of Maps. If you had walked into the Vaults at that moment it would not have been clear who actually was the Chief Hermetic Scribe. Beetle's long blue-and-gold coat of office had been banished to a nearby hook because its gold-banded sleeves scratched the delicate *Live Plan* and he was wearing his comfortable old Admiral's jacket, which kept out the chill of the Vaults. With his dark hair flopping forward over his eyes, Beetle looked very much at home as he leaned over the *Live Plan*, concentrating hard.

Suddenly Romilly—a slight girl with light brown hair and what Partridge thought was a cute, goofy smile—squeaked with excitement. A faint luminous splodge was moving along a wide tunnel below the Palace.

"Well spotted," said Beetle. "Ice Wraiths are not easy to see. I reckon that's Moaning Hilda."

"There's another one!" Romilly was on a roll. "Ooh . . . and look, what's that?" Her finger stabbed at a tiny shadow near the old Great Chamber of Alchemie and Physik.

Partridge was impressed. There was a minuscule blip at the end of Romilly's finger. "Is that an Ice Wraith too?" he asked.

Beetle peered closer. "No, it's too shadowy. And slow. Look—it is hardly moving at all compared to Moaning Hilda, who is way over there now. And it is too well defined; you can see it actually has a shape."

Romilly was puzzled. "Like a person, you mean?"

"Yes," said Beetle. "Just like a—*bother*!"

"It's gone," said Romilly sadly. "That's a shame. It can't have been a person then, can it? Someone can't suddenly disappear. It must have been a ghost."

Beetle shook his head; it was too solid for a ghost. But the *Live Plan* was telling him that all the Ice Tunnel hatches remained **Sealed**, so there was nowhere the person could have gone. Only a ghost could disappear from the middle of an Ice Tunnel like that.

"Weird," he said. "I could have sworn that was human."

It was human—a human named Marcellus Pye.

Marcellus Pye, recently reinstated Castle Alchemist, had just dropped down through a hatch at the bottom of an unmapped shaft, which went close enough to an Ice Tunnel to show on the *Live Plan*. As soon as he was through the hatch Marcellus knew he was safe—the *Live Plan* did not show anything lower than this level.

A pole with foot-bars led down from the hatch and Marcellus climbed down it with his eyes closed. He reached a flimsy metal platform and stood, not daring to open his eyes, not believing that after nearly five hundred years he was *back in the Chamber of Fyre.*

However, Marcellus did not need to open his eyes to know where he was. A familiar metallic sweetness that found its way to the back of his tongue told him he was back home, and brought with it a flood of memories—the tear that had run up from the base of the Cauldron, the sharp *crack* of the splitting **Fyre** rods and the heat of the **Fyre** as it spun out of control. Swarms of Drummins working ceaselessly, trying to contain the damage. The smell of burning rock as the flames spread beneath the Castle, setting the old timber houses alight. The panic, the fear as the Castle threatened to become a raging inferno. Marcellus remembered it all. He prepared himself for a scene of terrible devastation, took a deep breath and decided to open his eyes on the count of three.

One . . . two . . . three!

A jolt of surprise ran through him—*it was as if nothing had happened*. Marcellus had expected black soot to cover everything, but there was none—quite the reverse. Illuminated by the neatly placed **Fyre** Globes, which still burned with their everlasting flames, the metal platform shone. Marcellus picked up a **Fyre** Globe, cupping it in his hands. Marcellus smiled. The flame inside the ball licked against the glass where his hands touched it, like a faithful dog welcoming its owner home. He replaced the ball beside his foot and his smile faded. He was indeed home, but he was home alone. No Drummin could have survived.

Marcellus knew that he must now look over the edge of the dizzyingly high platform on which he was standing. This was when he would know the worst. As he gingerly walked forward, he felt the whole structure perform a slight shimmy. A feeling of panic shot up through his feet—Marcellus knew exactly how far he had to fall.

Nervously he peered over the edge.

Far below lay the great **Fyre** Cauldron, its mouth a perfect circle of blackness ringed by a necklace of **Fyre** Globes. Marcellus was immensely relieved—*the* ***Fyre*** *Cauldron was* *intact.* He stared down into the depths, allowing his eyes to become accustomed to the dark.

Soon he began to make out more details. He saw the metal tracery that was embedded in the rock and covered the cavern like a huge spider's web gleaming with a dull silver shine. He saw the peppering of dark circles in the rock that marked the entrance to the hundreds, maybe thousands, of Drummin burrows. He saw the familiar patterns of **Fyre** Globes that marked out paths of the walkways strung across the cavern hundreds of feet below and, best of all, he could now see inside the Cauldron the graphite glitter of one hundred and thirty nine stars—the ends of the **Fyre** rods that stood upright like fat little pens in an inkpot.

Marcellus shook his head in utter amazement. He had found his **Fyre** Chamber cleaned, repaired, neatly put in mothballs and, by the look of it, ready to go. The Drummins must have survived much longer than he had realized. They had worked so hard and *he had never even known*. Something caught in his throat; he swallowed hard and wiped his eyes. Suddenly Marcellus experienced what he called a Time Slip—a flashback to all those years ago, when he had been standing on the very spot where he was now.

His loyal Drummins are swarming around him. Julius Pike, ExtraOrdinary Wizard and one-time friend, is on the upper platform, yelling above the roar of the flames, "Marcellus. I am closing this down!"

"Julius, please. Just a few hours more," he is begging. "We can control the **Fyre**. *I know we can." Beside him on the platform old Duglius Drummin is saying, "ExtraOrdinary, we Drummins do guarantee it, we do."*

But Julius Pike doesn't even recognize a Drummin as a living thing. He completely ignores Duglius. "You have had your chance," Julius yells. "I am **Sealing** *the water tunnels and* **Freezing** *them. It is over, Marcellus."*

He is dragged toward the hatch by a bunch of thickset Wizards. He grabs hold of Duglius, determined to save at least one Drummin. But Duglius looks him in the eye and says sternly, "Alchemist, put me down. My work is not done."

The last thing he sees as the hatch slams shut is the old Drummin sadly returning his gaze—Duglius knows this is the end.

After that, Marcellus had cared no more. He had handed Julius his Alchemie **Keye**; he had even helped to **Seal** the Great Chamber of Alchemie and done nothing more than shrug halfheartedly when Julius, smiling the kind of smile a pike would if it could, had told him that all memories of the Chamber of **Fyre** would be expunged. *"Forever, Marcellus. It shall never be spoken of again. And in the future, no one will know what is here. No one. All records will be destroyed."*

Marcellus shook himself out of the memory and the distant echoes of the past faded. He told himself that all were long gone. Even the redoubtable Julius Pike was now no more than a ghost, said to have gone back to where he grew up—a farm near the Port. But he, Marcellus Pye, was still here, and he had work to do. He had the **Fyre** to start and the Two-Faced Ring to destroy.

Marcellus swung himself onto the metal ladder that led down from the upper platform and cautiously began the descent into the **Fyre** Chamber—or the Deeps, as the Drummins had called it. The ladder shook with each step as Marcellus headed doggedly downward toward a wide platform far below from which yet more **Fyre** Globes winked up at him. Some ten long minutes later, he set foot on what was known as the Viewing Station, and stopped to take stock.

Marcellus was now level with the top of the **Fyre** Cauldron. He peered down at the star-shaped tops of the **Fyre** rods glistening with the dull shine that undamaged **Fyre** rods possessed. The last time he had seen them they were on fire, disintegrating before his eyes and now . . . Marcellus shook his head in admiration. How had the Drummins done it?

A narrow walkway known as the Inspection Circle ran around the rim of the Cauldron. It was made of metal lattice, which Marcellus could see had been repaired where it had buckled in the heat. Very carefully, he stepped down onto it, holding tight to the guardrails on either side. From his tool belt he took a small hammer, known as a drummer, and clasping it tightly he set off. Every few paces he stopped and tapped the metal rim of the **Fyre** Cauldron, listening intently. To his ears it appeared to be sound, although he knew his hearing was nowhere near as acute as it needed to be for the job.

This was what the Drummins had done all day, all night, all the time. They had swarmed over the Cauldron, drum, drum, drumming with their tiny hammers, listening to the sounds of the metal, understanding everything it told them. Marcellus knew he was a poor substitute for a Drummin but he did the best he could. After walking the Inspection Circle, he returned to the Viewing Station, knowing that he could put off no longer the thing he had been dreading the most. He must go down to the floor of the Chamber of **Fyre**.

A flight of curved metal steps wound their way around the belly of the Cauldron down into the dimness below, which was lit by a few scattered **Fyre** Globes. Slowly, Marcellus descended into the depths and the smell of damp earth came up to meet him. On the bottom step, he stopped, gathering the courage to step onto the ground. Marcellus was convinced that the cavern floor must be strewn with the remains of the Drummins and he could not bear the thought of crunching their delicate little bones like eggshells underfoot.

It was some minutes before Marcellus stepped off. To his relief there was no sickening crunch. He took another step—on tiptoe—then another, and felt nothing below his feet but bare earth. Carefully, Marcellus tiptoed around the base of the Cauldron, tapping it with his hammer, listening, then moving on. Not once did he tread on anything remotely crunchy. He supposed that the delicate bones had already turned to dust. After a circuit of the underside of the Cauldron, Marcellus knew that all was well.

It was now time to begin the **Fyre**.

Back on the Viewing Station, Marcellus headed off along another frighteningly flimsy walkway that was strung out across the cavern, thirty feet up. He walked cautiously, glad of the light from a corresponding line of **Fyre** Globes placed on the ground. At last he arrived at a chamber burrowed into the rock face at the back of the cavern and stepped inside. He was back in his old control room.

Below the coating of hundreds of years' worth of dust, Marcellus could see that the walls had been repainted white and everything shone—there was no sign of the greasy soot that had covered everything. Marcellus walked across to the far wall where, beside a line of iron levers, there was a large brass wheel set into the rock. Taking a deep breath, Marcellus grasped the wheel. It moved easily. As he slowly turned it, Marcellus could feel the slip and slide, the *clunk* and the *thunk* of the chain of command, which reached up through the rock into the depths of the UnderFlow. Somewhere far above him a sluice gate opened. A great gurgle echoed around the sooty darkness of Alchemie Quay and the sluggish waters began to move. Marcellus felt the rumble inside the rock face of the tumbling water as it poured through ancient channels and began to fill the reservoir deep within the cavern walls.

Now Marcellus turned his attention to a bank of twenty-one small wheels farther along. Once the **Fyre** was begun, he must have a way of getting rid of excess heat. In the old days the heat had been dispersed through what were now the Ice Tunnels and used to warm the older buildings of the Castle. Marcellus had given the current ExtraOrdinary Wizard, Marcia Overstrand, his word that he would preserve the Ice Tunnels. This meant he needed to open up the secondary venting system—a network of pores that snaked up to the surface of the Castle.

Marcellus dared not risk discovery yet. He needed precious time to set the **Fyre** going, time to prove that it was not a danger to the Castle. Although Marcia had agreed that he could start up the **Fyre**, Marcellus knew that she assumed that the **Fyre** was the small furnace in the Great Chamber of Alchemie and Physik. Indeed, that was what he had led Marcia to think. Julius Pike had told Marcellus that he would make sure that no ExtraOrdinary Wizard would *ever* give permission to open up the Chamber of **Fyre** again—and Marcellus had believed him.

And so now Marcellus turned his attention to the little brass wheels that would open heat vents scattered throughout the Castle and wick excess heat safely away from the awakening **Fyre**. Marcellus had given this some thought—the trick was to open vents in places where the unusual heat could be explained away as something else. He took a rumpled piece of paper from his pocket and consulted a list. Counting carefully along, he spun nine selected wheels until they stopped. Marcellus checked his paper again, checked the wheels and stood back satisfied.

By now a red pointer on a dial was telling him that the reservoir was nearly full; Marcellus turned the wheel to close the sluice gate, rechecked his list and left the control room. Job done.

Two hours later, the water was flowing through the Cauldron and the **Fyre** was beginning the slow, gentle process of coming alive once again. Wearily, Marcellus pushed his Alchemie **Keye** into the dip on the lower **Fyre** hatch. He remembered the time, when they were both growing old, that Julius had come to see him. He had given Marcellus back the Alchemie **Keye** because, "*I trust you, Marcellus. I know you will not use it.*" And he hadn't.

Well, not until now.

Romilly and Partridge had long gone back to work, but in the Vaults, Beetle still watched the *Live Plan*—he knew that what goes down must come up. Beetle's stomach rumbled and as if on cue, Foxy, Chief Charm Scribe, poked his head around the half-open door. Beetle looked up.

Marcellus climbed through the lower **Fyre** *hatch. Once again, he was a blip on* The Live Plan of What Lies Beneath.

"Ta-da!" said Foxy. "Sausage sandwich!" He put a neatly wrapped package beside Beetle's candle. It smelled wonderful.

Marcellus closed the lower **Fyre** *hatch and began to climb—fast.*

"Thanks, Foxy," said Beetle. He looked back at the plan but his eyes, tired after so much staring, did not focus well enough to see the Marcellus blip. He glanced at the sausage sandwich longingly. He had no idea he was so hungry.

"I'll unwrap it for you," said Foxy. "You don't want sticky stuff on the *Live Plan*."

Beetle peered at the plan once more.

"Seen something?" asked Foxy.

"Yeah—I think . . ." Beetle pointed to the Marcellus blip.

Foxy leaned forward and his beaky nose cast a shadow over the blip.

Marcellus reached the upper **Fyre** *hatch.*

"Shove over, Foxy," said Beetle, irritated. "You're blocking the light."

"Oh. Sorry."

Beetle looked up. "Sorry, Foxo. Didn't mean to snap. Thanks for the sandwich."

*Marcellus was through the upper **Fyre** hatch and off the* Live Plan.

Beetle bit into his sausage sandwich.

And down in the Deeps, the **Fyre** began to wake.

2
A White Wedding

T*he Big Freeze had come* in, covering the Castle in a deep blanket of snow.

On a sunny late afternoon in the breathtakingly still air, pencil-thin columns of smoke rose from a thousand chimneys up into the sky. Along Wizard Way a crowd had gathered to watch a wedding procession walk from the Great Arch to the Palace. As the procession passed by, people from the crowd dropped in behind and followed, chattering about the young couple who had just gotten married in the Great Hall of the Wizard Tower: Simon and Lucy Heap.

Simon Heap, with his curly straw-colored hair neatly tied back in a ponytail, wore new blue robes—which, as the son of an Ordinary Wizard, he was entitled to do on his wedding day. The freshly dyed blue was bright and trimmed with traditional white wedding ribbons, which trailed behind him. Lucy Heap (née Gringe) was wearing a long, white, floaty woolen dress, which she had knitted herself and edged with pink fur. She had lovingly embroidered entwined blue and pink letters "S" and "L" across the skirt. Her mother had objected to this, saying it was bad taste, and for once in matters of taste Mrs. Gringe was probably right. But it was Lucy's Big Day and what Lucy wanted to do, Lucy was going to do. *No change there, then,* her brother, Rupert, had remarked.

The wedding party progressed down Wizard Way toward the Palace, crunching through newly fallen snow. The sky was a brilliant winter blue, but a small snow cloud directly above obligingly provided a few fat snowflakes, which floated down and landed on Lucy's beribboned long brown hair, where they settled like confetti. Lucy and Simon were laughing and talking happily to each other, Lucy twirling in the snow to show off her dress and sharing a joke with her new brothers.

Next to Lucy walked her own brother, Rupert, and his girlfriend, Maggie. Simon had considerably more companions: his adoptive sister, Princess Jenna, and his six brothers, including the four Forest Heaps: Sam, twins Edd and Erik, and Jo-Jo.

Mrs. Theodora Gringe, mother of the bride, walked right behind her daughter, occasionally treading on Lucy's train in her eagerness to be at the front. When they had emerged from the Great Arch, Mrs. Gringe had had to be restrained from actually leading the wedding party down Wizard Way. Lucy's mother was the proudest mother of the bride that the Castle had seen for a long time. Who would have imagined, thought Theodora Gringe, that the guests at her daughter's wedding would have included the great dignitaries of the Castle? The ExtraOrdinary Wizard, the Princess and the Chief Hermetic Scribe, and even that weird Alchemist fellow: they were all here. There was no doubt about it—the Gringes were on the way up.

But it was a shame, she thought, about the Heaps. They were a disreputable-looking bunch, and there were so *many* of them. Everywhere she looked she saw the distinctive curly straw-colored Heap hair topping a scruffy-looking individual. The Gringes were massively outnumbered.

A shout of laughter drew Theodora Gringe's attention to a group of four noisy men who reminded her of Silas Heap and who, she supposed (correctly), were his brothers. Mrs. Gringe grimaced and cast her critical eye over the Heaps she recognized. She grudgingly admitted to herself that Silas and Sarah looked smart enough in their blue and white wedding clothes—if a little eccentric with Sarah carrying that ridiculous duck-in-a-bag. Mrs. Gringe eyed up the duck: ready-plucked, perfect for a stew. Deciding to suggest that to Sarah later, she scrutinized the Heap boys with mixed feelings. The two youngest, Nicko and Septimus, weren't too bad.

Septimus in particular looked rather fine in his impressive formal Apprentice robes with the long purple ribbons dangling from his the sleeves. He was taller than Mrs. Gringe remembered and she noticed that his typical Heap hair had actually been combed. She didn't approve of Nicko's sailor's braids wound through his hair, although she supposed that his sober navy-blue boatyard tunic with its rather fetching sailor's collar was acceptable.

But at the sight of the remaining Heaps, Theodora Gringe's mouth puckered in distaste. The four Forest boys were a *disgrace.* She tutted as she watched Sam, Edd, Erik and Jo-Jo straggle along beside the bridegroom like—she searched for the right words—yes, that was it, like a pack of wolverines. At least they could have had the decency to keep to the back.

(While the wedding party had been in the Wizard Tower Courtyard, Mrs. Gringe had tried to push the Forest boys to the back. A struggle had ensued and her husband, Gringe, had had to drag her off. "Let it be, Theodora," he'd hissed. "They are Lucy's brothers now." Mrs. Gringe had felt quite faint at the thought. She had had to take a long look at their trophy guest, Madam Marcia Overstrand, ExtraOrdinary Wizard, to get over it—which had been a little embarrassing as Marcia had asked her, rather sharply, if there was something wrong.)

Mortified by the memory, Mrs. Gringe sighed and then realized that she had been overtaken by the crowd. Happily unaware that the tall, pointy felt triangle perched on top of her hat gave onlookers the impression that a shark was cruising through the wedding party, stalking the bride, Mrs. Gringe began to elbow her way back up to the front.

At last they reached the Palace Gate. The onlookers clustered around, offering congratulations, gifts and good wishes.

Lucy and Simon accepted them all, laughing, exclaiming, handing the gifts to various friends and relations to carry for them.

Sarah Heap linked her arm through Silas's and smiled at him. She felt unbelievably happy. For the first time since the day Septimus had been born, she had all her boys with her. It seemed as though a heavy weight had been lifted from her shoulders—in fact right then Sarah felt so light that she would not have been surprised if she had looked down and seen her feet floating a few inches above the pavement. She watched her gaggle of Forest boys, all young men now, laughing and joking with Simon as though he had never been away. ("Away" was the word Sarah used to describe Simon's **Darke** years.) She saw Septimus, confident in his Apprentice robes, talking with her little Jenna, who looked so tall and Queenly now. But best of all, Sarah saw her oldest son's eyes—bright green once more—shining with happiness as he looked around, no longer an outcast, back where he belonged. In the Castle. With his family.

Simon could hardly believe it himself. He was stunned at all the good wishes and the feeling that people actually seemed to *like* him. Not so long ago, when he had lived below the ground in a **Darke** place, he'd had dreams just like this. But he would wake from them in the middle of the night, distraught when he realized they were only dreams. Now, to his amazement, they had come true.

The crowd continued to grow and it looked as if Simon and Lucy were going to be at the Palace Gate for a while yet. On the edge of the crowd, Marcia Overstrand cut an imposing figure. She was wearing ceremonial ExtraOrdinary Wizard robes of embroidered purple silk lined with the softest, highly expensive Marshmouse fur. From below the robes two pointy shoes made of purple python skin peeked out into the white snow. Marcia's dark wavy hair was held back in a formal gold ExtraOrdinary Wizard headband, which glinted impressively in the winter sunlight. Marcia looked impressive—but prickly. Her green eyes found Septimus and she beckoned irritably to her Apprentice. Septimus excused himself from Jenna and hurried over to Marcia. He had promised Sarah that he would "make sure Marcia didn't take over," and he could see the warning signs.

"Septimus, have you seen that mess?" Marcia demanded.

Septimus followed the direction of Marcia's pointing finger, although he knew exactly what she was talking about. At the end of Ceremonial Way—which led straight up from the Palace Gate—a tall column of scaffolding covered with a brilliant blue tarpaulin reared up, garish against the snow. Around it were scattered untidy piles of bricks and a clutter of builders' equipment.

"Yes," Septimus replied—not very helpfully, in Marcia's opinion.

"It's Marcellus, isn't it? What is he doing starting already?"

Septimus shrugged. He didn't see why Marcia was asking him, especially as Marcia still hadn't set a date for him to begin his month with Marcellus. "Why don't you ask *him*?" he said.

Marcia looked a little guilty. "Well, I promised your mother when she came to see me that there would be no . . . er, arguments."

"Mum came to see *you*?" asked Septimus, surprised.

Marcia sighed. "Yes. She brought me the guest list and said that if there was anyone on it I didn't like, she would quite understand if I didn't come. Naturally I said that *of course* I was coming to Simon's wedding and it didn't matter at all who was there. She didn't look convinced, I must say. I ended up promising her that I would be, well"—Marcia pulled a face—"*nice* to everyone."

"Wow." Septimus glanced across at Sarah Heap with new respect.

"Apprentice! Marcia!" Marcellus Pye's voice caught their attention. Marcellus had escaped the clutches of Mrs. Gringe and was desperate to talk to someone—even Marcia. "Well, well," he said jovially. "You both look very splendid."

"Not quite as splendid as you do, Marcellus," said Marcia, eyeing the Alchemist's new set of black robes, the sleeves of which were slashed to show the red velvet shirt he was wearing underneath. Both cloak and tunic were liberally sprinkled with gold fastenings that glittered in the sunlight. Septimus could tell that Marcellus had made a big effort. His dark hair was freshly cut in a short bob and brushed forward over his forehead in the old-fashioned style that the Alchemist still favored on special occasions, and he was wearing his favorite pair of red shoes—the ones that Septimus had given him for his birthday two years previously. Marcia noticed the shoes and tutted. They still gave her an uncomfortable twinge of jealousy of which she was not proud.

Marcia waved her arm in the direction of the tarpaulin. "I see you have already begun," she said, a little disapprovingly. She forced herself to refrain from adding that Marcellus had agreed not to begin building the chimney until the Great Chamber of Alchemie had been reopened.

Septimus saw Marcellus give a guilty start. "Goodness! What, um, makes you say that?"

"Well, I should have thought it was obvious—that rubbish at the end of Ceremonial Way."

Septimus saw a look of relief fly across Marcellus's face. "Ah. The *chimney*," he said. "I'm merely making preparations. I know you do not wish to keep the Two-Faced Ring for longer than necessary. Keeping that ring safe must be a nightmare."

As she had promised Sarah, Marcia made an effort. "Yes, it is. But at least we have it, Marcellus. Thanks to you."

Septimus looked impressed. His mother had done a remarkable job, he thought.

Marcellus felt encouraged. He decided to ask a favor. "I wonder, Marcia, if you would object to a change of name?"

Marcia was flummoxed. "I am perfectly happy with Marcia," she said.

"No, no—I mean the Ceremonial Way. In the old days when the Great Chamber was operating and we had the chimney at the end of it—as we soon will again—it used to be called Alchemie Way. I wonder if you would allow it to resume its old name?"

"Oh," said Marcia. "Well, I suppose so. It was called Alchemie Way before so it is only right that it is Alchemie Way once more."

"Thank you!" Marcellus beamed. "And soon Alchemie Way will lead to the newly built Alchemie Chimney." He sighed. "Well, it will when the builders bother to turn up." A sudden outbreak of cheering and clapping signaled that the wedding party was beginning to head off to the Palace. Marcellus slipped away before Marcia had a chance to ask any more awkward questions.

Marcia felt dismal. An evening spent with a mixture of Heaps and Gringes did not figure anywhere on her good-nights-out list—not even at the very bottom. She glanced back longingly toward the Wizard Tower, wondering if she could make a run for it.

Septimus intercepted her glance. "You can't leave *now*. That would be very rude," he told her sternly.

"Of course I'm not leaving now," Marcia said tartly. "Whatever gave you that idea?"

* * *

The wedding supper carried on late into the night. Heaps and Gringes did not always mix well and there were a few tricky moments, particularly when Mrs. Gringe put the duck stew suggestion to Sarah Heap. But nothing, not even Mrs. Gringe's insistence that *it would be no trouble at all to take the duck home, and seeing as it was nice and plump it would do enough for everyone and she could bring the stew over the next day to save Sarah the bother of cooking* could dent Sarah's happiness for long. She had all her children with her for the first time *ever*, and that was enough for her.

Marcia was surprised to find that her evening was not as bad as she had feared. After some very tedious speeches by various increasingly merry Heap uncles, a welcome distraction appeared. Through the long windows of the Ballroom, which reached to the floor and looked out across the Palace lawns down to the river, a barge ablaze with lights was seen drawing up at the Palace landing stage.

"Goodness, who can that be?" Marcia commented to Jenna, who was sitting next to her.

Jenna knew who it was. "It's my father. Late as usual."

"Oh, how nice," said Marcia. And then, hurriedly, "Not

nice that he is late, of course. Nice that he has made it to the wedding."

"Just about," said Jenna.

Silas and the four Heap uncles, glad of an excuse to escape, went to inspect the barge and escort Milo back to the wedding supper. He arrived resplendent in what some people thought was the dress uniform of an Admiral of the Fleet and others were sure they had seen in the window of a fancy dress shop in the Port—but whatever it was he was wearing, Milo caused a stir. He strode up to the bride, bowed, kissed her hand and presented her with a tiny ship of gold in a crystal bottle, much to Lucy's delight. Then he congratulated Simon and took his seat next to Jenna.

It was not long before Jenna made an excuse to go and talk to the Forest Heaps at the far end of the table. Milo then took Jenna's place next to Marcia and from that moment Marcia found the evening was much improved. So much so that she stayed rather longer than she had planned.

3
PUDDLES

It *was nearly two o'clock* in the morning when Marcia made her way toward the Palace Gate across the well-trodden snow. A cold wind zipped in off the river and she pulled her winter purple cloak, lined with indigo blue fur, tightly around her. Her companion, the Chief Hermetic Scribe, did the same with his thick dark blue cloak. They made an impressive pair as they strode across the snow, cloaks fluttering in the wind. The new Chief Hermetic Scribe was now very nearly as tall as the ExtraOrdinary Wizard. Marcia was convinced that Beetle had grown since he had been **Inducted** as Chief Hermetic Scribe—or maybe, she thought, he now stood up straight and held his head high. Either way, Beetle could easily look Marcia in the eye, as he was doing right then.

"I'd like your advice," he was saying. "There's one not too far out of your way, if you wouldn't mind taking a look."

Septimus was spending the night at the Palace and Marcia was only too happy to put off the moment she returned to her rooms alone, to the ghost of Jillie Djinn, the previous Chief Hermetic Scribe, sitting mournfully on her sofa. "Beetle," she said. "I'd be glad to."

As they walked out of the Palace Gate together, Marcia thought how this conversation would never have happened with the late (and little lamented) Jillie Djinn. She realized how much easier, how much more pleasant and, yes, how much *safer* it felt to have someone she liked and understood as Chief Hermetic Scribe. She turned and smiled at Beetle. "So glad the **Pick** got it right this time," she said.

"Oh!" Beetle blushed. "Well, thank you."

The pair walked up the middle of the newly named Alchemie Way, making fresh footprints on the snow. The Way stretched out before them, empty, wide and lit only by the brightness of the snow reflecting the moonlight. Near the Palace it was particularly desolate. Here once was the Young Army Barracks, now boarded up and falling into ruin. Beetle and Marcia hurried by and the army buildings soon gave way to large houses, which were equally run-down and, at that time of night, dark and quiet. Many of the houses had boarded-up shopfronts on the ground floor. These were shops that had once serviced the thriving industry generated by the Great Chamber of Alchemie. But after the Great Chamber was closed down, the life went out of Alchemie Way and it had become an empty, windswept place—only to be briefly revived as the drilling ground for the Young Army and a venue for the lavish processions and displays that the Supreme Custodian enjoyed holding.

Beetle found it eerie and sad. He was pleased when a lantern hanging from a post showed the entrance to Saarson's Scurry, the alley he was looking for. The Scurry, as it was commonly known, was much more cheerful. It was clearly occupied by sociable night owls: a hum of conversation and the merry *clink* of glasses drifted out of the tiny but well-kept houses. Lighted candles in the windows reflected off the snow and lit their path. A short distance into the alley, Beetle came to a halt by a puddle of water lying incongruously in the snow. Marcia crouched down and dipped her finger in the water. She looked anxiously up at Beetle. "How many of these did you say there were?"

"There are eight that I know about."

Marcia made a teeth-sucking noise. "And you think they are all—what did you call them . . . vents?"

Beetle nodded. "Yes. Apparently it's a system of cooling."

"Really? What does it cool?"

"Well, that's the thing," said Beetle. "I don't know. Romilly Badger found an old plan and—" A movement caught his eye. He looked around and saw three amazed faces at a window, staring out at the sight of the Chief Hermetic Scribe and the ExtraOrdinary Wizard inspecting a puddle outside their front door. "Best if I tell you as we go, I think."

"Oh?"

Beetle nodded toward the window.

"Ah." To the shock of the onlookers, Marcia—still buzzing from the excitement of the evening—gave them a cheery wave. Then she put her arm around Beetle's shoulders and said, in a manner reminiscent of Milo Banda, "Righty-ho, Beetle. Fire away."

As they wandered along the snowy alleyways, heading toward Wizard Way, Beetle began to explain.

"Frankly, Marcia, the Manuscriptorium is in a real mess and we don't know where half the stuff is. I decided to recatalogue everything, and last week I began with the Vaults. I was shocked. There are piles of paper all over the floor and in the tunnel section there's a stack of stuff that's been left to rot in a pool of water, which even Ephaniah says he can't fix."

"It must be bad," said Marcia. Ephaniah Grebe was the Manuscriptorium's Conservation Scribe, who was known to be able to restore pretty much anything.

"It is," said Beetle. "We have lost an awful lot of information about what's beneath the Castle. Anyway, I started with the Ice Tunnel shelves and I got Romilly Badger—she's the Inspection Clerk—to help because I wanted her to understand as much as possible about them. You wouldn't believe it, but she hadn't even been given a proper map."

"Unfortunately, I *would* believe it," said Marcia.

"Yes. Well. So, after she had cleared the shelves Romilly

found a scrunched-up piece of paper wedged down the back of one of them. It was black with soot and very fragile, and I couldn't shake off the feeling that it was important. Luckily Ephaniah said he could fix that one."

"And how *is* Ephaniah?" asked Marcia.

"He's getting stronger now. Still gets nightmares, I think."

"That, unfortunately, is to be expected," said Marcia.

They had reached Terry Tarsal's shoe shop and Marcia stopped a moment to peer through the door and see what was on the shelves inside. Something rocked under her feet.

"Careful!" said Beetle. "There's another one!"

Marcia leaped nimbly onto firmer ground. "At least Terry's had the sense to put something over it," she said, poking the wobbly piece of wood with her foot. "That makes nine, then. Tell me, Beetle, what *is* on this bit of paper?"

They set off along Footpad Passage toward the bright lights of Wizard Way and Beetle began to explain. "At first I thought it was a drawing of a spider's web, but then Romilly pointed out that it fit the shape of the Castle. So Ephaniah floated it in the **Enhancing Tray** to see if he could get anything else to show up. And it did. A very faint map of the Castle appeared and *then* we saw the title."

"Which was?" asked Marcia.

"Vents: Cauldron cooling system."

"*Cauldron* cooling—is this some kind of witch thing?"

"I don't think it is. It is far too technical to be a witch thing and besides, they don't really write stuff down, do they?"

"True," said Marcia.

"Romilly pointed out that there were lots of breaks in the web and they all ended in a dot—as if someone had rested the pen on the paper for just a little too long. And we noticed that all the dots were in quiet alleyways. It was intriguing. So Romilly and I went out hunting, to see if there was anything visible aboveground."

"And was there?" asked Marcia.

Beetle sighed. "No. It was the day after the Big Freeze came in and the snow had covered everything. At the time I thought that was really bad luck and that we'd have to wait until the thaw. But then last week Foxy came into work soaking wet and said he'd fallen into a puddle. Well, we all laughed—how could he possibly have fallen into a puddle with everything frozen solid? But Foxy got really annoyed and insisted on taking me to see the puddle."

"I'd have thought a Chief Hermetic Scribe had better

things to do than go and see a *puddle*, Beetle," Marcia teased.

"Yeah. Well, it was either go and see the puddle or no more sausage sandwiches. Not from Foxy. Ever."

"Ah. I see."

"To my amazement there *was* a puddle. So sausage sandwiches were on me that day. The next day I heard about another one from Partridge and then another and another. It felt like all the scribes were at it, finding puddles. I got Partridge to draw a map of where they were and I had a weird idea. I superimposed it on the Vent web. And every puddle matched the dot at the end of a line. *Every single one.*"

"Well, well, well," said Marcia.

They had reached Bott's Cloaks, which proudly proclaimed above the door: WIZARD CLOAKS: OLD AND NEW, GREEN AND BLUE. PERFECT, PRELOVED CLOAKS ARE OUR SPECIALITY. Bott's Cloaks was a large and normally rather exuberant shop opposite the Manuscriptorium, but now it was sadly subdued because its proprietor, Bertie Bott, was missing, presumed eaten. Mrs. Bott had draped the usual garish statues in black cloth, and a solitary candle burned in the window.

"Poor Bertie." Marcia sighed and gazed at the window. "I feel responsible. If I hadn't insisted on him being on guard . . ."

"But *someone* had to be on guard," said Beetle. "If it hadn't been Bertie it would have been another Wizard. And it wasn't *you* that killed him. It was—well, actually, it was Merrin."

"No," said Marcia. "It was the **Darke**. Merrin was its tool, just as Simon was. The **Darke** finds people's weaknesses and exploits them."

"I guess so," said Beetle. The talk of the **Darke** had made Beetle a little spooked and the thought of the empty Manuscriptorium was not inviting. Even though it was late, he said, "Ephaniah is doing a final **Enhance** on the Vent diagram tonight. He thought he saw the shadow of some handwriting and he's going to have a closer look. I know it's late, but would you like to come and take a look?"

"Most definitely," Marcia said without hesitation. The thought of the ghost of Jillie Djinn staring at her empty-eyed when she came home was no more inviting for Marcia than the Manuscriptorium was for Beetle.

Down in the quiet, still whiteness of the Conservation basement, a bulky shape swathed in white robes was holding a transparent tray up to the light. Ephaniah Grebe, half man, half rat, turned to Marcia and Beetle. The lower half of

Ephaniah's face was, like his body, swathed in white. The shape beneath the silk wraps betrayed its ratness but his human brown eyes sparkled behind his spectacles as he gave a thumbs-up sign. Ephaniah put the tray down on the workbench and pushed a small white card across to Beetle and Marcia. It said: MILK, NO SUGAR, PLEASE.

"Huh?" said Beetle, puzzled.

Ephaniah made a sound that could have been a rat-laugh. He turned the card over. It now said: THE ENHANCEMENT IS COMPLETE.

Beetle and Marcia peered at the now thick and shiny piece of white paper lying in front of them. Ephaniah's long, narrow ratlike finger traced some faint handwriting that was scrawled across the foot of the drawing like an afterthought. Marcia drew out her **Enhancing Glass** and offered it to Beetle.

Beetle shook his head. "No, you first."

Marcia held the **Glass** close to the writing and peered intently. She tutted to herself as she read, then handed the **Glass** to Beetle. When he had finished reading, she said, "What did *you* think it said?"

"Julius FYI, M. Is that what you thought?"

"It is. Who was Julius Fyi, I wonder? Unusual name."

"It's not a name," said Beetle. "It's an old-fashioned abbreviation: For Your Information. No one uses it anymore."

"I see. So, how old do you think this paper is, Ephaniah?" asked Marcia.

Ephaniah flicked through his number cards and placed "475" in front of Marcia.

"Days? Weeks? Months?"

Ephaniah flipped a card from his calendar box: YEARS.

"Aha! Now that makes sense," said Marcia.

"Is does?" asked Beetle.

"Well, not all of it. But Julius must be Julius Pike, who was ExtraOrdinary Wizard at that time. And I'd bet the Wizard Tower to a wine gum that I know who the M is."

"Marcellus?" offered Beetle.

"Indeed. Our very own newly reinstated Castle Alchemist. Beetle, he *has* to have something to do with these puddles." Marcia turned to Ephaniah, who was rifling through his cards. "Thank you so much, Ephaniah," she said.

Ephaniah's eyes wrinkled with a smile. He placed a grubby card in front of her. IT HAS BEEN MY PLEASURE.

Beetle and Marcia headed back up to the Manuscriptorium.

They walked through the empty room, its tall desks like dark sentries as the night candles burned down. Beetle pulled open the flimsy door that led into the Front Office; the moonlight from the snowy Way outside shone in, sending sharp shadows across the boxes of papers and reconditioned **Charms** waiting for collection in the morning. Beetle followed Marcia through the pattern of light and dark and as she reached the main door she stopped and said:

"I shall call Marcellus up to the Wizard Tower first thing tomorrow. I shall require an explanation."

Beetle was not sure. "I think we should wait for a while and see what happens. I don't expect Marcellus will admit to anything."

Marcia sighed. "No, I don't suppose he will."

Beetle risked a joke. "No one likes to be accused of making puddles everywhere."

To Beetle's surprise, Marcia giggled. "Especially not when you have made a map of where they all are." She pulled open the door and stepped out into the snow. "I will allow Septimus to begin his month with Marcellus tomorrow—that way I can keep a close eye on what that man is up to. We will keep this under review. Let me know if any more puddles appear. Thank you, Beetle."

With that, Marcia closed the door and Beetle heard the sound of her pointy python shoes crunching away through the snow. They sounded kind of lonely, he thought.

⁜ 4 ⁜
MIGRATION

Number One, Snake Slipway.

From the desk of Marcellus Pye, Castle Alchemist.

Dear Marcia,

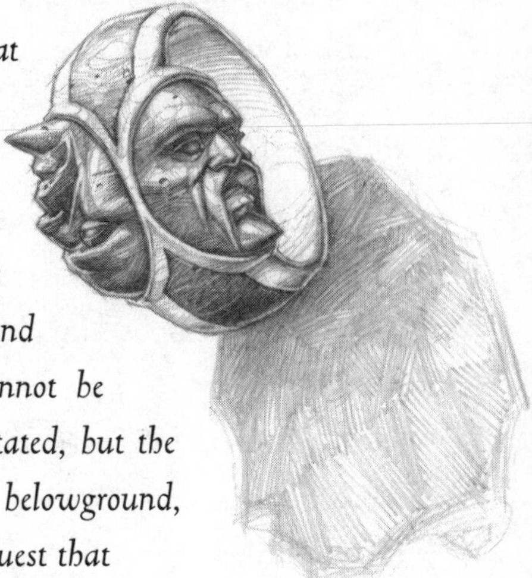

Work has now begun on the Great Chimney and I suggest that, with a view to **DeNaturing** *the Two-Faced Ring as soon as possible, we consider opening the Great Chamber of Alchemie and Physik. Of course, the* **Fyre** *cannot be started until the chimney is reinstated, but the sooner we get going on the work belowground, the better. To this end I would request that*

~~*my Apprentice*~~ *Septimus commence his month working with me as soon as* ~~*possible*~~ *is convenient.*

Yours,

Marcellus

Marcia read the letter while she drank her second cup of breakfast coffee. She handed it to Septimus, who was finishing his porridge. "Well," she said, "how about going to Marcellus today?"

Septimus had been looking forward to the break in routine. He was doing the advanced analytical **DeCyphering** module of his course and was finding it very tedious. "Might as well," he said, not wishing to appear too eager and hurt Marcia's feelings.

"Off you go and pack, then," Marcia said briskly.

"Okeydokey."

Marcia watched Septimus jump up from his chair and scoot out of the kitchen. She was not looking forward to the next four weeks without him.

Up in his room, Septimus was having trouble closing his backpack.

"Toothbrush?"

He looked up and saw Marcia's head peering around the doorway. "Yes," he grunted. "*And* my comb. Just like you said."

Marcia's gaze wandered around Septimus's room. It was not big—Apprentices' rooms in the Wizard Tower were always small—but it was, she was pleased to see, well organized and businesslike. The shelves were stacked with labeled boxes and papers from Septimus's various **Magykal** projects and assignments; they also boasted a line of small lapis pots (a MidWinter Feast gift from her), which contained his slowly growing collection of **Charms** and **Talismans**. There was a large, shiny black desk under the window with six legs, which Septimus called "the insect," on which were perched a pot of pens and stack of unused paper. Marcia avoided looking at the desk; with its spindly, hairy legs and its shiny, flat black top it put her in mind of a giant cockroach. Instead she glanced up at the dark blue ceiling with the constellations that Septimus had painted when he first arrived. The silver stars were still bright and they shone in the sunlight that was pouring through the window.

Marcia suppressed a sigh. She really was going to miss Septimus. Her gaze alighted on a folded pile of green woolen cloth with a telltale purple flash peeping out from it. "You've forgotten your spare Apprentice robes," she said. "It's the new set that arrived this morning. I ordered them specially."

"Well, no. I haven't forgotten," Septimus said a little awkwardly. He pulled the last backpack buckle closed and heaved the pack onto the floor, where it landed with a hefty *thud*.

Marcia jumped. Septimus was getting very big and clumsy, she thought. Everything he did sounded so loud. "I suppose you don't have room," she said. "I'll send a Wizard over with them later."

"Actually," Septimus said, "I won't be needing them."

Marcia sighed. "You cannot possibly wear the same robes for a whole month, Septimus."

"No. I know, so—"

"So I'll send them over."

"Marcia, no. I won't need them. I . . . I'll be wearing my Alchemie Apprentice robes."

Marcia nearly choked. "You'll be wearing *what*?"

"My Alchemie robes. You did agree that I would be Marcellus's Apprentice for a whole month."

"I agreed to no such thing," spluttered Marcia. "I agreed to send *my* Apprentice to help him for one month, and that is an entirely different matter altogether. And during that month you will remain my Apprentice, Septimus. You will *not* be an Alchemie Apprentice."

"That's not how Marcellus sees it," muttered Septimus.

"I don't give a brass baboon how Marcellus sees it," snapped Marcia. "I shall send the spare robes over later. And I expect you to wear them."

Septimus suppressed a sigh. He wished Marcia and Marcellus would stop fighting over him. "I thought you might say that," he said.

Half an hour later, Septimus was perched on the old oak chest by the purple front door waiting for Marcia. In the past he would have found something interesting to read and sprawled comfortably on the squashy purple sofa while Marcia finished fussing about in her study, but now the dumpy ghost of Miss Jillie Djinn, the ex-Chief Hermetic Scribe, occupied Marcia's once much-loved sofa. Jillie Djinn had, unfortunately, died on Marcia's sofa a few months previously. And because ghosts must remain for a year and day in the place where they entered ghosthood, Marcia had nine long months of Jillie Djinn's company still to go before the ghost was free to move on.

As a new ghost, Jillie Djinn was a bright figure: her dark blue robes had a crisp outline and the expression on her round face was easy to see—she looked annoyed, as though she were about to tell someone off. To Septimus and Marcia's relief, Jillie Djinn had not yet spoken, although she was now reacting to what went on around her and had even managed to get rid of her recent companion on the sofa—Septimus's jinnee, Jim Knee. One evening Jim Knee, who had been hibernating there, had suddenly got up and sleepwalked off to the spare bedroom, where he now lay snoring.

Jillie Djinn's dark little eyes stared unblinkingly at Septimus. It was most disconcerting and it had not occurred to him before that ghosts do not need to blink. He was relieved when Marcia appeared.

"Ready?" she asked.

"Yep." Septimus picked up his backpack.

Marcia glared at Jillie Djinn. "Come along, Septimus, let's get out of here."

Marcia and Septimus stood silently on the silver spiral stairs as they gently revolved, taking them down through the Wizard Tower. Septimus breathed in the scent of **Magyk**, which was stronger than usual due to the extra energy being expended keeping the Two-Faced Ring secure in the **Sealed Cell**. Down and down the stairs took them, past each floor where the **Magykal** business of the day went purposefully on as the ExtraOrdinary Wizard and her Apprentice glided quietly by.

As they stepped off the stairs onto the soft floor of the Great Hall, Marcia—loath to give up tutor mode just yet—stopped and said, "You haven't seen the **Sealed Cell**, have you?"

"No, I haven't."

"Time you did, I think. The Two-Faced Ring is due a check before we go."

The long tunnel that led to the **Sealed Cell** was reached through the **Seal** lobby—a small room behind the spiral stairs. Outside the lobby, two Wizards were on guard. Marcia was taking no chances.

Inside the **Seal** lobby the atmosphere was hushed. The silver-walled room was suffused with **Magykal** purple light that shone from the **Seal** covering the door to the tunnel. Its polished silver walls and rounded corners were designed to confuse any entities or Live Spells that might escape—it certainly confused Septimus. When he walked in, he had the odd experience of seeing about five or six most peculiarly shaped versions of himself come in. And when Marcia closed the door behind them, it felt as though he were in the middle of a purple bubble.

Inside the lobby, a Wizard stood staring at the **Seal** to the tunnel, watching for any changes that would indicate a disturbance on the other side. **Seal Watch** was a boring task requiring little skill but a lot of concentration, and it was not a popular duty. A rotation of half-hourly shifts was kept, which used up a lot of Wizards every twenty-four hours.

Marcia approached the watcher. "I have come to do an inspection. If you would like to stand aside, please?"

There was nothing that Thomasinn Tremayne, the **Seal Watch** Wizard, would have liked better. She stepped to one side and shook her head. The flickering lights made her feel nauseous and gave her a thumping headache. It was a horrible job.

"I am taking my Apprentice with me to inspect the **Sealed Cell**," Marcia said in a low voice. "You are to remain on guard. If we do not exit within ten minutes I authorize you, for security, to **ReSeal** the door."

Septimus glanced at Marcia in surprise. That seemed a

little drastic, he thought.

"Very well, Madam Marcia," whispered Thomasinn. And then, "Shall I watch your backpack, Apprentice?"

"Oh—thank you." Septimus shrugged off his backpack and it fell to the floor.

"Ouch!" gasped Thomasinn. "My *foot!*"

"Shhh!" shushed Marcia.

"Oh, gosh. I'm so sorry," Septimus apologized.

"Really, Thomasinn, it's only a little backpack," said Marcia. "Come along, Septimus."

Marcia held her hands out about an inch above the shimmering **Seal**, concentrating hard. Suddenly, she pushed her hands through and pulled them rapidly apart, unzipping the **Seal** as she did so, to reveal a narrow silver door.

Marcia pushed the door open and squeezed through, "Come on, Septimus. Quickly."

Septimus slipped inside and Marcia closed the door with a soft *ker-lunk*. She pressed her hand onto its smooth surface and a temporary **Seal** flashed across like purple lightning. Then she took a lamp from a hook beside the door, **Lit** it and set off. Septimus followed. Lamp held high, Marcia walked along the sloping brick-lined tunnel that snaked down to the **Sealed Cell**, which was buried in the bedrock below the Wizard Tower. They walked quickly, the sound of their footsteps absorbed by the thin clouds of **Magyk** hanging around the tunnel. Every seven yards, Septimus saw a small door set into the tunnel wall, beyond which he knew was a chamber used for storing all manner of potentially troublesome objects. Septimus was excited. He knew how the **Sealed Cell** worked and he had even, in the first year of his Apprenticeship, made a small model of it, but he had never actually been to the end of the tunnel and seen it—let alone been inside.

The **Sealed Cell** was the most secure place in the Wizard Tower. It was used for imprisoning the most dangerous and powerful **Magykal** objects, entities, **Spells** and **Charms**. Its last occupant had been Septimus's jinnee, Jim Knee, securely confined until he had agreed to do Marcia's bidding. But now it was the Two-Faced Ring that languished behind the tiny door to the **Sealed Cell** at the very end of the tunnel.

For more effective use of the **Sealing Magyk**, this door was only three feet high and even narrower than the entrance door. Not all previous ExtraOrdinary Wizards had actually been able to fit through it—DomDaniel himself had once got stuck, much to his then-Apprentice's amusement (a memory that Alther still cherished). What the door lacked in height and width, it made up for in thickness. It was, like the great doors into the Wizard Tower, made from solid silver, which shone through the misty purple haze of the **Seal** that encased the door.

Marcia placed her lamp on a small shelf beside the door; then she put her hand into the purple and with a deft flick of her wrist she broke the **Seal**. She took three small silver keys from her ExtraOrdinary Wizard belt and placed them in three keyholes: one at the top of the door, one at the foot and one in the middle. Marcia turned the middle key and Septimus heard three old-fashioned barrel locks rotate in unison. The door swung open with a small squeak.

Marcia lifted off the long pair of **Protected** forceps (known as the Bargepoles) that hung on a hook beside the door, picked up her lamp and squeezed through the narrow opening into the cell. Septimus quickly followed.

With the door closed the lamplight turned the dark space—which was lined in two-inch-thick solid silver—into a sparkling, shining jewel. But its brilliance did not disguise the fact that the **Sealed Cell** was tiny. Septimus felt sorry for Jim Knee, although it was, he supposed, better than the inside of a silver bottle. In fact, it felt not unlike being inside a very big silver bottle, for the shining walls were molded to the rounded contours of the end of the tunnel.

Set into the curved wall was a wide shelf, in the middle of which was the container that held the Two-Faced Ring: the **Bound** Box. It was a small black box made of layers of ebony interleaved with silver and secured with silver bands. Holding the Bargepoles in front of her, Marcia advanced upon the box rather as one might approach a small but deadly snake. Suddenly she gasped and said a very rude word. "Oops. Shouldn't have said that. Look at this, Septimus."

Septimus peered over Marcia's shoulder. Erupting through the **Bound** Box like a nasty green boil was the Two-Faced Ring. Marcia pounced. Striking at the ring like a mongoose, she stabbed the Bargepoles into the boil-on-the-box and held them up triumphantly.

"Got it!"

At the end of Marcia's forceps the Two-Faced Ring glittered angrily, its evil green faces glaring at them. Septimus looked away. He felt as though the faces could actually see him.

"I'm glad they're not real," he said with a shiver. The **Sealed Cell**'s peculiar echo whispered his words back to him.

Real real real.

Marcia flipped open the box and dropped the ring back in. Septimus imagined he could hear a stream of curses as the metal hit the wood. Marcia slammed the lid closed and began securing the bands around the box.

"They will be soon at this rate," she said grimly. "Marcellus will have to get a move on."

Move on move on move on.

Septimus was shocked. "You mean those two Wizards might actually come to life?"

Life life life.

Marcia put her fingers to her lips to shush him. She muttered a new **Lock** for the box. "Let's go," she said.

Go go go.

Septimus was more than happy to agree. He clambered out and waited for Marcia while she backed awkwardly out the narrow doorway, then slammed the door shut with a satisfying *thunk* and hung up the Bargepoles.

Back in the lobby, Marcia looked quite pale. "Madam Marcia, are you all right?" asked Thomasinn.

Marcia nodded. "Fine." But her hands were trembling as she **Sealed** the door to the tunnel.

Marcia was angry with herself. She realized she had delayed opening the Great Chamber of Alchemie dangerously long. Like all Wizards, Marcia had sworn an oath at her induction to "abjure all things Alchemical" and she took it seriously. It had been a difficult decision to allow Marcellus to light the **Fyre** once more in order to **DeNature** the Two-Faced Ring, and even though she knew it was the only way to destroy the ring, the lighting of the **Fyre** frightened her and she had hesitated to begin. It was a huge step for a Wizard to take and before the Chamber was opened, Marcia had wanted to understand what she was doing. However, the more she tried to find out about the **Fyre**, the less she understood. Nothing quite made sense. So many documents were missing, so much seemed to have been altered and she had been left with an unsettling impression that something was missing—something *big*. But now, whatever her fears, Marcia knew she could wait no longer.

Septimus shouldered his backpack and walked across the Great Hall with Marcia. "Did you mean that about the two Wizards?" he asked. "Could they really come back to life?"

Marcia sighed. "It is a possibility, that is all. The **Darke Domaine** has theoretically given it the power, which is why we are keeping it so securely."

"So . . . could it happen soon?"

"No, no, Septimus. These things take years."

Septimus felt relieved. "Marcellus won't take *that* long to get the **Fyre** going," he said.

Hildegarde Pigeon—sub-Wizard, but soon to be an Ordinary Wizard—stepped out from the porters' cupboard.

"Still on door duty, Hildegarde?" asked Marcia. "I thought you were up at **Search** and Rescue now."

Hildegard smiled. "Next month, Madam Marcia. But I enjoy it here. I have a letter for you. Mr. Banda left it this morning."

"Did he? Well, thank you, Hildegarde." Septimus thought Marcia went a little pink.

Hildegarde Pigeon handed an impressive envelope with a red-and-gold border to Marcia. Septimus noticed Hildegarde's delicate blue lace gloves. Hildegarde was self-conscious about her fingertips, which had been damaged when the **Thing InHabiting** her had chewed them. They reminded Septimus how destructive the **Darke** was—and how important it was to get rid of the Two-Faced Ring.

The huge silver doors to the Wizard Tower had swung

open. Marcia was dallying on the top step, reading Milo's note. Septimus was impatient to be off.

"Come on, Marcia," he said.

"Yes, yes. In a moment."

Septimus set off down the steps. Marcia put the letter carefully in her pocket and followed. "It shouldn't take too long to open a dusty old door to a chamber," she said.

Septimus waited for Marcia at the foot of the steps. "I think opening the Great Chamber of Alchemie and Physik might be a bit more complicated than that. And anyway, it hasn't got a door."

"All the better, then," said Marcia. "I shall just declare it open and then I'll shoot off. I shall be busy this evening."

Septimus had the distinct impression that Marcia was expecting to cut some kind of ceremonial ribbon and then go home. But he knew better than to say anything. He set off quickly.

Marcia hurried across the Courtyard, trying to keep up with her Apprentice. As she hurried through the Great Arch, her Wizard Induction vow came back to her. Marcia sighed. She felt as though she were on her way to betray the Castle.

5
The Great Chamber of Alchemie

T*he atmosphere was strained but* polite as Marcellus Pye ushered Marcia and Septimus into his house on Snake Slipway.

"Welcome, Marcia. Welcome, Septimus, or should I say, *Apprentice*," he said, smiling.

Septimus heard a *tut* from Marcia but to his relief she said nothing more. He lugged his backpack inside and dumped it on the floor with a crash. Both Marcia and Marcellus winced. Septimus saw his black-and-red-velvet Alchemie Apprentice cloak with its heavy gold clasp hanging ready in the hallway. He gave Marcia an anxious glance and saw that luckily Marcia did not recognize what it was.

"Let's get going, shall we?" said Marcia impatiently.

"Get going?" asked Marcellus.

"Yes, Marcellus. To the Great Chamber of Alchemie. Isn't that the idea?"

Marcellus looked shocked. "What—are *you* coming too?" he said.

"Naturally I am coming too, as you put it. Surely you didn't think I would allow you to open up that place on your own?"

That was precisely what Marcellus had thought. He fought down panic. The Chamber of **Fyre** was below the Great Chamber of Alchemie and the **Fyre** was beginning to come to life. What if Marcia noticed the warmth that had begun to spread upward—wouldn't she think it was odd? Marcellus told himself sternly that Marcia would not know what was odd and what wasn't. He must not give her any cause for suspicion.

"Er, no. Of course not, Marcia. Absolutely not," he said. And then he added tentatively, "You . . . you're not planning on *staying* there, are you?"

"I have *much* better things to do, thank you," snapped Marcia, remembering Milo's note.

"Then *of course* you must come," he said, as if magnanimously inviting Marcia to a party where she had been left off the invitation list.

"Yes," said Marcia stonily. "I must."

It was not easy to get to the Great Chamber of Alchemie, which was one of the most successfully concealed Alchemie Chambers in the world. Septimus and Beetle had once thought they had stumbled across the empty iced-up Great Chamber of Alchemie in the Ice Tunnels, but it was the decoy Chamber, installed in ancient times when traveling bands of marauders would target Alchemie Chambers for their gold. Enough gold objects would be left in the easily found decoy Chamber to satisfy the thieves, and the true Great Chamber would remain undiscovered.

After the Great Alchemie Disaster the hidden entrances to the Great Chamber were erased from Castle maps, so that they were eventually forgotten—except by Marcellus. But he was not about to divulge any of them to Marcia. As far as she knew, the only entrance was through a murky, smelly underground stream called the UnderFlow, and that was the way they would be going. The old Alchemie Boat had long ago rotted away, so Marcellus went next door to Rupert Gringe's boathouse to hire a paddleboat.

Rupert was doing winter maintenance on his fleet of brightly painted paddleboats, which he hired out in the summer for fun trips along the Moat. Rupert was used to his eccentric next-door neighbor, but Marcellus's request for a paddleboat, just as the Moat was beginning to ice up, floored him.

"You *what*?" he said, running his hand through his short, spiky red hair.

"I wish to hire a boat," Marcellus repeated.

"What, *now*?" Rupert looked at Marcellus as though he were crazy.

"Yes. Right now, in fact."

"But there's ice out there."

"Ice can be broken," said Marcellus.

"It will cost you. I've got them all laid up now and I'll have to winterize it again."

"Very well." Marcellus handed Rupert a very heavy gold coin.

Rupert looked at it and whistled through his teeth. "Blimey. Don't have change for a triple crown. Sorry."

"Keep it," said Marcellus. "Just give me the boat."

"Okeydokey. No worries. Right away."

Rupert Gringe shook his head as he watched the ExtraOrdinary Wizard, the Castle Alchemist and their disputed Apprentice squash uncomfortably into a bright pink paddleboat and head unsteadily along the Moat, while the ExtraOrdinary Wizard smashed at the ice with a pointed stick. He was glad it wasn't him wedged between those two fusspots, doing all the paddling. He wished his new brother-in-law a silent *good luck* and went back in to his warm boathouse.

The UnderFlow was dark and cold, but it was ice free. The paddleboat only just fit the narrow tunnel and the sound of the paddles turning was magnified a hundred times by the brick walls. Marcia sat in the prow like a large purple dog. She leaned forward, pointing her **FlashLight** so that it illuminated the low-arched tunnel that ran before them. The sound of the paddles rebounded off the walls, filling their heads with noise. Septimus paddled fast, churning up the murky water and sending it splashing up against the slimy brick and dripping into the boat. It was the first time he had been underground since his time in the **Darke Halls**, and he was surprised how scared he felt.

Ten long minutes after Septimus had steered the paddleboat into the UnderFlow, the tunnel widened out and he sensed the faint, acrid smell of smoke. He slowed his paddling and took the boat into a wide, low-roofed cavern—they had reached the UnderFlow Pool. Relieved, Septimus let go of the paddles and sat up straight to get his breath back.

Septimus knew exactly where they were—he had last seen this place five hundred years ago. But then it had had a beautiful lapis-lazuli-domed roof; now all was dismal and dark. He took hold of the paddle handles again and maneuvered the little boat alongside the Quay. Marcellus leaned out and tied it up.

No one spoke. Marcellus felt too emotional. Marcia had been overcome with a sense of mystery—she was entering a part of the Castle about which she knew nothing. That, for an ExtraOrdinary Wizard, was strange in itself. But what was even odder was the sense that this had once seen something so terrible that it had very nearly destroyed the Castle. And now here they were, three people in a ridiculous little pink paddleboat, the first to come back to the scene for nearly five hundred years.

Septimus jumped out of the boat. The Quay was slimy underfoot and he skidded and slipped. He broke his fall with his hands and when he stood up he saw in the light of the **FlashLight** that his palms were black.

"Soot," said Marcellus grimly.

Suddenly, Septimus realized why everything was black. He looked around, seeing the cavern with new eyes. "Everywhere," he whispered.

"Yes," said Marcellus heavily. He had forgotten just how bad it was—there had been no Drummins *here* to clean up. He took out a tinderbox and a sheet of metal gauze, which he folded to make a pyramid shape. From his pocket he produced a small fat candle, which he lit and placed in a candleholder, then put the pyramid of metal gauze over it.

"What are you doing?" asked Marcia.

"Preventing any explosions."

"*Explosions?*" Marcia's voice took on a slight squeak.

"Gases. Flammable. Just in case," explained Marcellus.

"We can use my **FlashLight**. That won't explode."

"Thank you, Marcia, but I want to do this my way. With my light only, if you don't mind."

Marcia heard the strain in Marcellus's voice. She imagined how she would feel going back to the Wizard Tower after some terrible disaster had ruined it—a disaster that *she* had caused. It did not bear thinking about.

"Of course, Marcellus," she said. "I don't mind at all." And she switched off her **FlashLight**.

There were three smoke-blackened arches on Alchemie Quay, two of which were bricked up. Marcellus headed for the open left-hand archway, where he stopped and turned, his face eerily illuminated by his candle—something that always gave Septimus the creeps.

"We will now enter the Labyrinth," he said, his voice hushed. "Please be aware that it does not run to a standard pattern. There are branches off to other smaller labyrinths and tunnels. Be sure to follow me and keep close. If you lose sight of me, stay where you are and call out. I will come and find you."

Septimus remembered the Labyrinth well, but then it had

been a beautiful, sinuous snake of a tunnel—brilliant with smooth, blue lapis lazuli walls shot through with gold and rare streaks of red and lit by rushlights. Now, like everything else, it was black with soot. Even though Septimus could recall all the tunnels and turnings, it looked so different that he doubted he would be able to find his way now.

Together Marcia and Septimus followed Marcellus through the arch and kept close behind him, the sound of their footsteps dulled by the carpet of soot. Marcellus trod carefully, after his first footsteps had raised a cloud of soot into the air and set everyone coughing and spluttering. The three walked slowly through the black coils of the Labyrinth, as subdued as if they were following a body on its way to its Leaving Boat. Even so, the soot rose into the air and tickled its way into their lungs, making them taste the fire of so long ago.

As the twists of the passageway became ever tighter Septimus knew they must be nearing the center—then suddenly they were there. Shocked, Septimus saw Marcellus staring at the blackened archway that was once the entrance to the Great Chamber of Alchemie. But now the archway led nowhere—it was blocked by a thick slab of heat-damaged metal, curled away at the bottom like a half-opened tin can.

Marcellus crouched down to inspect it. "The barricade has blown," he said.

"It's done a pretty good job, all the same," said Marcia.

"Possibly. I need a closer look." Marcellus disliked the use of **Magyk** in the Great Chamber and the areas nearby—he was convinced it disrupted the fine balance of Alchemical reactions. But now a little bit of **Magyk** seemed nothing compared to the devastation surrounding them. "Perhaps, Marcia, you would care to use your **FlashLight**?"

Marcia switched it on and a guffaw escaped from Septimus.

"What?" asked Marcia irritably.

"You. Marcellus. Me. . . ."

Marcia realized that all three of them were covered with soot from head to toe. "Great," she muttered.

For once Marcellus didn't care what his robes looked like. He ran his sooty sleeve over his face, leaving behind a black streak across his eyes like a mask.

Marcia touched Marcellus on the arm. "I'll do a **Remove**, shall I?" she offered gently. "The barricade is far too heavy for us to shift any other way."

"Yes. Thank you, Marcia."

Marcellus and Septimus stepped back and watched Marcia **Throw** a purple flash of **Magyk** across the metal slab. She waited a moment for the glimmering cloud to settle and then beckoned the barricade away from the archway.

The slab of metal began to shift and a sudden niggle of worry attacked Marcellus—there was something he must be careful about. But *what*?

"Septimus," he said. "Get out of the way. Take cover."

Septimus heard the warning in Marcellus's voice and slipped into the entrance of the Labyrinth. He peered out to see what was happening. Marcia was concentrating hard, unaware that Marcellus was now anxiously hopping around.

"Marcia!" said Marcellus. "*Marcia.* Can you do a protection thing?"

"Huh?"

"You need to do some kind of shield thingy."

Marcia shot Marcellus an angry look. What was he doing? Didn't he realize he was disturbing her concentration? If he carried on twittering like that he'd be lucky if he didn't get the barricade dropped on his stupid shoes. "*Thingy?*" she snapped.

"Spell. I don't know. Whatever you call it."

"I'm doing *this* now," Marcia said. "I can't be doing something else as well. Be quiet and let me concentrate, Marcellus."

Marcellus gritted his teeth. The slab was shifting and he could see the gap between the stone of the arch and the metal widening: in a moment the barricade would be out. He knew that this was the dangerous part. *But why?*

Suddenly the barricade was floating in midair and Marcia was conducting it across the space in front of the arch like a seasoned builder directing a heavy weight swinging on the end of a chain. Marcellus breathed out in relief: *nothing bad happened.* "It's all right, Septimus, you can come out now," he said.

The thick slab of black metal, still smooth and bright on the inside, was slowly shepherded by Marcia across to the opposite wall and lowered to the ground. It left behind a dark space, beyond which lay whatever was left of the Great Chamber of Alchemie.

Marcellus gulped. "I'll go in first," he said.

"We'll go in together," said Marcia.

Marcellus nodded. Sometimes he liked Marcia. He raised his candle up and saw something in front of him glimmering.

There was someone there, deep in the dark, holding a candle—*looking at him.* Who was it? Who was in the Great Chamber of Alchemie, *waiting for him*?

The hairs on the back of Marcellus's neck stood up as he saw a dark and desperate-looking creature, with eyes staring so wide that the whites glittered in the candlelight. Bravely, Marcellus took a step forward, then another and—"Ouch!" he gasped.

Marcia put out her hand. "Thought so," she said. "Glass."

"Glass?" Marcellus ran his hand over the smooth yet wavy surface.

"Yes. A second seal of glass. I'll get rid of that too."

Suddenly Marcellus understood. "Stop!" he yelled.

Marcia leaped back.

"Sand," said Marcellus.

"*Sand?*"

"The fire stop. Sand. Above the Chamber we kept a huge hopper of sand. If it all went out of control we could release the sand and fill the Chamber. To protect it. We had all kinds of fail-safes, you know. We were very careful, despite what people said."

"But clearly not careful enough," Marcia said crisply. She was shocked at what she had seen so far.

Marcellus slumped back against the wall. He looked defeated. "The heat has vitrified the sand."

Septimus was intrigued. He pushed his nose right up against the glass and peered in. "You mean the Chamber is full of *solid glass*? Like those paperweights they sell in the Traders' Market?"

"Yes," said Marcellus. "The whole thing is . . ." He searched for something to say and could think of nothing that didn't involve a rude word. He borrowed one of Septimus's recent phrases, ". . . a dead duck."

Marcia looked horrified. "But what about the Two-Faced Ring?"

"Oh, that will be all right," said Marcellus wearily. He knew when he was beaten. It was time to tell Marcia the truth about the Chamber of **Fyre**. "You see, Marcia. The real **Fyre** is—"

But Marcia was not listening. She was busy shining the **FlashLight** beam onto the glass. "I'm sure there is sand behind this glass," she said.

Marcellus stopped his confession. "Is there?"

"I'll check, shall I?" suggested Septimus.

"Be careful," Marcellus and Marcia said together—to their annoyance.

Septimus took a **HeatStick** from his Apprentice belt and placed it on the glass. The glass melted below the point and Septimus carefully pushed the **HeatStick** farther into the glass, making a hole. Deeper and deeper the **HeatStick** went until it had very nearly disappeared and Septimus began to think that the Chamber was indeed filled with solid glass. Then suddenly, the end of the **HeatStick** hit something solid. Septimus pulled the **HeatStick** out and a trickle of sand began to flow.

"Ta-*da*!" he announced.

Marcellus laughed with relief.

"I trust you have a couple of large wheelbarrows, Marcellus?" Marcia said.

Marcellus grinned. He didn't care how many wheelbarrows he was going to need—his precious Great Chamber of Alchemie had survived. The fact that it lay buried beneath hundreds of tons of sand was a mere irritation. His Apprentice would fix that.

Marcellus led Marcia and Septimus back through the sooty snake of the Labyrinth to Alchemie Quay. Marcia looked at her Apprentice and shook her head—his clean-this-morning Apprentice robes were completely blackened with soot.

"I give you permission to wear your Alchemie robes this month, Septimus," she said. "Frankly, after a day down here, I don't think anyone will be able to tell the difference."

6
LISTENING

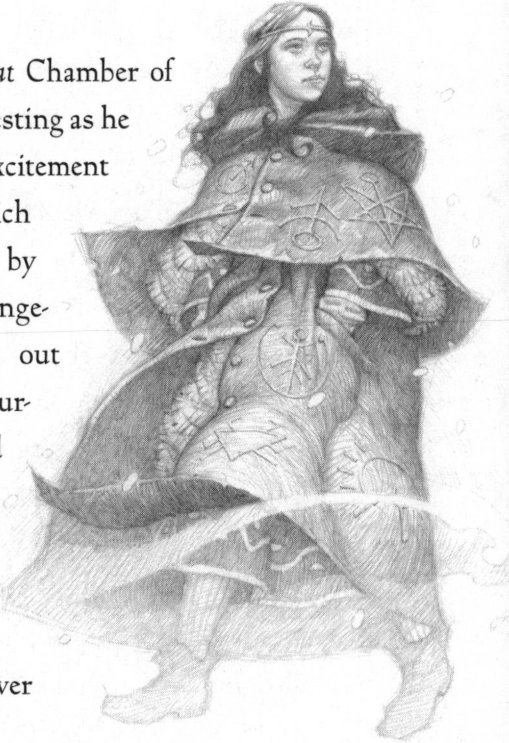

Septimus's month in the Great Chamber of Alchemie was not as interesting as he had hoped. After the initial excitement of removing the sand—which he managed in three days by fixing up a siphoning arrangement that drew the sand out through the Labyrinth, scouring it clean as it went, and sending the sand into the UnderFlow Pool—Septimus spent his time cleaning, unpacking and doing more cleaning. Marcellus was forever disappearing—*checking things, Apprentice*—and Septimus spent a lot of the time on his own. He began to count down the days to his return to the Wizard Tower.

Marcellus's disappearances were, of course, when he was tending the **Fyre**. It was going well but he dared not leave it for too long. The water flow was good—he had been a little anxious about dumping the sand in the UnderFlow Pool, but it was deep enough to take it. His main concern now was venting the Cauldron heat, which was growing daily. Toward the end of Septimus's month, Marcellus took a reluctant decision to open four more vents. He chose their positions carefully and hoped that no one would notice.

On a beautiful, bright dawn two days before the end of his month with Marcellus, Septimus was trudging to work, heading for the entrance to the Great Chamber that Marcellus had recently opened. His journey took him past the Palace and the bizarre collection of snow sculptures that were being created on the lawns in front. He stopped for a moment to look at the new ones and then reluctantly set off. It was going to be another beautiful day, but he would spend it underground in candlelight and it would be dark by the time he returned.

* * *

On the other side of the Palace, Jenna was drawing back the curtains from her bedroom window. She saw the sun climbing over the snow-covered hills in the distance, the pinky-green streaks of cloud low in the sky and the sparkling orange glints of light on the shining black surface of the river. It was beautiful—but it was *cold*. Jenna shivered. She was not surprised to see ice frosting the windows; it was now more than four weeks into the Big Freeze and a deep chill pervaded everything. She dressed quickly in her winter robes and, wrapping herself in her fur-lined cloak, was out of her bedroom fast.

The ghost of Sir Hereward, who guarded her bedroom door, woke with a start. A ghostly "Good Morning, Princess" followed Jenna as she strode briskly down the corridor.

"Morning, Sir Hereward," she called back over her shoulder, and disappeared around the corner.

Sir Hereward shook his head. The Living were always in such a hurry, he thought. The ghost performed an old-fashioned military about-turn and began a slow march down to the Palace doors where, once the Princess had left her room, he now spent his days on guard.

Downstairs, Jenna grabbed a few leftovers from the supper

table, pulled her red winter fur-lined cloak tighter around herself, and headed out, winding her way through the assortment of snow sculptures, stopping briefly to admire her favorites. As she drew near the Palace Gate, Jenna saw two large, ungainly figures loitering on either side. She approached cautiously, wondering who they might be. And then she remembered—it was the day of the annual Castle snowman competition. She pushed open the Gate and walked out through two guard snowmen.

"Happy Snowman Day, Princess!" one of the snowmen said.

Jenna jumped in surprise. Then she saw the bob of a red bobble hat followed by the cheeky grin of a small boy peering from behind the bulk of the snowman. Perched on the shoulders of a much taller friend, he was in the process of putting the finishing touches to his snowman.

"Happy Snowman Day," Jenna replied, smiling in return. "He's good," she said, pointing at the snowman.

The boys laughed. "We're going to win!"

"Good luck!" Jenna walked off into Wizard Way, her fur-lined boots pressing the fresh snow beneath. With her red cloak standing out against the more sober colors of most people's winter robes, Jenna was easy to spot as she made her way along the freshly cleared path that ran beside the shops. She passed by a motley assortment of snowmen. Larry's Dead Languages sported a surprisingly upbeat snowman with a large melon-slice grin and Larry's favorite scarf. Jenna suspected that once Larry saw it, both the scarf and the grin would rapidly vanish. Wizard Sandwiches boasted an eye-aching snowman made from rainbow-colored snow, and outside Sandra's Palace of Pets was a disconcertingly giant rabbit complete with a supersize carrot. Jenna walked slowly on past a trio of small printing shops, each with an identical little snowman wearing a printer's apron and reading a book. As she neared the Wizard Tower, she saw a familiar figure heading toward the Great Arch. He was wearing the still—to Jenna—unfamiliar dark blue robes of the Chief Hermetic Scribe and had a long metal cylinder tucked under his arm.

"Hey, Beetle!" she called, picking up speed.

The Chief Hermetic Scribe turned and waved, then waited for Jenna to catch up.

"Hello," puffed Jenna. "How's it going?"

Beetle smiled. "Good," he said. "Really good. And you?"

"Great. Yes, fine, thanks." Jenna regarded Beetle shyly. He

seemed so very different in his official robes. It was hard to believe this was the same Beetle who had been working for the irascible Larry not so very long ago. He seemed taller, older, and his brown eyes regarded her with an expression that was strangely distant. Beetle used to look so happy to see her, thought Jenna, but now that he was Chief Hermetic Scribe he was much more reserved. She wasn't sure if she liked that. The gold bands on the sleeves of Beetle's robes glittered as he raised his free arm to shield his eyes against the bright morning sun and then, in a happily familiar gesture, run his hand through his unruly black hair. Jenna smiled.

"Better get going, got to meet Marcia in"—Beetle looked at his timepiece—"five minutes and forty-two seconds precisely."

Jenna looked horrified.

Beetle broke into a broad smile. "Gotcha!" he said.

"Oh, you *pig*," said Jenna, laughing—happy to see a glimpse of the old Beetle. "For a horrible moment I thought you'd turned into Jillie Djinn!"

"Nope. Not *yet*, anyway."

"Um . . . so how are you? I haven't seen you for ages. Since . . . gosh . . . Simon's wedding, I suppose. Are you busy? Well, I guess you must be—"

The old Beetle disappeared and the Chief Hermetic Scribe looked at his timepiece. "I'm sorry, Princess Jenna. I really must go. Stuff to do and all that."

Jenna could see that Beetle was longing to be off. She felt as if she was being a nuisance, and that wasn't good. Jenna had an uncomfortable sense that she had once made Beetle feel just like she was feeling now.

"Oh, yes, of course," she said. "Well. I'll see you around, then. Have a nice day."

"You too." With that, the Chief Hermetic Scribe strode off, his long blue robes brushing the snow, leaving a softly flattened wake behind them. Jenna watched Beetle walk into the shadows of the lapis lazuli–lined Great Arch and disappear into his new, unknown world. She took a deep breath, trying to shake off the melancholy that had settled on her, and walked on toward the gap between the last two houses on Wizard Way. Here she made a left-hand turn into a snow-filled alleyway, which led to the Castle Wall. The alley was about a foot deep in snow, which Jenna waded slowly through. She was in no hurry to get to where she was going.

But soon enough Jenna reached a flight of stone steps that led up to the path that ran along the top of the Castle walls, just behind the battlements. Kicking newly fallen snow away so that she could see where the steps were, Jenna climbed up and found herself standing on a wide, flat snow-covered path, which bore traces of footsteps blurred with snow from the previous night's fall. Jenna stopped at the top of the steps and looked around. She loved this part of the Castle. Not many people chose to walk along the walls. It had been forbidden during the rule of the Custodians in the Bad Old Days—as they were now known—and many people still believed that only the ExtraOrdinary Wizard and the Princess were allowed to use the path. Jenna was happy with that. It was one of the few places in the Castle where she could wander without feeling she was public property.

The battlements were low at this point and Jenna could easily see over them. She looked across the iced-up Moat to the tall trees on the opposite bank: the outriders of the Forest. Their branches were laden with snow, thick and stark against the black bark of their trunks. Jenna thought of her four Forest Heap brothers. She was so glad that Sarah had persuaded them to stay in the Castle for the Big Freeze. She shivered. Even with a campfire burning day and night, even with all the smelly furs they wore, they must have been so *cold* in the Forest.

Jenna pulled her cloak closely around her and set off slowly along the path, following the tracks she had made the day before, and the days before that. The path on top of the Castle walls followed the curve of the Moat. The Moat slowly folded in toward her, turning always a little to the right like the python in the Marram Marshes. On her right-hand side the path was bounded by the back walls of typical tall, narrow Castle houses, which regularly gave way to unnerving sheer drops that could rapidly deliver the unwary walker to an alleyway twenty feet below. At these points she kept close to the battlements and took care not to look down.

Jenna passed softly—and unknowingly—over the ancient Hole in the Wall Tavern, a popular meeting place for ghosts that was hollowed out in the wall below, and approached a bend in the path. She rounded it and suddenly, laid out below, she saw Jannit Maarten's boatyard, which was now no more than a collection of boat-shaped snowy mounds. Jenna walked on, following her old, snow-covered footsteps until she came to a widening of the wall, open like a plateau, where her footprints ended in a circle of well-trodden snow. She stopped for a moment and glanced around. The open space was deserted, as it always was. And yet, as she walked slowly forward, Jenna could not shake off the feeling that she was pushing through a crowd.

And she was—a crowd of ghostly Queens, Princesses and Princesses-in-Waiting were waiting anxiously for her. With each careful step that Jenna took, the ghosts of her grandmothers, great-grandmothers, aunts and great-aunts fell back to avoid being **Passed Through**. Ghostly violet eyes followed their descendant as she made her way slowly to an icy spot in the middle of the space from which the snow had been scraped away. Jenna stopped, shivered, looked around once more, then took a few steps across to the battlement at the edge of the wall. She leaned over and looked down to check she was in the right place—just in case she had got it wrong. Some six feet below she saw a burnished gold disc set into the wall. Jenna stood back from the battlements and sighed. She was in the right place; of *course* she was. The crowd of royal ghosts parted as she returned to the icy spot, kneeled down and began to unlace her fur-lined winter boots.

High up in one of the houses set back from the path, Jenna added one more to her audience—a small boy. He peered out of an attic window and saw *the Princess.* Again. Soon he was joined by his mother and grandmother. Noses pressed against the glass, they watched the Princess take off her boots and a pair of furry purple socks, then stand barefoot on the cold stones.

"See, I *told* you she did that," whispered the little boy.

"Oh, dear," whispered the mother. "I do hope she's not going to be a crazy one like that Datchet."

"*Shh*," scolded the grandmother. "She'll hear you."

"Of course she won't," retorted the mother.

But down in the crowd of ghosts, the ghost of Queen Datchet III did hear. It is a fact that those who have been a little paranoid in Life develop a wonderful ability in ghosthood to hear their name mentioned many miles away. But Jenna heard nothing—neither the mother in the attic nor the sound she longed to hear—the *ther-umm . . . ther-umm . . . ther-umm* of the Dragon Boat's slow but steady heartbeat, pulsing through the stone and the soles of her feet as it always had—until the last few days. Jenna willed herself to feel that unmistakable *thump*. She thought of the Dragon Boat lying beneath the path, immured in her lapis lazuli Dragon House. She remembered the last time she had seen the Dragon Boat. In her mind's eye she could still see the great green dragon head resting on the marble walkway that ran along both sides of the barrel-vaulted Dragon House, and the thick dragon tail coiled like a massive green rope, laid on the marble ledge that ran along the back wall. Jenna remembered how perfect the boat had looked—so beautifully repaired by Jannit Maarten—and yet how limp and lifeless the dragon had been.

And then Jenna thought about how Aunt Zelda had *still* not let her have the **Transubstantiate Triple** bowls so that she could use the **Revive** she had gotten from Broda Pye so long ago. A wave of exasperation washed over her, but Jenna pushed the bad feelings aside, took a deep breath and emptied her mind of everything—everything except what she could feel through the soles of her feet. She stood stone-still, silent, immersed, but once again, she could feel *nothing at all.*

In the attic room the three watchers fell silent. The grandmother knew what the Princess was waiting for. She had not lived above the Dragon House without thinking about the beautiful Dragon that lay beneath and, especially on long, cold winter nights, wondering if the creature was still alive. And that was exactly what Jenna was wondering now.

The ice numbed Jenna's feet but still she waited for a small *ther-umm* of hope. A sudden gust of bitter wind blew a flurry of snow off the battlements; it sprinkled her bluish toes with icy white frosting and Jenna realized that her feet had gone numb. There was no hope of feeling anything now. The wind—or something—brought tears to her eyes. Slowly she kneeled down, pulled on her furry socks and her brown leather boots. She stood up, irresolute for a moment and then, watched by the family far above, and the ghosts of fifty-four Queens, Princesses and Princesses-in-Waiting, she began to retrace her snowy footsteps.

The small boy watched Jenna go. "She looks sad, Gramma," he whispered.

The grandmother watched Jenna walking slowly back along the path, her red cloak a splash of color against the monochrome whites and grays of the snow-covered walls and the dark Moat and wintry trees beyond.

"Yes, she does," the grandmother agreed. "It is not good for the Princess to be so sad."

7
FALSE TRAILS

Marcia watched Terry Tarsal wrap up her new shoes in his special *By Appointment to the ExtraOrdinary Wizard* gold tissue paper.

"Thank you, Terry," she said. "You've done a lovely job."

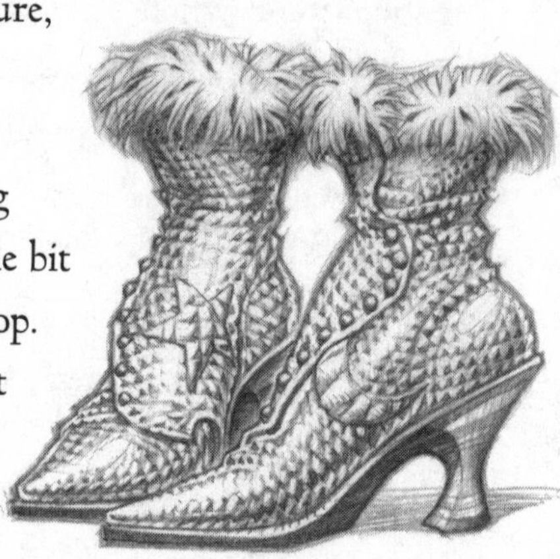

Terry glowed with pride. It wasn't often Marcia handed out praise. "It's been a real pleasure, Madam Marcia; it's always nice to do something special. I think the glitter really adds something to them. And I just *adore* the little bit of blue fur peeking out at the top. Inspired." Terry sighed as he put the neatly wrapped shoes into a smart gold box. "These have been a lifesaver. I've had twenty-nine pairs of brown galoshes to waterproof for the Ramblings Roof Gardening Society. Highly depressing."

"I can imagine," said Marcia. "Nothing worse than galoshes."

"Especially brown ones," said Terry, tying his best bow around the box with the dark blue ribbon he kept for special customers. He handed the package to Marcia, who took it excitedly. "That will be half a crown, please."

"Goodness!" Marcia looked shocked but she handed over the exact money. It was worth it.

Terry quickly put the money in the cash register before Marcia had the chance to change her mind. "Going somewhere nice this evening?"

Marcia was. Milo Banda had asked her to accompany him to a new show at the Little Theater in the Ramblings, but she wasn't about to let Terry know. "That's for me to know and you to wonder, Mr. Tarsal," she replied. Feeling flustered at the thought of the evening, Marcia hurried off. The door threw itself open and she rushed out.

Splash!

Terry Tarsal went pale. He knew exactly what had happened.

It was the wretched kids next door. They'd done it again. They had moved the puddle cover. Terry rushed outside to find his worst nightmare. His most prestigious customer was up to her neck in icy, muddy water right outside his shop. She didn't look too pleased about it.

"Get me . . . *out*!" spluttered Marcia.

Terry was small and thin but he was stronger than he looked. He grabbed hold of Marcia's arms and pulled hard. Marcia landed on Terry with a soft, obliterating *therwump*.

"Oof!" gasped Terry.

Marcia picked herself up and, like a large purple dog, shook as much water as she could off her **Magykal** cloak. Painfully, Terry crawled over to the puddle and extricated the gold shoebox floating forlornly on top. He should have known that a week occupied by twenty-nine pairs of brown galoshes was not going to end well.

Terry got to his feet. "I am so, *so* sorry, Madam Marcia. It's this blasted puddle. I've tried filling it in. You wouldn't believe the amount of trash I've put down there, but it just stays right there—a great big hole filling up with water. I don't understand. We shouldn't even *have* puddles at this time of year." Terry looked down at the soggy gold mess in his hands.

"I'll make these as good as new for you, I promise."

"Thank you," said Marcia, wringing out the furry hem of her cloak. "No chance of having them by this evening, I suppose?"

"I'll work through until I've done them. What time are you going out?"

"Seven thirty," said Marcia without thinking.

Terry smiled. "They'll be with you by then. I'll bring them to you. And once again, I am *so* sorry."

"Not as sorry as *someone* is going to be," muttered Marcia, as she dripped away along Footpad Passage and bumped into the Footpad communal snowman—which sported an uncomfortable pointy stick.

Beetle climbed the wide white marble steps of the Wizard Tower. At the top he stopped to savor the moment. He turned and looked at the beautiful snowy Courtyard with its freshly cleared path winding from the Great Arch to the foot of the steps. Beyond the high wall of the Courtyard he could just see the snow-covered roof of the Manuscriptorium, with its lazy skein of smoke from the blazing fire in the scribes' new sitting room drifting skyward. Beetle felt indescribably happy—and only very slightly unsettled from having just bumped into Jenna.

Pushing Jenna from his mind, he turned back and looked up at the huge silver doors that soared up above him. The Wizard Tower was particularly striking that morning. It was bathed in a shimmering silvery-blue light, with delicate flashes of purple shooting across the surface. Beetle could scarcely believe that here he was, about to give the Wizard Tower password for the very first time—and that the **Magykal** doors would open just for him. He smiled and savoured the moment just a little longer.

"Forgot the password, Chief?" a cheery voice came from behind him.

"No, I—"

Silas Heap bounded up the steps, his curly straw-colored hair disheveled as usual and his green eyes smiling. Silas liked Beetle. "Allow me," Silas said. And before Beetle could say anything, the double doors had swung silently open, Silas had taken his arm, and marched him across the threshold.

The words WELCOME, CHIEF HERMETIC SCRIBE materialized at Beetle's feet. And then WELCOME, SILAS HEAP flashed up and faded quickly away.

"**Seal Watch**," said Silas in explanation. "A bit late, but you know what they say."

Beetle hazarded a guess. "You're late? What time do you call this? Where on earth have you been?"

Silas looked baffled. "No. Better late than never."

Beetle watched Silas Heap head across the Great Hall toward the **Sealed** lobby and heard one of the guard Wizards demand, "Silas Heap—*where on earth have you been*?"

Beetle smiled and headed for the silver spiral stairs. He had an appointment to keep on the twentieth floor.

Marcia met Beetle at the door. She ushered him in, and for the very first time Beetle met the ghost of his ex-employer, Jillie Djinn. Marcia put a warning hand on Beetle's shoulder.

"Move across the room slowly. Try not to alarm her."

The ghost stared at Beetle, taking in his Chief Hermetic Scribe robes. She looked down at her own ghostly Chief Hermetic Scribe robes and then back at Beetle. A bewildered expression settled over her face like a fog as she watched Beetle's careful, almost apologetic progress across the room. Beetle was very nearly out of the room when he stumbled against a small table and caused Marcia's collection of Fragile Fairy Pots to wobble. It was then that Jillie Djinn, ex-Chief

Hermetic Scribe, realized that she was dead. She opened her mouth and a great howl of grief came from deep within: "*Aeiiiiiiiiiiiiiiiiiiiiieeeeeeeeeeeeeeeeeeeeeeeeeeeeeee . . .*"

The scream did not stop. Marcia hurried Beetle out and quickly closed the door. She looked pale and—Beetle now noticed—rather damp. Her dark hair was shiny and wet, hanging in tendrils about her shoulders. But before he had time to ask what had happened, Marcia ushered him into her study and closed the door against the desolate wail outside. Marcellus Pye was there, sitting on a small chair in front of the desk. He seemed, thought Beetle, a little tense.

He was. Marcellus had just sent Septimus on an errand and he had been about to check on the **Fyre** Cauldron while he was away. Time was ticking by.

"Thank you for coming at such short notice, Beetle," said Marcia.

"He is not the only one who has come at short notice," Marcellus observed tetchily.

"Beetle has not brought it upon himself, Marcellus. Unlike you," Marcia riposted. Keeping her gaze on Marcellus she said, "Beetle, perhaps you would like to show Mr. Pye the *Vent cooling system.*"

By not even a twitch of a muscle did Marcellus betray any familiarity with what Marcia had said. His studied expression—seventy percent annoyance, twenty-five percent bemusement, five percent boredom—remained the same.

Beetle took the gleaming white piece of paper out from his folder and laid it in front of Marcellus, who looked at it with no more than a natural curiosity. "What is this?" he asked politely.

Marcia stabbed her finger onto the title. "Vent cooling system," she read out very deliberately. "As you *know*, Marcellus."

Marcellus picked up the sheet of paper and perused it. "How strange. It looks just like a spider's web." He looked up at Marcia. "And why do you think I know about this"—he glanced deliberately down at the title—"vent cooling system?"

Marcia fought down her mounting irritation. She had expected Marcellus to cave in when confronted with the diagram, or at least look guilty. Either he was a very good actor or this actually was nothing to do with him—Marcia was not sure which. She stabbed her finger at the scrawled note at the foot of the page.

"Because, Marcellus, you have written on it. *There!*"

Very slowly—playing for time, Marcia suspected—Marcellus

fished out his little round spectacles and put them on, carefully fitting the curled earpieces behind his ears. Marcia tapped her foot impatiently.

Marcellus peered at the note. "Julius FYI—Vent Cooling System. M," he muttered. "FYI . . . strange name." Beetle began to correct Marcellus, but Marcia held her hand up to stop him. Marcellus looked up at Marcia. "And no doubt you think that the 'M' is for Marcellus?"

"Yes," said Marcia. A waver of uncertainty wandered into her voice.

Marcellus scented victory. He smiled and put the paper back down on the desk. "Well, I do hope you don't call me out to inspect every little note in the Castle signed with the letter 'M.' I shall be spending all my time going up and down Wizard Way. There must be so many notes out there from . . . let me see now . . . Milo, Morwenna, Marissa, Maureen, *Marcus*—"

Marcia blanched at the mention of Marcus. Marcus Overland, ex-Ordinary Wizard, had once been given Marcia's ExtraOrdinary Wizard robes by the Wizard Tower laundry in error. He had paraded around the Castle in them, acting very badly indeed. There were still people who were convinced that Marcia had once run screaming down Wizard

Way, waving a large pair of bloomers above her head. "That's enough of that, Marcellus," Marcia told him. "There is no need to be sarcastic."

"I was merely pointing out the infinite possibilities of the letter 'M,'" said Marcellus.

Beetle watched with a mixture of admiration for Marcellus's cool head and annoyance at how Marcellus was putting Marcia off. It was time for some straight talking. From his folder he took a translucent piece of paper on which he had marked the position of all the puddles, and placed it on top of the Vent diagram.

"We had hoped you might be able to help us, Marcellus," he said smoothly. "For the last few weeks I have been monitoring a very strange occurrence. Puddles have appeared throughout the Castle."

Marcellus looked genuinely surprised, and then—Beetle was sure—a brief flash of panic crossed his face. Feeling more confident, Beetle continued, "At the beginning of the Big Freeze we had nine. My scribes have been checking on them daily and despite temperatures well below freezing, they report that no puddle has frozen over. And then two days ago four more were reported. Two appeared in scribes' back gardens, and two in iced-up alleyways. It is odd, don't you think?"

"I suppose it is," said Marcellus. "But I don't know why you are telling *me*."

Beetle pointed to the papers lying in front of them. "You will see that on this top tracing paper I have a map of the Castle. On it I have placed a red dot where each puddle is." Beetle looked up at Marcellus. "There are thirteen in all."

There would be, thought Marcellus grimly. "Indeed?" he said coolly. "Is thirteen significant?"

"You tell me," said Beetle.

Marcellus said nothing.

Beetle continued. "Now, if we place the tracing over the Vent diagram, like so . . . we can see that each red dot is on top of the end of a line on the diagram."

"So it is," murmured Marcellus. "How very interesting."

"And I presume each line ending is a Vent."

Marcellus shrugged. "Whatever a *Vent* is."

Beetle knew he had to keep cool, but it was not easy. Fighting to keep any vestige of irritation out of his voice, he continued, "I—*we*—believe that the note is indeed from you and we believe that you wrote it to Julius Pike. FYI is, as I am sure you do actually remember, archaic shorthand for 'For Your Information.' Marcia and I are convinced that there is a connection between these puddles and the **Fyre** in the Great Chamber of Alchemie. We would like an explanation as to why the puddles occurred *before* the **Fyre** has even been lit. Before, in fact, the Chamber was opened."

For a few seconds, Beetle thought he had done it.

Marcellus sighed and said, "Indeed, there is a connection. Perhaps I may demonstrate?"

Beetle nodded.

Marcellus took a pen and proceeded to add a series of thick black crosses to the red dots on Beetle's Castle plan. He then joined them up so that they formed a wavy line that meandered from the South Gate by the river to the Wizard Tower.

"You will find that *all* these places will have melting snow," he said, looking at Beetle over the top of his spectacles. "You will also see that by no means all these spots have a—what do you call it—a *Vent* beneath them as shown on the diagram. It is an unfortunate coincidence that the ones you have found just happen to be above one of these Vent things. Whatever they may be." He shrugged. "Coincidences happen."

"Coincidences?"

Marcellus took off his spectacles and looked up. "Dragon blood."

"*What?*"

"Dragon blood. After his fight with the **Darke** dragon, Spit Fyre left a trail of blood from the South Gate to the Wizard Tower. Each red dot, and now each cross, marks a spot of blood. You will find the snow has also melted at every cross I have drawn. I agree there is a link between the opening of the Chamber and the melting snow, but only insofar as that the flight made by Spit Fyre led to us being in the happy position of being able to do this at all." Marcellus looked at Marcia. "No doubt you know all about the eternal heat of dragon blood?"

Marcia was not sure she did, but she was not going to give Marcellus the satisfaction of admitting it. "Of course I do," she snapped.

Marcellus knew the interview was at an end. He took off his spectacles and put them back in their red velvet case. "Dragon blood is a wonderful thing, but it does have a tendency to lead to puddles in snow, which is most annoying for those who fall into them. I suppose your shoes were ruined, Marcia?"

"How did you know I—"

Marcellus stood up. He had won and he wanted to get out of Marcia's study as soon as possible. "Now, if you will excuse me, I have important work to continue. I hope next time we meet it will be to do the job that we all wish to do—**DeNature** the Two-Faced Ring."

Marcia opened the study door. "Yes, indeed." She took a deep breath and said, "I apologize for interrupting your work, Marcellus. I'll see you out."

Beetle sat down with a sigh. Quietly, he put the Vent diagram and his tracing, now covered with taunting black crosses, back in his folder. He had made his first mistake as Chief Hermetic Scribe. It was not a good feeling.

Marcia returned without Marcellus. Beetle leaped to his feet. "Marcia, I am *so* sorry."

"Nothing to be sorry about, Beetle," said Marcia. "It's all for the best. Marcellus knows we have our eye on him now. Please do not let this put you off. You must let me know about anything else suspicious—anything at all."

Beetle felt very relieved. "Yes. Yes, of course I will. I will check out all the crosses he made."

"Thank you, Beetle. Now I think we have both earned a strong cup of coffee."

By the time Marcia escorted Beetle down the stairs he felt a little less embarrassed about the interview with Marcellus. As they spiraled down into the vaulted space of the Great Hall, Beetle saw that something had caught Marcia's attention: Milo Banda was coming out of the duty Wizard's cupboard.

Beetle saw Milo catch sight of Marcia and stop dead. Milo dithered. It seemed to Beetle that Milo wanted to skip back into the cupboard but was unsure whether Marcia had seen him. Marcia decided it for him. She jumped from the stairs and set off across the Great Hall at top speed. Beetle kept a tactful distance—something was going on, but he wasn't sure what.

Milo was floundering. "Marcia, how nice. Goodness. Fancy seeing you here."

Marcia looked confused. "I generally *am* here. This is where I live. And where I work."

"Yes, yes. Of course. What I meant was that I didn't expect to bump into you."

"No?"

"No. I, um, have some business here. A small project of mine."

"Oh. You never said. I might have been able to help."

"No . . . no, I don't think so."

"Oh."

"But of course, er, thank you for the offer. I do hope you understand," Milo said anxiously. "I didn't want to disturb you. I know how busy you are. That's why I come here in the mornings."

"Morn*ings*?"

"Er, yes. Hildegarde said it was the best time."

"*Hildegarde?*"

"Yes. But of course if you prefer I can see Hildegarde other times."

"It matters not a jot to me *when* you choose to see Miss Pigeon," Marcia said icily. "However, I will be having words with Miss Pigeon about using work time for social engagements." Marcia turned on her purple python heel and strode off.

Milo caught up with her at the foot of the stairs. "But it's not a social—"

Marcia glared at Milo. "I find that I have other commitments this evening. Double speed!" The stairs did Marcia's bidding and took her whirling upward. A distant scream followed by a *thump* came from somewhere far above as a Wizard was thrown off by the sudden change of speed.

Beetle and Milo watched Marcia's purple cloak disappear.

"Bother," Milo said. "Bother, bother, bother."

"I'll second that," said Beetle.

On the way back to the Manuscriptorium, Beetle saw Jenna's distinctive red cloak going past the Manuscriptorium, and he decided to take a detour to check out the nearest of Marcellus's crosses. After a fruitless hour he discovered that the three closest to the Wizard Tower were not possible to verify. Two were on top of roofs and one was actually inside a building. He suspected that the others would be the same. Beetle walked slowly back to the Manuscriptorium. He *knew* that Marcellus Pye was up to something. But what was it?

8
KEEPER'S COTTAGE

S*arah Heap was fiddling around* in the herb garden potting shed when Jenna let herself into the garden from the side gate. From Jenna's expression Sarah knew what the answer to her question would be, but she asked anyway.

"Hello, love. Any luck?"

"No."

"Well, it's *so* cold. Look at the frogs."

"*Frogs?* What frogs?" Jenna sounded touchy.

"Exactly—*what* frogs. They are all hiding in walls, asleep. Their hearts hardly beat at all in the winter, *you* know. And the Dragon Boat, she's cold-blooded too, like a frog."

Jenna was indignant. "She's nothing *like* a frog, Mum."

"Well, obviously she doesn't look like one but—"

"And anyway, I heard her all through the last Big Freeze and the one before. I'm worried that the **Darke Domaine** might have seeped into her somehow." Jenna took out a tiny blue glass bottle. On its small brown label was written: **Tx3 Revive**. "I've had this for *so* long now and every time I tell Aunt Zelda that we should use it and revive the Dragon Boat properly she makes an excuse. But I am not being put off *any longer*. I am going to see Aunt Zelda. Right now." Jenna strode off.

"Jenna!" Sarah called after her.

Jenna stopped at the walled gate that led into a covered way to the Palace. "What?"

Sarah picked her way along the icy gravel path to where Jenna waited impatiently. Unlike Sarah, Jenna liked to get things done as soon as she had thought of them. Sarah put her hand on Jenna's arm.

"Aunt Zelda is not quite as . . ." Sarah searched for the right word. "Er, *Aunt Zelda-ish* as she used to be. She is getting very forgetful—you know she forgot to come to the wedding. She doesn't always realize she forgets, but it upsets her when she does. Don't . . . well, don't expect too much."

"But she *has* to do it, Mum. It is her job as Keeper."

Sarah looked at Jenna fondly. "I know. When will you be back, love?"

"As soon as I can," Jenna replied. She gave Sarah a quick kiss and ran off along the covered way toward a small door at the foot of the east turret.

Sarah watched her go. She thought how Jenna had grown up during the past month. She thought how *Queenly* she looked. Sarah smiled at the idea of her little girl being Queen. It will suit her, she thought. She is ready now.

Inside the Palace, Jenna ran up the winding turret stairs. She arrived breathless at the top landing and from a pocket deep in her tunic she took a gold key with a large red stone set into its bow. She stepped forward, pushed it into what appeared to be a blank wall and quickly jumped backward. She waited for a few seconds, then walked forward and disappeared through the wall.

Many miles away, in a stone cottage on an egg-shaped island at the southern edge of the Marram Marshes, Jenna emerged from a tiny cupboard under the stairs.

"Aunt Zelda," she called softly. There was no reply. Jenna looked around the room she knew so well. A fire was burning in the hearth, the floor was neatly swept and the potion bottles that lined the walls sparkled with different colors. The room itself was long and low with a flight of stairs going up the middle, below which was the Unstable Potions and Partikular Poisons cupboard from which Jenna had just emerged. Aunt Zelda's cottage only had two rooms—one upstairs and one downstairs. Jenna did not count the kitchen, which was tacked onto the back and felt more like Sarah Heap's potting shed than a real room. She walked up the stairs and glanced around the long, low attic room. The beds were made, the room neat and tidy—and completely empty of Aunt Zelda.

Jenna went back downstairs. "Aunt Zelda?" she called once more, but there was still no reply. She must be out with Wolf Boy, thought Jenna, probably cutting cabbages or making sure there was a hole in the ice for the ducks. She decided to wait for them to come back.

Jenna wandered around, enjoying just being in the cottage on her own. Aunt Zelda's cottage was a special place for her. That morning it was alive with light reflected from the snow piled up outside, which, combined with the smell of the woodsmoke and the underlying odor of boiled cabbage, took her right back to the happy weeks that she had once spent in the cottage during a previous Big Freeze. Jenna loved the quiet orderliness of the cottage, the walls lined with books and hundreds of potion bottles, the low rough-hewn beams hung with all manner of interesting things, some that reminded her of Aunt Zelda: bags of shells, gardening hats, bundles of reeds, cabbage cutters, bunches of herbs, and some that announced the fact that the cottage was now Wolf Boy's home too: a selection of fishing rods, nets and a fine collection of catapults.

Jenna walked over to the fire and stood warming her hands, careful not to disturb the duck asleep on a cushion by the hearth. A sudden gust of wind brought down a shower of frozen snow from the cottage roof; it clattered against the thick green windowpanes and made her jump. Jenna decided she had had enough of being alone in the cottage—she would go and find Aunt Zelda and Wolf Boy.

The icy cold shocked Jenna as she stepped outside. She had forgotten how much colder the Marram Marshes were than the Castle, especially when the east wind blew. Today the east wind was blowing hard, sending flurries of ice particles scooting across the top of the snow and a raw chill into her bones.

She set off along the cleared path, which led down to the plank bridge that crossed the frozen Mott—the large ditch that surrounded Aunt Zelda's cottage. Jenna stopped and, shielding her eyes against the glare of the snow, she looked around for Aunt Zelda or Wolf Boy. There was no sign of them, nothing except the great expanse of white blurring out in front of her. She turned and looked back at the small stone cottage piled high with snow, which reached up to its low eaves and made the cottage look like an igloo. The warm glow from the fire shone through the windows and Jenna was very tempted to go back inside, but she told herself sternly that the sooner she found Aunt Zelda, the sooner she could get back to the Dragon Boat.

Jenna knew that on Draggen Island—the island on which Aunt Zelda's cottage stood—all paths eventually led to a cabbage patch; and a cabbage patch was where she was sure to find Aunt Zelda. Deciding to keep the biting wind behind her, Jenna turned right and began to walk along the path beside the Mott.

Jenna had forgotten just how much she loved being out on

the Marshes. She loved the wide windswept sky that seemed to go on forever, the exhilaration of being alive in the middle of so much wildness, but most of all she loved the quietness. In the summer it was punctuated by the *gloops* and *glugs* of unseen Marsh creatures, but in the winter the denizens of the Marsh buried themselves deep in the cold mud. They drifted into a long, slow sleep and the Marshes fell silent. The snows of the Big Freeze brought the thickest, softest, most perfect silence of all and Jenna reveled in it. She walked slowly, carefully placing her boots upon the snow so that they made no sound, and pulled her cloak up to quiet the soft *swish swish* it made as it brushed across the snow.

So, when a heavy *thud* sounded behind her, Jenna very nearly fell onto the frozen Mott in shock. She spun around and gave a loud shriek. Septimus stood on the path with a just-landed-out-of-nowhere look to him. He was swaying slightly, wreathed in a weird purple glow.

"Sep!" Jenna gasped. "What . . . I mean . . . where did you . . . how did you?"

Septimus was speaking but no sound emerged. Only when the last wisp of **Magyk** evaporated could Jenna hear what Septimus was saying.

". . . was a close one, Jen. Really sorry, I didn't expect anyone to be out here—especially you. What are you doing here?"

"What am *I* doing here?" Jenna laughed. "I'm just walking. You know, boring stuff, one foot in front of the other? *I*'m not suddenly appearing out of nowhere with little purple lights flickering all over me."

"Just my job, Jen." Septimus grinned.

"Was that one of those **Transport** things?" Jenna asked.

Septimus looked a little smug. "Yep, it *was* one of those **Transport** things."

"All the way from the Castle?" Jenna sounded impressed.

"Yep. Pretty good, huh?" Happy to be out in the sunshine at long last—and doing something interesting—Septimus linked his arm through Jenna's and began walking toward the cottage.

"If you want Aunt Zelda, she's not there," said Jenna. "I've come out to look for her."

"Oh. Well, I do want to see Aunt Zelda, of course I do, but really it's her flask I want," said Septimus. "Or rather, that Marcellus wants."

"Flask? What flask?"

Septimus shrugged. "I don't know. I've never seen it but Marcellus says she keeps it in a cupboard. One that he built especially for it."

"Marcellus built a cupboard for Aunt Zelda?" Jenna was amazed. "She never said."

"No, not for Aunt Zelda; he built it for Broda, his wife. You know, she was Keeper when Marcellus was young. I mean when he was first young—in Queen Etheldredda's time. Your lovely ancestor, Jen," he teased.

"I know all about Broda—I *met* her. And if you're not careful, Septimus Heap, when I am Queen I will be just like Etheldredda and make all Wizard Apprentices come and weed the Palace garden every Saturday." Jenna laughed.

"She didn't do that, did she?"

"Yep. It says so in my book."

"Ah, your *book*." Septimus smiled. He knew all about Jenna's book, *The Queen Rules*. Jenna had an annoying habit of quoting passages from it.

They walked along the Mott path, skirting the mound of snow that covered the remains of the ancient Roman temple where the Dragon Boat had once lain. Septimus stopped a moment and looked at the mound, remembering the first time he had seen the beautiful boat. "That's why you're here, isn't it?" he said quietly.

Jenna nodded.

"You still can't hear her?"

"No. It can't go on any longer, Sep. We need to do the **Triple** properly this time—with the **Tx3 Revive** I got from Broda. No more excuses. No more 'when the time is right, dear' from Aunt Zelda. I'll need you there, of course."

"Just say when and I'll be there. You know that, Jen."

Jenna smiled. "Thanks, Sep. I do."

At the far end of the island past the cottage, two figures, dark against the snow, came into view.

Jenna waved. "Hey! Wolf Boy! Aunt Zelda!"

The shapes were unmistakable. The large slow triangle was Aunt Zelda and the thin, loping creature topped with a mane was clearly Wolf Boy, helping the triangle up the steep slope to the cottage.

"Jen," said Septimus, "does 409—I mean Wolf Boy—does he know?" He still thought of his old friend by his Young Army number: 409. Just as Wolf Boy thought of Septimus by *his* Young Army number: 412.

"Know? About the Dragon Boat?"

"No, Jen—about being a triplet, with Marcus and Matt."

Jenna slowed down. With all her worries about the Dragon Boat she had forgotten about Wolf Boy's lost brothers. "Well, no, I don't see how he *can* know. We were going to tell him at Simon's wedding, weren't we? Only Aunt Zelda forgot to come."

"I thought you might have seen him already," said Septimus.

Jenna shook her head. "Nope."

"I really want to tell him myself. Do you mind?"

"Of course I don't mind, Sep. It's only right that you tell him."

"Thanks." Septimus remembered the time he had discovered who his family was—it had been on this very island almost four years ago. Now, he could hardly imagine being without his family and with no identity—but 409 still was. Septimus had suggested to Wolf Boy that he go to the Young Army Record Office to see what he could find out, but Wolf Boy had refused. He knew he was alone, he'd said, and he didn't see the point of finding *that* out for sure.

They arrived at the cottage just as Wolf Boy was helping Aunt Zelda inside.

"Well, look who's here," said Aunt Zelda, breaking into a

big smile. "How lovely to see you both." She perused Septimus with a puzzled air. "You look different somehow. It's . . . well, I don't know why, but you do, dear."

"Oh, it's my Alchemie Apprentice robes, Aunt Zelda," explained Septimus.

"Alchemie Apprentice. Goodness. Is that what you are now?"

"Only for this month, Aunt Zelda. In fact, only until tomorrow."

Aunt Zelda shook her head. Things changed too fast for her nowadays. "Well, come inside, dears, and we'll have some tea."

After what Sarah had said, Jenna was relieved to see that Aunt Zelda seemed to be her normal self as she bustled about. Jenna sat by the fire and listened while Wolf Boy, pleased to have new company after many weeks of solitude with Aunt Zelda, talked nonstop.

Aunt Zelda brought in buttered toast for Jenna and Wolf Boy and a cabbage sandwich for Septimus, then she settled down beside the fire with her own favorite—a bowl of pureed cabbage leaves and marshberry jam. She regarded her visitors with a happy smile.

"It is so wonderful to see you," she said. "What a lovely surprise. Now, tell me all the news."

Jenna knew that she should tell Aunt Zelda all about Simon and Lucy's wedding, but the Dragon Boat had to come first. She took a deep breath. "Aunt Zelda, it's not good news. I've come because I can't hear the Dragon Boat's heartbeat anymore."

Aunt Zelda paused with a spoonful of purple puree halfway to her mouth. Jenna saw a flash of concern in her blue witch's eyes. "It can be very faint in the winter, you know, dear. And very slow," she said.

"I know," said Jenna. "I'm used to that. This is the third winter I've listened to her. But I have heard nothing for four days now. *Nothing*."

Aunt Zelda put the spoon back in the bowl. "Are you quite sure?"

"I am *absolutely* sure."

Aunt Zelda put the bowl of puree down on the floor. "Oh, dear," she murmured to herself. "Oh, deary deary dear."

"Aunt Zelda," Jenna said. "*I think she's dying*."

Aunt Zelda gave a small moan and put her head in her hands.

Jenna pressed on. "We *must* do the real **Revive** now, with the potion I got from Broda. Please, Aunt Zelda, can you get the bowls for the **Triple** and come back with me and Sep now—*please*?"

Aunt Zelda looked distraught. She heaved herself out of her seat, walked slowly over to the Unstable Potions and Partikular Poisons cupboard and squeezed inside with some difficulty. Jenna glanced anxiously at Wolf Boy.

"Is Aunt Zelda all right?" she whispered.

Wolf Boy waggled his hand to and fro in a so-so gesture. "She forgets stuff and loses things. It upsets her, you know?"

"But she still keeps the cottage really tidy," said Septimus, thinking that he had never seen the bookshelves look so organized. "And the potion bottles so sparkly."

Wolf Boy grinned. "I'm not a bad housekeeper," he said. "And I wield a mean duster."

Aunt Zelda emerged from the cupboard carrying a very battered ancient wooden box on which was written in old script: THE LAST RESORT. She sat down by the fire and handed it to Wolf Boy. "Here, dear. You're good at opening things."

Wolf Boy slipped the catch and went to give the box back

to Aunt Zelda, but she was reluctant to take it. "No, dear. You take the bag out for me."

Wolf Boy drew out an old leather pouch.

"Take out the bowls for me, would you, dear?" asked Aunt Zelda.

Wolf Boy took out a bowl and balanced it snugly in the palm of his hand. Jenna and Septimus recognized the small hammered-gold bowl with the blue enamel edging that they had last seen when they and Aunt Zelda had performed the **Transubstantiate Triple** on the gravely injured Dragon Boat.

Jenna felt relieved. Aunt Zelda's reluctance to do the **Triple** had made her wonder whether she had lost the bowls, but all seemed fine.

Wolf Boy plunged his hand back into the pouch and brought out another bowl identical to the first. "Pretty, aren't they?" he said, balancing a bowl in each hand.

"Yes. And there's one more," said Jenna.

Aunt Zelda closed her eyes and began to mutter something under her breath.

Wolf Boy shook his head. "No more," he said. "That's it."

"*No more?*" asked Jenna.

"No. Sorry. Here, take a look." Wolf Boy passed the bag across to Jenna. She put her hand inside and felt nothing more than cold, dusty leather. Hoping that maybe the bowl was hiding in some obscure **Magykal** way, Jenna handed the pouch across to Septimus, who felt inside. He shook his head.

"Sorry, Jen. No bowl."

"Aunt Zelda," Jenna said gently. "You know there should be three bowls in the bag? Do you know where the other one is?"

Aunt Zelda sighed. "The Marsh Python ate it," she said.

9
TRIPLETS

Night was closing in. Wolf Boy got up from the gloomy group by the fire and lit the lanterns in the deep-set windowsills, while Aunt Zelda began to explain.

"It was a lovely sunny day and I'd left the door open. I was organizing the potion cupboard and I thought I would give the bowls a clean, so I put them on the desk over there"—she waved at an odd-looking desk that had feet like a duck—"and I went to get the **GoldBright** from the top shelf at the back behind the stairs. Well, I couldn't find it, so then I had to sort through everything. I suppose I took a while looking for it. You see, it was hidden behind the **Frog Fusions**, which was next to the **Marvel Mixture**, which I am sure it never used to be, but the **Marvel Mixture** always shines so much that you can't see anything unless you almost close your eyes and of course **Frog Fusions** is a really big bottle as we have so many frogs here and it seems a shame to waste them but the trouble is you can't see anything through that murky green stuff, but I found it at last wedged behind the bottle in a little crevice thingy and when I went back to the desk I tripped right over it."

"Over what?" asked Septimus, who had got lost on the **Frog Fusions**.

"The Marsh Python. Great ugly green thing, thick as a sewer pipe, snaking in through the door all the way to the desk, with its horrible flat head staring around and its long green tongue flicking in and out." Aunt Zelda shuddered. "The wretched thing stretched all down the path to the Mott; in fact most of it was still in the Mott. I think it had been after Bert, because later I found her under my bed with her feathers in a terrible state."

"What did you do?" asked Septimus.

"I gave her some milk and Balm Brew. It always calms her down."

"You gave the python some *milk*?"

"What?"

"Zelda means she gave Bert some milk and Balm Brew," said Wolf Boy. He turned to Aunt Zelda. "So what did you do with the python?"

"I swept it out with the **BeGone** broom," said Aunt Zelda, shuddering at the memory. "Later I found that a bowl was missing and I realized what had happened. That disgusting snake had swallowed it. So I put the two bowls away with a **Return Spell**. It's only a matter of time—the bowl will come back one day; things that belong together always do."

"It will be too late by then," said Jenna flatly.

Aunt Zelda looked desolate. "Jenna dear, I am so, so sorry. I know I should have told you, but I hoped the Dragon Boat would recover her strength in her own way and we would never need to use the **Triple** again."

"Now I understand why you wouldn't do the **Revive**," said Jenna. "It wasn't about it being better for the Dragon Boat to heal herself at all. It was because you'd lost a bowl. I wish you'd told me the truth." Jenna was trying not to feel angry, but she could not believe that Aunt Zelda had kept something so important from her. She remembered what Sarah said about witches: *they tell you what they want you to know—not what you want to know.*

Jenna had been stroking Bert, who lay sleeping on the cushion beside her. But being stroked by someone who was upset made Bert feel edgy. Suddenly the duck gave Jenna's hand a sharp peck. Jenna, to her utter embarrassment, burst into tears.

"Hey, Jen," said Septimus, "it's okay."

"No, it's *not.*" Jenna sniffed.

"We can fix it, I know we can," Septimus insisted.

"But *how*?" Jenna asked, blowing her nose on her red silk handkerchief.

Septimus picked up one of the bowls and turned it over in his hands. "When he's got the **Fyre** going, I bet Marcellus could make another one."

"I'm afraid he can't, dear," said Aunt Zelda. "A new bowl would not belong. It couldn't communicate with the others. You see, they are all from one original piece of ancient gold."

"Ah . . . **Cloned** gold."

"Gnomed gold?" asked Aunt Zelda, whose hearing was not as good as it had been.

"***Cloned***. Each one belongs to the other. Like identical triplets. Oh!" Septimus suddenly realized what he had said. He glanced at Jenna.

The shock at the disappearance of the third bowl had put all thoughts of Wolf Boy's brothers out of Jenna's mind. But now she was glad to think of something else for a while. She nudged Septimus. "Go on."

"Ahem," said Septimus nervously. Suddenly, it seemed such a big thing to tell Wolf Boy.

The little cottage fell silent. Aunt Zelda stared mournfully at the fire.

"Triplets," said Jenna, trying to get Septimus to speak.

"Weird. Don't you think?" said Wolf Boy.

"What's weird?" Jenna asked.

"Triplets. Twins. People being identical." Wolf Boy shook his head. "I dunno why, but whenever I see twins or triplets it always gives me a peculiar feeling. Right here." Wolf Boy pushed his fist against his stomach. "Something about people looking the same, I guess."

Septimus and Jenna exchanged glances. *Tell him*, Jenna mouthed.

Wolf Boy was a good lip reader. "Tell him what?" he asked suspiciously.

Septimus looked at Wolf Boy. "Um. There might be another reason why you feel like that." He pushed his fist against his stomach just as Wolf Boy had done.

"Yeah?" said Wolf Boy, picking up a bowl and twirling it to catch the reflections from the firelight.

"Identical triplets," said Septimus. "I mean . . ."

Wolf Boy put the bowl down and stared at Septimus, puzzled. "What?"

Septimus floundered. "Well, some people actually are triplets but they don't know they are but even so they still kind of know deep down because even though they can't remember it they were together once I mean so close together you can't imagine it and so that's why they get this weird thing when they hear about triplets and . . ."

"You all right, 412?" Wolf Boy asked.

"Yep. Fine."

Jenna could bear it no longer. "Sep, just tell him straight."

Wolf Boy looked worried. "Tell him *what* straight?" he asked.

Septimus took a deep breath. "*You* are an identical triplet. We've found your brothers—well, Beetle has. He went to the Young Army Record Office. And there are two more like you: 410 and 411."

"Jeez." Wolf Boy slid down to the floor with a bump.

Septimus grinned. "I suppose you're the lost bowl," he said.

"Swallowed by the python," Jenna added.

Aunt Zelda looked up, shocked. "Swallowed by the python? Who?"

"It's all right, Zelda, no one's been swallowed by the python," Wolf Boy said gently. "But it seems . . . wow, it's so *weird* . . ." He grinned. "It seems I got two brothers. Just like me."

"Oh, yes, so you have. I forgot." Aunt Zelda smiled.

"You *knew*?" asked Septimus.

"I remember now. There were two boys at your fourteenth birthday party. They worked in a cave place . . . what was its name?"

"Gothyk Grotto," Jenna supplied.

"That's it, dear. I thought at the time, Wolf Boy, that your voices sounded so alike. But it slipped my mind."

"Two more of *me* . . ." Wolf Boy was muttering.

Septimus could not stop smiling. "Yep, two more of you. Except they've got less hair. And they're not so thin. And they are really pale compared to you."

"That's right," said Aunt Zelda, pleased that she could at least remember this. "At the party—you were sitting opposite them, Wolf Boy dear."

"*Opposite?*" said Wolf Boy, shocked.

"They're really nice," said Jenna.

"Yeah. Yeah . . ." Wolf Boy mumbled.

"You could do a lot worse," said Septimus. He was an expert in long-lost brothers.

Wolf Boy shook his head. "Yeah. I know. I really liked them. Matt and, er, Marcus, yeah?"

"That's right."

Wolf Boy put his head in his hands. "It's . . . it's so *horrible*."

Jenna glanced anxiously at Septimus. "What's horrible?" she asked, putting her arm around Wolf Boy's shoulders.

"It's so horrible that I met my brothers and I had *no idea*. They could have been anyone. I should have recognized them," he said, sounding upset. "But I didn't. I *didn't*."

"How could you?" said Septimus. "You were only three months old when they took you away."

"Took me away?"

"Your father was a Custodian Guard. He made a joke about the Supreme Custodian and they took his children away. You and your brothers."

Aunt Zelda reached out and took Wolf Boy's hand. No one said anything for some minutes.

At last Wolf Boy spoke. "You know, 412, it was bad what they did to us. Really, *really* bad."

"Yes, it was," said Septimus. "It was disgusting."

Jenna picked up the two gold bowls and cradled them in her hand. "Sep," she said. "I want to take these to Marcellus. We have to go. *Now.*"

Septimus sighed. He wanted to stay and talk to Wolf Boy. "But, Jen, I told you. Marcellus doesn't have the **Fyre** going yet. It will be weeks before there is any chance of making another one."

Jenna shook her head stubbornly. "I have to try, Sep. *I have to.*"

It was Wolf Boy who settled the argument. "Why don't we check out the **Triple** rules first?" he suggested. "There are lots of books here that you don't have in the Castle—you know, witchy books. We might find a way around needing the third bowl. Witches are good at finding their way around things."

"That's a good point, Jen," said Septimus.

Jenna could only agree with Wolf Boy. Witches clearly were very good at finding their way around things. "Okay," she said. "We'll stay tonight. And look through all the books.

Supper was pig-foot pie garnished with steamed eel heads followed by a large communal bowl of cabbage leaf and marsh-berry jam puree, into which Aunt Zelda suggested they dip dried wormsticks, although no one did. The usual pushing of food around plates occurred, and even Septimus, who had once loved Aunt Zelda's cooking, found the pig foot on his plate hard to swallow. They helped Aunt Zelda clear the table and wash the plates; then Aunt Zelda went upstairs to bed, leaving them feeling queasy but still very hungry.

Wolf Boy fetched three straw mattresses and laid them out beside the fire along with three pillows and quilts. As the gentle sound of Aunt Zelda's snores drifted down the stairs, Wolf Boy began setting up a tripod over the fire, from which a large hook dangled.

"What's that for?" Jenna asked.

"The cooking pot," said Wolf Boy. "Like we had in the Forest. 'Scuse me a moment." He got up and went into the kitchen, returning with a round black pot, which he carefully hung on the hook. He threw another log on the fire and they watched the flames jump up and curl around the side of the pot. "Rabbit stew," said Wolf Boy. "*Proper* rabbit stew. With good stuff in it like—"

"Rabbit?" asked Jenna.

"Yep. With potatoes and onions and carrots and herbs."

"No eels?" asked Septimus.

"No eels," said Wolf Boy firmly. "No wormsticks and positively *no* pigs' feet."

As the cooking pot bubbled gently, a delicious smell filled the room and ushered out the lingering taint of eel. Jenna felt ravenous. "Do you always cook your own stuff?" she asked.

"I'd be as thin as one of those brooms up there if I didn't," said Wolf Boy. "Zelda doesn't mind. She goes to bed early, I clean up and then I sit here with my cooking pot and memorize some potions or something."

"You don't get lonely?" asked Jenna.

"Nah. I'm not alone. Zelda's upstairs, Bert's here and the marsh is outside. I love it."

To Jenna's dismay, the search through Aunt Zelda's witchy library yielded nothing at all. As the moon rose high above the snow and its silver light filled the cottage, they settled down for the night, pulling the quilts around them to keep off the chill that was creeping in. The cottage grew quiet and they began to drift off to sleep, lulled by the silence of the frozen marsh.

Suddenly Wolf Boy sat up. "Hey!" he said.

"Wassamatter?" Septimus mumbled blearily.

"So what am *I* called?" asked Wolf Boy.

"Huh?" asked Jenna.

"My name? What's my name?"

"Wolf Boy," said Jenna, confused.

"No. I mean my *real* name. There's Matt and Marcus, but what about me?"

"Ah," said Septimus. He glanced at Jenna.

"Your surname is Marwick," said Jenna. "That's a good, ancient Castle name."

"Marwick . . . yeah, that's nice, feels right, somehow," said Wolf Boy. "But what is my first name?"

"Well." Septimus sounded reluctant.

Wolf Boy was getting impatient. "Oh, spit it out, 412. It can't be that bad."

Septimus thought it could. "Mandy," he said.

"Mandy?" Wolf Boy sounded incredulous. "*Mandy?*"

"Yeah. Sorry, 409."

Wolf Boy buried himself in his quilt. "Sheesh . . ." Jenna and Septimus heard him muttering. "*Mandy . . .*"

⳨ 10 ⳨
THE CLOUD FLASK

"Morning, Mandy," said Septimus, *stepping* over the recumbent Wolf Boy. A wiry arm shot out and a hand fastened itself around Septimus's ankle. A growl came from beneath the quilt. "Don't . . . call . . . me . . . Mandy."

"Ouch, 409, that *hurts*."

"Good." Wolf Boy sat up, his long matted tails of hair fuzzed by sleep.

"So what *do* we call you?" Jenna's voice came from the far end of the room. The marsh light had woken her early, as it always used to, and she was gazing out of the window watching the snow falling thick and fast across the marsh. "You've got three different names now."

Wolf Boy considered the matter. "Yeah. Well, Marwick's good. I like Marwick. Or Wolf Boy is fine. Don't think much of 409 anymore—not after what they did to us. No more numbers, hey, 412?"

"Yeah," agreed Septimus. "No more numbers."

"That's a deal," said Wolf Boy. "So . . . I think I'll use Marwick officially, like when I have to sign my Keeping papers and stuff like that. But Wolf Boy's good for the rest of the time."

"Until you're too ancient to be called 'boy' anymore," said Jenna.

"Yeah. Then I'll be plain old Marwick. Sorted."

Aunt Zelda got up late. She looked tired and drawn, Jenna thought, as she walked slowly and heavily down the stairs, her grizzled hair unbrushed and her large patchwork dress looking gray around the edges. A pang of pity went through Jenna—suddenly, Aunt Zelda was old. Jenna rushed over and wrapped her arms around her great-aunt.

Aunt Zelda looked a little overcome. "I thought you might have gone. I was afraid . . ." The words seemed to catch in her throat. "I was afraid you might never come to see me again."

"Of course I'll come to see you again," said Jenna. "And don't worry about the bowl. Marcellus will make another one."

Aunt Zelda didn't think such a thing was possible, but she merely sighed and said, "Well, I do hope he can, dear."

"Okay, Sep?" said Jenna. "Shall we get going now?"

Aunt Zelda twisted a patchwork handkerchief in her knobbly fingers. "Come and tell me when the bowl's ready, won't you? Please?"

Jenna gave Aunt Zelda another hug. "We'll need you to do the **Triple** with us, Aunt Zelda. Come on, Sep. I'll take you through the Queen's Way."

"Yes—oh, bother. Wait a minute, Jen; I've got to get the flask. I promised Marcellus."

"Okay. But hurry up."

Jenna waited impatiently by the fire while Septimus explained to Aunt Zelda what he wanted. Aunt Zelda looked surprised. She led him over to a door set into the wall at the back of the cottage and, fumbling in her pocket, she drew out a set of small brass keys. Septimus waited impatiently while Aunt Zelda frowned at the keys.

"Would you like me to find the key?" Wolf Boy asked gently.

Gratefully, Aunt Zelda handed him the keys. "Yes, please, dear."

A moment later Wolf Boy had unlocked the door and opened it to reveal the flask.

"It's massive!" Septimus gasped.

Wolf Boy shrugged. "Yeah, well, it is quite big, I suppose. But then Cloud Flasks have to be, don't they?"

"Do they?" Septimus knew nothing about Cloud Flasks and Marcellus had certainly not enlightened him. He had imagined a small glass jar that he could put in his pocket. But the thick glass flask that sat on the cupboard floor was as wide as Aunt Zelda and a good foot taller. Its round bowl filled the cupboard completely and its tall neck rose up above Septimus's head.

Septimus glanced anxiously over to Jenna, who was pacing up and down by the fire—there was no way he could get something this big back through the Queen's Way. "Um, Jen . . ." he ventured. "Can you come over here, please?"

Jenna was not pleased. "It won't go through the Way, Sep."

"I know." Septimus sighed. "I'll have to take it back to the Port on a sled and then get the Port barge."

Jenna was aghast. "No, Sep! We have to get to Marcellus today. It's a matter of *life and death.*"

"But Jen, like I said, Marcellus hasn't got the **Fyre** going yet. He can't do it until then."

"Sep, we have to ask—*we have to!*"

Wolf Boy stepped in. "Septimus," he said, feeling strange using his friend's real name for the first time, "have you looked outside?"

Septimus glanced across at the window. Snow was falling fast. He went over to the front door and pulled it open. All he could see was a grayish-white blanket of snow falling so thick that the air looked almost solid. "Bother," he said.

"It's a real marsh blizzard," said Wolf Boy, joining him. "You'd be crazy to go out in that. In ten minutes you and that flask would be just a weird-shaped pile of snow."

"How long will it last?" asked Septimus.

Wolf Boy shrugged. "Who knows? But I'd guess all day. We've had a few of these recently and once they start, the snow keeps falling until the cold night air comes in."

Septimus would have happily waited the blizzard out in the comfort of Aunt Zelda's cottage. He would have loved to spend a day by the fire talking to Wolf Boy, catching up with his life and finding out what he was doing. But one look at Jenna told him that that was not an option. "I'll have to come back for it," he said. "Tomorrow, when the blizzard's blown out."

Jenna pushed Septimus into the little cupboard under the stairs, closed the door and lit a small lamp. The light flared up in the dark and Septimus saw the familiar shelves with their orderly bottles of Unstable Potions, and below them he saw in the dark wood a line of drawers, in which he had always supposed the Partikular Poisons were kept. He watched as with a practiced air, Jenna reached down to the bottom drawer and opened it. He sensed something move within the drawer and heard a soft click behind them as the cupboard door locked itself and they were plunged into darkness.

The next thing Septimus knew was Jenna pushing the door open again. He guessed she had forgotten something. She stepped out and he waited for her to go and get whatever it was.

Jenna looked back into the cupboard. "Are you coming, Sep?"

"Huh?"

"We're here."

"Where?"

"Back at the Castle. In the Palace."

"Already?"

Jenna grinned. "Yep. Good, isn't it?"

Septimus followed Jenna out of the cupboard and stepped into a small, cozy room. It possessed a little fireplace with a fire burning in the grate, and a comfortable, somewhat worn-looking chair placed beside it. What he did not see was the occupant of the chair: the ghost of a Queen—a young woman, wearing a red silk tunic, with a gold cloak wrapped around her shoulders. Around her long dark hair was a gold circlet—the one that Jenna now wore.

At the opening of the cupboard door, the ghost jumped up. She had been waiting for this moment. Her daughter had rushed past her so fast on her way into the cupboard that she had not had time to react. Now she was ready. The ghost of the Queen got to her feet and stepped in front of Jenna.

Jenna stopped dead—*something was in the way.*

Septimus was just behind Jenna. "What is it?" he whispered.

Jenna remembered something the ghost of Queen

Etheldredda had once said to her. "I think that maybe my mother is here," she whispered. Tentatively she put her hand out in front of her.

The ghost of Queen Cerys stepped back to avoid being **Passed Through**. "Yes, *yes*, I am here!" she said—but no sound emerged. What the ghost did not realize was that it takes some practice to speak without **Appearing**. And Cerys knew that the Time was not yet Right for her to **Appear** to her daughter.

Jenna turned to Septimus. "Do *you* feel it?" she whispered.

Septimus nodded. The little room felt strangely full of movement, as though currents of air were swirling around.

Jenna took a deep breath and said out loud, "Is anyone there?"

"*I* am here," said the ghost of the Queen, silently and somewhat irritably. "Daughter, our mothers tell me the Dragon Boat is dying. You must save her!"

Beside the ghost of Queen Cerys stood the ghost of her own mother, Jenna's grandmother, the redoubtable Queen Matthilda. The rotund ghost, gray hair awry, crown slightly askew as it always had been in Life, was agitated. "For goodness' sake, Cerys, say something," the ghost told her daughter.

"I am *trying* to, Mama."

"Well, try harder, dear. She'll be gone in a moment. The young move so fast."

Queen Cerys concentrated hard. "Daughter. Listen to me!"

Jenna glanced at Septimus. "Was that you?" she asked.

"Was *what* me?"

"A kind of whisper."

Septimus shook his head. He longed to get out of the oppressive little room; it held bad memories for him. "Let's go, shall we?" he said.

Jenna nodded.

Queen Matthilda was exasperated. "Cerys, *tell* her!"

"How can I concentrate when you keep *going on at me*?" Cerys demanded crossly, as she watched her daughter and the Alchemie Apprentice edge past her.

"Well, *I* shall tell her," snapped Queen Matthilda.

"No, you will *not*."

"I shall. She is *my* granddaughter."

"And she is *my* daughter."

"Sadly neglected if you ask me," Queen Matthilda huffed. "You really should make more of an effort with her. Poor child. You know I would happily stay here in your place so that you could go to her. She needs you, Cerys."

Jenna took the few steps across to the blank space in the wall where the hidden door to the outside lay. Septimus followed, glancing backward uneasily.

Cerys was fast descending into one of the legendary fights that she used to have with her mother. "Mama, you know *The Queen Rules* perfectly well. We do not **Appear** until the Time Is Right. You *know* that. How can my daughter ever become a true Queen if we keep **Appearing** to her, telling her what to do, preventing her from finding her own true path?"

"Absolute twaddle," harrumphed Jenna's grandmother. "I never did agree with that part of the *Rules*. Never."

"You cannot cherry-pick from the *Rules*, Mama. It is all or nothing. Wait!"

The ghost of Queen Cerys saw her daughter take hold of the Apprentice's hand and heard her say, "Let's go, Sep!" Cerys began whirling around the room in frustration. Why couldn't she speak? *Why?* As her daughter headed toward the wall, a faint, despairing cry found its way into the room: *"Hear me! Only you can save the Dragon Boat!"*

On the other side of the wall Jenna stared at Septimus openmouthed. "That was my mother!"

"Are you sure?"

"Sep, I know her voice. *I know it.* It's my mother!"

"It was only her ghost, Jen."

"So why doesn't she **Appear** to me, Sep? *Why?* She must have seen me often enough. She's just like my father. They're both the same. They *both* keep away. It's *horrible.*"

"Oh, Jen," said Septimus, at a loss for words.

"And now—now all she does is *tell me to do something that I can't do!*"

⁜ 11 ⁜
DRAGON Fyre

S*eptimus held a burning rushlight* to light the way as he and Jenna walked through the coils of the lapis lazuli Labyrinth. The last time Jenna had been there was five hundred years in the past, and the flickering of the flame lighting up the blue lapis walls brought back terrifying memories of being dragged through it by the murderous ghost of Queen Etheldredda.

At last they reached the arch that led into the Great Chamber of Alchemie. After Septimus's descriptions of all the soot and sand, Jenna was expecting to see a wreck, but what met her was a bright glittering chamber, full of gold—a testament to Septimus's cleaning skills.

Jenna's gaze was at once drawn to the two huge, patterned gold doors set in the wall opposite: the Great Doors of Time that had once been the gateway to the Glass of Time itself. Even though she knew that the Glass had shattered and no one could now pass through them to another Time, they still had a presence that gave her goose bumps. Jenna shivered and looked away to the neat ebony workbenches that lined the walls, clean and polished, with unpacked boxes stacked up neatly.

Jenna loved all the gold gleaming softly in the candlelight—gold catches, handles and hinges, tiny gold drawers below the workbenches, gold brackets that held up the shelves and even the scuffed strips of gold that ran along the bottom of the ebony benches, protecting the precious wood from the boots of Marcellus's ancient and long-gone junior Apprentices.

Jenna and Marcellus shared a fascination for gold.

To Jenna's right was the furnace—still unlit—with its funnel of a chimney snaking up through the domed ceiling. In the center of the Chamber was a long table on which a line of candles was burning brightly. But something was missing.

"Where's Marcellus?" asked Jenna.

Septimus shrugged. "I dunno. He's always going off somewhere. He'll be back soon."

Jenna sat down at the long table. "So, where does he go, then?"

"I don't know. He never says."

"Don't you ask?"

Septimus laughed. "I know *you* would, Jen. But it's not polite for an Apprentice to ask things like that. He'd tell me if it was important."

"Sounds weird to me," Jenna said. "I mean, what *else* is there to do down here?"

The sound of footsteps in the Labyrinth stopped their conversation. A few seconds later, Marcellus Pye appeared through the archway. He looked startled.

"Septimus! What are you doing back so *soon*? Oh! And Esmeralda!" Marcellus was spooked. In the candlelight Jenna looked so much like his long-gone sister, Esmeralda, that he had forgotten for a moment what Time he was in. Being in the **Fyre** Chamber still took him back to the old times. Marcellus recovered from his Time Slip and offered Jenna the seat at the head of the table. "Please, Princess Jenna, sit down."

Jenna took her seat and Marcellus sat down a little shakily on the bench at the side of the table, leaving Septimus to take his usual place on the right-hand side.

"Welcome to the Great Chamber, Princess Jenna," Marcellus said rather formally. "I am delighted that you have come to see it so soon. It is an integral part of the Castle in which the Queens have always taken a great interest. Much greater, I believe, than in the Wizard Tower."

Jenna nodded—she could believe that. Remembering what she had come for, she placed the leather bag on the table and took out the two bowls.

Marcellus looked at them with interest. "Ah," he said. "The **Triple**. How nice." He waited for Jenna to put the third bowl on the table.

"There isn't another one," she said. "The python ate it."

Marcellus looked shocked. "You must get it back right away. Kill the wretched snake if you have to."

"It's not that easy," said Jenna. "You see—"

Marcellus got to his feet. "Well, Marcia will just have to go without her silly shoes."

"Shoes?" asked Jenna, confused.

"Her purple pythons. Isn't that the only reason Terry Tarsal keeps that ghastly snake? Marcia may not believe it, but some things are worth more than shoes and this set of bowls is one of them. Terry Tarsal will just have to kill his precious python."

Now Jenna understood. She sighed. "It's not Terry Tarsal's python, Marcellus. I wish it were."

"Then whose python is it?"

"It isn't anybody's python. It's the giant Marsh Python."

Marcellus sat down. "Ah. Unfortunately not quite so easy to catch."

"No."

"Well, that's a great shame. To lose the **Triple** after all this time."

"I told Jenna that you could **Clone** them," Septimus said anxiously.

Marcellus laughed. "You have great faith in me, Apprentice. But there is much to do before we can even think of that." He sighed and stood up as if to end the meeting. "I am so sorry, Princess," he said. "I cannot **Clone** the gold for you now. We are not yet ready."

"So that's it, then," said Jenna flatly. "She's going to die."

Marcellus looked shocked. "Who is going to die?"

"The Dragon Boat."

"What, the Dragon Boat of Hotep-Ra?"

Jenna nodded, too upset to speak.

"If you will forgive the question, Princess, why do you think she is going to die?" Marcellus asked.

"I haven't heard her heart beat for a whole five days now. I go every day in the Big Freeze. Aunt Zelda said I should. And I do hear it. Even though no one else can, *I* always do. And now . . . now it's stopped. And the only thing my mother has ever asked me to do, I *can't*."

Marcellus thought that Jenna had the same look that his sister Esmeralda used to have when teetering on the edge of a tantrum. He decided to tread carefully.

"Tell me, Jenna, what is it that Sarah has asked you to do?" he asked gently.

"Not Sarah—not *mum*. My mother. The Queen."

"The Queen? Her ghost has spoken to you?"

"We *think* we heard something," Septimus said doubtfully.

Jenna was distractedly tracing her finger around the design of the sun cut into the ancient wood of the table. "Sep, I heard my mother. I *know* it was her." She looked up at Marcellus. "Her ghost spoke when we were in the Queen's Room."

"Ah. Then it *is* your mother," said Marcellus. "That is where the ghost of the previous Queen always resides."

"Does she? Why didn't you tell me?" asked Jenna.

"Well, I assumed you knew," said Marcellus.

"No. No one tells me anything," Jenna declared. "Not even my *mother*."

Marcellus stood up. "Then it seems to me, Princess, that as your nearest relative on the *royal* side, it is time I stepped in. I will tell you all I know from my dear dead sister and my, ahem, less dear but thankfully dead mother."

Jenna looked surprised. She had never thought of Marcellus as a relative, but it was true; he was in fact a great, great—and then some—uncle. Suddenly she felt a weight lifted from her shoulders. The Dragon Boat was no longer her worry alone. "Thank you," she said, smiling for the first time that day.

"My pleasure, niece," said Marcellus. "Now, I suggest we repair to the boatyard and open the Dragon House."

"But what for? We've lost the **Triple** so we can't revive her," said Jenna, exasperated. She wondered whether Marcellus had actually listened to what she had been saying.

"There is more than one way to skin a cat," said Marcellus.

Jenna's patience ran out. Angrily, she stood up, scraping the old oak chair back across the stone floor. "Stop talking in riddles, Marcellus," she snapped.

Marcellus put his arm out to stop Jenna from going. "Forgive my obscure speech, Princess," he said. "What I mean is, there is more than one way to revive a dragon." He stood up and put his arm around Jenna's shoulders. "The **Magyk** way is beyond us now, so I shall show you the Physik way."

Jannit Maarten was sitting in her snow-covered hut in the boatyard, cooking her favorite sausage and bean stew when, to her dismay, she saw the new Castle Alchemist walk by with the Princess, the ExtraOrdinary Apprentice and then—as her tiny snow-dusted window filled with green—*ohnonotthatwretcheddragon*. Jannit muttered a sailor's curse and got to her feet.

During the Big Freeze, Jannit hibernated like a tortoise in her hut. She looked forward to the peace and quiet that the first flakes of snow brought with them. She sent her Apprentices and dockhands home, and waited happily for the day the Moat froze over and not even the Port barge could disturb the serenity of the boatyard. For the rest of the year Jannit worked day and night, eating, sleeping and dreaming boatyard business, but the Big Freeze was her holiday. As she had grown older, Jannit had begun to look forward to it so much that she had recently considered barring the way through the tunnel to ensure she was not disturbed by anyone from the Castle. The sight of three Castle dignitaries walking by her tiny snow-dusted window, accompanied by a notoriously heavy-footed dragon, made her wish she had done just that. There was a sharp rap on her door and Jannit briefly toyed with the idea of pretending she was not there in the hope they would go away. But the thought of them poking unsupervised around her boatyard and, even worse, the heavy-footed dragon trampling on the delicate shells of the upturned boats, got Jannit opening the hut door with a growled, "*What?*"

The new Castle Alchemist spoke. "Good day, Mistress Maarten, I—"

Jannit bristled. "I am no one's *mistress*, Alchemist." Jannit, who disapproved of Alchemie, managed to make "Alchemist" sound like an insult. "Jannit Maarten is my name and Jannit Maarten is what I answer to."

"Ah. Forgive me. Jannit Maarten. Yes. Indeed. Ahem."

Jannit, who was nearly a foot shorter than Marcellus, folded her arms belligerently and squinted up at the Alchemist. "What do you want?"

Marcellus looked down at the small, wiry woman swathed in a thick blue-black woolen sailor's coat that was far too big for her and reached almost to the ground. He could see she meant business. Her iron-gray hair was scraped back into a sailor's pigtail that seemed to bristle with annoyance, and every deep-set, wind-burned line in her face showed just how displeased she was to see him. Marcellus took a deep breath. He knew that what he had to say was not going to go down well.

"We have come to open the Dragon House," he said. "I am sorry for any inconvenience it may cause."

Jannit looked flabbergasted. "You what?"

Jenna decided to step in. "I'm really sorry, Jannit," she said. "But I think the Dragon Boat is dying. We have to get into the Dragon House. We *have* to try to save her."

Jannit liked Jenna, who reminded her of how she had been as a girl: a confident, taking-charge kind of person. That, thought Jannit, was how girls should be.

"Well, Princess, I am most sorry to hear that. Of course you must open the Dragon House, though how you propose to do that I have no idea. You do realize there is no opening anymore—just a solid wall?"

Jenna nodded. "Yes. That's why we have Spit Fyre with us."

"So I noticed," said Jannit drily. She looked up at the dragon, and Spit Fyre's green eyes with their red ring of **Fyre** around the iris met her disapproving stare. Spit Fyre shifted uneasily from one foot to another. He felt as though he had done something wrong, although he wasn't sure what. He finished chewing the cow bone that Septimus had just fed him and a large glob of dribble headed for Jannit's sealskin boot.

Jannit moved her boot just in time. "Well, I suppose if you must. Don't let him tread on anything, will you?" she said. "I don't want anything broken."

"We shall naturally take great care," said Marcellus and gave a small bow. Jannit—who thought bowing was an affectation—harrumphed and turned to go back inside her hut.

"Thank you, Jannit," said Jenna. "Thank you so much."

Jannit thawed a little more. "I hope you find your boat is well, despite your fears, Princess Jenna," she said. She stood at the hut door, watching the group pick its way across the boatyard as they headed toward the Castle wall within which the Dragon House was secreted. Jannit was just closing the hut door (and looking forward to her sausage and beans) when she saw Spit Fyre about to step on a large pile of snow, under which lay her favorite rowboat.

"Stop!" she yelled, running out of the hut and waving her arms. The group did not hear. Jannit saw that Spit Fyre was about to lower his foot—suddenly she remembered something from her childhood. "Freeze!" she screamed. It worked. Everyone stopped in midstep, including Spit Fyre, whose great foot hovered a few inches above the pile of snow. Jannit raced out into the snow. "Wait right there!" she yelled. "Don't move an inch."

Spit Fyre stood with his foot swaying uncertainly in midair, looking increasingly unsteady. Jannit hurtled to a halt beside them. "Don't step there!" she said.

Spit Fyre looked down at Jannit and wobbled. Any minute now, Septimus thought, he will topple over and squash someone.

"Easy now, Spit Fyre," said Septimus. "Put your foot down here—next to mine." He looked at Jannit. "It's okay there?"

Jannit sounded relieved. "Yes, thank you, Apprentice."

"Ouch!" Septimus gasped. Spit Fyre's foot had come to rest on his boot.

Jannit now insisted on piloting the party across the yard. Dragons and boatyards did not mix, she told the visitors sternly. They reached the other side without any breakages and came to the edge of the Cut, which was a short and apparently dead-end run of water that led off the Moat and ended at the high Castle wall. Because the water in the Cut was virtually unaffected by the Moat's currents it froze early. It was, Jannit informed them, easily thick enough to support the weight of a dragon.

Septimus was not so sure. Spit Fyre was—as his throbbing foot was telling him—extremely heavy. But it was true; the Cut was an ideal spot for the dragon to take off from, safely away from the boatyard clutter. To get to the nearest alternative takeoff area, Septimus would have to walk his dragon back through the boatyard, and he didn't relish telling Jannit that. The Cut it would have to be.

Septimus climbed up into the dragon's Pilot Dip. "Okay, Spit Fyre. Forward. One foot at a time and *slowly*."

Spit Fyre looked at the ice and snorted doubtfully.

"Come on, Spit Fyre," Septimus urged. "Foot down."

Spit Fyre stretched out his huge right foot; its green scales glistened against the smooth white snow that covered the Cut. He leaned out from the icy edge, tipped forward a little and suddenly Spit Fyre went sliding onto the Cut. A groan came from deep within the ice and Septimus felt the surface beneath the dragon's feet shift.

"Up!" he yelled to Spit Fyre. His shout was lost in the *craaaaack* that spread across the ice like the sound of the ripping of a thousand sheets. Spit Fyre needed no urging to go. He thrust his wings down just enough to raise his weight off the ice at the very moment it fell away beneath his feet. In a spray of ice splinters and snow Septimus and Spit Fyre were airborne.

Jenna, Marcellus and Jannit watched Spit Fyre rise up and head slowly toward the blank wall at the end of the Cut. Jannit, who appreciated how difficult it was to maneuver odd-shaped craft in confined spaces, was impressed. When Spit Fyre was only a few feet away from the wall, he stopped and hovered so that his nose was level with the burnished gold disc set into the Castle wall. The disc was just above a line of dressed stones that arched gracefully through the Castle wall—this was the only clue to the hidden entrance to the Dragon House.

A thrill of excitement ran through Septimus. He and Spit Fyre were going to make **Fyre** for real, not some practice run trying to hit the metal **Fyre** target in the Dragon Field. This was actually going to do something—it was going to open the Dragon House. He steadied Spit Fyre and patted his neck. "**Ignite!**" he yelled.

A deep rumble began inside Spit Fyre's fire stomach, taking the phosphorus from the bones that Septimus had hastily fed him on his way to the boatyard, and turning it into the gases that would combine to make **Fyre**. The plume of gas swept up through Spit Fyre's fire gullet and hit the air where it spontaneously **Ignited** with a loud *whuuuuuumph*. A thin, blindingly bright jet of **Fyre** streamed from the dragon's mouth and hit the very center of the gold disc. The disc began to glow and turn from a dull gold to a dusky orange, to bright red, to a blinding white. Then there was a sudden flash of brilliant purple, which caused everyone to flinch and shut their eyes—Spit Fyre included.

When the watchers beside the Cut opened their eyes there was a collective sharp intake of breath. The wall was gone and the Dragon House was revealed: a towering lapis lazuli–domed cavern, covered in golden hieroglyphs. And below, held fast within clear blue ice, lay the Dragon Boat, her head resting on a marble walkway, where it had been laid almost three years earlier.

A sudden shout came from below. Septimus looked down to see Jenna running toward the Dragon House.

"She's covered in ice!" he heard Jenna yell. "She's *dead*."

12
The Chamber of the Heart

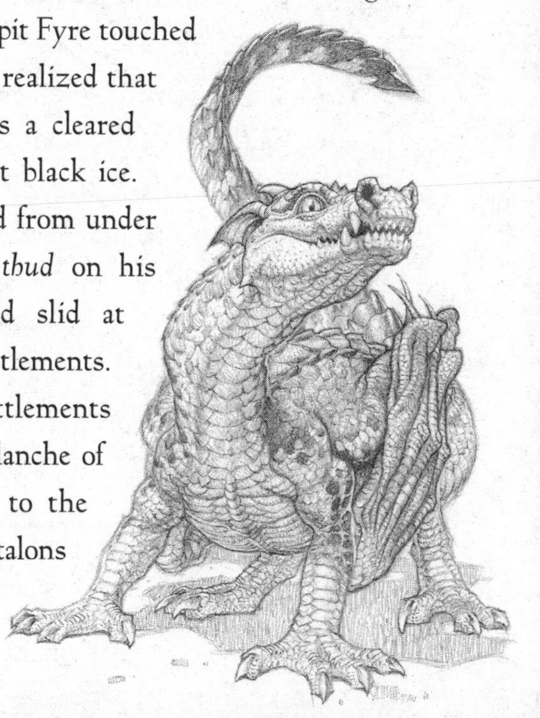

Septimus landed Spit Fyre on the broad space above the Dragon House where Jenna had listened for the dragon's heartbeat. It wasn't until Spit Fyre touched the ground that Septimus realized that what he had thought was a cleared patch of snow was in fact black ice. Spit Fyre's feet disappeared from under him. He landed with a *thud* on his well-padded stomach and slid at great speed toward the battlements. A moment later the battlements were gone, sending an avalanche of stones thundering down to the Cut. It was only Spit Fyre's talons digging into the ice—and a superb piece of tail-braking—that stopped Septimus and his dragon from following the stones into the Cut below.

A delighted face in an attic window watched the scene. "Gramma, Gramma, it's Spit Fyre! Gramma, *look*!" yelled the boy.

His grandmother was less thrilled. "That tail could put all the windows out," she said.

Septimus slipped down from the Pilot Dip and patted the dragon's nose. "Well done, Spit Fyre. Go home!"

But Spit Fyre didn't want to go home. He could see that there was another dragon right beneath his feet and he wanted to meet it. He thumped his tail in disapproval.

The little boy in the attic squealed with excitement. His grandmother threw open the window. "Careful!" she yelled.

"Sorry!" Septimus shouted. He looked at his stubborn dragon and a whisper of the **Synchronicity** between him and Spit Fyre came back—now he understood why Spit Fyre wanted to stay. Septimus put his hand to his ear, which was the sign that told Spit Fyre to listen. Spit Fyre dutifully dropped his head down so that Septimus could talk at dragon-ear height.

"Spit Fyre. The dragon is very ill. She may even be dying. If you stay you must be very quiet. You must not move. No tail thumping, no claw scratching, no snorting, no *anything*. Do you understand?"

Spit Fyre blinked twice in assent. Then he lay down on the ice and mournfully rested his head over the parapet: a dying dragon was a terrible thing. Septimus patted Spit Fyre's neck and left his dragon to be watched over by a nervous grandmother and her excited grandson.

With Jenna's cry of "she's dead" still echoing in his head, Septimus raced down a narrow flight of stone steps that led to the opposite side of the Cut. As he made his way along the foot of the wall toward the Dragon House, a faint movement and a slight cooling of the air told Septimus that he was walking through a throng of ghosts. And from the restrained, somewhat regal atmosphere he guessed they were ancient Queens and Princesses, anxiously watching.

Septimus moved slowly through the ghosts toward the open mouth of the Dragon House. He now saw what Spit Fyre's **Fyre** had revealed. It was eerily beautiful. The Dragon Boat, stark white against the deep blue lapis of the Dragon House, lay deathly still, encased in a frosting of ice. A shaft of light from the winter sun glanced in and made the ice sparkle with such movement that for a moment Septimus thought that all was well and the Dragon Boat was breathing. But the concerned faces of Marcellus and Jenna—and even Jannit Maarten—on the opposite side of the Cut told him otherwise.

Septimus walked quickly across what was left of the ice, reached the boatyard side of the Cut and followed Marcellus and Jenna into the chill of the Dragon House. The air inside reminded Septimus of the Ice Tunnels—stale, strange and icy cold. He made his way along the icy marble walkway and joined Jenna and Marcellus where they stood, looking down at the Dragon Boat's head.

Her head rested on a rug laid on the marble walkway. The swanlike curves of her neck, the fine detail of the scales, the intricate contours of the head all showed through the ice frosting, like a finely carved statue. In fact, it seemed to Septimus that the dragon had turned to marble, so cold and stonelike did she look.

Marcellus nodded to Septimus. "I have been explaining to Jenna that a dragon is a reptile with blood that cools but does not freeze, with blood that allows her to become deeply unconscious and yet still return to life. Indeed, some say dragon blood has the property of eternal heat. What I am saying is that it is *good* she is covered in ice."

This made sense to Septimus, but from Jenna's expression he could see that Marcellus still had some persuading to do.

"So," said Marcellus, "shall we go aboard?"

"*Aboard?*" The thought of stepping onto the Dragon Boat made Jenna feel very uncomfortable. It felt disrespectful—like walking over a grave.

"Naturally. It is what we need to do. Or rather, what *you* need to do."

"Me?"

"It is the Queens who have the touch. And, I believe, a small bottle of **Revive**."

"Oh!" Jenna took the tiny the blue bottle from her pocket. On its small brown label was written **Tx3 Revive**. "So I can use it, even without the **Triple Bowls**?"

"Of course. There are many ways to use the **Revive**."

"So, what do I do? Put it on her nose or something?"

"Something," said Marcellus. Very carefully, he stepped onto the deck of the Dragon Boat and held out his hand for Jenna, who took it and stepped lightly in beside him, followed by Septimus. Almost reverentially, Marcellus moved toward the center of the deck, where there was a pair of tiny doors leading to a locked cabin. No one had ever been able to open the doors. When Jannit had repaired the boat, she had become quite spooked by the fact that there was a part of it she could not get to. And there were times when she thought she could *hear something in there.*

Marcellus kneeled down at the doors, which were mistily visible through the ice. He unwrapped his black velvet scarf and began to gently rub the ice until it was clear of hoar frost, and peered through the glassy surface of the ice to the mysterious azure blue doors below. "Apprentice, I wonder if you have something that would melt this ice?"

Septimus fished a small candle-end out of his pocket. "I've got my tinderbox. I can light this."

Marcellus heaved a sigh. "That will take hours, Apprentice. Do you have, er, anything else?"

Septimus grinned. So much for Marcellus insisting on *no* **Magyk** *while you're my Apprentice.* "You mean something like a *spell*?" he asked.

"A spell will be fine, thank you."

Septimus kneeled down beside Marcellus and placed his hands on the ice that covered the doors. With his palms threatening to stick fast, he quickly muttered a simple **Melt**. Then he leaned all his weight onto his hands and pressed hard. He felt the heat of his palms spread out into the ice and soon there were two rapidly growing hand-shaped holes in the ice, water was running down the inside of his sleeves and his hands were through to the smooth wood below. Septimus rocked back on his heels, shook the warmth back into his freezing hands and watched the ice retreat to reveal two shiny, deep blue lacquered doors, each with a simple dragon symbol enclosed in a lozenge shape.

"Stop now," said Marcellus. "I think it is safer to keep the temperature low until we find out what . . . what we are dealing with."

"You mean, until we find out if she's dead," said Jenna.

"Personally, I do not believe she is dead," said Marcellus. "Now we must open the doors."

Septimus shook his head. "They don't open. In fact, I think they're false doors. Just one piece of wood."

"That, Apprentice, is what they are made to look like. But they are not. I have opened them once before."

"*When* before?" asked Jenna.

"You forget I was the husband of a Keeper," Marcellus

answered. He took off the heavy gold disc that hung around his neck—his Alchemie **Keye**—and placed it in a shallow indentation where the doors joined, saying, "My dear Broda once had a similar panic as you, Princess."

"I am *not* panicking."

"During a particularly cold Big Freeze she too was sure that . . . *aha*, the doors are opening!"

Jenna and Septimus crouched down beside Marcellus and watched the doors swing open to reveal a deep, red-tinged darkness. Gingerly, Marcellus leaned forward and looked inside; then he sat back on his heels and beckoned to Jenna to come closer. "Can you hear anything now?" he said in a hushed voice.

Jenna leaned forward through the hatchway into the dark. A sense of being deep inside the Dragon Boat made the hairs on the back of her neck rise. She could smell something like warm iron; it was rich and strange and made her feel a little queasy. "Is this where her heart is?" she whispered.

Marcellus nodded. "Wait a few minutes. Her heart beats slowly when it is so cold."

Like surgeons gathered around a patient on an operating table, they waited for a heartbeat. Marcellus took out his timepiece and looked at the second hand moving round. It made three sweeps of the dial, then four, then five.

"Nothing," Jenna said miserably. "*Nothing.*"

"No," said Marcellus heavily. "You are right, Princess. Of course."

"She's dead," said Jenna despairingly. "She's *dead.*"

"I do not think so. If she were dead I believe she would be frozen all the way through. But possibly she is getting near to it." Marcellus looked up at Jenna, a serious expression in his eyes. "As your mother so rightly said, only you can save her."

"But *how*?"

"It is something the Queens pass down one to another."

"But *no one's* passed it down to me."

Marcellus was soothing. "I know. But I can tell you. That day in the Big Freeze when my Broda could no longer hear a heartbeat, she went to get my sister Esmeralda, who was Queen. I came with Esmeralda because she always panicked in the Queen's Way. And I watched what Esmeralda did." Marcellus gave a wry smile. "And what a fuss she made about it."

"About *what*?" asked Jenna, irritated. Sometimes she thought that Marcellus enjoyed being obscure.

"I will tell you."

By the time Marcellus was nearly through his explanation Jenna had a good deal of sympathy with Esmeralda. So did Septimus.

Marcellus finished with, "So now, Princess, you too must enter the Chamber of the Heart."

Jenna looked at the reddish darkness beyond the two little doors and for a moment wished that she had never asked Marcellus for help. Like most Castle Queens and Princesses, Jenna had a squeamish side to her, and right then she felt quite sick. But she must do what she must do. She took a deep breath, ducked through the low opening and crept inside, where she found the wide, flat rib that Marcellus had described and crawled gingerly onto it. Below her, Jenna now knew, lay the Dragon Boat's heart.

Following Marcellus's instructions, Jenna tipped a few drops of the brilliant blue **Tx3 Revive** onto her palms and rubbed it in. The fresh smell of peppermint cut through the thick, meaty fug of the Chamber and took away her nausea. She reached down into the darkness, and her hand met something firm to the touch, cool but not ice-cold and not, as Jenna had feared, at all slimy. It felt like touching the side of her horse, Domino, on a chilly night. This was, she knew, the Dragon Boat's heart. Stretching out both hands, Jenna dropped forward and leaned all her weight onto the heart for a few seconds, then released the pressure. She repeated it twice and then sat back and waited. Nothing happened. Jenna counted to ten slowly and did it again. One . . . two . . . three . . . Once more she waited and once again, nothing happened. Jenna dropped forward for a fifth time and leaned all her weight onto the stilled heart, willing it to respond. *One . . . two . . . three . . . wait, count to ten, then ready to begin again.* Just as she was reaching the end of her count to ten, Jenna became aware of something happening below in the darkness. A flutter, a twitch . . . and then a low, slow *ther-umm* pulsed through the Chamber. Jenna was out of the doors as fast as she could go.

"It worked!" she whispered excitedly. "*It worked.* Her heart just did a beat. She's alive!"

"A true Queen," said Marcellus, smiling. "No one else could have done that. I suggest we wait for another beat before we close the doors. Just to make sure."

They waited. And waited. "Two minutes." Marcellus's whisper echoed around the cavern after what had felt like at least ten to Jenna. "Three . . . four . . ."

And then at last—another *ther-umm* resonated through the Dragon House.

"Thank goodness," whispered Marcellus. "Now, let us quickly close the doors. It is not good to expose such delicate areas to the air." Marcellus placed his **Keye** on the doors to lock them once more. "Perhaps you could ice them over, Apprentice," he said to Septimus.

"An **Ice *Spell*** you mean?" asked Septimus, grinning.

"Whatever," said Marcellus, who, like Marcia, had now caught Septimus's slang.

Ther-umm came another heartbeat.

Septimus completed his spell and a fresh skin of ice crept across the doors. Marcellus, Jenna and Septimus stepped off the Dragon Boat and walked along the walkway toward the brightness of the snowy boatyard where the small, anxious figure of Jannit Maarten waited. As they stepped down from the marble walkway, a strange sound like the rustling of autumn leaves greeted them—the sound of ghostly applause from the crowd of Queens and Princesses.

Ther-umm.

The ghosts parted to let them through, all passing

favorable comments on Jenna's Queenly abilities. Her grandmother, Queen Matthilda, who had left her daughter sulking in the turret, could resist no longer. She **Appeared** to Jenna. "Well done, my dear," she said.

Jenna looked shocked. No ghost of a Queen—apart from the ghastly Etheldredda—had ever spoken to her. There was, as she knew from section 133 in *The Queen Rules*, a ban on ghosts speaking to Living Princesses and Queens. It was put there for the very good reason that all Queens were convinced that they knew best and would have no hesitation in telling the current incumbent so. But Queen Matthilda—who had watched over her granddaughter since the day she was born—could keep silent no longer. Her granddaughter needed to know she was doing well and Queen Matthilda intended to tell her. She lightly patted Jenna's arm and smiled. "You will make a good Queen," she said.

"Oh!" said Jenna. "Thank you!"

Ther-umm.

A sudden gasp from Jannit broke the moment. "My hot pot!" she yelled and took off running across the yard, leaping over the upturned boats, heading for her hut. A cloud of black smoke was billowing from the stovepipe in the roof and suddenly everyone could smell burning.

Septimus went to help.

To the background of sailor's curses and the sound of a metal pot hissing in the snow, Marcellus and Jenna looked at the Dragon Boat, lying white and majestic in the blue of the Dragon House.

Ther-umm.

"I don't want to wall her in again," Jenna said. "I want to be able to come and talk to her. To watch over her, just like Aunt Zelda would do if she were here."

"I understand, Princess," said Marcellus, "but perhaps you should seek advice from the Keeper first."

Jenna was not sure. "Aunt Zelda forgets stuff now," she said. "I don't know if she knows what's best anymore."

Marcellus was still annoyed with Marcia, but he knew he must give as good advice to Jenna as possible. "Then ask Marcia," he said. "She will know."

Septimus took a very reluctant Spit Fyre back to his Dragon Field and arranged to meet Jenna by the Great Arch. Jannit retreated to her hut, locked the door and embarked upon cooking sausage-and-bean hot pot take two.

* * *

It was later that evening that Jannit, to her utter dismay, found she had two dragons in the boatyard. Spit Fyre had returned and was sitting, perfectly quietly, at the entrance to the Dragon House. Jannit was not pleased, but there was something about the two dragons together that touched her. It was almost, she thought, as if they were mother and son.

13

WELCOME BACK

Alther Mella, ex-ExtraOrdinary Wizard, ghost and mentor was up in the Pyramid Library with Marcia. Alther's presence broke the convention that ExtraOrdinary Wizard ghosts did not return to the Wizard Tower, but after her old tutor's shocking death, Marcia had missed Alther so much that when he was released from his year and a day in the place where he had entered ghosthood,

Marcia had asked Alther to come back to the Wizard Tower and to use it just as he had when he was Living. She had never regretted it.

The tall, purple-clad ghost with his white hair tied back in a ponytail was hovering over a large book with tissue-thin pages, wafting them over one by one. He was helping Marcia search for something—*anything*—that would explain the puddles. It was a thankless task. They had found nothing. But Marcia could not shake off the feeling that deep below the Castle *something was going on.* It was even giving her nightmares: fires burning out of control and monsters coming out of the deep regularly invaded her sleep.

Marcia knew that everything relating to What Lies Beneath the Castle was stored either in the Manuscriptorium Vaults or in the Pyramid Library. Beetle had done a complete search of that section in the Vaults and found nothing more than his Vent diagram—so whatever information there was had to be in the Pyramid Library.

What puzzled Marcia was that although she and Alther had found nothing positive, they had found some strange absences. In many of the shelf indexes there were unexplained gaps, even complete empty pages. The Alchemie section was almost nonexistent apart from some very basic student primers, and the notes relating the Ice Tunnels went back no further than when they were **Frozen** after the Great Alchemie Disaster, which was very odd, Alther said, because they were as old as the Castle itself. It seemed to both Marcia and Alther that a large chunk of Castle history had been systematically removed. And Marcia was beginning to suspect that the lack of information about the **Fyre** and the Vents was linked. They must be, she thought, part of the same system and were therefore removed at the same time. *But why?*

"The funny thing is, Marcia," Alther said as he wafted through the pages of yet another index, "you wouldn't know things were missing unless you were looking for them."

"Exactly," Marcia agreed. "And if you didn't know about them to start with, you wouldn't be looking for them, would you?"

"If you ask me," said Alther, "someone has spent a long time up here, systematically removing anything relating to Alchemie and ancient structures beneath the Castle. It must have been an ExtraOrdinary Wizard—no one else would have had the access. I wonder who it was?"

"More to the point, I wonder *why*," said Marcia. She

thumped a pile of pamphlets down and a cloud of dust **Passed Through** Alther. The ghost spluttered. "Careful, Marcia. I'm allergic to dust."

Marcia laughed. "You can't be, Alther. You're a ghost."

Alther looked a little offended. It was not polite to remind a ghost of their ghosthood. "Well, I *am*," he said huffily. "Ever since that ghastly Drago Mills place."

"It's not totally ghastly," said Marcia. "I got a very nice rug from the sale. Oh, hello!"

The little door to the Library had swung open and Septimus and Jenna came in.

"How lovely to see you both!" said Marcia. She looked at her Apprentice, who she had not seen for some weeks. "Oh, Septimus, you look so *pale*."

Septimus fielded a barrage of questions about whether he was eating properly and did he ever get outside in the daylight, and then went to talk to Alther, leaving Jenna to ask Marcia's advice about the Dragon Boat.

Ten minutes later, Septimus, Jenna and Marcia were out in the corridor, waiting for the stairs to change direction. They were on slow mode due to the arrival of the elderly parents of one of the Wizards, and Marcia was polite enough to wait until they had got off. Septimus watched the silver treads rise sedately upward; the shafts of sunlight coming in through the azure-blue glass of the stairwell window threw lazy, glimmering patterns onto the solid silver treads. He loved this time of day in the Wizard Tower; there was something **Magykal** about the evening sun when it came in low through the windows. Septimus took a deep breath and breathed in the scent of **Magyk**—sweet with a hint of sandalwood.

"Have you seen him acting suspiciously?" Marcia said suddenly.

"Huh?" said Septimus, heady with the **Magyk**.

"Marcellus. Have you noticed anything . . . strange?"

It was a difficult question for Septimus to answer: many things that Marcellus did could be thought of as strange—especially by Marcia. But Septimus did not like to tell tales. "No," he said.

The stairs changed direction and Marcia hopped on. "I'll look forward to seeing you back here tomorrow evening, Septimus." She looked at her Apprentice critically as he stepped back to let Jenna get on before him. "It's not good for you, being buried like a mole under the ground."

Marcia was beginning to disappear from view. Jenna jumped on after her and made her way down a few steps until she was near enough to talk. "It really is all right, then?" she asked Marcia. "The Dragon House staying open?"

"Fresh air and some sunshine—just what the Dragon Boat needs," Marcia said. "And Septimus too."

The stairs were now approaching the fifteenth floor. Dandra Draa, the new Sick Bay Wizard—headhunted by Marcia for her skills in **DisEnchantment**—had just finished an emergency callout to a Wizard who had been convinced he had **Enchanted** himself by reading an ancient text. Dandra had diagnosed Papyrophobia and was now on her way up to see Marcia. She was waiting patiently for the stairs to change direction when she saw the distinctive purple pointy pythons appearing above her.

"Good afternoon, Madam Marcia," said the Sick Bay Wizard. She waited politely for Marcia to rotate past.

"Jump on, Dandra," said Marcia. "I'm sure you've got better things to do than wait there."

Dandra Draa was new to the Wizard Tower and was unsure of protocol. She had recently arrived from the Dry, Hot Countries in the South where she had lived in a beautiful, star-encrusted, circular tent beside a deep pool on the edge of a desert. Life there had been so much simpler. It had certainly not involved stairs of any description—or ExtraOrdinary Wizards with weird shoes. Dandra hesitated. Surely it was not right to stand *above* the ExtraOrdinary Wizard? But it was impossible to step on below as those stairs had already passed. And *oh, no*, here came the Princess, slowly revolving down. Dandra did a confused half bow, half curtsy. What was she to do now? Could she jump on in front of the Princess? Oh, it was all too much.

"Get on, Dandra, do," said Marcia impatiently.

Dandra took a deep breath and jumped nervously onto the empty stair between Marcia and Jenna. It was an embarrassing squash and Dandra hardly dared breathe. She decided to deliver her message, whatever the protocol.

"Madam Marcia. What we hope for happen. Syrah Syara wake."

Marcia took a moment to digest Dandra's way of speaking. But Septimus understood at once.

"Syrah's awake?" he asked. "You mean she is **Dis-Enchanted**?"

Dandra looked up to see the big brown boots of the

ExtraOrdinary Apprentice. "Yes," she said. "Syrah is **DisEnchanted**."

"Dandra, that is marvelous news," said Marcia. "I shall go and see her at once."

"So shall I," said Septimus.

Marcia stepped off the stairs, closely followed by Dandra Draa, who performed an awkward jump and to her embarrassment landed on Marcia's cloak hem.

"See you tomorrow, Sep," Jenna said, as she carried on down.

"See you, Jen," Septimus called, as he jumped onto the seventh floor.

Jenna saw Marcia put her arm around Septimus's shoulders and lead him down the dimly lit corridor that led to the Sick Bay. She was glad to see Septimus back with Marcia in the Wizard Tower; it suited him better and, she had to admit, it felt safer. Jenna pushed away a niggle of anxiety at the thought that he still had one more day to go in the Great Chamber of Alchemie and Physik—Septimus would soon be back, she told herself.

Jenna jumped off the stairs in the Great Hall and wandered across to the tall silver doors, watching the flickering images on the walls—which showed important and often dramatic moments in the history of the Tower—fade in and out of focus. One that she had not seen before came into view: Septimus and Spit Fyre attacking the **Darke** Dragon. She smiled and wondered if Septimus had seen it yet.

Jenna had an idea. She scribbled a Welcome Back party invitation for Septimus and knocked on the door of the duty Wizard's cupboard. Hildegarde Pigeon peered around the door.

"Oh!" she said, looking surprised and glancing back into the cupboard. "*Princess Jenna*," Hildegarde said, oddly loudly. She peered out. "How can I help you?"

A muffled cough came from inside the cupboard. Jenna thought it sounded familiar, although she couldn't place it. "Can you give this to Septimus, please?" she asked.

Hildegarde's hand shot out of the narrow gap between the door and the doorjamb and hurriedly took the invitation.

"Um, thank you," said Jenna. "Sorry to interrupt whatever it is you're doing."

"Doing?" Hildegarde squeaked. "I'm not *doing* anything!" The door to the duty Wizard cupboard slammed shut.

Jenna shook her head—now that Hildegarde was almost

a proper Wizard she was as weird as the rest of them, she thought. Pleased to be leaving the **Magykal** mist that always hung around the Great Hall of the Wizard Tower, Jenna whispered the password and waited while the huge silver doors to the Wizard Tower swung open and the floor bade her GOOD-BYE, PRINCESS. HAVE A NICE DAY.

Moments later she was running down the white marble steps in the brilliant, breathtakingly cold winter sunshine, heading back to the Dragon Boat—which was, amazingly, *alive*.

✣ 14 ✣
DisEnchantment

In *the* **DisEnchanting** *Chamber, Syrah* Syara lay in her cocoon, suspended from the ceiling by the wispy strands of Forrest Bands. She looked just as she had done when Septimus had said good-bye to her before he left to be with Marcellus: her face was bone-thin, her hair pulled back into two tight little plaits and her skin was tinged blue by the light in the Chamber. Nothing had changed except for one important thing: Syrah had her eyes open.

Syrah looked up at the three faces staring down at her. Her gaze traveled blankly from Marcia, to Dandra Draa and on to Septimus.

"Syrah," said Septimus. "It's me, Septimus. Syrah, you're safe. You're in the Wizard Tower."

Syrah frowned and struggled to speak.

"Is enough now," Dandra said. "I watch Syrah tonight and if all go well, we move her. Is good. Out, please." In her own domain, Dandra Draa had confidence. She shooed Marcia and Septimus out like a couple of annoying bluebottles. They emerged into the Sick Bay, smiling.

"Wonderful," said Marcia. "Dandra has done all I hoped she would. I'll see you tomorrow evening, Septimus, six o'clock sharp, please, in time for Dandra and Hildegarde's Wizard Warming Supper." She strode across the Sick Bay, giving a cheery wave to Rose, the Sick Bay Apprentice, and was gone. Septimus sighed. He wished he did not have to go back to Marcellus. He *so* much wanted to be there when Syrah came out of the **DisEnchanting** Chamber.

Loath to leave, Septimus stopped to say hello to Rose. Rose—tall and skinny with brown hair so long that she could sit on it—looked very efficient. Her hair was tied back into the regulation Sick Bay plait and she wore a white tabard over her green Apprentice robes.

"Still here?" Septimus asked. He knew that Rose, who was on the new Apprentice rotation scheme, had been hoping to go on to the **Charm** Desk.

"Still here," agreed Rose. She glanced around. "Worse luck," she whispered.

"I'm sorry." Septimus stopped. That didn't sound right. "I mean, I didn't mean I'm sorry to see you. I meant—"

Rose smiled. "That's okay. I know what you meant. I say stupid stuff like that all the time. Oh! See, I did it right then."

"Quits then," Septimus said, grinning. "Anyway, maybe it's not so bad still being here. Maybe you'll end up upstairs."

"Upstairs?"

"Yes. With Marcia. She's put the Pyramid Library onto the scheme."

"Wow!" Rose looked amazed. The **Charm** Desk paled into insignificance compared with the Pyramid Library. "Oh, gosh, I must go and get some sheets," she said. "We've got a scribe coming up. Broken leg."

Rose rushed off and headed for the cupboard between beds twelve and one. The beds in the Sick Bay were ranged around the room like numbers on a clockface. There were only two occupants, both elderly Wizards and both asleep. Septimus watched a large pile of sheets stagger over to bed three.

"Need any help?" he offered the stack of sheets.

"Oh, *yes*, *please*," it said.

Septimus helped Rose make the bed in the approved Young Army fashion. Rose surveyed the result. "You're good," she said, surprised.

Septimus very nearly gave Rose a Young Army salute but stopped just in time. "Thank you," he said. "I'd better go. I'll be back tomorrow evening."

Rose smiled. "Syrah will be out then."

"Yes, isn't that great?"

"Yes. Miss Draa has been amazing." Rose watched Septimus breeze out and tried not to wish that he was coming back to see her rather than Syrah.

Down in the Great Hall, Septimus bumped into Beetle. "Hey, Beet!" He smiled. "What are you doing here?"

"Hello, Sep. Just seen poor old Barnaby Ewe onto the

stretcher lift. Broke his leg. He fell into one of those puddles—there's a really deep one in a dark corner of Little Creep Cut. Be careful if you go down there. People cover them up, then some joker gets an idea it would be fun to move the covers."

Septimus fell in with Beetle as he walked across to the doors. "Marcia was going on about puddles too," he said. "She thinks it has something to do with Marcellus."

"It has," said Beetle. "I am convinced of it. He's doing something he's not telling us about."

"Really?"

The double doors swung open and a rush of fresh, cold air met them. Twilight was falling as Beetle and Septimus headed down the wide steps and the great doors closed silently behind them. They walked across the Wizard Tower Courtyard, their boots crackling through the frosted snow, the ice crystals sparkling in the light from the rushlights that lined the wall.

"I suppose you haven't noticed Marcellus doing anything unusual?" asked Beetle. "Like disappearing and not saying where he's been?"

Septimus did not reply.

"Sorry," said Beetle. "I know I shouldn't ask. Confidentiality between Master and Apprentice and all that."

"It's okay. I'm not his Apprentice, and I'm not going to be either. I was thinking about what you said. Well, Marcellus comes and goes, you know? Nothing unusual, really. He's just busy, I guess."

Beetle sensed a "but." He was right.

"But . . . well, yesterday Marcellus sent me off to Aunt Zelda's to get a flask. He didn't tell me it was so huge that I'd have to bring it back across the Marshes. He must have known it would take days. And he didn't seem pleased that I was back so soon. It made no sense—until I thought that maybe he didn't want me around for some reason. You know?"

"Well, well. Fancy that," said Beetle.

At the Great Arch both Beetle and Septimus stopped and turned around to look up at the Wizard Tower. It was one of those crystal-clear nights when the lights of the Tower were dazzling; they glittered and sparkled in the frosty air, brilliant against the Tower's silver sheen, turning the gently falling snowflakes a soft purple and blue.

"Wow," breathed Beetle. "Sometimes I forget how beautiful this place is."

"Yeah," said Septimus. After a month underground, he too

had forgotten. He felt a pang of homesickness for the Wizard Tower and had a real desire to turn around and go back . . . home. He sighed. He had one more day with Marcellus. That was all. It would soon be over.

Septimus and Beetle walked through the inky shadows of the Great Arch and emerged into Wizard Way. They looked down the snowy Way, quietly busy with people closing up their shops for the night, and at the far end they saw the unmistakable red flash of Jenna's cloak as she disappeared through the Palace Gate. Septimus was in a reflective mood.

"You never did say anything to Jenna, did you?" he said.

Beetle looked at his friend, surprised. "About what?"

"Beetle, you *know* what. About *liking* her."

Beetle shot Septimus a look as if to say, *How did you know?* "Well. No," he said. "She didn't want me to. I could tell."

"Could you? How?" Septimus really wanted to know.

"I just *could*. And then . . . well, I suddenly knew for sure that she didn't care. Not in that way. But it's fine now. I've got better things to do."

"So that's okay, then?" Septimus sounded doubtful.

Beetle smiled. He realized what he had said really was true.

"Actually, Sep, it *is* okay. What I love is being Chief Scribe. Most days I wake up and I still can't believe that's what I am. Most days I don't even *think* about Jenna."

"*Really?*"

"Well . . . maybe that's not totally true. But it's okay. And anyway, she's very young."

"She's not *that* young—she's nearly fourteen and a half now."

"Yeah . . . well. Even so."

"Same age as me." Septimus grinned.

"You're six months older, remember—after your time with Marcellus?"

"Oh, yeah." That was not something Septimus liked to remember much—being stranded in another Time. The more he thought about it the less he wanted to go back to Marcellus's house in Snake Slipway, which—especially at night—reminded him of that Time. He took a deep breath of the Wizard Way air from *his* Time and wandered along with Beetle toward the Manuscriptorium.

At the door, Beetle said with a grin, "Want to come in and have a **FizzFroot**? I've got buckets of 'em upstairs now."

Septimus shook his head. "I should really be getting back to Marcellus. I have to tell him that Marcia won't let me do another month with him."

"Oh, come on, Sep. Just one little **FizzFroot**. You haven't seen my new place yet."

Septimus needed no excuse to change his mind. "Okay, Beetle. Just one."

The new Chief Hermetic Scribe took the ExtraOrdinary Apprentice through the Manuscriptorium with a proudly proprietorial air. The large room with the tall desks was empty. Unlike the previous Chief Hermetic Scribe, Beetle did not believe in keeping scribes at work after dark had fallen. It was brightly lit with fresh candles placed in the ancient candleholders set into the wall and the room no longer had the air of suppressed boredom and gloom that had pervaded it in Jillie Djinn's time. Beetle and Septimus headed toward the short flight of steps that led up to a battered blue door.

The rooms of a Chief Hermetic Scribe were modest in comparison with the rooms of an ExtraOrdinary Wizard, but Beetle loved them. There was one long, low-ceilinged room with a multitude of beams that spread almost the entire length of the Manuscriptorium. The room had a line of three low dormer windows on either side. One side looked out across the rooftops to the Moat and the dark Forest beyond, and the other looked out on Wizard Way. Off the main room was a small, beamed bedroom, a bathroom and a tiny kitchen where Beetle kept his stash of **FizzBom** cubes to make up the **FizzFroot**.

"Wow," said Septimus, admiring the minute kitchen dominated by the large bucket of refurbished **FizzBom** cubes on the shelf. "You can do just what you want. Without Marcia banging on your door telling you not to."

"Let's hope so," said Beetle with a grin. "Chocolate Banana, Apricot Ginger or a weird blue one—no idea what it is."

"Weird blue one, please."

"Thought you'd say that. Cheers, Sep."

"Cheers, Beetle. Happy new home."

It was much later when Septimus finally left the Manuscriptorium and headed back to Marcellus's house in Snake Slipway. As he approached the tall, thin house, with its windows ablaze with lighted candles, Septimus felt very guilty for being so late. He looked up to the little attic window where his bedroom was and saw the lighted candle in the window, which

Marcellus always placed there at night. He thought of the welcoming fire in the grate, the sloping eaves, his desk and his bookshelf full of Physik books, and he felt a stab of sadness. He realized he had loved being there too. He thought about the great Chamber of Alchemie and Physik where the **Fyre** was ready to be lit—which he was going to miss. He sighed. There were two places in the Castle where he belonged, but he had to choose one. And he had chosen. But it didn't mean he liked the other any less. And it didn't make it any easier to tell Marcellus.

Septimus let himself into the house with a sinking feeling in his stomach. Marcellus was waiting. "You look frozen," he said as he ushered Septimus into the small front room. "Your lips are quite blue." He made Septimus sit beside the fire and drink some of his special hot ginger. While Marcellus was putting another log on the fire, Septimus took the opportunity to rub the **FizzFroot** blue off his lips.

"That's better," said Marcellus, settling into his old armchair opposite Septimus. "You've got some color back now."

Septimus took a deep breath. "I have to leave tomorrow," he said.

"Ah," said Marcellus.

"I'm sorry," said Septimus.

Marcellus gave a rueful smile. "I am not surprised, Apprentice. I had a little, ah, contretemps with Marcia recently and to tell the truth, I was not expecting anything else." He raised his glass to his old Apprentice. "Here's to you, Septimus. And my thanks to you for all your work. I know this last month has not been quite what you had hoped for, but I have so enjoyed having you to help me." Marcellus paused. "I did hope you might decide to . . . what is the phrase . . . jump ship. Become my permanent Apprentice."

"I did think about it," said Septimus. "A lot."

"But you decided not?"

"Yes."

Marcellus nodded. "I understand. One has to make choices. You will be difficult to replace, Apprentice. However, I do have someone in mind."

Septimus looked surprised. It had not occurred to him that Marcellus would replace him with someone else. He wasn't sure how he felt about that.

Late that evening, when Septimus had gone up to his room to pack his bag, the new residents of the house opposite

Marcellus Pye got an unexpected visit from their neighbor.

Lucy Gringe, resplendent in a beribboned dressing gown she had just finished making, opened the door. "Oh!" she said. And then, remembering her manners, "Hello, Mr. Pye. Do come in."

"Thank you." Marcellus stepped inside. "Goodness," he said. It was chaos.

"Excuse the mess. Wedding presents," said Lucy cheerfully. "It's nice to see you. Would you like some herb tea? Come through."

"Oh, well, actually I wondered if Simon was—" But Lucy had already set off. Marcellus followed her along the dark, narrow corridor, catching his long pointy shoes on various objects strewn across the bare floorboards.

"Ouch!"

"Sorry, Mr. Pye. You okay?"

"Oof. Yes. Thank you, Lucy."

They negotiated the obstacle course and reached the tiny kitchen, which consisted of a fire with a large pot hanging over it and a deep stone sink set on tree-trunk legs, in which sat the remains of supper. The kitchen was a jumble, covered with pots and pans that had nowhere to hang, half-open boxes and stacks of plates. Lucy saw Marcellus's gaze travel around the room. "We'll get it sorted," she said cheerfully. "I'll call Si; he'll be really glad to see you."

"Ah," said Marcellus, still lost for words.

Lucy opened the back door and yelled into a tiny yard enclosed by a high brick wall, "Si . . . *Si!* Mr. Pye!"

Simon, who had been trying to unblock a drain, emerged from the shadows, wiping his hands on his tunic.

"Si, Marcellus is here to see you," said Lucy.

Simon smiled. "Good evening, Marcellus. Good to see you. Would you like some tea?"

Marcellus, a fastidious man, had decided it might be safer not to risk the tea. "Your good lady wife . . ."

Lucy, still not used to being called Simon's wife, giggled.

". . . kindly offered me some, but I mustn't stay long. I have a proposition to put to you, Simon."

Lucy and Simon looked at each other.

Simon cleared a pile of plates off a rickety chair. "Please, do sit down, Marcellus."

Marcellus saw the sticky ring left on the chair and shook his head. "No, no. I really must get back. This won't take a moment."

Five minutes later Simon and Lucy watched Marcellus Pye cross the snowy slipway back to his house, the moonlight glinting off the gold fastenings on the back of his shoes.

Simon was lost for words. In his hand was a precious copy of the Alchemist's oeuvre, the *I, Marcellus*, with instructions to read it thoroughly and meet Marcellus at six o'clock the following evening.

"Well," said Lucy. "Who'd have thought it?"

15
THE LAST DAY

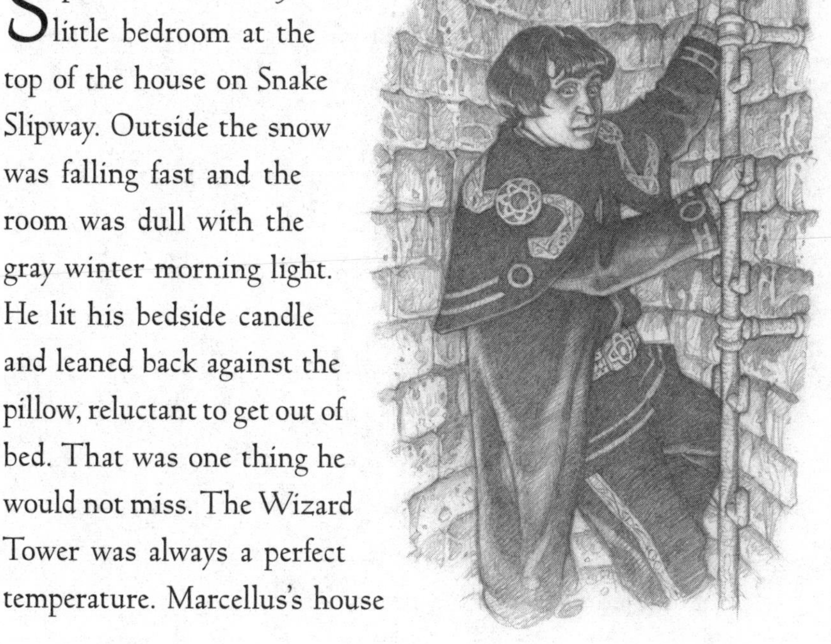

Septimus awoke early in his little bedroom at the top of the house on Snake Slipway. Outside the snow was falling fast and the room was dull with the gray winter morning light. He lit his bedside candle and leaned back against the pillow, reluctant to get out of bed. That was one thing he would not miss. The Wizard Tower was always a perfect temperature. Marcellus's house was, like all old Castle houses during the Big Freeze, bitterly cold.

An hour later Septimus was with Marcellus in an old lock-up at the end of Gold Button Drop—a dead-end alleyway just off the end of Alchemie Way. The lock-up was a cover for a secret entrance to Alchemie Quay, which Marcellus had recently reopened. After locking the little iron door behind them, Marcellus pulled open the circular manhole cover in the center of the earthen floor. A glow of red light shone upward, lighting the rough stones of the lock-up's conical roof. Carefully, Marcellus unhooked a small **Fyre** Globe from its peg just below the manhole cover, clipped it onto his belt, and began the descent down the iron rungs set into the brick chimney. Septimus swung himself in after Marcellus and pulled the trapdoor shut with a clang.

There followed a long descent down a brick-lined shaft, eerily lit with the red light from the Globe. Eventually Marcellus and Septimus reached a wide, brick-lined tunnel and set off along it. Some minutes later, they emerged into the first curve of the Labyrinth, but instead of turning left, as they normally did for the Great Chamber, Marcellus turned right and led Septimus out onto Alchemie Quay.

"It is your last day, Apprentice," Marcellus said.

"It is," agreed Septimus, wondering what Marcellus had in mind. He hoped it was going to be more interesting than cleaning sand out from cupboards with a toothbrush.

"Septimus," said Marcellus. "I wish to apologize for sending you off on a wild-goose chase to collect the Cloud Flask. I needed time to think."

"Oh?" said Septimus.

"Indeed. And your absence made me realize how much I valued you. I have made an error in not telling you everything that I am doing here."

"Ah," said Septimus, not entirely surprised.

Marcellus took a deep breath, aware that he was taking an irrevocable step. "I want to show you the **Fyre**," he said.

Septimus did not understand. "But you haven't lit it yet."

"Apprentice, the furnace that you see in the Great Chamber is a decoy. The true **Fyre** has already begun."

Suddenly things began to make sense. "*Where?*"

"Come. I will explain." Marcellus led Septimus over to the edge of the Quay, where the pink paddleboat bobbed quietly, tethered to its ring. Marcellus kept it just in case— an Alchemist always had an emergency escape route. The

UnderFlow Pool lay dark at their feet and the familiar feeling of vertigo that always got to Septimus when he stood on the edge of the UnderFlow Pool made him feel dizzy.

"See the currents in the water?" asked Marcellus.

Septimus nodded.

"A hundred feet down from here is a sluice gate. Some weeks ago I opened it. Now water is flowing through it, pouring down a channel bored through the rock to a reservoir far below. This is the water that is making the **Fyre**."

"But water doesn't make **Fyre**," said Septimus.

"Alchemical **Fyre** is different," said Marcellus. "It is a beautiful, living thing. And life needs water. Before you leave me, Septimus, I want you to see it. So that when you return to the Wizard Tower, you will understand that whatever they may tell you about the **Fyre**, it is not true."

Septimus was puzzled. "But no one has ever told me anything about the **Fyre**," he said.

"They do not speak of it," said Marcellus. "But if they ever do, I would like you to understand that it is not the terrible thing they say it is."

"Right."

"But . . . there is one little thing."

"Yes?" said Septimus warily.

"Promise me that you will tell no one what you see today." Marcellus glanced around as though he expected to find Marcia lurking in a corner. "Not even Marcia."

"I can't promise that," Septimus said regretfully. "Not now that I am going back to Marcia. Anyway, Marcia asked you to start the **Fyre**, didn't she, so she knows already."

"Marcia thinks the **Fyre** we are lighting is in the Great Chamber of Alchemie. She does not know that the true **Fyre** is in the place that all ExtraOrdinary Wizards fear and have promised to keep **Sealed** forevermore—the Chamber of **Fyre**. If she knew that she would close it down, just as Julius Pike once did."

"I don't think Marcia would close it down, because she doesn't know anything about it."

"Of course she knows about it," said Marcellus. "She is the ExtraOrdinary Wizard."

"But before I was coming here I asked her about the **Fyre** and she said she didn't know a thing. *Nothing*."

"There are many things Apprentices are not told," said Marcellus.

Septimus was not convinced. He knew when Marcia

was deliberately not telling him things—she had a certain "don't go there" warning look in her eyes. But when they had discussed the **Fyre**, Marcia's expression had been one of bemusement. He remembered her saying, "*There is something about this* **Fyre** *stuff that we just don't know anymore. I wish I knew what it was . . .*"

"Apprentice, let me explain," said Marcellus. "After the Great Alchemie Disaster, the ExtraOrdinary Wizard, Julius Pike—who was once my dear friend—told me that he would make sure that all future ExtraOrdinary Wizards would never allow the **Fyre** Chamber to be **UnSealed**. Never again would the **Fyre** Cauldron be used. The only reason Marcia has agreed to the **Fyre** is because she thinks it is the one in the Great Chamber of Alchemie. And I know that, like any other ExtraOrdinary Wizard, Marcia would never let the Chamber of **Fyre** be opened. All I ask you is to keep it secret for"—Marcellus did some quick calculations—"another month? After that I will reveal it to Marcia, I promise."

"But why in a month—why not tell Marcia *now*?"

"It will not be ready until then. Alchemical **Fyre** is delicate in its early stages of Life and takes time to reach maturity. But once the **Fyre** is ready and Marcia sees that it has been burning safely for some time, then I have a chance to prove to her that all is not as she has been told. Do you understand?"

"I suppose so. . . ." Septimus understood, but it did not make keeping the secret feel any better.

Marcellus was uneasy; it felt decidedly risky having Septimus go back to Marcia at such a delicate time. "That, Apprentice, is why I am so sorry you are leaving me now. Before it all begins. Perhaps, when you see the **Fyre**, you will reconsider your decision to leave."

"It's not really my decision," said Septimus.

"Indeed, no. While you are Marcia's Apprentice it is not your decision. It is hers. But if you were to decide to become the Castle's first Alchemie Apprentice then that would be different." Marcellus left the offer hanging in the air.

"Sometimes," said Septimus, staring at his reflection in the dark waters of the UnderFlow, "I wish there were two of me. I wish I could be in the Wizard Tower and here at the same time."

Marcellus smiled. "Even the greatest **Magyk** cannot make that happen," he said.

"Not for longer than seven seconds," said Septimus.

Marcellus looked impressed that it could happen at all.

Septimus thought for a while. "Okay," he said.

There were three arches leading off from the Alchemie Quay, each one lit by a **Fyre** Globe. Marcellus headed for the right-hand archway. Inside the archway, he turned to Septimus apologetically.

"I know you do not like building work, Apprentice, but I assure you this is the last you will have to do." Marcellus opened the old carpetbag in which every day he brought their lunch, and to Septimus's surprise, from underneath the neatly wrapped sandwiches he took out a hammer and heavy chisel, which he handed to Septimus.

"Thanks," said Septimus ruefully.

Marcellus indicated a shallow arch within the bricks, just above head height. "Remove the bricks below the arch, please, Apprentice. They should come out quite easily."

Septimus sighed and got to work. He was pleased to find that the bricks did indeed come away easily.

"Alchemist's mortar—never sets," said Marcellus. "It began as a mistake when we had to do a lot of building ourselves. Looks solid, but is as soft as butter. Very useful at times."

Septimus took away the rest of the bricks below the arch.

Behind them was a black shiny surface reflected in the flames of the **Fyre** Globe.

Marcellus smiled. "I understand you have seen something like this before."

Septimus looked suspicious. "It's not some kind of Time Glass, is it?" he asked.

Marcellus looked guilty. "Oh, dear. I am so sorry about the way we met, Apprentice. It was, I see now, very wrong. You do know I would never do that again, do you not?" Marcellus picked up the chisel, counted down from the top brick on the right-hand side of the doorway. He levered out the seventh brick and placed his hand on the smooth black substance behind it. A faint green light began to glow beneath it.

Septimus stared at it, astonished.

"You recognize it, Apprentice?" Marcellus smiled.

"Is . . . is this a moving chamber?"

"Indeed it is."

"Like the one on the Isles of Syren?"

"Pretty much. Unfortunately I cannot remember the finer details of its operation. I used to know it, but like many memories, it has faded. I was hoping you might remember. I would like to get it working again. So much more pleasant than the long climb down."

"To the Chamber of **Fyre**?"

"To the Chamber of **Fyre**. So, Apprentice. Shall we go?"

Gingerly Septimus stretched out his hand and placed his palm on the opening plate—the worn part of the smooth, cool surface behind the brick. The green light sprang up below once again; it grew bright and then began to fade.

"Oh," said Septimus. "That shouldn't happen." He took his hand away and rubbed it on his tunic; then he put it back and leaned his whole weight against the surface. This time the green light immediately glowed bright and suddenly, silently, a concealed oval door slid open revealing a tiny, blue-lit chamber.

"Oh, well done!" said Marcellus, excited. "Shall we step inside?"

Septimus followed Marcellus through the door into a virtually spherical space. Its walls were a smooth, shiny black material with no obvious features. It was, as far as Septimus could tell, identical to the one he had known on the Isles of Syren.

"Perhaps you would like to close the door, Apprentice?"

Septimus was not sure that he would. "Marcellus, when did you last use this?" he asked.

Marcellus looked surprised. "Oh, goodness. Well, it's all a bit of a blur, really. There was a lot going on at the time. Esmeralda was with me; I remember that."

"So, about four hundred and seventy-five years ago?"

"About that, I suppose."

For someone who had dabbled in moving from one Time to another, Marcellus was always annoyingly vague about time, Septimus thought. "I'm asking because Syrah said that it needed to be used every day to keep it, er, alive."

"Alive!" Marcellus laughed. "Superstitious nonsense. It is a piece of machinery."

"I know," said Septimus, "but that was how she explained it. And it makes sense to me. She said its life drained away unless it was . . . what was the word she used? Recharged."

Marcellus was skeptical. "Septimus, you must remember that Syrah was **Possessed**. She was just saying words like a . . . Oh, what are those birds with many colors?"

"Parrots. Syrah was *not* like a parrot," said Septimus, annoyed.

"No, of course not. Not the real Syrah," Marcellus said soothingly. "However, I can assure you that this chamber is *not* alive."

Septimus felt that it would be wrong to back out now. There was a worn spot beside the door, and he placed his palm onto it. A red light glowed beneath, lighting up his hand, and the door closed silently. A small orange arrow pointing downward now appeared on the other side of the chamber. Septimus went over to it and reluctantly raised his hand to press it. "Are you sure about this?" he asked.

"Yes," said Marcellus. "Of course I am."

Taking a deep breath, Septimus placed his hand on the orange arrow and pressed. The floor of the chamber gave a sickening lurch and his stomach did the same. The chamber was falling fast and Septimus had forgotten just how terrifying it was. When he had been in the one on the Isles of Syren, he had been with Syrah, and she had known what she was doing. Now he was with Marcellus, who looked just as scared as he was. Septimus watched the orange arrow plummeting down the wall, like a bird hit by a stone.

It is going too fast, he thought. *It is going too fast.*

Suddenly the descent stopped with a bone-jarring *thud*

that set their teeth rattling in their skulls. Marcellus staggered back and grabbed hold of Septimus. This brought them both slithering to the floor, which—being shiny and slightly tilted—sent them cannoning across the chamber, where they fetched up in a pile against the wall.

"*Aaaaah*," Marcellus groaned.

Septimus extricated himself from Marcellus's shoes. He stood up shakily and shook his head, trying to clear the buzzing inside.

"Do you think it's landed all right?" Marcellus whispered from the floor.

Septimus didn't think it had, but there was only one way to find out—open the door. He saw a telltale worn patch on the opposite side of the chamber from where they had come in; he walked gingerly across the sloping floor and placed his hand on the wall. Septimus waited for the green light to appear that would signal the opening of the door. A glimmer of green rose briefly beneath his hand, then faded away. Septimus rubbed his hand on his tunic to remove any dust and pushed it back on the patch, leaning all his weight on it.

Nothing happened. No green light. No opening door. Nothing.

A sharp intake of breath came from Marcellus. "Try again, Apprentice," he urged.

Septimus tried again. Nothing happened.

"Maybe there?" said Marcellus, pointing to another spot.

Septimus tried there. Nothing. He told himself to keep calm.

"Perhaps that might be the place," said Marcellus, indicating a slightly less shiny spot that was not, Septimus thought, anywhere near where the door should be.

Nothing.

"Apprentice," said Marcellus, "we should ascend."

Septimus thought they should too. He put his hand on the orange arrow, which was still pointing downward, and moved his hand in an upward direction, which should have flipped the arrow around to point up. The arrow stayed just as it was. Septimus tried again but still the arrow did not move. And neither did the chamber.

"You're not doing it right," Marcellus said.

"You do it, then," Septimus replied, irritated.

Marcellus—whose hand, Septimus noticed, was trembling—had no luck with the arrow either. It stayed where it was, pointing resolutely to the floor.

"Sheesh," muttered Marcellus.

"Perhaps it needs to go down a bit more first," Septimus suggested, running his hand down from the orange arrow. But whether the chamber needed to or not, it would not budge.

It was then that the blue light illuminating the inside of the chamber began to fade. The last glimpse it showed Septimus was the flash of panic that shot across Marcellus's face. And then it was dark—no orange arrow, no green light, nothing but a total blackness.

Septimus waited for the glow from his Dragon Ring to kick in. It was strange, he thought, because he didn't usually have to wait at all. His left hand found his right index finger and he checked that the ring was still there. It was. So why wasn't it glowing like it always did? *Why?* Septimus felt a flicker of panic in his stomach and fought it down. The total darkness took him straight back to a terrifying night that he had spent, age seven, in a Young Army wolverine pit.

"My ring," he said into the darkness. "My Dragon Ring. It's not doing anything."

"No," came Marcellus's voice, dismal in the dark.

Septimus felt as though he could not bear being trapped inside the blackness a moment longer. He had to do something.

"I'm going to do a **Transport**."

He heard the Alchemist sigh and mistook the reason.

"Marcellus, I'll come back; you know I will. But I have to get some help. Marcia will know what to do."

Another sigh.

"Marcia will have to know now, Marcellus. We've got no choice. I'll **Transport** right back here. I won't leave you, I promise."

There was silence.

"You do believe me, don't you?"

At last Marcellus spoke. "Yes, I do believe you, Apprentice. I believe you because I trust you absolutely. But even if I didn't trust you I would still believe you—because unfortunately I *know* you won't leave me. Not with a **Transport**."

"What do you mean?" Something about the way Marcellus had spoken made Septimus feel very scared.

There was a long silence and then Marcellus spoke. "Apprentice, **Magyk** will not work in this chamber."

"No. That's not true!"

"So . . . does your Dragon Ring shine?"

"That isn't the same."

"It, too, is **Magyk**, Apprentice."

Septimus ran his fingers across the Dragon Ring. It sat cold and unresponsive on his finger, just like any other ring. The little buzz of **Magyk** that he always felt from it was no longer there. A feeling of doom swept over Septimus. He knew Marcellus spoke the truth—**Magyk** did not work inside the chamber.

They were trapped.

++16++

MISSING

That evening at five past six, Lucy—who was trying to hang up an interesting experiment in knitted curtains—watched from the window as Simon Heap waited on Marcellus's doorstep. She saw Simon knock for a third time, step back and look up at the windows, shake his head and cross the road back to their house.

"He's not there," Simon said forlornly, as he wandered into their tiny front room. Lucy was inspecting her curtains with approval—she particularly liked the holes where she had dropped the occasional stitch. "Don't worry, Si," she said. "He'll be back soon."

Simon took the *I, Marcellus* out of his pocket and looked at it. "I thought it was too good to be true," he said gloomily.

"Don't be silly, Si. If Marcellus didn't want you to be his Apprentice, he wouldn't have given you his precious book, would he? We'll sit and wait for him to come back."

Simon made a pot of herb tea and set it down on the table next to a small, battered box that bore the label SLEUTH. He opened the box, took out his old and worn **Tracker Ball** and began gently throwing it from one hand to the other as he always did when he felt unsettled. Lucy poured the tea and together they sat at the window, watching for the return of the Alchemist.

Night began to fall and candles were placed in the windows of the houses on either side of Marcellus's, but his remained dark. Suddenly Lucy saw a cloaked figure stride quickly down the slipway and walk up to his front door.

"There he is!" she said. Simon threw Sleuth into its box and was heading out of the room when Lucy said, "Oh. It's Marcia."

The sound of the angry rapping of Marcellus's doorknocker carried across the snowy slipway. They watched Marcia wait and then step back and peruse the dark windows, just as Simon had. Then they saw the ExtraOrdinary Wizard spin around and head across the slipway toward their door. Simon rushed into the hall, leaping over a rolled-up rug, a potted plant and a box of books. He opened the door just as Marcia was about to knock.

"Oh!" she said, surprised.

"Sorry," said Simon. "It falls off its hinges if you knock hard."

Marcia did not waste words. "Have you seen Marcellus?" she asked.

"No, I haven't."

"It's too bad, Simon. It's Septimus's last day and I'm expecting him back for a Wizard Warming Supper. We have two new Ordinaries to welcome."

"Right." People becoming Wizards were still a sore spot for Simon.

"I'd be very grateful if as soon as they come back you would kindly tell Septimus to get straight over to the Wizard Tower?"

"Yes, of course."

"Thank you, Simon." With that Marcia turned and strode away up Snake Slipway. Simon closed the door.

"What was that about?" asked Lucy.

"I'm being a messenger for my little brother, that's all," said Simon glumly. "And it looks like that's all I'm ever going to be."

"Oh, don't be silly, Si. Just because Marcellus is late home it doesn't mean he's changed his mind about making you his Alchemie Apprentice, does it? We'll watch for him to come back and as soon as he does you can go and see him."

"All these new Wizards, Lu. It's not fair."

"You don't want to be a boring old Wizard," said Lucy. "Alchemie is much more exciting."

"I guess so."

"Besides," Lucy said with a smile, "you look really good in black."

But Marcellus did not come back. Simon watched all evening from the front-room window and, much to Lucy's annoyance, would not let her draw her new curtains. Lucy wanted to see the effect of the moonlight through the holes, but Simon was adamant—he had to watch for Marcellus. By the time midnight was drawing on, Simon was worried.

"I'm going to the Wizard Tower, Lu," he said. "Something's not right."

Simon had not even reached the end of Snake Slipway when he saw the unmistakable figure of Marcia striding toward him.

"Simon! Oh, good, I see you are on your way to tell me. Thank goodness they're back. Whatever was Marcellus thinking of? It really is too bad. Septimus must be exhausted and—"

Simon interrupted as soon as he could. "No, Marcia—they're not back."

Marcia stopped. She looked shocked. "*Not* back?"

"No."

"Simon, are you *sure*?"

"Yes. I've been watching all evening. The house is still in darkness. That's what I was coming to tell you."

Even in the moonlight, Simon could see that Marcia had gone pale. "Something's happened," she muttered. "Something in that awful underground pit has gone wrong." She shook her head. "I should never have agreed to this. *Never*."

Sixty seconds later Simon was standing alone on the Snake Slipway ice, feeling very odd. He had just witnessed Marcia's **Transport** to the Great Chamber of Alchemie and he'd forgotten how exciting **Magyk** could be. With the feeling of **Magyk** still buzzing in his head, Simon walked slowly back to the only house with a lighted downstairs window and went inside. Lucy met him anxiously.

"What's going on, Si?" she asked.

Simon shook his head. "I dunno, Lu. But it doesn't look good."

Marcia's fizzing purple **Magyk** was the first light the Great Chamber of Alchemie had seen all day. She waited for the last vestiges of the **Transport** to wear off, then she pulled a **FlashLight** from her pocket and swung its beam around to check if anyone was there—perhaps they were lying overcome by noxious fumes or victim of a bizarre Alchemical accident. Marcia wasn't quite sure what an Alchemical accident would look like but she figured she would know one if she saw one. However, it was soon clear that nothing untoward had occurred and that the place was deserted. She headed out of the Chamber and into the Labyrinth, walking quickly, the tippy-tapping of her python shoes echoing through its deep blue coils.

Although Marcia knew that there were tunnels running off the Labyrinth she had never actually been along them and she decided to explore what she knew first. Marcia knew all about the planning of Labyrinths—it had been a hobby of hers when she was a girl—so finding the way to Alchemie Quay was no problem. She emerged through the left-hand tunnel and stood a moment surveying the deserted Quay. Marcia was beginning to think that maybe Marcellus and Septimus had done something completely stupid like running away, when she saw a flash of color and movement against the stone of the Quay—the gently bobbing pink paddleboat.

Marcia rushed over and looked down at the paddleboat—its chubby, childish shape and its vibrant pink sitting incongruously on the deep, dark waters of the UnderFlow Pool.

"So they *are* here," she muttered to herself. The worm of worry that had been niggling Marcia since Septimus's nonarrival at the Wizard Warming Supper turned into a fat snake of fear. Something was wrong. She *knew* it. She peered into the inscrutable black waters below her and a horrible conviction came over her. Septimus was somewhere below—somewhere *deep.* Marcia gave a gasp and sat down on the steps, trembling.

They had fallen in and drowned. It explained everything.

No doubt it was Marcellus in those ridiculous shoes who had lost his footing and dear, darling, brave Septimus had dived in to save Marcellus—who had surely grabbed on to him with those long bony fingers and pulled him down with him. Marcia stifled a sob and sat staring into the water for some minutes.

When she'd calmed down a little, Marcia—who was a naturally optimistic person—began to wonder if there might be another explanation. She got to her feet and paced the Quay, trying to empty her mind of panic. There were, she told herself, other possibilities: they could be trapped somewhere, or even lost in one of the old tunnels off the labyrinth. The most sensible thing was to go back to the Wizard Tower and do a **Search** from the **Search** and Rescue Center. Marcia walked quietly along the edge of the Quay, her purple pythons no longer tippy-tapping in their usual exuberant way. She was loath to leave, which was odd, she thought, as the Alchemie Quay gave her the creeps. And then Marcia realized why she didn't want to go; it was because she **Felt** that Septimus was still here. And that meant that he was still alive. Close by.

The art of **Feeling** that someone you love is near (and it only works if you really do love them) is easy to learn with a good teacher, and Marcia had been taught by one of the best—Alther Mella. But it was what he had called a Fugitive Art, which meant that the more you thought about it, the less certain you were. So as soon as Marcia realized she **Felt** that Septimus was close by, she no longer **Felt** it. And then she began to wonder if she ever had.

"Don't be silly, Marcia," she muttered. "You **Felt** it. You know you did."

Marcia decided to check out the other two arches even though she knew that they were both bricked up. She shone her **FlashLight** across the central arch and gave it a tentative shove, remembering something she had once read about Alchemists' Mortar. It was solid and—*eurgh*—still greasily sooty. Marcia wiped her hand on her handkerchief and moved on to the right-hand arch, shining her **FlashLight** into the darkness.

To her shock, Marcia saw that there was a gaping hole in the brickwork below the archway. She felt a huge feeling of relief—so *this* was where they were. Marcellus had opened up an old tunnel and presumably they had got lost. She hurried into the opening and suddenly the ground disappeared below her right pointy python. Marcia toppled forward. A cold gust of air came up to meet her as she teetered, arms flailing, on the brink. She grabbed hold of the wall beside her but it gave way, sending bricks hurtling down into the dark. Some seconds later she heard the clang as they hit something far below.

Panic shot through Marcia. She knew that she was balanced on the edge of a precipice.

⊹17⊹
FALLING

A *sudden* boom *woke Septimus* from an uncomfortable doze. He jumped up.

Marcellus groaned. "What was what?"

"Something landed on the roof!"

"You were dreaming, Apprentice," said Marcellus.

"No. No, I'm sure I heard—"

Booooooomboomboomboooooom!

Suddenly the chamber reverberated to a hail of objects slamming onto its roof, ending with a huge *whuuump* of something heavy and soft, which sent shudders through to their

feet. Marcellus and Septimus felt the chamber tilt, and then the brief but sickening sensation of free fall.

What Marcellus and Septimus did not know was the moving chamber had become lodged just above the top of the exit door where, over the centuries, a fat helictite had formed so that it obstructed its path. The falling objects had provided enough force for the chamber to snap the helictite and continue on its way. Fast.

Luckily it was only a ten-foot drop.

There was a bone-jarring *crump*. Marcellus and Septimus picked themselves up from the floor. They looked at each other in the darkness but saw nothing but the total absence of light that had oppressed them for almost fifteen hours.

"It's not tilting anymore," said Septimus. "That must be a good sign."

"Let us hope so," muttered Marcellus.

"I'm going to try again and see if the door will open," said Septimus.

"It won't," Marcellus said flatly. "There's no orange arrow. That means no power."

"We may as well try," said Septimus. "Unless there's anything else exciting you had in mind?"

"There is no need to get tetchy, Apprentice."

"I am *not* tetchy."

"No. Of course not. Well, you take one side and I'll take the other."

They had already done this countless times before the chamber fell for the second time—desperately pressing their palms over the cold, smooth surface of the chamber with absolutely no response—but now they began again. Septimus took one side of the chamber and Marcellus the other. Suddenly the darkness took on a faint orange hue. Marcellus gasped.

"The arrow—it flickered! Quick, quick, Apprentice. The door's on your side. We may have a chance. Press it now! Now!"

The problem was that without being able to see the telltale worn patch—the dim orange glow did not give out much light—Septimus could not know whether his hand was in the right place or not. Marcellus joined him and frantically they pushed their palms onto the glasslike surface in increasingly wildly improbable places, desperately seeking the spot that might—just might if they were lucky—open the door. And all the time the orange arrow flickered, reminding Septimus of the distress lights on the Wizard Tower.

"It's going! It's fading!" Marcellus sounded desperate as his hands slapped frantically against the wall.

Septimus knew they were never going to find the right spot by panicking. "Stop," he said. "I want to find it a different way."

"I told you, Apprentice, **Magyk** does not work in here."

"But my mind still works," said Septimus. "Marcellus, please. Stop and be quiet a moment. Let me . . . let me **Find** it."

The orange arrow was fading away and Marcellus knew they were getting nowhere. He let his hands drop to his sides. "Very well, Apprentice. Over to you."

Septimus closed his eyes. It made no difference as to what he could see, but it sent him back inside his head—deep into another place. He held out his right hand and remembered how he had once opened a similar door far below the Isles of Syren. He remembered how the smooth, cold material of the chamber had felt beneath his hand; he imagined that he was there now, in its bright blue light, and he allowed his hand to guide itself where it wanted to go. Then he pressed his palm down hard, throwing all his weight behind it. He heard a soft swish and Marcellus's gasp.

"It's open! Apprentice, you've done it. *You've done it!*" Terrified that the door would suddenly close, Marcellus pulled

Septimus out of the chamber. As soon as they were safely across the threshold, Marcellus sat down very fast and put his head between his knees.

Septimus collapsed, giddy with relief, on a wobbly metal platform that felt dizzyingly high up. But for once he didn't care how high he was—he was free. He was not going to finish his life trapped in a box hundreds of feet below the ground. Slowly, he began to take in his surroundings. He could feel a vast arena all around him; it was hot, and suffused with a deep red glow that shone up from below. His overwhelming impression was of a heavy sense of stillness where a quiet and purposeful process was slowly unfolding.

Septimus walked carefully along what felt like a very rickety platform to a line of **Fyre** Globes placed below a guardrail, and gingerly looked over. His head swam. Far, far below, a huge red circle stared up at him, as bright and intense as a sun. Across the top of the red ran tiny, vibrant flames of blue, licking and jumping up into the air. Septimus felt overawed. So *this* was the real **Fyre**. He looked away and saw a perfect green afterimage in front of his eyes. It was then Septimus realized that he was standing on a perforated metal platform as flimsy as a sieve. The bones in his legs felt as if they had turned to water and he retreated back to Marcellus.

"Wow," he said. "That is so . . . beautiful."

"It is," agreed Marcellus.

"And **Magykal**. So alive and delicate . . ." Septimus was lost for words.

Marcellus smiled. "You understand," he said. "I thought you would, even though most Wizards don't understand the **Magyk** of **Fyre**."

Septimus was overwhelmed. "I wish you had shown me before."

Marcellus was silent for a while. "I should have done. So I cannot tempt you to change your mind and become my Apprentice. Forever?"

Septimus so much wanted to say yes. And yet, the thought of what he would have to give up was too much. "I . . . I really want to."

"Wonderful!"

"But . . ."

"Ah, a 'but.'" Marcellus smiled ruefully. "I thought there might be."

"But I can't. I have promised Marcia."

"Oh, well," Marcellus said sadly.

"But . . ."

"Yes?"

"Will you let me come back here sometimes?" Septimus asked.

"Of course, Apprentice. I want no more secrets—not after next month, anyway. Both you and Marcia will be here when I **DeNature** the Two-Faced Ring." Marcellus began to get to his feet, then he swayed and sat back down. He looked very pale.

"Are you all right?" Septimus asked, sitting down beside him.

"I will be in a minute. I just need . . . a little fresh air."

"Not much of that down here."

"No . . . but more than in that . . . coffin."

Septimus shuddered. That had been his thought too. "I wonder what fell on it?"

"Bricks. Sounded like bricks," said Marcellus.

"But why? Something must have made them fall."

"Probably Marcia looking for you. It's late." Marcellus looked at his timepiece. "One hour past midnight."

Septimus looked at Marcellus aghast. "Yes. Of *course* she would look for me. I was due back for the Wizard Warming Supper."

"Don't look so concerned, Apprentice. It's good that she came, surely? Without her we'd still be stuck."

Septimus now matched Marcellus's pallor. "Oh, Marcellus. Supposing . . . supposing what you said is really true. *Literally* true."

"Huh?"

"That without Marcia we would still be stuck." Septimus put his head in his hands, trying to get the sound of the last thing that fell onto the chamber's roof out of his head: heavy, yet soft.

Marcellus's thoughts were on a different track. "Of course I would prefer that Marcia did not know about the moving chamber, Apprentice, but given the circumstances I—"

"Marcellus—the last thing that fell onto the roof . . . it wasn't a brick, was it?"

"I can't remember."

"Well, it *wasn't* a brick. It was heavy. But . . . kind of soft."

"Soft?"

"Yes. Soft. And up there at the top, you couldn't see the drop, could you? You wouldn't be expecting it, would you? It would just be dark. You'd probably think it was a tunnel. In fact, you'd probably think that was where we had gone . . . got lost maybe. So you'd step in and there would be *nothing there*. You'd grab hold of the bricks, they'd fall away in your hand and then . . . and then . . ."

Marcellus suddenly got it. "Oh, great Alchemie! No!"

Septimus felt sick. He had hoped Marcellus would have an explanation. "So you think so too?"

"I can't think of anything else," said Marcellus, clutching his head with a groan.

They sat in silence. "We have to get back to the Alchemie Quay," said Septimus after a while. "We have to see what's happened."

"If something *has* happened, then we won't see anything," said Marcellus. "It's a long climb, Apprentice. I suggest we get going. Follow me." He went to get up, but Septimus stopped him.

"Marcellus, I am going to do a **Transport** to the Alchemie Quay. I have to know what's happened—*now*."

"A **Transport**. Yes, of course. I will follow you by more normal methods."

Marcellus watched Septimus begin his **Transport**. He saw his Apprentice close his eyes, and watched a strange shimmering purplish light begin to run across him. Marcellus shivered. This was serious **Magyk**. The thought of moving a human being from one place to another—blood and bone through brick and stone—made Marcellus feel very odd. He was in the presence of something he did not understand. It was right, he thought, that Septimus returned to Marcia as her Apprentice; there was more **Magyk** to him than he had ever realized. At the thought of Marcia, Marcellus remembered the soft yet heavy *thud* of something falling and a stab of dread shot through him.

If Marcia was there to return to.

⁺⁺18⁺⁺

TRANSPORTS

Septimus arrived in the middle of Alchemie Quay. As the blanketed feeling of the **Transport** wore off he was relieved to find he had judged it perfectly. **Transports** into confined spaces were difficult and dangerous; Septimus was not officially allowed to do them. But—unlike much **Magyk**, which required a clear head—a

Transport was made more accurate by distress. And right then Septimus had *that* by the bucketful.

He stood still, allowing the last vestiges of **Magyk** to drift away. Septimus did not want to move. He wanted to stay right where he was and never, ever have to walk over to the right-hand arch and peer down into the depths. But he knew he must do it. He *had* to know what had happened.

Feeling as if he were wearing lead boots, Septimus walked slowly across the Quay to the right-hand archway. A terrifying feeling of vertigo came over him as he approached the black hole in the middle of the bricks—unlike Marcia, thought Septimus, he knew about the huge drop that lurked behind them.

Septimus inspected the jagged hole in the bricks. There was a large bite out of the bricks at about shoulder height, exactly at the place where he would have expected Marcia to grab hold of them. Very, very carefully, Septimus leaned forward.

"Marcia . . ." he called down into the darkness, tentatively. The sound fell into the blackness and died. "Marcia!" Septimus called more loudly. And then, "Marcia, Marcia, can you hear me?"

There was no response, just a heady sense of the emptiness

below his feet. Septimus stepped back from the drop and leaned against the wall to steady himself. Of course there was no reply, he told himself; how could there be? Maybe, he thought, Marcia hasn't been here at all. Maybe the mortar had suddenly given way and the bricks had fallen on their own. Maybe . . .

It was then that Septimus saw something he really did not want to see: a small jade button lying on the ground beside the **Fyre** Globe. He bent down to pick it up and cradled it in his hand. He knew what it was—a button from Marcia's shoes. She had been complaining that Terry Tarsal had not sewn them on properly. A wave of despair washed over him. Recklessly, Septimus leaned into the darkness of the shaft.

"Marcia!" he yelled. "Mar . . . seeee . . . *aaaaaaaaaaaaaa!*" As the sound died away, Septimus stumbled out from the archway and heard a very faint something that made him think his mind was playing cruel tricks.

"*Septimus . . .*"

He stopped. A shiver ran down his spine. It was Marcia's voice. *It was her ghost calling to him.* Septimus stared at the gaping hole in the brickwork, half expecting to see Marcia's ghost float out of it.

"Septimus . . ." There it was again. *Behind him.*

Septimus spun around. Nothing. The Quay was empty. Slowly, silently, he walked out of the arch, listening hard.

Tippy-tap, tippy-tap, tippy-tap-tap . . .

The lapis lazuli of the Labyrinth lit up, glowing a brilliant blue with its streaks of gold glistening. A figure in purple hurried out—and screamed.

"Septimus! Oh, Septimus!" Marcia hurled herself toward Septimus and enveloped him in her cloak. "You're alive. I thought . . . I thought you were dead. I thought you'd fallen . . ."

"Me too," said Septimus, holding on to Marcia. "*Me too.*"

Marcellus awoke, aching all over. He lay in his bed staring at the winter sunlight that shone through the window and he felt an odd feeling of happiness. He was not sure why. And then he remembered. *The carpetbag*—his soft carpetbag heavy with a crowbar and a lump hammer. It was the carpetbag that had fallen onto the roof of the moving chamber. Marcellus sank back into his pillow with a sigh of happiness. He remembered his long, slow, dismal climb through the tiny shafts that led up to Alchemie Quay. He remembered how as he had gotten nearer he had been convinced that Marcia had fallen to her death; and then he had been overcome with worry that Septimus, too, might have fallen while looking for her. By the time he had emerged onto the Quay, Marcellus was very nearly in a state of collapse. And at the sight of Marcia sitting on the edge of the Quay with her arm around Septimus, he had felt happier than he had could ever remember—which was odd, considering how annoying Marcia was. But it had been wonderful when Marcia had grabbed his hands and told him in response to all his questions that yes, it *was* her. Yes, she *was* real.

"Well, well, well," muttered Marcellus, smiling to himself. He reached out for his timepiece on his bedside table and squinted at it. Nine o'clock. He had three more hours in bed before he was due to see his new Apprentice. The old Alchemist closed his eyes and soon the sound of snoring filled the room.

In the house on the other side of Snake Slipway, Lucy was excited. She had just found a note that had been pushed under the front door. She rushed into the kitchen. "Si, Si! Look, it's from Marcellus."

At the kitchen table, over a pot of coffee, Simon read out the note to Lucy.

"'Dear Simon, my sincere apologies for breaking our appointment last night. I regret to say that I was detained by circumstances beyond my control and could not get a message to you. However, all is now resolved. Would it be convenient for you to renew our appointment for midday today?'"

"Yaay!" yelled Lucy, jumping up and punching the air. "Didn't I tell you? Didn't I say it would be all right?"

Simon grinned. "Yes, Lu, you did. You said it quite a lot, I seem to remember."

At the Wizard Tower, Septimus slept on.

Up in the Pyramid Library, Marcia was very happy indeed. She had her Apprentice back and now things could get back to normal. Marcia was preparing the next stage in Septimus's **DeCyphering** course—the practical. For all Apprentices, this meant having a go at the hieroglyphs inscribed into the flat silver top of the golden Pyramid that crowned the Wizard Tower. It was generally agreed that they were indecipherable—or as Marcia preferred to call them, gobbledygook. But it was a tradition and she supposed they should stick with it.

In front of Marcia was the old rubbing that a long-ago ExtraOrdinary Wizard had made of the hieroglyphs. It wasn't, thought Marcia, very clear. No wonder no one had figured out what they meant. She remembered ruefully a comment she had made to Septimus about "going back to original sources" and she had a nasty feeling that was what he might do. He would take himself to the very top of the Pyramid and sit there, working it out. Or, at the very least, go up there to do his own rubbing. A shiver went right through Marcia—she had had enough nightmares about Septimus falling to last her a lifetime. Marcia came to a decision. She scribbled a note for Septimus in case he woke before she returned, then she was off—tippy-tapping down the stone stairs, pinning the note on Septimus's door, then back up to the Library to pick up an envelope she'd forgotten, down the steps again, rapidly past the ghost of Jillie Djinn and out of her rooms.

In the Great Hall, Marcia rapped on the door of the duty Wizard's cupboard. Hildegarde answered.

"Ah, Miss Pigeon," said Marcia frostily. "I thought you might have company this morning."

"No, Madam Marcia. It is very quiet this morning."

"Mr. Banda otherwise engaged, is he?"

"I think so, Madam Marcia. Did you want to leave a message in case he drops by?"

"No," said Marcia. "I don't."

"Is there anything I can help you with?"

Marcia handed Hildegarde an envelope. "My choice for the rotation scheme Apprentice for the Pyramid Library. Send it up to the Sick Bay, will you?"

"Of course, Madam Marcia. Right away."

"I'll be back in about an hour."

"Very well, Madam Marcia."

Hildegarde called for the duty Message Apprentice and gave him the envelope; then she went into the duty Wizard's cupboard and sat down with a sigh. She knew she had done something to offend Marcia but she had no idea what. She sat down and finished a note.

Dear Milo,

Thank you for your message. I will meet you at the old bakehouse at two o'clock this afternoon.

Hildegarde

Marcia ignored Hildegarde on the way back. She hurried by, put the stairs on *fast* and zoomed straight up to the twentieth floor. She found Septimus in the kitchen, making porridge.

"Aha, Septimus!" she said cheerily.

"Morning," said Septimus, blearily scraping the porridge into his bowl.

"Coffee?" asked Marcia brightly.

"Oh! Yes, please." Septimus looked surprised. Generally it was his job to make the coffee.

Marcia snapped her fingers at the coffeepot, which was loitering in the shadows with the sugar bowl. "For two!" she told it. The coffeepot scooped in a couple of spoons of coffee, added three teaspoons of sugar, stood under the tap, which obligingly turned on, then scuttled over to the stove and settled onto a ring. "Light!" Marcia told the stove.

Septimus smiled. When *he* made coffee, he had to do it himself. The coffeepot was a one-Wizard pot and took absolutely no notice of him.

Marcia waited until Septimus had finished his porridge—which was drenched in syrup—and two tiny cups of hot, sweet coffee were sitting on the table; then she took a dark blue velvet drawstring pouch from her pocket, which Septimus recognized as a standard Manuscriptorium **Charm** bag. Marcia pushed the bag across the table to Septimus. "For you," she said.

"Oh. Thank you . . ." Septimus was touched. Marcia didn't often give presents.

He wiped his hands on his tunic, then loosened the drawstring and tipped the **Charm** out onto his palm.

"Wow! Oh, *wow!*"

Septimus could not believe it. Lying in the middle of his slightly sticky palm was the **Flyte Charm**. He had forgotten how delicate and beautiful it was—a simple gold arrow covered with intricate swirling patterns. But what Septimus loved most about it were the two delicate little silver wings that sat on top of its somewhat misshapen flights—fluttering gently as if to greet him after its long sojourn inside a dark urn in the Vaults of the Manuscriptorium. These were the wings that Marcia had given him when she had first asked him to be her Apprentice, and it was these that Septimus had missed so much after Marcia had confiscated the **Flyte Charm**.

"There are conditions to its use," said Marcia. "You are only to use it when on Apprentice duties *in the Wizard Tower.* At all other times it is to be kept on the **Charm** shelf in the Library. Understood?"

"Yes, *yes,* totally understood." Septimus didn't care about any conditions. *He had the **Flyte Charm** back.*

"There's another thing," said Marcia. "Last night."

Septimus gulped, convinced that Marcia was about to ask some very awkward questions. "Yes?" he said.

"It was awful."

"Yes."

"And it made me realize that you have been working far too hard. It has been a lovely Big Freeze and you have missed so much . . ." Marcia searched for the right word, a word she did not often use. "Fun."

"Fun?" Septimus sounded surprised.

"*Fun*, Septimus," said Marcia adopting the word with enthusiasm. "You need to go out and have *fun*. You have spent a month underground, and now I want you to take a month aboveground to do what you want."

Septimus looked puzzled. "Like what?"

"That is entirely up to you. It is *your* vacation—"

"*Vacation?*"

"Yes. Vacation."

Septimus was at a loss. "But what am I going to do?"

Marcia had it worked out. "What you are going to do, Septimus, is *fun*."

Septimus smiled. "All right," he said. "I can do fun. If you insist."

"You look better already," said Marcia. "Off you go. And forget all about that ghastly underground stuff."

"I'll try." Septimus wished he could forget, but the unblinking red eye of **Fyre** was imprinted on his brain—whenever he closed his eyes he saw it. He longed to go back and see it again. He longed to know what it was, crouching below the Castle like a living creature. And most of all, he longed to tell Marcia all about it.

19
WHAT MIGHT HAVE BEEN

Septimus was on his way to have fun. He stood waiting by the spiral stairs, because unlike Marcia he was not allowed to change their direction, and before long he saw the green Apprentice robes of their passenger.

"Rose!" he said.

Rose stepped off, her green eyes shining with excitement. "Hello, Septimus." She stopped and looked around. "Wow, it's amazing up here. So bright. And kind of . . . sparkly."

"It is, isn't it?"

"I can't believe I'm going to be up in the Pyramid Library. With you and Marcia."

"Ah. It's just Marcia for the next few weeks."

Rose's face fell. "*Just* Marcia? On her own?"

"I have to be on vacation. Marcia told me that I have to go and have, um, fun."

"Marcia said you had to go and have *fun*?" Rose looked astonished.

"Yep. That's what she said."

"Crumbs."

"Yes, I know."

Until Rose had arrived, Septimus had felt quite excited at the prospect of his vacation. Now it just felt like another job he had to do. And then he remembered something. He fished Jenna's Welcome Back Party invitation out of his pocket, took a pencil from his writing pocket and added Rose's name to it. He handed the invitation to Rose.

"Would you like to come?" he asked.

"Oh. Wow. *Yes, please.*"

"Tell Marcia I asked for you to have a late pass," said Septimus.

"Oh. Right. Yes, I will." Rose stood clutching the invitation.

"I'll pick you up later?"

"Yes. Crumbs." Flustered, Rose rushed off along the corridor toward the big purple door.

Marcia was right, Septimus *had* missed a lot of fun.

While he had spent his month belowground, Septimus had missed a sunny Big Freeze—what people in the Castle called a Bright One. Most Big Freezes were dull and overcast with biting winds and freezing fog, but every now and then along came one with clear blue skies and brilliant winter sunshine. This Bright One was particularly welcome: it felt to the Castle inhabitants as though it was chasing away the very last shadows of the **Darke Domaine**.

Everyone had been determined to make the most of it. Nicko had arranged a series of Moat skating races (much to Jannit Maarten's annoyance). Jenna had organized a snow-sculpture park on the Palace lawns and the Chief Hermetic Scribe had held a series of Manuscriptorium sled races down

Wizard Way and allowed the scribes to leave two hours before sunset every day to enable them to enjoy the snow. Hot food carts selling chestnuts, sizzling sausages and warm toffee bananas had been set up along Wizard Way and proved highly popular. More controversial was the igloo village populated by young teens that had sprung up on Alchemie Way, which, according to the disapproving older people who lived nearby, was the source of much loud music and bad behavior. The long ice-slide that zigzagged down the Municipal rubbish dump, ending outside Sally Mullin's Tea and Ale House, was probably the most popular—and dangerous—innovation. Sally took advantage of this by setting up an outside hot-barley-cake stand and, after the first few days when the slide had become treacherously fast, a first-aid tent.

After the **Darke Domaine**, Sarah and Silas Heap had moved out of the Palace back to their old room in the Ramblings, leaving Jenna in sole possession of her Palace for the very first time. When the four Forest Heap boys came to the Castle for Simon and Lucy's wedding, Sarah had insisted they, too, stay in their old home in the Ramblings. But after only one night, she had had to admit defeat: even half her family no longer fit into one room, so Jenna invited Sarah, Silas and the Forest Heaps into the Palace for the duration of the Big Freeze.

The Palace began to fill up. Simon and Lucy visited almost every day and the Forest Heaps—Sam, Jo-Jo, Edd and Erik Heap—roamed the corridors in much the same way as they had roamed the Forest paths, loping along and blending into the shadows.

For Sarah, it was a magical time. At long last she had all her children back in the Castle. She stopped worrying that something awful was going to happen to one—or all—of them and began to unwind. Silas was pleased to see the change in Sarah; her permanent air of concern had lifted and she had even stopped carrying *that daft duck-in-a-bag* around everywhere. Silas, too, became less distracted, he enjoyed getting to know his Forest sons once more; he even broached the subject of them considering Wizard Apprenticeships, although only Sam showed any interest. Silas didn't mind; he was just pleased to have his boys back.

Jenna, too, was pleased to have her brothers back, but she was less happy about Sarah. Jenna thought of the Palace as her territory now and she did not like the way Sarah had taken charge as soon as she had returned. The way Jenna saw it,

Sarah had moved out and was now back as her guest. Sarah, however, did not see it that way.

It was the little things that annoyed Jenna.

For instance, Jo-Jo Heap had developed a fascination with Gothyk Grotto, the shop at the end of Little Creep Cut, and soon some members of the staff became regular visitors to the Palace. Sarah Heap did not object to two of them: Matt and Marcus Marwick, Wolf Boy's brothers, were "nice young men," she said. What she did object to was "that sulky young witch, Marissa."

"But Mum," Jo-Jo protested, "Marissa's left both Covens."

"*Both?*" Sarah was horrified. "You mean she's a Port Coven witch as well?"

"No, Mum. I *told* you. She not with either of them anymore," Jo-Jo insisted.

"Once a witch, always a witch," Sarah declared. "And no witch is going to set foot in *my* house."

Jenna pointed out that the Palace was her house now and *she* would decide who was welcome in the Palace, not Sarah. Ever since Marissa had helped her escape from the Port Witch Coven, Jenna had come to like her. To prove a point she had invited Marissa over that very evening. Jo-Jo was delighted.

Sarah was not.

Another day Jenna found Sarah in one of the disused kitchens, loading Lucy up with a pile of saucepans. "We don't need all this stuff," Sarah told Jenna when she had come to see what all the noise was. Jenna felt annoyed. Even though she was perfectly happy for Lucy and Simon to have things from the Palace, she did think Sarah should have asked her first.

While Sarah managed to irritate Jenna in a hundred little ways, Milo Banda was having the same effect on Sarah. "He's hovering round the Palace like a bad smell," Sarah complained to Silas one afternoon, after bumping into Milo in the shadows of the Long Walk for the fifth time that day, carrying something covered with a cloth. "And he's always got some kind of junk with him. And when I ask him what it is he just smiles and goes *shhh.* What's *that* about, Silas?"

"Don't ask me," said Silas. "The man's a total fruitcake."

Sarah sighed. "I know I shouldn't complain. He *is* Jenna's father—oh, Silas, don't look so crotchety—and this is his home. But usually he's here one day and gone the next."

"The sooner he's gone the better, if you ask me," said Silas. "He unsettles Jenna."

Silas was right; Milo's presence did unsettle Jenna. Some

mornings later, just as Septimus was getting his **Flyte Charm** returned to him, Jenna was leaning over the balustrade of the gallery that ran along the top of the Palace entrance hall. She was gazing at the patterns cast by the snow-bright sunlight glancing in through the windows when she saw Milo stride across the hall, his shiny black leather boots *click-click*ing on the stone floor, his red-and-gold cloak billowing out behind him as he rushed out of the Palace on yet more "business."

Suddenly Jenna had the oddest sensation. She felt as if she had been transported to the life she would have had if her mother, Queen Cerys, had not been gunned down by an assassin's bullet. It was so real that it made Jenna feel quite strange.

In the what-might-have-been world, Jenna (except she wasn't called Jenna. She had a longer, more ancient name) was the oldest daughter—the Crown Princess. She had two younger sisters and a brother, all of whom had dark hair, violet eyes and found **Magyk** weird, just like her. Her two sisters looked a lot like her and her little brother looked like a young Marcellus. The what-might-have-been Palace was a busy place, the center of Castle life with coming and goings, and somewhere close by—in the Throne Room, probably—she knew that her mother was getting on with the business of the day. In fact, her mother was waiting for her to go to her, to spend the morning helping with Castle business and learning how to be a Queen. All was as it should be and at that moment it seemed to Jenna that her whole life up until now was no more than a long and complicated dream out of which she had just stepped.

Jenna was so caught up by the sensation of what-might-have-been that when Milo—sensing she was there—looked up at her and smiled, she blew him a kiss. She saw Milo stop dead as though someone had hit him; then she saw his face break into a smile of happy amazement. Milo blew her a kiss in return, and was out of the door and gone.

"*Binkie-binkie-boo . . . binkie-binkie-boo . . .*"

The spell was broken. Maizie Smalls, the Palace and Castle TorchLighter, was wandering down the corridor. "Excuse me, Princess Jenna, have you seen Binkie?" asked Maizie.

"Binkie?" Jenna tried to pull herself back to reality.

"My cat."

Jenna was puzzled. "I thought Binkie had gone. In fact I thought all the Castle cats had gone. Jo-Jo said they were living in the Forest with the Wendrons."

Maizie tutted; she did not approve of the Wendron Witches. "My Binkie wouldn't do that," she said. "Anyway, he came home a few days ago." A frown flitted over Maizie's face. Binkie had not been exactly friendly since he had returned; she had the scratch marks to prove it. "But he's disappeared and I'm worried he might have gotten shut in a cupboard or something. So, if you do hear anything I'd be very grateful if you would check it out."

"Yes, of course I will." Jenna was not Binkie's biggest fan, but she knew how much Maizie loved her cat. She watched Maizie wander off along the corridor making *binkie-binkie-boo* noises.

Jenna's moment of what-might-have-been was not easily shaken off. For the rest of that day she was left with a feeling of sadness for what she had lost. And she began to understand that Milo, too, had lost his own what-might-have-been.

Evening arrived and the Palace grew quiet. Jenna's what-might-have-been thoughts began to fade as she got things ready for Septimus's Welcome Back Party. The party was, despite Sarah's objections, going to be in her room, and Sir Hereward was under strict instructions not to let any parents in, on any pretext whatsoever.

At eight o'clock a bemused Sir Hereward watched a succession of Young Ones, as the ghost called them, troupe past him. A wide assortment of Heaps came first: four Forest Heaps, Nicko, Simon and Lucy, then Septimus with Rose. Rupert Gringe came next with his girlfriend, Maggie, and after them the Manuscriptorium contingent arrived: Beetle, Foxy, Moira Mole, Romilly Badger and Partridge, who were followed by Marcus and Matt from Gothyk Grotto. Jenna and Marissa arrived a few minutes later pushing an old Palace trolley (once used for transporting documents down the long corridors) in which sat a huge flagon of what Jenna called "punch" and a box of pewter mugs from one of the old kitchens. It was greeted with a cheer as they pushed it through the doors.

On his way to the party, Foxy had ordered an extra-large bucket of sausage sandwiches from Wizard Sandwiches for delivery to the Palace. Foxy perused the trolley with a practiced eye—he could spot the lack of a sausage sandwich a mile off. "No sausage bucket?" he asked.

"I'll go down and check," said Jenna. "It might be in the hall, waiting."

"You don't want them to get cold," said Foxy anxiously.

As Jenna was descending the sweeping stairs to the Palace entrance hall a loud knocking started up on the old oak entrance doors and did not stop. Jenna picked up speed. "Coming!" she yelled. She threw open the doors and found not the Wizard Sandwiches delivery boy, but two bedraggled elderly men, clearly identical twins, who looked oddly familiar even though Jenna was sure she had never seen them before. They took it in turns to speak.

"You took your time, Miss."

"It's freezing out here."

"Can we come in?"

The twins made as if to step inside but Jenna stopped them. "Who are you?" she asked.

They both chuckled annoyingly. "We're a surprise. Now be a good girl and run along and tell Silas Heap there's someone to see him."

Jenna didn't like being spoken to like that. "I won't do anything of the sort."

"Can't get the servants nowadays, Ern," said one, nudging the other.

"You are not speaking to a servant," said Jenna frostily. "You can wait outside. I will go and find Silas Heap."

The twins turned to each other. "Hey, Eddie. I reckon she might be . . ." But Jenna never heard who they thought she might be. She slammed the door on them and set off, highly irritated, to find Silas Heap.

Silas was no more pleased than Jenna at the intrusion. He had been relaxing by the fire with Sarah in her old sitting room. Despite Jenna's fears, neither Sarah nor Silas had any intention of going anywhere near her party—they were savoring the prospect of a quiet evening together. Very reluctantly, Silas left the fireside and set off with Jenna along the icy cold Long Walk.

Jenna threw open the Palace doors to reveal the two scruffy men, each munching their way through a sausage sandwich.

"Goodness!" gasped Silas.

"What nerve!" said Jenna. She snatched up the rapidly cooling sausage bucket from the doorstep.

"Lovely."

"Ta."

"Not eaten all day."

"Been a bit of a hike."

"How are you, Silas?"

"Have we missed the wedding?"

"Can we come in?"

"Perishing out here."

Silas looked flabbergasted. He stood back and let the two scruffy tramps in. Jenna was not particularly surprised; Silas had some weird friends.

"I'm off upstairs, Dad," she said, setting off across the hall.

Silas collected himself. "Jenna! Wait a minute."

One of the twins elbowed the other. "See. It *is* her. Told you."

"Dad, I need to go," said Jenna, already on the staircase. "The sandwiches are getting cold."

"Well, come and say a quick hello before you rush off. This is Ernold and Edmund. Your uncles."

"My *uncles*?"

"Yes. My brothers. You know, the two that didn't make it to our Simon's wedding? Gosh, I haven't seen them since before . . . well, since before all the *stuff* happened."

It was on the tip of Jenna's tongue to tell Silas that the two rude old men were not actually her uncles and were nothing to do with her, but she knew how much that would hurt Silas. She bit back the words and hurried down the stairs—the sooner she said hello, the sooner she could get the sausage sandwiches up to where they belonged.

Jenna held out her hand, keeping her distance from Ernold and Edmund. They looked, she thought, like the sort of uncles who would lunge at you for a sloppy, sausage-sandwich-scented kiss. The very thought made Jenna feel sick. But Ernold and Edmund behaved themselves. They meekly shook Jenna's outstretched hand and mumbled:

"Sorry we . . ."

"Didn't recognize you."

Jenna slipped into gracious Princess mode. "Please don't worry about it. I didn't recognize you either. I hope you will excuse me; I have to go. I have some people waiting for me," Jenna said, making it sound as though she were returning to a board meeting. She picked up the bucket of sausage sandwiches and, carrying it as though it were a precious heirloom, she gracefully ascended the stairs. As soon as she was out of sight, Jenna broke into a run. Thirty seconds later she hurtled into her room yelling, "Sausage bucket!"

20
WITCHERY

"*You certainly know how to* throw a good party, Jen," Septimus said many hours later, as they led the revelers out along the shadowy upstairs corridor.

"Thanks, Sep!" Jenna was buzzing with excitement; it had been a wonderful evening. As the guests made their way out along the candlelit corridor, an assortment of Palace ghosts—old servants, ancient officials and a few of the more sociable

Queens and Princesses—looked on approvingly. The Palace was beginning to return to its old, lively self.

The party giggled its way down the sweeping stairs, out of the Palace and into the snow, where the icy night air hit them. With their breath hanging in the freezing air, they walked slowly across the broad plank bridge that led over the iced-up Palace moat, gazing at the strangely beautiful forms of the snow sculptures sparkling in the light of a full moon; the sight gave rise to a chorus of "wow" and "hey" and "spookieeeeeee" as everyone stopped and gazed. Some of the boys began a snowball fight and Jenna got out of the way. She found herself standing next to Beetle, who was laughing about something with Marissa.

Jenna tried to think of something interesting to say but couldn't. Beetle tried to as well, with the same result. Marissa, however, had no such problem. "Hey, Beetle; are you walking back to the Manuscriptorium?"

"Yep," said Beetle.

"I've got a room at Bott's Cloaks now. Just opposite. Walk with you?"

Beetle sounded surprised. "Oh. Yes. Of course. How's poor Mrs. Bott doing?"

Marissa shrugged. "Dunno. She doesn't say much."

Beetle turned to Jenna, the gold braid on his Admiral's jacket glistening in the moonlight. "Jenna. Thank you for a lovely party," he said, rather formally.

Jenna smiled. "Oh, thank you so much for coming, Beetle. It was very nice to see you," she said and immediately wished she hadn't. She had sounded so *Princessy*, she thought. No, worse than that, she had sounded *prissy*.

"Yeah, it was really great," said Marissa, giggling and linking her arm through Beetle's. "*Byeeee*." With that Marissa tugged Beetle off into the sculpture garden and Jenna watched them disappear behind a giant frog. Maybe, thought Jenna, she didn't like Marissa quite as much as she thought she had.

Jo-Jo, Matt and Marcus stopped their snowball fight. "Where's she gone?" they demanded.

"Where's who gone?" asked Jenna.

"You know who, Jens," said Jo-Jo. "*Marissa*."

"What's it to you?" demanded Marcus, eyeballing Jo-Jo.

"None of your business," Jo-Jo retorted.

"Hey, Forest boy, don't get clever with me—"

"Stop it!" said Jenna, stepping between Jo-Jo and Marcus. "She's gone off with Beetle if you must know."

"*Beetle?*" three voices chorused incredulously. "Jeez." They sloped off disconsolately and resumed their snowball fight, but with a lot more edge.

A succession of good-byes followed until Jenna was left alone with Septimus and Rose.

"Hey, Jen, you okay?" asked Septimus.

"Fine, thanks."

"It was great, wasn't it?"

"Yep," said Jenna. "I mean, yes, really great."

"Time we went, Jen," said Septimus. "Got to get Rose back before her pass expires."

Jenna had an idea. "If you hurry you can catch up with Beetle."

Septimus grinned. "Maybe he doesn't *want* catching up with, Jen."

"Don't be silly, Sep," said Jenna snappily.

"Ah. Well, g'night, Jen," said Septimus. "And thanks. Great party."

"Thank you," said Rose. "It was really lovely."

Septimus gave Jenna a hug; then he and Rose wandered off, weaving their way through the sculptures. After following a well-trodden path past the giant frog, a large chicken, a rowboat, a huge crown, three fat bears, a large, rude Water Gnome and something that bore a remarkable resemblance to Marcia Overstrand with a pile of saucepans on her head—much to their amusement—they reached the Palace Gate. In the distance Septimus saw Beetle and Marissa walking arm in arm up Wizard Way. After a few moments' thought, he took Rose's arm and followed slowly, in no more hurry than Beetle was.

Jenna felt decidedly unsettled. She looked up at the Palace, which was blazing with light from the candles in the windows, and sighed. It looked beautifully welcoming, but she didn't want to go to bed. Not just yet. She slipped into the entrance hall and took her thickest fur cloak from the coat cupboard under the stairs. Beside it hung her Witch cloak, which she grabbed and angrily scrunched up into a ball: *that* was going in the trash. She'd had enough of witches.

Witch cloak stuffed under her arm, Jenna took the path that led round the back of the Palace to the new kitchens where the trash was. As she bundled the cloak into the bonfire bin something brushed against her dress. Jenna looked down. "Binkie!"

Maizie Smalls's cat stared balefully up at Jenna. Jenna felt a little spooked—Binkie was not the kind of cat you wanted to meet alone at night. If it had been any other lost cat she would have picked it up and taken it into the warmth of the Palace, but there was no way she was going to touch Binkie. Jenna watched the cat stalk off toward the thicket of trees that bordered the Palace gardens. A feeling of unease made Jenna reach into the bonfire bin and take her Witch cloak out again. She threw it over her red fur cloak and set off toward the river—somehow, she didn't know why, she felt protected by her Witch cloak.

There was a disused jetty just past Spit Fyre's dragon field where Jenna liked to sit and think, and right now that was where she wanted to be. As she cut across the Palace lawns, Jenna glanced over to the thicket of trees that bordered the Palace grounds. She shivered, and felt glad of her Witch cloak surrounding her like a shifting shadow.

Deep in the darkness of the thicket, Binkie, chief of the Forest Cats and new familiar to Morwenna Mould, the Wendron Witch Mother, was purring loudly. Morwenna stroked the cat and crooned, "Well done, my little spy. Well done." She eased her bulk off a fallen log and moved silently out of the trees. Morwenna was determined that this time, the Princess would not get away, unlike a few years back, in the Forest.

All Witch Covens crave a true Princess—it gives them great power among other Covens—and Morwenna knew that this was her last chance. Soon enough Jenna would no longer be a Princess and then the Wendron Witches would have to wait for Jenna's daughter. The Witch Mother smiled grimly. The Wendrons would get in fast next time—**CradleSnatching** was so much easier. If only she hadn't once made a promise to that lovely young Wizard, Silas Heap, they would have **CradleSnatched** this one fourteen years ago. How different things would have been.

Morwenna followed Binkie down toward the river. Tail held high, Binkie tiptoed over the ice-crusted snow while Morwenna sank down so deep that the snow fell into the tops of her boots. As they drew closer to their quarry, Morwenna was shocked to see that the potential Wendron Witch Princess was *wearing a Port Witch Coven cloak*. She had heard a rumor that Jenna had kidnapped the Coven's youngest witch and stolen a cloak—and it looked like it might be true. Morwenna smiled. This Princess was going to be worth having.

As Jenna walked below the trees that led to the Dragon Field, her cloak was doing what Witch cloaks do best—blending in with the shadows—and Morwenna could no longer see her. Horrified at losing sight of the Wendrons' Princess, Morwenna made a decision. She would have to do some **FootFollowing**.

FootFollowing is an ancient witch skill. It involves following a quarry by stepping into their exact footprint. Once a witch has **FootFollowed** three consecutive footsteps she knows that her prey can never escape, wherever they go: through the densest forest, up the tallest mountain, under the deepest river. Always, the witch will be **Following** in their footsteps. Like most witch **Magyk**, it has both advantages and disadvantages. The advantage is that the witch is sure to find her victim. The disadvantage is that she has no choice but to do so. She must **FootFollow** in every footstep until she reaches her target. It can at times be dangerous: for example, if the **FootFollowed** happens to fall off a cliff, the **FootFollower** will have no choice but to do the same. Morwenna was aware it was not something to be undertaken lightly, but Jenna's Witch cloak had worried her—there was more to this Princess than she had realized. She must take no chances.

Finding three consecutive footprints was not as easy as Morwenna had expected, because the Witch cloak was doing its job well. As Jenna moved through the snow it had brushed across her footprints, blending them together—as Witch cloaks are meant to do. But Jenna had then stopped to open a gate, and Morwenna got lucky—three perfect Princess footprints planted in the snow. The witch whispered the **FootFollow** and set off. This, she thought, was going to be a pushover.

It probably would have been a pushover if Morwenna had not been encroaching on dragon territory. While Spit Fyre was perfectly happy to allow Jenna to walk through his Dragon Field—Witch cloak and all—he felt very differently about a real witch.

When one is **FootFollowing** it is not possible to look up from the footprints. Morwenna's brilliant blue witchy eyes were fixed firmly on the ground, so she got quite a shock when she suddenly saw planted in front of her two huge green dragon feet with very large claws indeed. (No one cut Spit Fyre's toenails anymore. Even Billy Pot, the dragon keeper, had given up—they blunted his hacksaw.)

Morwenna said a very rude Forest curse and slowed

down—but she could not stop. Her feet were **FootFollowing** and she was heading straight for the underbelly of a nasty-looking dragon. This was not what she had planned. It was not what Binkie had planned either—tail puffed out like a bottlebrush, the cat shot off into the night.

Spit Fyre snorted threateningly. A tendril of dragon dribble landed on Morwenna's winter fur cloak and scorched a trail of holes. A nasty smell of burning wolverine hit Morwenna's nostrils, but she had no choice but to keep on going. With some difficulty, she squeezed beneath Spit Fyre's tummy and headed for his frighteningly spiky back legs. Morwenna began to feel scared—those spikes were sword sharp. *She would be cut to pieces.*

After his recent fight with the **Darke** Dragon, Spit Fyre had grown his adult leg spurs. He was very proud of them, but although they were extremely sharp they were also soft and new, and Spit Fyre did not want a witch anywhere near them. And so, to Morwenna's surprise and great relief, the dragon carefully lifted his feet and stepped aside. Morwenna was out of the Dragon Field as fast as she could go—but not before a well-aimed stream of dragon spit had hit her squarely on the back. Spit Fyre watched the witch go in disgust, then he took off for the boatyard, where he had taken to spending every night keeping the Dragon Boat company.

Morwenna moved fast and silent along the dark footpath that ran along the riverbank. The moonlight showed nothing more than shifting shadows as she went, her Forest Witch cloak merging with both the snow and the river beyond. She was now walking along a well-trodden path and was pleased she had chosen to **FootFollow**—the Princess could be anywhere. As Morwenna came to a bend she was surprised to find that her feet took her away from the path and through a gap in the hedge. She pushed through the snowy leaves and stepped silently onto the old jetty. The witch smiled. How very convenient, she thought. Earlier that evening, she had tied up her coracle to the mooring post at the end of that very jetty.

Jenna was sitting, leaning against the mooring post, watching the breaking reflections of the moon in the mirror-black river and wondering why she felt so upset about Marissa asking Beetle to walk home with her. Jenna remembered that when Marissa had said that she was renting a room above Bott's Cloaks, she had been pleased for her—until later when she had realized that Bott's Cloaks was opposite the

Manuscriptorium. And then, unaccountably, she had felt distinctly *not* pleased. She had even caught herself thinking how nice it would be to have the freedom to rent a room opposite the Manuscriptorium, rather than having to live so far away, in the Palace. This had thrown her into confusion. She loved the Palace—how could she possibly compare it with a tiny room above smelly old Bott's preloved cloaks? Why would she want to live *there*?

While Jenna was pondering the merits of the Palace versus Bott's Cloaks, the jetty gave a sudden lurch. She turned around and a flash of fear went through her. She saw the large bulk of Morwenna Mould creeping forward, carefully placing her feet into the snow in a rather peculiar way. Jenna knew at once she had to get away— there was no doubt in her mind that being crept up on by a witch when it is way past midnight and you are alone, perched over an icy river, was not good.

Very slowly, so as not to disturb Morwenna—who seemed to be in some kind of trance—Jenna got to her feet. If she had been anywhere else, she would have run for it, but unfortunately the only escape involved actually going *toward* Morwenna, who pretty much took up the width of the landing stage. Jenna hesitated. She was sure that Morwenna hadn't seen her—the Witch Mother was staring intently at the old planks as though she had lost something. But she was moving ever closer in an oddly deliberate way that frightened Jenna. Jenna decided that her best chance was to take Morwenna by surprise. She would wrap her Witch cloak around her like a shield and run straight at her. With any luck she could push past Morwenna before the Witch Mother had time to do anything.

Jenna took a deep breath and ran. As she got to within arm's length, Morwenna looked up. "Princess!" she gasped.

Jenna stopped. She eyed up the available space on either side of the witch—there were maybe six inches of landing stage, certainly no more. And below was the icy river.

Morwenna took a step forward and Jenna took a step back. "Morwenna," she said, playing for time. "How . . . nice to see you."

Morwenna did not reply. She was trying to remember the Rules of **FootFollowing**. Could she grab her prey now or did she have to **Follow** *all* the footsteps? Would she have to go to the end of the jetty first and then come back? She wished she could remember.

"Yes," said Morwenna, distracted, "very nice." And then,

"*Bother,*" as her feet began to take her past Jenna. She was going to have to **Follow** every single step. What a stupid spell, she thought. "Excuse me a moment, Princess Jenna. Um, don't go away."

Politely, Jenna stepped aside to let Morwenna by and smelled the earthy scent of leaf mold and decomposing fungus as the witch squeezed past her. Jenna was confused. She had been convinced that Morwenna was stalking her and yet clearly that was not the case. Lulled into a false sense of security, Jenna headed for the path back to the Palace.

Behind her Morwenna had put on a surprising turn of speed. The witch raced to the end of the landing stage, wheeled around and headed right back. The next thing Jenna knew was the smell of leaf mold behind her as Morwenna placed her dainty witch foot into Jenna's last footstep. As Jenna wheeled around in surprise, the heavy hands of the Witch Mother descended on her shoulders and her talonlike grip dug into the top of her arms.

"Got you!" Morwenna crowed triumphantly. "At *last.*"

21
What Is to Be

"Get off me!" *yelled Jenna*, twisting and turning, trying to get free.

"You can't get away; I have put a **Grasp** on you," hissed Morwenna.

Jenna could not believe it—she had been so *stupid*. She

should have run away while she could. Morwenna propelled her back along the jetty and Jenna was convinced that the witch intended to drown her. They reached the mooring post and Morwenna—keeping her **Grasp** on Jenna—leaned down and pulled a small coracle out from underneath.

"Get in!" she puffed.

There was no way Jenna intended to get into something that looked like a large teacup floating on the river—especially with a witch. "No!" she said and gave Morwenna a shove backward. But the witch's **Grasp** held firm and Jenna found herself teetering on the very edge of the rickety planks. She grabbed hold of the mooring post with both hands. If Morwenna wanted to take her, she would have to take the post too.

Suddenly a movement on the riverbank, dark against the snow, caught Jenna's eye. Two figures were moving fast toward the landing stage. With a sinking feeling Jenna guessed it was witch reinforcements—witches always traveled in threes. An old rhyme came into her head:

*One Witch to **Find** you,*
Two Witches to pay,

Three to remind you
You won't get away.

And she'd bet anything that one of them was Marissa. But suddenly a very un-Marissa voice boomed out. "*Stop right there!*"

Never had Jenna been so happy to hear that voice. "Milo!" she yelled. "Help, *help!*"

The rickety planks shook as Milo pounded toward them. Morwenna gave Jenna a massive shove, but Jenna was ready. Using the momentum—and the fact that Morwenna could not let go—Jenna swung around the mooring post in a full circle, taking the witch with her. She had heard that witches and water did not mix well. Her only hope was that the shock of the water would make Morwenna break her **Grasp**. As Morwenna began to topple, Jenna prepared herself for the fall into the icy water.

Milo's heavy hand suddenly landed on Morwenna's shoulder, pulling her back from the edge. "Eerf ym dlihc!" he yelled.

Morwenna gave a cry of fury and Jenna felt the witch's **Grasp** fall from her arm. She jumped back and both she and Milo gave Morwenna a hefty push. The witch landed neatly in her coracle, feet sticking out, arms flailing like a beetle stranded on its back. The coracle began to do what coracles do best: go round in circles. Around and around it went, spinning off into the middle of the river. Milo and Jenna watched the witch twirl through the moon's reflection; then the current took the coracle and pulled it rapidly along, bouncing through the choppy waters in the middle of the river, taking the Witch Mother back to the Forest.

"What was it you said that made her let go?" asked Jenna.

Milo had made a decision that morning after Jenna had blown him her kiss. At last, Jenna was allowing him to be her father, and he would start acting like one. Probably for the first time ever, he answered a question directly. "I said, 'Free my child.' In **Reverse**."

Jenna had not expected that. "Oh . . ."

It was not easy, but Milo made himself continue. "When . . . yes, when Cerys, your mother, was first expecting you she got very worried about **CradleSnatching**. It is something that the Wendron Witches used to do, snatch baby girls from their cradles to bring them up as witches—and they particularly liked to take Princesses. A Princess is a great prize for a Coven, so they say."

Jenna nodded. She knew all about that.

"By the time Cerys was Queen, the Wendrons had stopped taking Castle babies, but your mama was afraid that they might still be tempted by a baby Princess. So she told me a powerful **Reverse**." Milo smiled at the memory. "Well, actually, she sat me down and made me learn it over and over again."

Once again Jenna was overwhelmed with the what-might-have-been feeling. "And you remembered. After all this time."

Keeping to his resolve to be straight with Jenna, Milo had something to admit. "Well, I almost did. Actually, I'm sure I *would* have done. But luckily your mother reminded me. It's something you want to get right the first time. There's not always a second chance with a witch."

Jenna knew she'd been lucky: she had escaped from the Port Witch Coven once and from the Wendrons twice now. "Third time *un*lucky," was another well-known witchy saying. But something Milo had said did not make sense to Jenna. And as he seemed to be actually answering her questions for once, she asked,

"What do you mean, *my mother reminded you*?"

Milo looked at Jenna with an odd expression in his eyes.

She seemed so young to him, *too* young. But what did he know? The Queen was always right. "Jenna, your mother, or rather the ghost of your mother, is here."

"*Here?*"

"There." Milo gently guided Jenna around so that she was looking toward the Palace.

"Oh!" Jenna gasped.

Standing on the riverbank at the far end of the landing stage was the ghostly figure of a young woman wearing the long red robes of a Queen.

Milo asked softly. "Shall we go and meet her?"

Jenna was lost for words. She nodded.

Milo put his arm around Jenna's shoulders and together they walked toward the ghost. As they drew nearer Jenna saw that her mother was just as she appeared in her dreams. She was surprisingly young, her long dark hair was caught up in a golden circlet, and her large, violet eyes did not leave her daughter for a moment.

With every step Jenna took, she felt as though she were walking out of one life and into another. The ghost of Queen Cerys stretched out a translucent hand and in response Jenna held her hand out to meet it, careful to allow the ghost to make the first touch, if she wished. Cerys did wish. She placed her hand on Jenna's and Jenna felt something fleeting, like a warm breeze on a winter's day.

"Daughter . . . dearest. My . . . *Jenna*." It was hard for Cerys to say Jenna's name, because it was not the one she had chosen for her. Milo and Cerys had decided that Jenna would be named after her two grandmothers, but the Naming Day had never happened.

Jenna stood silently. She did not know what to call her mother. "Mother" felt too formal, "Mum" was Sarah Heap and "Cerys" felt too much like a friend.

The ghostly Cerys guessed what Jenna was thinking. "Perhaps you would like to call me Mama?" the ghost asked.

Jenna was not sure. Mama sounded kind of babyish. "I . . . I don't know."

Cerys withdrew her hand and looked downcast. "Of course. You already have a *Mama*. For more than fourteen years you have lived your life with another family. A family that I would never, *ever* have . . ." The ghost's voice became faint with emotion. Marcia's selection of Sarah and Silas Heap as adoptive parents had horrified Cerys when she had first found out from the ghost of her own mother—who had wholeheartedly approved. "They will love her as their own," Queen Matthilda had told her grieving daughter. "And that is the most important thing for a child." But Cerys did not agree, and the choice of the Heaps still rankled.

Milo could see that Cerys was working herself up into what he used to call one of her "states." "What's done is done," he said quietly. "The Heaps are a good family. And it is *your* time now, Cerys."

Jenna watched her parents together with a feeling of disbelief. Ever since she had been given *The Queen Rules* on her fourteenth birthday, she had known that one day soon she would meet the ghost of her mother, but she had never expected to see her mother and her father together as a couple. It was a shock. There was none of the easy, happy banter that she was used to between Sarah and Silas. Jenna at first supposed it was because one of them was a ghost, but they seemed to slip into their roles with such ease that she began to suspect that they had always been like this—her mother edgy, and her father conciliatory.

Milo's soothing words had their intended effect and Cerys calmed down. The ghost held out her hand to Jenna, saying, "Come, daughter, we have a Journey to make."

Jenna was not surprised—a Journey was mentioned in the Arcane section of *The Queen Rules*, although no details were given. She wondered where the Journey would take them. She placed her hand into the shadow of her mother's and allowed the ghost to lead her along the riverbank toward the Palace. Milo watched his daughter and the ghost of his wife walk away together, then set off after them at a discreet distance. He sighed, overcome as Jenna had been earlier, by the sense of what-might-have-been.

Sarah and Silas were dozing by the fire in Sarah's sitting room. Ernold and Edmund Heap had long gone to bed but Sarah knew that Jenna was still out, *and I can't go to bed until I know she is safely home, Silas. You go on up without me.*

But Silas had stayed with Sarah. He wasn't going to leave her alone in that sitting room ever again. So when the door creaked open and Silas looked up to see Jenna peering round, he nudged Sarah.

Sarah opened her eyes and smiled at Jenna. "Nice time?" she asked.

Jenna did not return her smile. She came into the sitting room and—using the tone that announces something no parent wants to hear—she said, "Mum. Dad."

Sarah and Silas were on their feet in an instant. "*Ohmygoodnesswhatisit?*"

In reply Jenna stepped to one side and pushed the door behind her wide open.

"Oh!" gasped Silas.

"Your . . . Your *Majesty*," said Sarah. "Oh . . . *my*."

"Sarah Heap. Silas Heap." The ghost of Queen Cerys smiled uncertainly.

"Oh, Your Majesty. Please come in."

The ghost drifted into what had once been her (immaculately tidy) sitting room and stared at the chaos in horror. Sarah saw the Queen's gaze settle on the remains of that night's supper, which was piled on the floor beside the fire, and she quickly threw a towel over it. A red stain from some pickled beetroot (Silas loathed pickled beetroot) spread up through the towel as though someone had shot it. And that made Sarah even more embarrassed. She glanced at Queen Cerys, trying unsuccessfully not to look at the great dark bloodstain over the ghost's heart.

"Um . . . Mum, Dad," Jenna said again, not knowing where to start.

"Yes, love?" Sarah said anxiously.

"My mother. The Queen. She has something she would like to say to you and Dad."

"Oh, dear . . ." This was a moment that Sarah had been dreading—the moment the past came back to haunt them.

"It's nothing bad, Mum," Jenna said hurriedly. "Really."

Sarah was not convinced.

Queen Cerys looked upset—she could not believe what Sarah Heap had done to her beautiful sitting room. Was this how her daughter had lived too? She was silent for a moment as she tried to compose herself. Sarah and Silas waited nervously.

"My husband and I . . ." the ghost began, and then turned and beckoned someone in from the corridor. "Come *in*," she said, a little impatiently, Sarah thought. Milo squeezed in through the door and tried to hold it open with the fluffy pink rabbit doorstop, with little success. With some difficulty, he found a place to stand, wedged between two stacks of dog-eared romance novels, which were liberally splattered with duck poo. The ghost started again. "My husband and I wish to thank you both, Sarah and Silas Heap, for looking after our daughter."

Sarah glanced at Silas. She didn't like Jenna being described as someone else's daughter. Silas raised his eyebrows in response. Neither did he.

The ghost continued. "We are both deeply grateful for the love and care you have given her. And we are well aware of the hardships that have befallen you as a result of your guardianship . . ."

Sarah flashed a look of dismay at Silas. They were not Jenna's guardians—they were her *parents.*

". . . of our daughter. We trust those difficulties are at an end and that you will now be able to resume your simple, yet happy life." Silas let out a spluttering sound. Sarah looked like a goldfish that had been thrown out of its bowl.

Silas spoke for them both. "Your Majesty, Jenna has brought us nothing but good. And we have always considered Jenna to be our daughter. We always *will* consider Jenna to be our daughter. Nothing is at an end."

"Things end, Silas Heap," said Cerys. "Things begin. It is the way of the Castle. The way of the world."

Sarah was becoming increasingly agitated. "*What do you mean?*" she burst out.

"I mean that today things begin."

"What *things*?" demanded Silas.

"That is not for you to know, Silas Heap."

Silas thought differently. "If it affects our daughter, it most certainly *is* for us to know."

The Heaps were not quite what Cerys had expected. She had assumed that they would curtsy and bow respectfully, gratefully hand over her daughter, and she would see no more of them. Cerys felt quite rattled: when she had been Queen no one would have dreamed of speaking to her like that—especially Sarah and Silas Heap. Stranded at the doorway by the sheer amount of junk she would have to **Pass Through** in order to go any farther into the room, Queen Cerys raised her voice and spoke very slowly.

"It is time for our daughter to go on her Journey," she said.

"What journey?" Sarah demanded. "Where?" Memories of a similar visit by Marcia Overstrand to take Jenna away from their room in the Ramblings some four years in the past had come flooding back. "You can't just come here and take Jenna away. I won't allow it; I *won't*."

"It is not for you to allow or disallow, Sarah Heap," Queen Cerys informed her.

Milo watched in dismay; he had become very fond of the

Heaps and did not like to see them upset. He had forgotten quite how bossy Cerys was. Time had thrown a rosy hue over his life with her—now he remembered why he had gone away on so many voyages. Milo was back to his role of fifteen years ago: smoothing the waters. He threaded his way across the room to the upset Heaps.

"Silas, Sarah," he said. "Please don't worry. All Princesses go on a Journey with the ghost of their mothers before they become Queen. They go back to where their family came from, I believe."

This did not make Sarah feel any better. "Where on earth is *that*?" she asked. "And how does Jenna get there? How long will she be away?"

"I don't know," admitted Milo. He shrugged just like Jenna, thought Sarah. "It's Queen stuff," he said with a rueful smile. "They do a lot of that, you'll find."

Jenna pushed past a stack of washing and hugged Sarah. "Mum, it's okay. Milo's right; it *is* Queen stuff. And that's what I have to do. You *know* I do."

"I know, love." Sarah noisily blew her nose into a large handkerchief and woke Ethel. Since the **Darke Domaine** the duck was easily frightened, particularly in Sarah's sitting room. Ethel now launched into full-scale panic. A frantic quacking filled the room and the duck rose up, flapping her little bony wings. She careered across the tiny room, bouncing from Milo's head to washing pile to flowerpot stack, and shot out of the door, **Passing Through** the astonished ghost of Queen Cerys.

The ghost of the Queen had never been **Passed Through** before. It is a shocking experience for any ghost the first time it happens, particularly when the **Passer-Through** is a hysterical duck. Queen Cerys fell out of the room with a groan and Milo rushed after her.

Jenna had a few moments with Sarah and Silas. "Mum. Dad. You mustn't worry. I will be fine. I know she—I mean, my mother, the Queen—seems a bit . . ."

"Rude," Silas supplied.

"Yes," Jenna admitted. "But she hasn't spoken to anyone for ages and I think things aren't quite what she expected." Jenna took a deep breath. She felt excited at what she was going to say. "And I think I am going to be Queen soon."

Sarah nodded. "I think so too, love."

"You do?"

"Yes. I can tell. There is something different about you. I

do understand that The Time *Is* Right."

Hearing this from Sarah made Jenna feel relieved and happy. "You don't mind?"

"Of course we don't. We knew it would happen one day. Didn't we, Silas?"

Silas sighed. "Yes, we did."

Milo appeared anxiously at the door. "All right?" he asked. "Ready?"

"Yes." Jenna nodded. "Bye, Mum. Bye, Dad. I'll be back soon." She hugged them both hard, then Sarah and Silas watched Jenna pick her way across the room.

Queen Cerys's pale hand stretched out toward Jenna. Jenna turned, blew Sarah and Silas a kiss and then she was gone.

Tactfully, Milo slipped out, leaving Sarah and Silas together. There was a long silence in the sitting room.

After a while, Silas said gruffly, "I'd better go and find that blasted duck."

⊹ 22 ⊹

Relations

Now *that it was known* that the Princess was gone on her Journey, a strange collection of objects and people began arriving at the Palace.

Never a day went by when Sarah Heap was not called to the entrance hall—always hoping it would be Jenna—only to find someone holding some kind of pot, box or bizarre object. At the sight of Sarah the person would make a formal bow and say: "Comptroller, I bring you this Wonder for the Coronation. We, the family (*insert family name here*) are honored to be the Keepers of the Coronation (*insert description of object here, e.g. trumpet, fire shovel, broom, eggcup, shoehorn, stuffed*

ferret) and as is our bounded duty since Time Began, we now present this to thee, O Comptroller, for its sacred duty. Safe Journey." The donor would then bow three times, walk backward across the Moat bridge, taking care not to fall prey to the snapping turtles—and once out of role, he or she would either give Sarah a cheery wave and shout "Good luck!" or scuttle off in embarrassment.

Sir Hereward, on guard in the shadows, faithfully awaiting Jenna's return, had seen it all before. He watched the arrival of each object with approval, pleased to see the old traditions continuing. He was less pleased to see the precious objects carelessly thrown into an ever-increasing pile beside the doors.

Sarah had become almost used to the visitations. She had given up telling people she was not the Comptroller—whatever that was—she had even stopped telling people she was not going on a journey, thank you, when she realized it referred to Jenna's Journey, but she wished they would stop. As soon as she had begun to do something she would hear the tinkling of the bell in the entrance hall. If she ignored it the duty doorperson would come and find her—because no Keeper would leave without personally handing the object over to "the Comptroller."

Sarah could not help but be anxious about Jenna, but she did her best not to show it. She wanted her four Forest boys to enjoy their time "back home," as she called it. Sarah nursed hopes that they might decide to stay, so she tried to hide her fears. But Nicko understood how his mother felt. He knew how much she had fretted when he had been lost in another Time and he wanted to make things up to her.

A few nights after Jenna had gone, Sarah was sitting at her window watching darkness fall. It was a bad time of day for Sarah—yet another night was drawing in and she could not help but wonder where Jenna was and what she was doing. As Sarah gazed out toward the river, she saw lights flickering by the Palace landing stage. Excited, she sprang to her feet. Jenna was back already! She ran out of the room only to cannon straight into Nicko.

"Oof! Hello, Mum. Good timing," said Nicko with a big smile.

"She's back," said Sarah. "What a relief."

"Who's back?"

"Jenna!"

"Oh, that's brilliant. Sam's got plenty of fish."

"*Fish?*" Sarah was flummoxed.

"It's a surprise, Mum. We're having a Forest supper. For you."

"Forest supper?"

"Down on the riverbank. See?" Nicko pointed to the lights outside.

"Oh." Sarah gazed out at the lights. Now that she looked closely she could see the burly figures of her four Forest sons tending a fire and yes, standing beside the river, holding lanterns, were Simon and Septimus talking to Silas, Edmund and Ernold.

"Mum, are you all right?" asked Nicko.

Sarah shook off her disappointment. She knew that only a few months ago if someone had told her that she would have all her boys with her, safe and happy, she would have been ecstatic. Count your blessings, Sarah Heap, she told herself sternly. And *smile*.

"I'm fine, Nicko love. Thank you. Now, where's this wonderful supper?"

While the Forest Heaps cooked fish for Sarah and Silas, down on Snake Slipway another supper was in progress. Marcellus, Simon and Lucy were sitting in the long, narrow dining room that ran from the front to the back of the house, at an equally long, narrow table lit with so many candles that Lucy found it hard to see anything in the glare.

"I have some bad news," Marcellus announced.

Simon looked at Lucy anxiously. He still expected things to go wrong, and he braced himself, thinking that Marcellus was going to say that he no longer wanted him to be his Apprentice.

"The Alchemie Chimney has fallen down," said Marcellus.

"It's the frost," Lucy said. "The mortar won't set."

"So they say," said Marcellus gloomily.

"You need to put heaters inside the scaffolding tarpaulin," said Lucy.

Marcellus looked suddenly attentive—why hadn't the builder thought of that? "And you should make them build it like CattRokk lighthouse," Lucy added.

"Oh?"

"Yes. CattRokk has huge granite blocks as foundations, then bricks. They get smaller as they go up. You need the lower part of the chimney to be a good wide base for the upper part."

Marcellus was impressed. So much so that by the end of

the evening, Lucy was in charge of building the Alchemie Chimney. Later, as they walked across the road back to their little house, Simon said proudly, "There's no way the new chimney will fall down, Lu. Not with you in charge. It wouldn't dare."

While Sarah fretted about her Forest sons leaving, the one group of Heaps who Sarah would have been very happy to wave good-bye to showed no signs of wanting to go. In fact, to Sarah's dismay Ernold and Edmund Heap showed every sign of wanting to stay—permanently. They found themselves a suite of rooms at the far end of the Palace and set up camp, as Sarah put it. "The trouble is, Silas," Sarah said one afternoon, "we can't say we don't have the room, can we?"

"We won't when we move back home," said Silas. "They'll have to go then."

The morning after the supper by the river, Silas was due at the Wizard Tower on **Seal Watch**. Sarah begged him to take Ernold and Edmund with him. "They are driving me nuts, Silas—they follow me everywhere and they *don't stop talking*. All I want is a quiet morning in the herb garden without having to listen to a comedy double act." Silas dutifully took his brothers along to the Wizard Tower. He signed them in as visiting Wizards—which they both claimed to be—and left them to explore the open areas of the Tower. Half an hour later, when he had finished his **Watch**, Silas found himself in trouble.

Head fuzzy from staring at **Magyk**, Silas emerged to find an angry Marcia Overstrand waiting for him with Edmund and Ernold standing sheepishly at her side.

"Are these yours?" Marcia demanded, as though Silas had left a pair of smelly socks on the floor.

"Er, yes. I signed them in," Silas had to admit.

"As visiting *Wizards*?" Marcia sounded incredulous.

"As indeed we are, Madam," Edmund piped up.

"Totally, utterly and entirely at your service, ExtraOrdinary Madam," Ernold supplied.

"I am *not* an ExtraOrdinary Madam," said Marcia severely. "I am an ExtraOrdinary Wizard. Silas, before signing people in as visiting Wizards I would expect you to at least check that they are bona fide Wizards. As these two persons"—with some effort, Marcia fought off the urge to refer to the visitors as idiots—"clearly are *not*."

"Oh, but we are," chorused the twins.

"We trained with the Conjurors of the Calm Green Seas . . ."

". . . in the Wayward Islands of the West."

"Absolute rubbish!" said Marcia.

"No, we did."

"Really, we did. Honest."

"You misunderstand me," said Marcia. "I meant that Conjuring is rubbish. It is mere trickery and bears no relation to **Magyk**. I do not doubt you know a few tricks—the singing pink caterpillar infestation in the fourth-floor communal houseplant is testimony to *that*—but that does not make you Wizards. Take them home, Silas. At once."

The thought of what Sarah would say if he returned with Edmund and Ernold after only an hour made Silas brave. "Marcia, my brothers are not here for long—"

"Oh, but we *are*," said Edmund.

"No, you're not," retorted Silas. He turned to Marcia. "My brothers would dearly like to learn about **Magyk**. Education is one of the purposes of the Wizard Tower, isn't it? They are willing to take their turn in all tasks and they humbly apologize for the caterpillars—" Silas kicked Ernold on the shin. "*Don't you?*"

"Ouch!" said Ernold. "Yes. Absolutely. Edmund didn't mean to do it."

"But I *didn't* do it!" protested Edmund.

"You *did*."

Marcia looked at the squabbling brothers. "How old are you?" she inquired.

Silas answered for them. "Forty-six, believe it or not. Marcia, please let them stay. I think it would be really good for them. I will never let them out of my sight, I promise."

Marcia considered the matter. Recently Silas had been frequenting the Wizard Tower on a regular basis. He had told Marcia that so very nearly losing the Tower to the **Darke Domaine** had made him realize how much he valued the place. Marcia knew that Silas had taken more than his fair share of the unpopular **Seal Watch** and there was a chronic shortage of Wizards available to do it. She supposed that even a couple of Conjurers might be trained to **Watch**. Marcia relented.

"Very well, Silas. I will ask Hildegarde to issue each of them with a Visitor Pass. It will restrict them to communal

Wizard facilities only. You can train them as **Watchers** and they can take their turn, providing they pass the elementary **Watch** test."

"Oh, Marcia, *thank you*," said Silas. It was more than he had hoped for.

"My condition is that you must, as you promised, accompany them at *all* times. Is that understood?"

Silas smiled. "Yes, it certainly is. Thank you *so* much."

++ 23 ++
THE ALCHEMIE CHIMNEY

Septimus's vacation flew by and soon his month was nearly over. The Big Thaw set in. Sarah Heap had been dreading it—now there was nothing to keep her Forest boys in the Castle. But determined not to think about it, Sarah busied herself by trying to organize all the "Coronation Clutter," as she called the multitude of offerings that were still arriving. Sarah was particularly pleased when she saw her old friend Sally Mullin coming up the drive—Sally always took her mind off things. Sarah hurried to the entrance hall, past the huge pile of "Clutter" watched over by a rather disapproving Sir Hereward. Barney Pot was on weekend door duty, sitting on a tall chair, happily swinging his legs and reading his new comic from the Picture Book Shop.

"Don't worry, Barney," Sarah told him. "I'll get the doors." She pulled them open and a gust of wind blew in. Sarah and Barney shivered. It was a dismal, raw day. "Come in, Sally, it's so nice to see you, I've been—"

"Comptroller," Sally began hurriedly in an oddly strangled voice. "I bring you this Wonder for the Coronation. We, the family Mullin, are honored to be the Keepers of the Coronation Biscuit Tin and as is our bounded duty since Time Began, we now present this to thee, Oh, Comptroller, for its sacred duty. Safe Journey." Sally handed over a very battered golden tin, which sported a beautifully engraved crown on its lid.

Sarah took the tin. "Oh!" she said, nearly dropping it. It was *heavy*. Clearly it was made from solid gold.

Studiously avoiding Sarah's amused gaze, Sally bowed three times and then walked backward across the plank bridge. As soon as she reached the other side, her suppressed giggles erupted and both she and Sarah collapsed in laughter.

"Oh, Sally," gasped Sarah, "I had no *idea*. Come in and have a cup of herb tea."

Sally scurried gratefully back over the bridge. "Ta. It's perishing out here. Blasted biscuit tin weighed a ton, too."

The slamming of the Palace front doors woke Septimus, who was sleeping in a large room at the front of the Palace. Blearily, he sat up in the creaky old bed—yet another dream of the red eye of **Fyre** still vivid in his mind—and remembered that it was the last day of his vacation.

Septimus had enjoyed his time off far more than he had expected. He had spent the first few days at the Wizard Tower pottering about the Library with Rose and dutifully visiting Syrah—who still did not recognize him—in the Sick Bay, until Marcia had shooed him off and told him to *take a break, Septimus*. So he had come to stay at the Palace, much to Sarah's delight. Soon he was hanging out with his brothers around their campfire on the riverbank, helping Silas to file his **Magyk** pamphlets, and spending time with Sarah in the herb garden. He had stayed over with Beetle and gone out with a bunch of scribes to the Little Theater in the Ramblings and had even ventured back to the Pyramid Library to visit Rose a few times. It was the very first time in his life that Septimus had been free to do what he pleased day after day, and he was sorry to think it was very nearly over.

Septimus got out of bed and padded across the threadbare rugs to the window. He drew back the moth-eaten curtains and looked out of the window onto a dismal scene. Overnight it had rained, turning everything soggy and miserable, and now a watery mist hung in the air. Along Wizard Way piles of dirty snow and gritty, gray ice were heaped up; the only color was the Wizard Tower at the far end, which shone with its indigo morning **Magyk** lights flickering gently through the misty gloom.

The Wizard Tower now had a strange twin: the Alchemie Chimney at the end of Alchemie Way. It sat in the middle of a large circular space, which people had begun calling by its old name, Alchemie Circus. The chimney was covered with a blue tarpaulin, which glistened with water and shone with its own, more basic lights—the lanterns that Lucy Gringe had had set up inside it to enable building work to continue all night. There were always a few onlookers but today Septimus saw that a fairly substantial crowd was gathered. Suddenly he heard the sound of Lucy Gringe yelling through a megaphone, "Stand back! Stand back! Will you all *get out of the way*!" There was a noise like thousands of flapping sheets, and the tarpaulin fell to the ground.

This was greeted by cheers evenly balanced with boos. Now revealed, the Alchemie Chimney stood tall and oddly out of place. It looked to Septimus like a stranded lighthouse.

Five minutes later, Septimus hurriedly looked into Sarah's sitting room. Sarah and Sally were giggling by the fire. "I'm off, see you later," he said.

"Bye, love," said Sarah. "Don't forget, I'm cooking a special supper for your last night."

"I won't. Bye, Mum, bye, Sally."

"Lovely lad," said Sally, as Septimus closed the door.

Septimus ran out of the Palace and headed up Alchemie Way, pleased that the mist—and Jo-Jo's old Forest tunic that he had taken to wearing—meant that people would be unlikely to recognize him. Something told him that Marcia would not be happy about where he was heading. As Septimus reached Alchemie Circus, he caught sight of Lucy's distinctive multicolored dress fluttering like a bright butterfly against the granite-gray stones of the base of the chimney. He weaved his way through the onlookers to get a closer look. The sound of Lucy making the scaffolders refold the tarpaulin reached him. "That's rubbish. Do it again—and do it right this time!"

Septimus was glad Lucy Gringe was not his boss—she made Marcia look like a softy.

"Hey, little bro!" Lucy called out. "Beautiful, isn't it?"

Septimus looked up at the chimney. Below the tracery of scaffolding, he saw stone cut so precisely that you could scarcely see the joints and above the stone, the neat circles of frostproof, heatproof and pretty-much-everything-proof brick began. The bricks were graded by size, getting smaller as they delicately traveled upward, each circle subtly different. "Brilliant!" Septimus called back.

Lucy beamed with delight.

Some lettering carved into the great granite slabs at the base of the chimney caught Septimus's eye. There was the date, followed by:

MARCELLUS PYE: LAST AND FIRST ALCHEMIST.

SIMON HEAP: ALCHEMIE APPRENTICE.

Lucy Heap: Architect.

Heather, Elizabeth and Samson Snarp: Stonemasons and Lighthouse Builders.

Septimus looked at the names for a few minutes, taking them in. There it was, set in stone—he was no longer anything to do with Marcellus. Or Alchemie. Or the **Fyre**. Where his name could have been, there was Simon's.

Lucy was so busy supervising the dismantling of the scaffolding that she did not notice Septimus wandering away disconsolately and disappearing into the shadows of Gold Button Drop. The mist in the Drop was thicker than in Alchemie Way. It settled around him like a blanket; it muffled the sound of his boots and set his Dragon Ring glowing in the dull light. The conical shape of the lock-up solidified out of the mist, flat at first like a cardboard cutout; then details came into view: the rough stone blocks, the dark arch of the door. And then he saw the door open and a black-and-red-cloaked figure emerge.

"Marcellus!"

"Ah, Septimus. Well, well, what a coincidence. I was on my way to find you."

Septimus brightened. "Really?"

"Indeed. The chimney is complete and we are about to bring the **Fyre** up to its operating level. I would like you to see this, so that when you become ExtraOrdinary Wizard—"

"ExtraOrdinary Wizard?" said Septimus. "*Me?*"

Marcellus smiled. "Yes, *you*. Do you not expect to be?"

Shaken by seeing Simon's name carved into the chimney, Septimus was full of regrets for Alchemie. He shook his head. "No. Oh—*I don't know.*"

"Well, just in case it turns out that way. I want the **Fyre** to be as much part of your life as it is part of mine or, indeed, Simon's. I want you to trust it and understand it, so that never again does an ExtraOrdinary Wizard even *think* of killing the **Fyre**."

"I would never do that. *Never,*" said Septimus. "The **Fyre** is amazing. It makes everything, even the Wizard Tower, feel dull."

"Ah. But you have made your decision, Septimus."

"I know," Septimus sighed. "And it's set in stone."

Marcellus and Septimus took the climbing shaft and tunnel down to Alchemie Quay and then transferred to a much narrower and steeply sloping tunnel that wound its way in a spiral, down between the web of Ice Tunnels that radiated off from below the Chamber of Alchemie. It was over half an hour later that they reached the end of the tunnel where the upper **Fyre** hatch, illuminated by a **Fyre** Globe, lay.

"This is but a short climb down, Apprentice," said Marcellus. "But we must make it a fast one. This is the one point where we can be seen on the *Live Plan*. And I do not wish to be seen just yet. You do understand?"

"Yes," said Septimus a little guiltily.

Marcellus placed his Alchemie **Keye** into the central indentation of the hatch and it sprang open. A waft of heat came up to meet them. Septimus waited while Marcellus swung himself into the shaft, then he quickly followed and pulled the hatch shut. He clambered down the metal ladder and waited while Marcellus opened the lower **Fyre** hatch, then dropped down after Marcellus onto the flimsy metal platform.

Simon, in his black-and-gold Alchemie robes, was waiting for them.

"Hello, Simon," said Septimus, not entirely pleased to see him.

Simon, however, looked happy to see his little brother. "Hello, Sep," he said. "What a place. Isn't it beautiful?" He pointed to the **Fyre** below.

"Yes, it is. It's amazing," said Septimus, thawing a little at Simon's enthusiasm.

"Apprentices," said Marcellus. "It is not safe for the secrets of the **Fyre** to be known by only one person. Or even two. By the end of today, I hope that there will be three of us who will understand all there is to know about the **Fyre**. 'Safety in numbers' is the expression, I believe. And safety is what we want."

And so, they became a team. Patiently, Marcellus took Simon and Septimus through all the stages of bringing the **Fyre** to its full power, which, now that the chimney was completed, it was safe to do. They worked through the day, methodically running through Marcellus's long checklist. They regulated the water flow through the Cauldron, cold when it entered, hot when it left to find its way out through the giant emergency drain into the river. They drummed the Cauldron, they measured the height of the **Fyre** rods, they checked the levers that operated the huge hoppers of coal buried in the cavern walls—the **Fyre** blanket, Marcellus called it—and a hundred other small things that Marcellus insisted upon. "For safety," as he said countless times that day.

It was late afternoon when Marcellus, Septimus and Simon stood once more on the dizzyingly high platform at the top of the **Fyre** Chamber. Above them was the huge oval opening to the Alchemie Chimney, which would take up the heat and the fumes and provide a much-needed airflow through the Chamber. But it was not the unobtrusive opening in the roof that claimed their attention—it was, of course, the perfect circle of the eye of **Fyre** far below, brilliant red brushed with its delicate blue flame, that returned their gaze. Underneath the blue they could see the dark twinkling of the graphite rods, each one a perfect five-pointed star, silently powering the **Fyre** around it. Marcellus smiled. All was well. They climbed up the pole to the lower **Fyre** hatch, sweaty, tired and longing for fresh air once more. But there was one more thing to do.

An hour later, the decoy fire in the furnace of the Great Chamber of Alchemie and Physik was lit and burning well. Marcellus lowered the conical fireguard over it so that the flames were safely contained. "Good," he said. "That will produce enough smoke to satisfy everyone. Time to go."

They headed wearily up the long incline back to the

lock-up. Septimus had been so impressed with Marcellus's insistence on safety that—even though he knew Marcellus did not like to talk about it—he said, "I just don't understand how the Great Alchemie Disaster ever happened."

Marcellus sighed. "That, Septimus, makes two of us. I don't understand either. It makes no more sense to me now than it did all those hundreds of years ago. But what I do know is that if the ExtraOrdinary Wizard had not intervened in such a high-handed manner—excuse me, Septimus, it rankles to this day—and closed down the **Fyre**, then many lives would have been saved. And my house in Snake Slipway would not be so perishing cold every Big Freeze." Marcellus smiled at Septimus's bemused expression. "The Ice Tunnels were not just the old communication tunnels between the ancient Castle buildings; many of them were also part of the Castle heating system. As you know, they run beneath every old house. The hot water from the **Fyre** kept us all warm. People loved the **Fyre** in those days."

"Ah," said Septimus, thinking that that made a lot of sense.

Evening was falling when they emerged from the lock-up. They hurried off to Alchemie Circus, where Lucy had been anxiously awaiting the first plume of smoke to appear from the chimney. She ran excitedly toward them.

"It's working—look!" Lucy pointed up to the thin wraith of white smoke that was climbing lazily up into the evening sky.

"Well done, Lu," said Simon. "It's a brilliant chimney."

"Thanks, Si," said Lucy.

"Yes," said Marcellus. "It's very nice. Very nice indeed."

People had been hanging around Alchemie Circus all day, waiting for the first breath of smoke to emerge from the chimney, but with the onset of dusk, most had drifted away. But although the Living had got bored and gone home for supper, Alchemie Circus was, in fact, still packed—with ghosts. They had come to see what many considered to be the very heart of the Castle come alive once more. Most approved, but there were some who did not. These were the ghosts who had been present at the Great Alchemie Disaster. Indeed there were some there who had entered ghosthood because of the disaster. Some had been burnt to death by the hundreds of subsidiary fires that had swept through the Venting system and burst, unannounced, up through the floors of houses. Others—like Eldred and Alfred Stone—had been frozen into the Ice Tunnels during the panic to **Freeze** them. But those who had lived before the disaster had good memories of the **Fyre**. It had been the beating heart of the Castle, and those who had known life with it considered the present-day, **Fyre**-free Castle to be a poorer place.

But nothing stayed secret in the Castle for long and word soon spread that the **Fyre** was lit. Later that evening, after Septimus had gone back to the Palace for Sarah's last-night-of-the-holiday supper, Marcellus, Simon and Lucy joined the edgy crowd at the foot of the chimney, many of whom were clutching the recently reissued *All You Need To Know About The Great Alchemie Disaster* pamphlet.

"Oi!" someone called out. "It's the Alchemist fellow."

A young woman carrying a toddler waved the pamphlet angrily. "Have you read this?" she demanded.

"Madam, I *wrote* it," said Marcellus.

"Rubbish!" yelled a bookish, elderly man wearing a fine pair of gold-rimmed glasses.

"Well, I'm sorry you didn't enjoy it. I did my best."

"I meant there is no *way* you wrote this. You *Alchemists!*" the man spat out the word in disgust. He waved his copy of the pamphlet under Marcellus's nose. Marcellus caught a waft of old paper—it was one of the original ones. "You Alchemists always covered everything up. And you, Mr. Pye, were one of the worst offenders."

Marcellus held his hand up in protest. "I am sorry," he said. "Please believe me, the Great Alchemie Disaster was not of our making."

"So whose fault was it, then?" demanded a teenage boy. "The tooth fairy's?" The crowd giggled.

Marcellus had known that the return of the **Fyre** to the Castle would not be popular. He had given the problem a lot of thought and he hoped he had a solution. He raised his voice above the murmurings of discontent. "To prove to you that we have nothing to hide, we will be starting guided tours of the Great Chamber of Alchemie."

There was a stunned silence.

"All will be welcome and it will be my pleasure to meet you at the UnderFlow Quay and show you around personally. You may book the tours with Rupert Gringe at the Boathouse. I look forward to seeing you all again shortly." With that Marcellus bowed and strode away.

Lucy ran after him. "Guided tours?" she asked. "Are you *sure*?"

"Just to the Great Chamber. It will make them feel involved.

We show them the furnace and all the gold. They'll *love* the gold. Give out a few souvenirs, that kind of thing. Simon can talk to the young women. They'll love that."

"Huh," said Lucy.

"People need to know that there are no secrets in the Great Chamber of Alchemie and Physik," said Marcellus.

"*Aren't* there?" asked Lucy.

"Of course not," said Marcellus. "Whatever gave you that idea?"

Lucy wasn't sure. All she knew was that something about the **Fyre** did not make sense. And that Simon said suspiciously little about what he did at work all day.

"Well, thank you, Lucy," said Marcellus. "You have done a wonderful job on the chimney. I really don't know what I would have done without you."

Lucy suddenly realized that her work was done. "Oh," she said. "Right."

"And to show my appreciation at this historic moment I would like to offer you . . ." Marcellus paused.

"Yes?" said Lucy, wondering if Marcellus was about to overcome the legendary stinginess of Alchemists and actually *pay* her.

"The chance to accompany me to the Wizard Tower tomorrow to collect the Two-Faced Ring. It is an historic occasion."

"Thanks but no thanks," snapped Lucy. "I have better things to do. Like knitting curtains."

Marcellus watched Lucy stride off down Alchemie Way, plaits flying. She looked annoyed, he thought. But he wasn't sure why.

24
NOT A GOOD MORNING

The next morning at the Palace, Septimus was up at dawn. He put on his new Apprentice robes—which Marcia had sent to him a few days earlier—checked through his Apprentice belt to make sure all was in order, and grabbed a quick breakfast. Yesterday's misty drizzle had given way to a beautiful morning, crisp and clear. As Septimus walked quickly up Wizard Way, he saw the Wizard Tower rearing up into the blue sky, gleaming pale silver in the early morning sun. Septimus felt excited to be going back to work at last and was even looking forward to his practical **DeCyphering**. It was a perfect morning to take the **Flyte Charm** up to the top of the Golden Pyramid and make a new rubbing of the hieroglyphs.

Hovering in the bright, still air above the hammered silver platform, Septimus managed to produce a very good rubbing using a thin but strong sheet of **Magykal** tracing paper and a large block of black wax. The hieroglyphs came up crisp and clear, but they still made no sense—particularly the strange blank square in the center. Undaunted, Septimus took the huge piece of paper back down to the Library, where he and Rose settled down to the prospect of a happy morning puzzling.

Back at the Palace, Silas Heap was feeling considerably less perky. Slowly surfacing after a night of vivid and horrible dreams, Silas could not shake off a fuzzy, disconnected feeling in his head and a high-pitched ringing in his ears. He wandered downstairs, convinced that he had forgotten something although he could not remember what. Silas was hoping for a quiet breakfast in the family kitchen and he was pleased to see that there was no sign of Edmund and Ernold anywhere. He was due at the Wizard Tower for yet another **Seal Watch** later that morning and needed some quiet time to clear his head. But Silas was not to get it. He had just poured himself a strong cup of coffee when Sarah breezed in, slamming the door behind her.

"Ouch!" Silas winced.

Sarah looked at her husband disapprovingly. "I don't know what you were doing last night, Silas Heap, but you deserve your headache this morning. *Really!*"

"What d'you mean?" mumbled Silas. He blinked a few times, trying to get rid of an odd blue fuzziness around Sarah. It made him feel queasy. "You know I was on midnight **Seal Watch**. And the twins were after me, so I had to wait for them too. You *know* that, Sarah. I explained at supper."

"Silas, you didn't get back until four o'clock in the morning. I had *no idea* you were going to be so late. You might have told me. What were you *doing*?"

Silas shook his head and wished he hadn't. "I . . . I don't know." He groaned. "**Watching** that **Seal**, it makes you feel really sick."

"Huh!" said Sarah. "Well, you can come and do something useful for a change. I need some help out here."

"Sarah. Please. Just let me finish my coffee. I have to get to the Wizard Tower soon."

"The coffee can wait, Silas."

Silas gave in. He knew that arguing with Sarah would take as long as actually doing what she wanted. He got up and followed her out into the Long Walk.

All kinds of weird and wonderful objects, many of them extremely valuable, were now piled up in the Palace entrance hall, spilling out across the floor and teetering in unwieldy stacks. Sarah had grown used to it but after Silas had tripped over a pyramid of musical Coronation Frogs and become entangled in a string of metallic red and gold Coronation Bunting and nearly strangled himself, even Sarah had had to admit that things were out of control.

At Sir Hereward's suggestion, Sarah had opened up a series of large rooms at the far end of the Long Walk to store the Coronation Clutter. With the old ghost's help—few people are brave enough to refuse a request from a sword-carrying ghost with one arm and a dented head—Sarah now had a band of helpers. Only the Uncles—as Ernold and Edmund had become known—had successfully eluded her, which had made her all the more determined to get Silas to help. She propelled him into the entrance hall, where a disconsolate group of Forest Heaps and assorted Palace helpers were getting to work under the eagle eye of Sir Hereward.

"Sarah, it's a mountain," protested Silas. "I really don't have the time."

Sarah was unmoved. "The sooner you start, the sooner you'll finish. You can help the boys with that." She waved toward a large upright piano, glittering with red and gold curlicues, and sporting some very fine gold candleholders. Sam and Jo-Jo were struggling to push it onto the old carpet that ran down the center of the Long Walk.

"What on earth is it?" asked Silas.

"It's the Coronation Pianola," sighed Sarah. "Apparently you press the foot-pedals and it plays the music for the Coronation Tea. Little Betsy Beetle and her grandmother brought it. They pushed it all the way from the Ramblings. And do you know, Silas, they live on the *top floor*?"

"Goodness," said Silas. Goaded by the thought of little Betsy Beetle—who had never grown taller than four feet high—he set to. "Right then, come on, boys—*heave*."

"So where's Milo when you need him?" Silas muttered grumpily as they maneuvered the Pianola onto the carpet. "As soon as there's work to be done he's gone. *Typical*."

"Stop wasting your breath, Silas," said Sarah. "You'll need

it to push." She gathered up a tall pile of silver plates on the top of which she had precariously balanced the Coronation Canary—long dead and now stuffed and living forever in a golden cage—and followed on behind the Pianola. Behind Sarah came Barney Pot pulling a trolley full of Coronation Cutlery, Maizie Smalls with the Coronation Bunting ("Keep it away from Silas, Maizie, *please*," Sarah had pleaded), Edd pushing the Coronation Puppet Theater, which wobbled along on three squeaky wheels, and Erik struggling with a huge sack of dusty Coronation Cushions, which made him sneeze.

At last the procession reached its destination. Just as Sarah was unlocking the big double doors that led to the old Conference room where she had decided to store the clutter, a door opposite opened and Milo emerged, blinking in surprise.

"About time," said Silas. "Give this a shove, will you, Milo? I really *must* go. Oh, hello, Hildegarde, what are *you* doing here?"

Everyone stared at Hildegarde, who had followed Milo out of the room.

"Nothing!" said Hildegarde quickly.

"Exactly," said Milo. He quickly locked the door and pocketed the key. "Excuse me, Sarah, Silas: I really must be off," and before either of them could protest, Milo ushered

Hildegarde rapidly away down the Long Walk.

"Typical!" said Silas. "Right, boys, one, two, three, *heave*."

By the time the Coronation Clutter was stored away in the Conference room, Silas was very nearly late for his **Seal Watch**. Edmund and Ernold were nowhere to be found—which did not surprise him. Like Milo, they were never around when there was work to be done. Silas decided to risk Sarah's ire at leaving the twins behind and hurried off to the Wizard Tower.

As Silas walked out of the Palace Gate he glanced up to the Alchemie Chimney and, to his amazement, saw a breath of smoke curl up into the sky. Silas felt a stab of excitement. The **Fyre** was lit! Very soon the tedious **Seal Watches** would be no more and the Two-Faced Ring would be confined to oblivion. Silas was surprised at the feeling of relief at the thought. He had not realized how much the brooding presence of the ring had gotten to him over the weeks.

A breeze coming in from the river obligingly bowled Silas quickly along Wizard Way and cleared his head in the process. He climbed the marble steps up to the Wizard Tower with a spring in his step, looking forward to lunch in the new canteen after his **Watch**. He whispered the password and the tall silver doors swung silently open to reveal a large crowd of Wizards in the Great Hall. This didn't worry Silas; it was getting near lunchtime and the newly refurbished canteen was proving highly popular. As Silas wandered in, whistling a happy tune under his breath, a nearby Wizard nudged a neighbor. The word spread, and in a moment the Great Hall fell silent and all eyes—green, every one of them—were on Silas Heap.

"Um . . . hello," said Silas, realizing that something was not as it should be. "Nice day. Well, actually a bit windy but lovely and—"

"Silas Heap!" Marcia's voice carried across the Great Hall.

"Good morning, Marcia," Silas called back, a little anxiously.

"No, it is *not* a good morning," came Marcia's reply.

The crowd of Wizards parted to give Marcia a clear run at her prey. As Silas watched the ExtraOrdinary Wizard advance toward him, an expression of fury on her face, he wished that he was still shoving the recalcitrant Pianola through a doorway—in fact Silas would have willingly shoved any number of recalcitrant Pianolas through an infinite variety of doorways in exchange for not being where he was right then.

Marcia reached him. "Where have you been?" she demanded.

"Sorry. Been moving stuff." Silas looked at his timepiece. "I know I'm cutting it a bit fine, but I'm not late."

"That, Silas Heap, is not the point." Close up, Marcia looked scary. Her green eyes glittered angrily and her frown cut a deep line between her eyebrows.

"What's wrong?" asked Silas nervously.

Marcia did not answer his question. "Silas Heap!" she announced. "You are under a Wizard Tower Restraint Order."

"*What?*" gasped Silas.

Marcia clicked her fingers and pointed at the three Wizards nearest to Silas. "Sassarin Sarson. Bernard Bernard. Miroma Zoom. The Ordinary Wizard Silas Heap will remain in your custody until further notice. Take him to the Stranger Chamber."

Silas gasped. This was a terrible insult. "But, *Marcia*. I'm not a Stranger. I'm Silas. You *know* me."

Marcia rounded on Silas. "I thought I did. Now I am not so sure. Take him away."

⳩25⳨ THE STRANGER CHAMBER

The *Stranger Chamber had been* set up some seven hundred years previously after a disastrous rampage through the Wizard Tower by a highly plausible Grula-Grula. It was a large, windowless room on the opposite side of the Great Hall from the duty Door Wizard's cupboard and was used for visitors who were considered a potential threat to the Tower. Although it showed no sign of being so, it was a completely **Shielded** and **Secure** area, and was the one place in the Wizard Tower that was devoid of **Magyk**. All the protective **Magyk** surrounding the room—and there was a lot—was sealed away in a second skin buried in the walls.

Behind its smart blue door, the Stranger Chamber looked comfortable and inviting. It was intended to put visitors at ease and give them no cause to suspect that they were, in fact, imprisoned. It was carpeted with a thick, finely patterned rug laid beside a fake fireplace, which contained a fire basket full of welcoming candles, burning brightly. There was a squashy sofa on the near side of the fireplace with its back to the door, and on the far side facing the door was a comfortable armchair strewn with cushions. Beside it was a table piled high with interesting books to read, a welcoming bowl of exotic fruits, a tin of biscuits and a jug of fresh water. It was to this armchair that the Stranger was always shown. The reason for this was that the Stranger's chair was placed on top of a large trapdoor over which the rug had been carefully cut out. Beside the entrance to the Chamber next to the Alarm button, and also beside the sofa, were discreetly hidden levers. These, if given a sharp tug, would open the trapdoor and send the Stranger, chair and all, hurtling down a chute. Depending on a master lever set in a small box beside the door, the chute would send the Stranger either on a rapid descent under the Wizard Tower Courtyard and eventually out into the Moat, or straight down into a cell hewn from the bedrock of the Castle.

No Stranger had ever realized the purpose of the Chamber—until it was too late. They would be offered the very best food that the Wizard Tower could supply and be provided with the companionship of a highly attentive Wizard. If the Stranger was thought to be potentially dangerous or **Darke**, very often the attendant would be the ExtraOrdinary Wizard herself.

The true purpose of the Stranger Chamber was a well-kept secret even within the Tower, and many of the junior Wizards assumed it was merely a waiting room. But Silas was an old hand: he had once been the ExtraOrdinary Apprentice. He had even once been Attendant Wizard in the Stranger Chamber to a particularly odd character that Alther Mella had been convinced was a Chimera. Alther had, of course, been right, and Silas had actually got to pull the lever that had sent the Chimera hurtling on her way to the Moat. The Wizard Tower had escaped with no more damage than a few scorch marks to the Stranger Chair inflicted when, at the very last moment, the Chimera realized what Silas was about to do.

So, as Silas was ushered into the Chamber by his three escorts, he knew that he was no longer trusted in the Wizard Tower. He was, in fact, considered to be no better than a foul-smelling, fire-breathing, malevolent hybrid that wore way too much lipstick. It was utterly humiliating.

The first thing that struck Silas as he stepped into the Stranger Chamber was its complete lack of **Magyk**. After so recently rediscovering his love for **Magyk** after many years, Silas felt its absence all the more keenly. As he walked slowly across the soft patterned rug and was shown to the comfortable blue velvet chair strewn with multicolored cushions, Silas felt desolate. He watched his three escorting Wizards take their place on the sofa opposite. But no one needed to try to fool Silas, so he did not receive the usual sociable chitchat. Instead, the Wizard guards sat like three stone monkeys, staring at him in a most disconcerting way—especially as Silas knew one of them quite well. Bernard Bernard was a regular player in Silas's Counter-Feet league and had even been to the Palace for supper. It was excruciating. Silas could not bear to look at them. He stared at his boots and tried to imagine what could possibly have happened to cause his incarceration. But his imagination failed him. All he knew was that it must be really, *really* bad. He would put a big bet on it being something to do with Edmund and Ernold—but what?

After what felt like hours, but was only ten minutes, the door opened and Marcia came in.

Silas leaped to his feet. "Marcia!"

To Silas's horror, Marcia immediately placed her hand on the lever. "Sit!" she barked, as though Silas were a dog. Silas sat.

Marcia nodded to the three Wizards on the sofa. "You may go."

Silas watched the Wizards file out, each one avoiding his gaze. He saw them close the door and, although he heard nothing, he knew that they had **Locked** it. Silas looked up at Marcia. "Marcia, *please.* Tell me what has happened," he pleaded.

Marcia walked across to the fake fireplace and stood with her back to the candles, placing her hand on the other lever.

"I suggest *you* tell me, Silas," she said coldly.

"But I don't *know,*" Silas very nearly wailed.

"*You don't know?*" Marcia spluttered incredulously. "You are telling me that you don't know that your brothers are in fact two extremely skilled and daring **Darke** Wizards."

Silas's laugh bordered on hysteria. "*What?*"

"It is no laughing matter, Silas. You presented these as your two bumbling, Conjuring brothers eager to learn from us. When in fact they are two of the most skillful Wizards I have ever had the misfortune to come across."

"No, that's not possible."

"Unfortunately it is perfectly possible."

"Well, they certainly had me fooled," muttered Silas.

"It doesn't take a lot to do *that*," snapped Marcia.

Silas was about to say that they had had Marcia fooled too, but he stopped himself. He noticed with dismay that Marcia's hand was not only resting on the lever, but was impatiently drumming her fingers on it.

"Marcia . . ."

"Yes?" Marcia waited for what she thought was a confession coming.

"That lever—it is on a hair trigger."

Marcia looked surprised. She did not realize that Silas knew about the workings of the Stranger Chamber. She stopped drumming her fingers but Silas saw that she did not take her hand away.

"I will remove my hand when you convince me that you have not been party to this."

"Party to *what*?"

"Party to a conspiracy to introduce two **Darke** Wizards into the Wizard Tower for the purpose of theft and burglary of the most serious kind. Party to aiding and abetting the two said Wizards in pursuit of their plan. Party to expediting their escape from the Castle."

Silas spent some seconds trying to work out exactly what it was that Marcia had said. But his brain was in panic mode. All he could manage was, "Marcia, please. I don't understand. *What have they done?*"

Marcia did not reply. There was an odd look in her eyes that Silas found disconcerting. Silas had never progressed to the **MindScreen** level of his Apprenticeship and he did not realize that Marcia was trying—without the aid of any **Magyk**—to catch a glimpse of his thoughts.

Marcia just about managed it. She got panic, anger with his brothers, but overriding everything was utter bewilderment. The bewilderment was, she could tell, completely genuine. Marcia took her hand off the lever and sat down on the sofa opposite Silas. Silas breathed a sigh of relief and fell back into the cushions. *Marcia believed him.*

"Silas Heap," she said, "I accept that you have not conspired against the Wizard Tower."

"Oh, thank goodness," breathed Silas.

Marcia held up her hand. "*However . . .*"

"Oh," muttered Silas.

"You have neglected your duty as an Ordinary Wizard. On your Induction all those years ago you promised to protect the Wizard Tower at all times. You promised to honor your word. At some time in the last twelve hours you have broken both those promises with disastrous consequences."

"No! No, I *haven't*."

"You have. You promised to accompany your brothers in the Wizard Tower at all times."

"But I *have*."

"If that is so, then that makes your position even worse."

"But—"

Marcia cut in. "If you were with them at all times then that makes you an accomplice, does it not?"

All Silas could do was to shake his head.

"You understand that breaking your Induction vows can lead to permanent **Barring** from the Wizard Tower?"

Silas nodded miserably.

"And I assume you are aware that the **Barring** of a Wizard will also affect their immediate family?"

Silas was horrified. "No! No, you can't make Septimus suffer for my stupid mistake."

"I don't make the rules, Silas. If you are **Barred**, then it is highly probable that Septimus will find he cannot access the arcane secrets of the Tower. This will mean that, should he wish it—and right now I don't know if he ever will—he will never be able to become ExtraOrdinary Wizard. He will be **Tainted** by you."

Silas groaned.

"It's not fair, but that's how it goes. You *know* that. There would be nothing I could do about it. The Tower has a mind of its own, and the deepest **Magyk** is not available to all. Why do you think we still have a Wizard Tower after it was inhabited by DomDaniel? He never got to its heart. *Never.*"

Silas was aghast. "You can't lump Septimus in with that awful old Necromancer!"

"Of *course* I don't. But the Wizard Tower might."

Silas put his head in his hands. *What had his brothers done?*

Marcia spoke. "I want you to know that it is only for

Septimus's sake that I am not **Barring** you from the Tower."

Silas sat up. "You're *not*?"

"I'm not. I give you my word. So I suggest you try to fix things as soon as you can."

Silas felt bleary, as though someone had hit him on the head. "Fix what?" he asked.

"Come on, Silas. Now you have my word that I'm not going to **Bar** you—and *I* keep my promises—you can be straight with me. You knew what Ernold and Edmund were planning. You're their brother, they've been living with you, working with you—of *course* you knew. Just tell me where they are and what they've done with it and all will be fine."

Silas leaped to his feet. He had had enough. "Knew *what*?" he demanded. "Done with *what*? Marcia, what are you talking about? *What have my idiot brothers done?*"

At last Marcia was convinced that Silas had no part in his brothers' deed.

She stood up and looked Silas in the eye. "Edmund and Ernold have stolen the Two-Faced Ring."

26

BAD TIMING

The door to the **Sealed** Tunnel in the Wizard Tower swung to and fro like a broken window in a hurricane as the last eddies of **Magyk** drained away. A somber group of senior Wizards stood at the door, waiting until it was possible to close it once more. It was essential that the tunnel be drained of all contamination before it was **ReSealed**.

Septimus—extricated from the Pyramid Library—was there. It was important, Marcia had told him, that he saw the correct procedure for **DeContaminating**. Marcia had then hurried off to the Stranger Chamber where, Septimus guessed, she had the culprit.

Bernard Bernard—a big bear of a man with squashy features and dishevelled hair—appeared. "Anyone need a break?" he inquired. And then, seeing Septimus, he added sympathetically, "Ah, hello, lad. Don't you worry, now. He'll be all right."

"Who'll be all right?" asked Septimus.

Bernard Bernard suddenly realized that Septimus did not know that Silas was in the Stranger Chamber. He looked embarrassed. "Ah. Well, I meant to say, *we'll* be all right. All of us."

"So Marcia's got the you-know-what back?" someone inquired. (Some of the more superstitious Wizards considered it bad luck to name the Two-Faced Ring.)

"Just being, er, optimistic," Bernard Bernard flannelled.

"That's a no, then," observed the Wizard. A sigh ran through the group.

"It's those two idiot Heaps in there, is it?" asked another, and then glanced apologetically at Septimus. "Sorry, Apprentice. I forgot."

"That's okay," said Septimus. He wished *he* could forget.

"Not sure how many exactly," said Bernard Bernard awkwardly. "Must go." And he hurried off.

An embarrassed silence descended, broken only by the mournful squeak that the door to the **Sealed** Tunnel had developed: *eek-erk, eek-erk, eek-erk.*

Marcia was determined that to any visitor to the Wizard Tower it must appear to be business as usual. It was Septimus's job to deputize for her, so when Hildegarde came to tell him that there were some important visitors for Marcia and *would he come now, please*, he felt very relieved to leave the group of **Watchers**.

Septimus found Marcellus and Simon sitting on the visitors' bench next to the discreet door to the Stranger Chamber—and he knew what they had come for.

Marcellus got straight to the point. "Septimus. You know that I would normally be very happy to deal directly with you. But as I am sure you realize, this particular errand demands I speak to the ExtraOrdinary Wizard herself. Is she available?"

Septimus felt very uncomfortable. He wanted to say to Marcellus, *No, she's not, she's in a real panic, someone has stolen the Ring*, but of course he couldn't. "Well . . . um," he began,

"Marcia is busy at the moment." He decided to buy some time. "Would you like to come upstairs to her rooms?"

Marcellus was dismayed; he knew that Septimus was not telling him something. His hopes for complete trust between the Wizard Tower and the Alchemie began to falter. Marcellus had somewhat grumpily accepted Septimus's offer when the door to the Stranger Chamber was thrown open and Marcia strode out.

"Marcia!" said Marcellus leaping to his feet. "Got you!"

Marcia jumped. "Ah!"

Silas appeared tentatively around the door.

"Dad!" gasped Septimus and Simon together.

"Oh," said Silas, feeling as though he had been caught red-handed.

Marcellus had seen the panic that had flashed across Marcia's face when she first saw him. "Marcia," he said, "I thought you'd be *pleased* to see me. The **Fyre** is lit. All is now ready for the **DeNaturing** of the Two-Faced Ring."

"Jolly good," said Marcia.

"I was just taking Marcellus and Simon upstairs," Septimus told Marcia, "so you can talk to them in private."

But Marcia could not bear the thought of having to tell

Marcellus that the ring had gone. "Tomorrow," she said.

"*Tomorrow?*" Marcellus and Septimus chorused, one indignant, the other shocked.

"Tomorrow," said Marcia. "Now excuse me, Marcellus, Simon. I really must get on." Silently, she gave the password to the Wizard Tower doors and they swung open. The fresh outside air drifted in.

Very deliberately Marcellus looked Marcia in the eye. "To save me another wasted journey, I would be most grateful if you would send someone with the ring when you find . . ." He paused meaningfully.

"Find what?" Marcia dared him.

"The . . . *time*. Good-bye, Marcia."

"Bye," said Septimus apologetically as the doors swung silently closed, leaving Marcellus and Simon standing on the top step.

"Well!" Marcellus exclaimed.

Alchemist and Apprentice walked swiftly across the Courtyard and emerged from the Great Arch. A gust of wind blew up Wizard Way and Marcellus raised his cloak to shield himself from the chill—and eavesdroppers.

Marcellus had not defeated all eavesdroppers, however. Not

far above him—returning to the Wizard Tower after a fruitless aerial search of the Castle—flew the **Unseen** ghost of Alther Mella. Alther had a Wizard's mistrust of Alchemists and he wondered if Marcellus had anything to do with the theft of the ring. Now, he thought, was the time to find out. Still invisible, Alther swooped down low and followed Marcellus and Simon, flying no more than a few feet above their heads.

"She's lost it," he heard Marcellus say in a low voice.

"I thought she was quite calm, really," Alther heard Simon reply. "I've seen her much worse than that." Not entirely successfully, Alther fought back a laugh. Simon glanced up. "There's some weird birds about," he said, puzzled.

Marcellus looked at his Apprentice sternly. "Simon, right now there are far more important things to think about than wildlife. I meant that I believe our ExtraOrdinary Wizard has lost—" Marcellus stopped and looked around. "*It*," he whispered.

Simon stopped dead. "No! Not the . . ." He, too, looked around and lowered his voice. ". . . *ring*. She can't have."

"She was panicking; I saw it in her face. She couldn't get rid of us fast enough. Septimus wanted to tell us but couldn't.

And the Wizard Tower was in turmoil. Did you not notice?"

"Well, yes. It did seem a bit . . . frantic."

"Frantic? It was like someone had poked an ant's nest."

"Yes. I suppose it was."

"It's an utter disaster," said Marcellus angrily. "Marcia has lost the Two-Faced Ring—and she doesn't even have the decency to tell us."

Alther saw a look of horror spread over Simon's face as he realized that what Marcellus said had to be true. "Oh, *Foryx!*" muttered Simon.

"Quite," said Marcellus.

Alther had heard enough to convince him that Marcellus had nothing to do with the theft of the ring. He did a quick backflip and, breaking Rules numbers Two and Five in the *EOW Post-Living Handbook*—that ghosts of ExtraOrdinary Wizards do not use the door password or frequent the public areas of the Wizard Tower—he did first one, then the other. Alther then proceeded to break a few more rules for luck. He interrupted Marcia (Rule Twelve: Disrespecting the Current Incumbent). He told her she should not have sent Marcellus and Simon away (Rule Eight: Seeking to Influence and/or Criticize the Current Incumbent) and then he insisted she send Septimus out after them to bring them back (Rule Six: Interfering with the Policy of the Current Incumbent). He very nearly broke Rule One, which was about foul language, but Marcia backed down just in time.

From the Front Office of the Manuscriptorium, Beetle, who was showing his new clerk how to operate the Day Book, saw Marcellus and Simon stride angrily by. A few minutes later he saw Septimus chase down Wizard Way. Some minutes after that he saw Marcellus and Simon walking swiftly back, with Septimus beside them. A few seconds later the Manuscriptorium door crashed open, and Septimus came into the Front Office, breathless.

"Beetle!" said Septimus, and then, seeing that Beetle was with a scribe, Septimus thought he should be more formal. "Chief Scribe. The ExtraOrdinary Wizard requests your presence. At once."

Beetle looked surprised. "Yes. Of course. I'll come right now." He turned to his new clerk, Moira Mole. "Moira, when's my next appointment?"

Moira looked at the Day Book. "Not until two thirty, Chief. It's Mr. Larry."

Beetle's ex-employer had taken to booking appointments to discuss the finer points of translation. Beetle was not at all sorry to miss him. "Moira, I'm going to the Wizard Tower. If I'm not back by then please give Larry my apologies."

"Okay, Chief." Moira smiled.

"Any problems, ask Foxy."

"Will do."

Moira Mole—a plump girl with short, dark curly hair, and tiny bottle-glass spectacles perched on her nose—watched Beetle and Septimus leave. She peered around the Front Office nervously. She hoped no one else came in.

But at two o'clock Marissa turned up. Marissa scared Moira. She reminded her of the big girls at school who used to pinch her when no one was looking. Moira told herself that she was not at school anymore and, more comfortingly, there was a big desk between her and Marissa. Moira asked Marissa what she wanted but all Marissa would say was: "I want to ask Beetle something." Moira told her she didn't know when he would be back but, to her dismay, Marissa declared that she would wait.

At two fifteen, two rats knocked on the Manuscriptorium window. Moira recognized one of them as Stanley, head of the

Rat Office. The other rat, a little smaller and a lot leaner, she did not recognize. She let them in and they jumped onto the Day Book on the Front Office desk. Moira hoped they had wiped their feet on the way in.

Moira was gaining confidence. Marissa was sitting on a wobbly stool pretending to be interested in an old pamphlet. Moira had the comfortable chair and important things to do. And now she had a Message Rat.

"Speeke, Rattus Rattus." Moira said the words with such aplomb that no one would have guessed she had never said them before.

Stanley prodded the smaller rat. "Go on, Florence. Do what the Office Clerk says."

The small rat looked nervous and squeaked.

"Go *on*," urged Stanley. "No need to be shy. You can't be a Message Rat and be shy, Florence." Stanley looked at Moira apologetically. "Sorry," he said. "Staff training."

"Of course," said Moira with the air of one who knew all about the problems of staff training. "Shall I say it again?"

"Oh, yes, please."

Moira looked at Florence, who was staring at her feet in embarrassment. **"Speeke, Rattus Rattus."**

"Come on now, Florence," Stanley said sternly. "Or I won't bring you out again. You will have to stay in the office and do the filing."

Florence gulped and took a deep breath. "First . . . I have to ask . . . er . . . is William Fox here?"

"Who? Oh, *Foxy*. Wait a mo, I'll go and get him." Moira disappeared into the Manuscriptorium and returned with Foxy.

"Is that him?" Florence whispered to Stanley.

"Now, Florence, I won't always be here to ask, will I? You must ask him yourself."

"So it *is* him?"

"Possibly. But you have to ask."

"First . . ." squeaked Florence, "I have to ask . . . er . . . is William Fox here?"

"Yep, that's me," said Foxy.

There was a silence broken by Stanley. "Go *on*, Florence."

Florence gulped. She stood up tall and took a deep breath. "Message begins: 'Foxy. Please close the Manuscriptorium immediately and initiate **LockDown**. Keep enough scribes with you to guard all entrances and send the rest home, right now. Let no one in, even if you recognize them. If it is me, I will give the password. If I don't, don't let me in. Keep **LockDown** active until I return. This message is sent from O. Beetle Beetle. Chief Hermetic Scribe. PS: don't worry.' Message ends."

"Don't *worry* . . ." said Foxy. "Yikes." And then remembering the Message Rats, he said, "Thank you. Message received and understood."

Stanley nudged Florence again.

"Oh!" said Florence. "Um . . . I regret that we are not at liberty to take a reply. The sender's whereabouts are confidential."

"Okay," said Foxy. "Thanks anyway."

"Well done, Florence," said Stanley. He looked at Foxy and Moira. "Thank you for your patience," he said. The rats jumped down from the desk and Moira held the door open for them to leave.

Foxy sat down in the Front Office chair with a thump. "Jeez," he said. "That was the most scary message I have ever heard."

Marissa, however, was rather excited by the message. "Can I stay too?" she asked.

Foxy was not sure. "Well, I don't know. Beetle said *scribes*."

"Oh, *please* let me. You never know, I might be useful. I *am* a witch, you know."

"I thought you'd given all that up," said Foxy disapprovingly.

"Yeah, I have. But you know what they say, *once a witch, always a witch.*"

Foxy reckoned that a witch might actually come in handy. "Okay," he said.

"Bother," said Moira, who was looking out of the door, watching the rats run off. "Larry's on his way."

Marissa jumped to her feet. "I'll get rid of Larry for you, shall I?"

"Oh, yes, please," said Foxy and Moira in unison.

Marissa shot out of the door. Foxy and Moira didn't know what Marissa did, but Larry never appeared. Half an hour later most of the scribes had gone home and a very nervous Foxy was starting the **LockDown**—a procedure that, as deputy, Foxy had had to learn. Foxy's hands shook as he peered at the new **LockDown** protocol that Beetle had worked out from some faded old documents, but with the help of Romilly Badger, Partridge, Moira Mole and Marissa, Foxy managed to get through to the end.

"I think it's called battening down the hatches," said Moira, who came from a fishing family. "It's what you do when a storm is coming."

Foxy had a bad feeling in the pit of his stomach. He didn't like storms.

27
MYSTERY READING

Up *in the Pyramid Library* a crisis meeting was in progress. Although it was only early afternoon, the windows were shuttered and the Library was dark except for a single candle that burned on a large desk in the center of the room. Gathered around the desk were Marcia Overstrand and the two people—Septimus and Beetle—and the one ghost in the Castle whom she trusted implicitly. There were also two other people she trusted less implicitly but had been persuaded to include by Alther.

"We have a problem," she said. "And it could be a big one."

The candle flame flickered in the air currents that circulated around the Library, wafting in through tiny vents in its golden roof. Marcia's green eyes, sparkling in the light, were worried. "Two things I don't understand: First, how did those idiot Heaps break the **Seal**? Second, they were on **Seal Watch** at half past midnight, so what happened between then and when I discovered them? And why can't we find them? **Search** and Rescue should have easily tracked them down by now. *I just don't get it.*"

"That's three things, Marcia," Alther pointed out.

"*What?*"

"Nothing. Sorry, just being pedantic."

"Alther, can't you at least try to be helpful?" Marcia was still annoyed with Alther for insisting they include Marcellus and Simon.

Alther floated around the end of the desk and settled himself onto an empty shelf. "I've been going to the Mystery Readings recently—you know, in the Little Theater in the Ramblings. They read a mystery story every week."

Marcia looked confused. If Alther had still been alive she would have suspected that he was going a little peculiar, but that could not happen to a ghost. A ghost remained as sane—or crazy—as he or she was on the day they entered ghosthood. And Alther had been absolutely fine on that day.

Marcia impatiently tapped the end of her pencil on the desk. "Well, Alther, I'm glad you are getting out and about. Now, please, we must get on."

"Yes, quite. So you see, every Mystery Reading begins with the audience being told a mystery—"

"Alther, enough!"

"Marcia, be patient. I am trying to explain. The person on stage tells us the mystery. Then two more people appear. One is clever, and the other is . . . well, not so clever, shall we say. The not-so-clever person is involved in the mystery in some way but they don't understand the significance of what they know or have seen. So the clever person makes the not-so-clever person tell them every little detail that happened. And then the clever person works out the solution purely from what the not-so-clever person has told them. Or even gets the not-so-clever person to work it out for themselves. It's very interesting."

Marcia looked displeased. "I think I know where this is going."

Alther had a distinct feeling that he had not explained things as well as he could have, but he plowed on. "So, Marcia, if you tell us everything that happened today, no matter how insignificant it may have seemed to you—"

"As the not-so-clever person."

"No! Goodness, Marcia, I don't mean that at all."

"Well, I seem to be fitting the part rather nicely. Which makes you, Alther, the *clever* person, who will soon be able to tell us where the Two-Faced Ring is. Right?"

"Not necessarily. But it might help us think. Besides, Beetle needs to hear everything that happened. As do Marcellus and Simon."

"You could have just said that in the first place, Alther. It would have saved you a lot of trouble. I am quite happy to go over everything for *Beetle*."

"Jolly good, Marcia. I suggest you begin at the beginning. When you woke up this morning."

Marcia took a deep breath. The morning felt a very long time ago. "I woke up late. I'd had my usual bad dream over and over again and I hadn't slept at all well."

"Describe your dream," said Alther.

"No, Alther. That's witchy stuff. Dreams are *not* important."

"*Everything* is important," Alter insisted.

"Oh, very well. It's the usual horrible dream. I've been having it since we discovered those puddles. There is some kind of fire under the Castle."

Septimus gave a start of surprise and Marcellus flashed him a warning glance.

Marcia, lost in her dream, did not notice. "I keep trying to put the fire out, but just as I think I have, I see flames coming up through the floor of the Wizard Tower. It gets hotter and hotter and then I wake up." Marcia shuddered. "It doesn't sound like much, but it is not nice."

"And then?" prompted the clever one.

"Well, I was not happy about waking up so late. I went straight downstairs and into the kitchen. Septimus had just come down from doing the hieroglyphs and he asked if I wanted some porridge but I wasn't hungry. I couldn't shake off the dream. I knew it was silly, but I had to go down to the Great Hall to check there were no flames coming up through the floor." Marcia laughed, embarrassed. "And of course there weren't. But I still felt something was not quite right so I decided to go and check on the **Seal** before I went back upstairs. As soon as I went into the lobby, I *knew* something was wrong—Edmund and Ernold were on **Seal Watch**."

"What was wrong with that?" asked the clever one.

"Plenty. First, they were not on the rota for that morning. Second, Silas was not supervising, as he was meant to do. Third, they looked . . . weird."

"They *always* look weird," said Septimus, who had not taken to his uncles.

"But it wasn't their usual weird," said Marcia, who knew exactly what Septimus meant. "There was a greenish light all around them and they kind of *glowed*. I asked them what they were doing, and where was the Wizard on **Seal Watch**. They laughed and said that there would be no need for **Seal Watch** anymore. And you know what was really horrible? They both spoke in unison. Like some kind of . . ." Marcia searched for the words. "Twin machine.

"I was actually quite scared and I decided to get help. I backed out of the lobby, intending to **Lock** the door on them. But I didn't get that far. They turned around and they looked so dangerous that instinctively I threw up a **Shield**." Marcia's voice caught in her throat. "I felt something hit me. Twice.

Like being punched. Here." She put her hand over her stomach. "I couldn't get my breath . . . it felt like forever. All I could do was watch them. They came toward me, moving in a really weird way, like those automatons that Ephaniah makes, and **Threw** something else at me. It shook the **Shield** and knocked me back against the wall. They walked by, laughing—I think they thought I was dead. As they went past I felt there was something absolutely, utterly terrifying about them."

Silence fell. Everyone, including Alther, looked shocked. Septimus glanced uneasily at the door, as if expecting his uncles to burst in at any moment.

"Where did they go?" asked Beetle.

"Out of the Wizard Tower—they knew the password, of course. Some Wizards chased after them but they had vanished. I got the **Search** and Rescue onto them right away. They were last seen outside Larry's Dead Languages and after that nothing—nothing at all."

"Is Hildegarde in **Search** and Rescue?" asked Alther.

"Yes, I insisted on it."

"So when did you discover the Two-Faced Ring was gone?" asked Alther.

Marcia sighed. "I *knew* it was gone. They had it when they

went by. That was what I could feel. It has a presence, does it not, Septimus?"

"Yes. It does."

"But you did check?" asked Marcellus anxiously.

"Of *course* I checked. They had left a false **Seal** on the door so that it looked okay, but when I put my hand on it there was nothing there. I did an **Override Command** to the door to let go of the false **Seal** and it took three goes for the **Override** to work. I guess I was a bit shaken up. And then, of course, I saw the truth. The door was open and beyond it I could see the tunnel snaking away. With the false **Seal** gone, the **Magyk** began to drain and the door started to bang to and fro. I left some guard Wizards at the entrance and I walked down to the **Sealed Cell**. I knew what I would find and I did. The door to the **Sealed Cell** was open; there was a hole in the Bound Box. The ring was gone."

Marcellus put his head in his hands. Simon sighed.

"What then?" asked Alther.

Marcia shrugged. "I informed **Search** and Rescue and called a meeting in the Great Hall. Just as it began, Silas walked in."

"And what did *he* have to say for himself?" asked Alther.

"Not much. He was here late last night. He did his own

Seal Watch, and he remembers supervising his brothers' **Watch** but he doesn't remember them finishing it. He remembers nothing else until this morning, when he woke up feeling very weird. He suspects he has been the victim of a **Forget Spell**. He has the classic symptoms. Which are, Septimus?"

"A blue fuzz around people. A slight ringing in the ears. An inexplicable sensation that something is missing."

"Very good. So it seems that the Heap uncles were not mere Conjurors after all," Marcia said. "Their actions have the stamp of powerful Wizards." She turned to Alther. "So, clever one, what do you make of *that* Mystery Reading?"

Alther shook his head.

There was silence while everyone thought about what had been said.

Marcia looked at Beetle. "Beetle—if you were the clever one in the Mystery Reading, what would you be telling the audience now?"

Beetle ran his hand through his hair. "I suspect I am the not-so-clever-one," he said ruefully. "It just doesn't make sense."

Simon coughed apologetically. It still felt strange to him to be included in a meeting like this. "Actually, I think it does," he said.

All eyes were on Simon. "Marcia, it's exactly what you said: *their actions have the stamp of powerful Wizards.*"

"Oh?"

"That, unfortunately, is the answer."

"Apprentice, what do you mean?" asked Marcellus.

"Please continue, Simon," said Marcia. "I suspect you know more about this than I do."

Simon nodded uneasily. He didn't like being the one with the **Darke** knowledge, but he knew that was the way it would always be. And if he could use it for good, then at least there was some purpose in what he had once done. "You said there was a hole in the box?" he asked Marcia.

Marcia stared at Simon, the awful truth beginning to dawn on her. Of *course*. She had been too focused on the Heap twins to think it through properly.

Simon saw Marcia's expression. He coughed apologetically. "I believe that the Two-Faced Ring has . . ." He glanced at Marcia.

"Migrated," Marcia finished for him.

"Surely not," said Alther. "It takes thousands of years for that to happen."

Marcia put her head in her hands. "It was on its way a few

weeks ago. Septimus and I had to put it back in the Bound Box."

Simon looked shocked. If he had been ExtraOrdinary Wizard he would not have left the ring alone for one second after that.

"But that still doesn't explain how Edmond and Ernold were able to get the ring," said Beetle. "I mean, they had to break the **Seal** to get it. And really I don't think they were up to that. They were just a couple of bumbling old . . ." Beetle trailed off, aware that they were Septimus's uncles.

"Fools," supplied Septimus, who shared Beetle's opinion.

"Exactly," said Simon. "The more foolish the better."

Marcia looked at Simon. "Simon. I think you know something about this ring that we don't."

Simon nodded. "When I was with, um, the ring's previous owner, he told me that the ring was very near what he called **Reversion**. I think he was quite scared of that happening. He knew that all it needed was something big for that to become possible."

"Like a **Darke Domaine**?" asked Marcia.

"Yes. Exactly. And I think that last night, the ring had an opportunity to enter the first stage of **Reversion**."

Marcia swore.

Septimus looked shocked.

"Sorry," said Marcia. "I shouldn't have said that."

"I would have done if you hadn't," said Alther.

Beetle looked confused. "What is a **Reversion**, exactly?" he asked.

Marcia indicated to Simon to speak.

Simon leaned forward. The candlelight lit up his green eyes and his fingers fiddled nervously with a stray thread from his tunic, twisting it around as he spoke, self-consciously aware that all eyes were upon him. "It is a return to a former state of existence. In the case of the Two-Faced Ring, its former existence was two **Darke** Warrior Wizards: Shamandrigger Saarn and Dramindonnor Naarn."

The candle on the desk guttered and spat: there were some names that were not to be spoken in the Pyramid Library and these were two of them. Silence fell. Beetle got goose bumps.

Quietly, Simon continued. "A **Reversion** is not straightforward. It must go through stages. The first would be to find something unresisting to **InHabit**, which—not surprisingly—appear to be my uncles. I assume they were **InHabited** last night when they were on **Seal Watch**. And of course, there were *two* of them. I suspect that the fact that they were twins actually made them a target."

"So it wasn't Ernold and Edmund who stole the Two-Faced Ring," Septimus said quietly. "It was the ring that stole *them*."

"Yes," said Simon. He looked upset. "Poor Ed and Ern . . . a **Consuming Habitation**. They do *not* deserve that."

Everyone was silent. A **Consuming Habitation** was a terrible fate.

But Septimus was still puzzled. "So why did the Ring Wizards wait in the **Seal** lobby all night?" he asked.

"They would need to get control of the **InHabitation**," said Marcia. "They would have to access the Wizard Tower password from the Heaps in order to get out."

Simon looked at Marcia. "That's true," he said. "But actually, I suspect they were waiting for you. They'd want to get rid of you as soon as they could. It's lucky you got the **Shield** right—and so fast."

Marcia nodded.

"I wonder why the other Wizards on **Seal Watch** didn't notice them?" Beetle said. "You'd have thought two **Darke** Wizards hanging around in that tiny lobby there would have been **Seen**."

Simon gave a rueful laugh. "Nope. Not being **Seen** by a few very Ordinary Wizards is easy for them."

Marcia got to her feet. "Right," she said. "It's not good but at least now we know what we are up against. First we get Edmund and Ernold. Then we do the **Committal** to get the Ring Wizards back in the ring. And then we **DeNature** the ring."

"Well, that's this evening taken care of," said Alther.

"But—" said Septimus.

"Alther, there is no need to be sarcastic," snapped Marcia.

"It's not as bad as it could be," said Simon, trying to smooth the waters. "At least Jenna is safely out of the way. They can't possibly find her on her Journey."

"Why would they want to find Jenna?" Marcia asked.

"They swore revenge on the Queen's descendants. One of Jenna's ancestors shot them. Both. In the heart," Simon said.

"Why doesn't that surprise me?" Beetle smiled.

"But we—" said Septimus.

"*What is it*, Septimus?" Marcia demanded. She was still a little snappy.

"Um. We don't have the ring. To put them back in."

Marcia groaned and put her head in her hands—she

was just not thinking straight.

"Do they *have* to go back into that particular piece of gold?" Beetle asked.

Marcia looked at Marcellus. "You're the gold expert."

Marcellus tried to remember his gold history—something he had once avidly studied. "Hmm. It is indeed possible that they *don't* have to go back into the ring. It is said that Hotep-Ra made the ring for the Queen from a lump of extremely old, **Magykal** gold that he had brought with him. A lump of gold so very ancient will develop a single identity, so that even when it is split and made into separate objects, it will recognize the other objects as itself."

"What else was made from that lump of gold—do we know?" Marcia asked.

"It is said that Hotep-Ra also made the circlet—you know, the one that Jenna wears—from it."

Everyone sighed. That was no good.

"Is this the same as **Cloned** gold?" Septimus asked.

"That is another word for it," said Marcellus.

"So what about the bowls—the **Transubstantiate Triple**?"

"Of course! I *knew* there was something. Apprentice, I believe you have it!" Marcellus said excitedly. He turned to

Marcia. "He's good, isn't he?"

Septimus looked embarrassed.

"He's not at all bad," Marcia agreed. "Which is, of course, why I chose him to be *my* Apprentice."

A look of irritation flashed across Marcellus's features. "I can get the bowls," Septimus said hurriedly. "They are in Jenna's room."

"Good," said Marcia. "Now all we have to do is find the Ring Wizards. Before Jenna gets back."

Marcellus was still riled. "It is impossible to find such beings if they do not want to be found, Marcia."

"So we have to make them come to us."

"And how do you propose to do that?" Marcellus asked.

"Bait," Marcia said.

"*Bait?*" said three people and one ghost in unison.

"And what—or who—did you have in mind?" asked Marcellus.

Marcia smiled. "Merrin Meredith," she said.

28
BAIT

"T*wo bacon-and-bean pies, please, Maureen,*" said Septimus, out of breath. He had just managed to get to The Harbor and Dock Pie Shop before it closed.

Maureen handed over two pies. "Here, try one of our new sweet pies, apple with marshberry jam. Let me know what you think."

"Thanks, Maureen. I will. Smells good. Do you have another one?"

"Hungry, eh? That's what I like to see." Maureen neatly wrapped the pies and handed them across the counter. "So, your brother—doing all right at the Castle, is he?"

Septimus did a quick mental run-through of his collection of brothers at the Castle and decided that Maureen meant Simon. "Yes. He's doing fine, thanks."

Maureen smiled fondly. "I'm glad. He and Lucy had some difficult times. They deserve a break. Got married too, I hear."

"Yep. A couple of months ago," he said, heading fast for the door.

"Lovely. Say hello to Simon and Lucy from me when you see them."

Septimus nodded. "Will do. Thanks. See you. Bye." Feeling bad that he hadn't told Maureen that Simon was no more than fifty yards away, Septimus was out the door before Maureen could ask him anything else. Simon had refused to come into the pie shop with him. "I like Maureen, Sep, but she gossips. And I don't want anyone to know I'm here, okay?"

Some ten minutes previously, Septimus and Simon had done a **Transport** to the harbor front—the nearest open space to where Merrin lived. As Septimus walked across the deserted Quayside, clutching the packets of hot pies, which the wind tried to snatch from his hands, he thought how strange it was to be doing **Magyk** with Simon. He was surprised that it actually felt good. Septimus had not expected Simon to have such good skills with **Magyk**; they were pretty much at a level of his own although Simon had his own slightly odd way of doing things, which came, Septimus figured, from him having taught himself—and, he suspected, not being too fussy about using **Darke** sources.

Septimus found Simon sitting on a bollard by the water, sheltered from the wind and out of sight of the pie shop. As they both bit into their bacon-and-bean pies they heard the clatter of the shutters of The Harbor and Dock Pie Shop as Maureen closed them for the night.

"I can't see Merrin coming with us without a fight," said Septimus.

"He can have a fight if he wants it," said Simon.

"Better not, though," said Septimus. "We don't want the neighbors getting involved."

"Gerk!" said Simon, his mouth full of bacon.

"Huh?"

"Just choking. At the thought of the lovely neighbors . . . but you're right. We don't want a scene. The last thing we want to do is to draw attention to Merrin." Simon glanced anxiously about. "You never know where . . . *they* might be," he whispered.

Septimus felt the hairs on the back of his neck stand on end. "We shouldn't use any **Magyk** either. The **Transports** were risky enough. **Magyk** attracts **Magyk**—particularly **Darke Magyk**."

"I know," said Simon a little curtly. He didn't like his kid brother telling him basic stuff he knew already. "So we have to scare him so much that he's not going to try anything at all. So that he's too scared to even speak."

"Yeah," said Septimus, handing Simon an apple and marsh-berry jam pie. "That's what I thought too."

Simon bit into his pie and red jam ran down from his mouth. "You thinking what I'm thinking?" he asked.

"I guess so," replied Septimus.

They sat in silence eating their pies, waiting. In front of them the fishing boats bobbed and clinked in the brisk wind that was blowing in off the sea. The tide was high and the harbor full of boats; all the fishermen knew that the wind was rising and the night was going to be wild. The metal fixings in the boats' rigging clinked against the masts and the taut ropes thrummed in the wind.

"Not a good night for flying ghosts," Simon commented, wiping his sticky hands on his robes.

"Nope," mumbled Septimus, spraying bits of pastry into the wind. He hoped that Alther and his companion were faring well on their flight to the Port. Simon was right—ghosts found gusts of wind very difficult. Alther would complain that it was like being **Passed Through** by pixies with boots on. How Alther knew what being **Passed Through** by pixies with boots on was like, Septimus had no idea.

Septimus was stuffing sticky pie wrappers into his pocket when he saw something big and white gliding in above the masts. A moment later a massive albatross swooped down; it skidded onto the Quayside but the ungainly bird did not stop. Its huge webbed feet acted like skis as it shot across the slippery cobbles—heading straight for Septimus and Simon. They leaped up just in time to avoid its beak, which was heading like a dagger straight for their knees.

With a soft *crump*, the bird's beak hit the bollard. Septimus winced—that must have hurt. The albatross then performed a most unbirdlike maneuver. It rolled onto its back, put its feet in the air and covered its beak with its wings.

"**Transform!**" said Septimus.

With a small *pop* and a flash of yellow light the bird **Transformed** into a willowy man wearing yellow and what appeared to be a pile of donuts of ever-decreasing size on his head. He lay on his back beside the bollard with both hands clamped over his nose. "Eurrrgh," he groaned. "By doze. By *doze*."

"That, Jim Knee, is what comes from showing off," said Septimus, sounding uncannily like Marcia. "Where's Alther?"

A small movement in the air answered his question.

"Here's Alther," said the ghost, **Appearing**. And then, noticing Jim Knee lying on the ground: "What's he done now?"

"Pit der Pollard," groaned the jinnee.

"I *told* you not to be an albatross," said Alther crossly. "It was asking for trouble with this wind. You need a lot of skill to fly a bird like that. A small gull would have been quite adequate."

Jim Knee sat up indignantly, leaving one hand on his nose. "I don't do gulls," he said. "Nasty creatures. They eat the most disgusting stuff. And given how hungry I am, goodness knows what some mangy gull would have picked up by now. Yuck." He shuddered and glanced over to the pie shop. "Shame it's closed," he said. "I'm starving. Haven't eaten for six months."

Septimus felt guilty. He had woken Jim Knee up from his hibernation and not thought about feeding him anything—he really should have bought him a couple of Maureen's pies. But Septimus had learned not to be too considerate with his jinnee. He had to keep up a tough act, even though it did not come naturally. "You can eat when you've done what you came for," he said gruffly, catching a look of surprise from Simon, who was seeing a tougher side to his little brother.

Jim Knee, however, merely sighed and said, "Very well, Apprentice. What is it that you wish?"

Septimus glanced at Simon. "I'll tell you on the way," he said. "It's time we got going. I have a feeling that Merrin probably goes to bed early nowadays."

Apprentices, ghost and jinnee set off across the harbor front and took a small lane leading off it. Port streets were dark and not particularly safe at night and Simon, who knew the Port well, led the way—heading for the Doll House, where Merrin now resided with his long-lost mother, Nurse Meredith—or Nursie as she was known to all in the Port.

"I don't agree with this," said Alther as they walked quietly down a narrow street that smelled strongly of cat pee. "I think you should tell Merrin the truth."

"Alther, he won't believe us," Septimus said in a low voice. "Think about it. The two people that Merrin loathes most—me and Simon—turn up on his doorstep at night and say, '*Oh, hello, Merrin. You know those two* **Darke** *Wizards who were in your ring? You know, the one we cut your thumb off to get back? Well, they've escaped and because you have worn the ring, you're on their hit list. But don't worry. Because we like you such a lot, we've come to take you to the Wizard Tower, where you'll be safe.*' I don't think he's going to say, '*Thank you so much. I will come with you right away,*' do you?"

Alther sighed. "If you put it like that, I suppose you are right. I just don't like your solution, that's all."

The party reached the end of the smelly street and took a turning into a long, marginally less smelly street with tall houses on either side, unlit apart from a pool of light at the far end. They walked swiftly along, heading toward the light. A few nosy residents twitched aside their curtains and saw a strange procession: a man who appeared, from the black and red robes he wore, to be a **Darke** Wizard, followed by a lanky Wizard Apprentice, and a man trying to keep a pile of yellow doughnuts on his head. But they thought little of it—living not far from the Port Witch Coven, they had seen much more bizarre sights. They soon closed their curtains and went back to their fires.

Toward the end of the road the group stopped opposite a garishly painted house on the other side of the street. This was the Doll House. It was, underneath its paint, a typical Port house: tall and flat-fronted, with the front door just a broad step up from the street. But the Doll House stood out from all the others in Fore Street by virtue of its freshly painted glossy pink and yellow bricks that shone in the light of a lone torch that burned brightly beside its front doorstep.

Septimus looked anxiously at the house next door—a gloomy, ramshackle building in urgent need of repair that, even from the other side of the road, smelled faintly of sewage. He was relieved to see it looked quiet, although he guessed that now that night had fallen the occupants would probably be stirring. This was the residence of the Port Witch Coven.

Septimus scanned the jaunty Doll House and searched for

clues as to what might be happening inside. The Doll House's cheery façade gave nothing away, but Septimus could not help but wonder if they were too late—were Shamandrigger Saarn and Dramindonnor Naarn already inside?

"It all looks very quiet," Alther whispered nervously.

Simon glanced around. "So far. Best not to hang around." He looked dubiously at Jim Knee, who was biting his nails. "Septimus, your jinnee does understand what he has to do?"

"He understands," said Septimus.

"Jolly good," said Alther. "Over we go, then."

They crossed the street to the doorstep of the Doll House and listened. All was quiet. Jim Knee, consumed with nerves, checked his reflection in the shiny surface of the brass letter box, bobbing up and down to get a full view of his face.

Septimus addressed his jinnee sternly. "Jim Knee, stop preening and *listen to me*."

"I am all ears, Oh Apprentice." Jim Knee prodded at his somewhat protruding ears. "Unfortunately. They never came back properly after that ghastly turtle you made me—"

"Good," Septimus cut in. "You will fit the part perfectly. Are you ready?"

Jim Knee looked sick. "As ready as I'll ever be."

"Jim Knee, I command you to **Transform** into the likeness of—"

"Septimus, are you absolutely sure about this?" Alther interrupted apprehensively.

"It's only a likeness, not the real thing."

"Even so . . ."

Septimus addressed his jinnee with a formal command. "Jim Knee. I wish you to **Transform** into the likeness of . . . DomDaniel!"

29
DOORSTEPPING

From an attic window in the house of the Port Witch Coven, Dorinda saw a portly man wearing a stovepipe hat, a purple ExtraOrdinary Wizard's cloak embroidered with **Darke** symbols and an impressive array of rings on his stubby, fat fingers. Dorinda's huge elephant ears twitched in amazement. *Surely that was DomDaniel?* Her mouth went dry. *But wasn't he dead?* She peered out again and saw the man lift the knocker and knock loudly on the door. Dorinda knew no ghost could do that. She sat down on her bed in horror. He's real, thought Dorinda. And then she thought: DomDaniel is visiting Nursie! Dorinda began to panic; clearly there was more to Nursie than she'd realized. She just wished she'd known that earlier—before she'd tipped a bucket of **Darke** spiders over her that afternoon while she was hanging out the washing. Dorinda groaned. She wrapped her elephant ears around her head and began to chew a soft ear-edge for comfort. Nursie had looked up and *seen* her—so that was what she had meant by "I'll get *you* for that, *you* little trollop!" *Nursie was going to set DomDaniel on her.* Dorinda shook her elephant ears free, leaped to her feet and *screamed*. And when Dorinda screamed, the whole of the Port Witch Coven knew it.

Down on Nursie's doorstep, Jim Knee was, to his surprise, enjoying himself. He had a penchant for rings and he rather liked his new collection. He raised his hand to knock once more and admired the flash of the diamond cluster that nestled on his little finger. As he was about to let the knocker go, the door surprised him by opening to reveal the back view of a lanky youth with short black hair and a neat dark tunic, who was yelling back into the house.

"*What?*"

"Answer . . . the . . . door!" a disembodied voice yelled from somewhere at the top of the house.

Septimus, who was standing hidden in the shadows behind Jim Knee, was relieved to see that Merrin Meredith seemed his usual self—clearly the **Darke** Wizards had not yet found him. Septimus thought that Merrin looked surprisingly neat and tidy—pretty normal, in fact—apart from a bandage around his left hand, which, as it grasped the edge of the door, showed an odd flatness where the thumb should be. But Merrin himself had yet to notice who had knocked. He was too busy yelling, "I'm *doing* it!"

"Merrin! Answer . . . the . . . *door!*" came the voice from upstairs.

"*I'veansweredthestupiddoorareyoudeaf?*" Merrin screamed into the gloom of the house. "*Jeez!*" He swung around grumpily and saw his visitor for the first time. His mouth fell open and stayed that way.

"*Who . . . is . . . it?*" yelled the voice from upstairs.

Merrin was in no state to reply—all he could do was stare at the apparition on the doorstep in terror.

Jim Knee perused his dumbstruck victim with an air of

satisfaction; things were going well. The jinnee drew himself up to DomDaniel's full height—which was not much, although the stovepipe hat added enough to be just taller than the boy at the door—and was surprised by the nasty little voice that came out of his mouth.

"Apprentice." Jim Knee coughed and tried to get the voice deeper and more scary. "Ahem. App*ren*tice."

Merrin emitted a small squeak and leaned against the doorframe. His long, thin legs wobbled as though they were made of rubber and looked ready to fold in half at any moment. From inside the house heavy footsteps could be heard coming downstairs accompanied by a voice yelling, "Merrin! Who *is* it?"

"Hurry *up*!" Septimus urged his jinnee.

"Apprentice," intoned Jim Knee. "You will accompany me to the Castle."

Merrin leaped back and tried to slam the door, but Jim Knee stepped forward and wedged his foot against it. Merrin stared at his old Master in horror. It was worse than his worst nightmare ever. "N-nah . . . ah . . ." he gurgled.

"Apprentice. Come with me!" Jim Knee boomed, getting control of the voice now. He leaned close to Merrin and said in a voice so laden with threat that even Septimus got goose bumps, "Do I have to make you, you little *toad*?"

Wide-eyed, widemouthed, Merrin shook his head. Very reluctantly, he began to edge forward. Suddenly footsteps could be heard on the stairs.

"Mum!" squeaked Merrin.

Septimus panicked—events were going a little too fast. In a moment Nursie would be there and they would have lost their chance. "Grab him, quick!" he told Jim Knee.

Jim Knee grabbed Merrin's arm.

Nursie's voice came echoing along the corridor. "Merrin! Tell them we're full!"

"Mum! Help!" Merrin at last managed a small yell.

Thud, thud, thud came the sound of hobnail boots on floorboards: mummy monster was coming to rescue her baby. "Oi, what's going on? You let go, you great big bully!"

"Ouch!" yelled Jim Knee.

A large fist landed square on the jinnee's nose, which was still very sore from hitting the bollard. To Septimus's dismay, Jim Knee collapsed in a heap on the doorstep. Septimus leaped forward and grabbed hold of his jinnee's collar—a greasy affair that protruded over the purple cloak.

"Get up, you idiot," he hissed. Merrin stared at Septimus

in amazement. He would never have dared call his old Master *that.*

A shadow fell across Septimus. He looked up and saw the substantial bulk of Nursie looming over him. "Get that horrible man away from my Merrin," she told Septimus. Nursie took in Simon. "And you can buzz off too. Blasted Heaps. Nothing but trouble." She turned to Merrin, who was leaning against the doorway, pale as a ghost. "Are you all right, my precious?" she asked.

Merrin nodded weakly.

It was at that moment that the door to the Port Witch Coven was wrenched open and the Witch Mother staggered out. "Master!" came the loud rasp of her voice. All on the doorstep turned in amazement to watch the Witch Mother—a round barrel of black robes smelling of cat poo—clatter precariously across to the Doll House in her tall, spiked shoes. The Witch Mother's face, creased from sleeping in her thick white makeup (which covered her allergy to woodworm) was set in an expression of extreme humbleness. She grabbed hold of the Doll House railings and hauled herself up, heading for Simon and Jim Knee. Jim Knee stared at the Witch Mother in horror. He did not like witches.

Neither did Nursie. "And you can buzz off too, you old carcass," Nursie informed the Witch Mother, and gave her a push. The Witch Mother wobbled precariously and grabbed hold of Simon to stop herself falling. Simon pushed her away and the Witch Mother clattered back against the railings.

Alther watched in dismay as a full-scale brawl threatened to break out on the doorstep of the Doll House. He decided to **Appear**, making himself as opaque as possible, for he was sure that Nursie was one of those who never normally saw ghosts.

"Madam," he said.

"What?" demanded Nursie.

"There seems to be some kind of misunderstanding."

"I understand perfectly. This horrible old *baggage*." Nursie stabbed her finger on Jim Knee's nose for emphasis.

"Ouch!"

"Not only kidnapped my little boy when he was a baby but now he has the nerve to come back and try it *all over again*. Well, I'm not having it. Not this time."

"Madam," said Alther. "Please let me explain. We have come to help your son; he is in grave danger from—"

"*Him!*" Nursie poked at Jim Knee again for emphasis.

"Ouch!"

"And he is lucky I don't do worse than poke—"

"Ouch!"

"Him—"

"Ouch!"

"In—"

"Ouch!"

"The—"

"Ouch!"

"Nose."

"Ouch, ouch, *ouch*!"

The Witch Mother watched Nursie's treatment of DomDaniel in amazement. A new respect for her neighbor began to dawn. "Er . . . Nursie," she ventured.

"What *now*?" demanded Nursie.

"Please accept my most humble apologies for any inconvenience that the Coven may have caused you in the past and my assurances that we will do all we can in the future to assist you in any way. Any way at all . . ." The Witch Mother made an awkward bow to Nursie.

Nursie was on a roll. Her enemies were falling before her

like bowling pins and she was going to make the most of it. "And you, you smelly old bat—you can buzz off an' all," she snapped at the Witch Mother.

The Witch Mother continued bowing frantically and began to back away. "Yes, thank you. I will indeed buzz off as you so kindly suggest."

The motley group on the doorstep of the Doll House watched the Witch Mother totter back next door, lift the **Darke** Toad doorknocker and let it go with a *bang*. The door opened and the Witch Mother staggered inside. As soon as the door to the Port Witch Coven closed Septimus told Jim Knee to **Transform**. There was a flash of yellow light on Nursie's doorstep and DomDaniel was gone; in his place stood an exotic-looking man dressed in yellow holding his red, swollen nose.

Nursie looked at her visitors quizzically. A few weeks back she had received a letter from Marcia explaining what had happened to Merrin and telling her that he was her son. Nursie, after all the years in the wilderness, searching for her son, had at last begun to think clearly. And the more she thought, the more she knew that she was never, *ever*, going to let Merrin out of her sight. She perused the Apprentices, the odd-looking man with the doughnut hat and the ghost. Taking the ghost to be the most reasonable of them all she addressed her comment to him.

"Is my Merrin really in danger?" she asked Alther.

"Unfortunately, madam, he is."

"Why?" demanded Nursie—quite understandably, Alther thought.

"It relates to the **Darke** ring he used to wear, madam."

"But he doesn't have it anymore. Look. Show them, Merrin."

Merrin meekly held up his bandaged hand.

"Indeed, madam. But the two **Darke** Wizards who were in the ring have escaped. This puts your son in great danger. Which is why we wish to take him to the Wizard Tower for his own protection."

Nursie was suspicious. "Why do you care about him all of a sudden? You never did before."

"It is to do with the ring, madam," said Alther, who tried to never tell a lie.

Nursie narrowed her eyes and looked at Alther. "If you wasn't such a nice, honest-looking gentleman, I'd say you was thinking of using my Merrin as bait," she said.

"Bait!" gasped Alther.

"To get the ring back."

"Oh. Goodness me!"

"Near the mark, am I?" asked Nursie.

"No, no!" Alther rapidly abandoned his principles for the greater good. "We would not dream of doing such a thing. Oh, dear me, no."

"And he'll be safe in the Castle?"

"As safe as we can make him, madam."

"Very well. On one condition," said Nursie.

"Yes, madam. And what would that be?"

"I will take him myself. I am not letting my Merrin out of my sight ever again."

Alther knew when to give in. Short of abducting Merrin by force—and with Nursie present he didn't give much for their chances—it was the best they were going get.

"Very well, madam. I beg the honor of escorting you."

"To make sure we don't escape?" asked Nursie.

"No, madam, not at all. To try to protect you from the **Darke** Wizards." And this time, Alther did indeed speak the truth.

* * *

They were just in time to catch the late Barge to the Castle. Merrin and Nursie joined the Barge's only passengers—two excitable women who were planning to join a **Magyk** tour of the Castle the following morning. They took their seats under cover and wrapped themselves in the rough barge blankets provided for nighttime journeys. Alther hovered above the barge, watching for any signs of trouble. But despite the wind and the spattering of rain that was beginning to fall, all was quiet. It seemed as though the whole Port had gone early to bed.

Septimus, Simon and Jim Knee watched the barge edge away from the Quay and head out into the choppy waters of the river. They saw the wind catch its huge white sail and send it plowing rapidly through the spray. Very soon it was gone into the night, heading upriver to the Castle.

"It won't take them long with this wind," said Simon. "It will blow them straight there."

Septimus and Simon headed away from the Barge Quay into the maze of alleyways that would take them back to the harbor front, where they could safely do their **Transports** back to the Castle. Jim Knee followed, debating with himself whether he might request being an owl for the return journey.

He was so hungry that the idea of fresh mouse was quite appealing. And then he thought about mousetail and changed his mind.

Septimus was pleased with the way things had gone. "Bait dispatched," he said. "Now all we have to do is wait for Edmund and Ernold to turn up for it."

But seeing Merrin shivering in the barge, setting off into the night—and who knew what danger—had made Simon thoughtful. "Poor Merrin," he said.

Septimus was not in the mood to feel sorry for Merrin. "None of this would have happened if he hadn't taken the ring in the first place."

"True," agreed Simon. "But then, you could say the same about many things. None of it would have happened if DomDaniel hadn't kidnapped him instead of you. Maybe you should be thankful to Merrin for taking your place."

Septimus fell into kid-brother mode. "I wouldn't have been such a little tick as him, even if it had been me," he retorted.

Simon smiled ruefully. "You can't know for sure. Not until you have walked the same road in the same shoes."

"But my feet are different from his," said Septimus.

"They are now. But baby feet are soft. You have to take care they don't get squashed." Simon grinned at Septimus. "Well, that's what Lucy says, anyway."

The alleyway narrowed and Septimus dropped back. They hurried, single file, through Fat Man's Crush and Weasel Slip Slide and soon emerged onto the deserted harbor front.

"Ready to go?" Septimus asked Simon.

Simon nodded.

Septimus decided to give Jim Knee the choice of bird to **Transform** to—the jinnee had done well. "Time to go, Jim Knee. I'll see you at the Castle—at the Port barge landing stage. We have someone to meet. **Transform**!"

There was a flash of yellow light, a small *pop*, and an albatross stood at Septimus's feet. Septimus heard a sharp intake of breath from Simon.

"Oh, *no*."

"It's okay. I said he could be what he liked."

"Not the stupid albatross. Over there. *Look!*"

Heart in mouth, Septimus looked up, expecting to see two wild Heap uncles heading their way. But hurrying out of the shadows came a very different Heap.

"It *can't* be," said Septimus.

"It is. It's *Jenna*."

30
Port Palace

"Oh, *Sep. It is so* good to see you!" Jenna threw herself at Septimus and hugged him hard. "And you too, Simon."

"What are you doing *here*, Jen?" Septimus whispered.

"You would not believe it, Sep. You just would *not*. She is totally, utterly *impossible*."

"Who is?"

"The Queen—my *mother*. She is a complete control freak. Mum never, *ever* behaved like that."

Septimus recognized the expression in Jenna's eyes. "You mean you had a fight with the Queen?"

"You bet I did," said Jenna.

"Wow."

"I stuck it out for *forever*, Sep, until I couldn't stand it a moment longer. I just *had* to come home."

"You *walked out*?" Septimus was amazed.

"Yep. But I was so mad that I didn't look where I was going and I ended up here. There's a kind of crossroads in the Queen's Way, I think." Jenna grinned at Septimus. "And now I'm really glad I did." She stood back and pushed her hair out of her eyes.

Jenna began to notice how oddly her brothers were behaving. They were standing really close to her—like a couple of guards—but neither of them was looking at her. Instead they were gazing around the empty harbor front like they were expecting someone else to arrive at any moment.

"Hey, you don't look very pleased to see me," Jenna said.

"We're not," said Simon tersely.

"Well, thank you, Simon Heap. Thank you *so* much."

"He didn't mean it like that, Jen," Septimus whispered.

"Well how *did* he mean it, then?"

"There's no time for this," said Simon, also whispering. "Right now we need to get somewhere safe."

Jenna was beginning to feel scared. She glanced around and thought for the first time how scary an empty harborside can be. "Why, aren't we safe here?"

"No."

"I guess it *is* creepy here. Anyway, I'm off. I've stayed here too long as it is—I really must get back and see Mum. I'm going to get the late Barge to the Castle."

"You've missed it," said Septimus.

A gust of wind whipped across the open harbor front, sending the ships rigging zinging, and a rumble of thunder drifted in from the ocean beyond. Jenna shivered. In her time away she had become accustomed to the heat. Suddenly she felt tired, cold and frightened. "Well, I suppose we can go back to the Port Palace," she said reluctantly.

"Where's that?" asked Simon, who knew the Port well, but had never seen or heard of a Palace.

Jenna pointed over to the Customs House, a tall building on the edge of the harbor front where Simon had, until recently, lived in one of the attic rooms. "There's an alleyway down there."

"No, there isn't," said Simon.

"Yes, there is," said Jenna. "But you don't see it—unless you're with me. So, do you want to go there or not?"

A flash of something by the side of The Harbor and Dock Pie Shop caught Septimus's eye. "Yes, we do. Right now," he said, accompanied by the bang of Maureen's broom as she chased out two rats she had found sleeping in the warmth beneath the pie ovens.

"Okay." Jenna set off across the harbor front. Flanked on either side by her guards and waddled after by a reluctant albatross, who longed to be spreading its wings and lifting off into the wind, she led them into the shadows of an old brick wall beside the Customs House. Jenna turned to her brothers.

"Is that yours?" she asked, pointing to the albatross.

"Yes." Septimus sighed. "It is."

Jenna grinned. "You can bring your, er, *bird* too, Sep. This place even has an aviary."

The albatross gave a raucous squawk of protest and pecked at Septimus's foot.

"Ouch!" he said. "Okay, Jim Knee. I give you permission to **Transform**."

With another *pop* and a yellow flash Jim Knee was once

more back in human form, shivering in the chill wind. Albatross feathers were remarkably warm.

"I thought it might be you," said Jenna with a smile. "The yellow beak was a giveaway."

Jim Knee bowed politely. "Good evening, Your Majesty."

To Septimus's surprise Jenna did not object—as she certainly would have in the past. She merely replied, "Good evening, Jim Knee."

Jenna turned to Septimus and Simon. "We'll go in now." She leaned forward and placed her hand on the old bricks. The bricks shimmered like stone on a hot day and slowly disappeared to reveal a ghostly archway. Septimus and Simon were impressed, Jim Knee less so—he'd seen plenty of these Arcane Alleys before, although this one looked rather smart compared to many of the dingy dives he had known. The name of the alley, he noticed, was The Queen's Way.

"Okay, now it's like going into the Queen's Room. We all need to hold hands to get across the threshold," said Jenna, holding out her hand to Septimus. He took Jim Knee's hand, who took hold of Simon's, and the chain followed on quickly, afraid that both the alley and Jenna would disappear. As Jenna crossed the threshold, a line of candles in golden holders sprang alight showing a narrow alley, glittering in tiny red and gold tiles snaking away into the darkness along the side of the Customs House.

Once everyone was safely in, Jenna waved her hand across the entrance and the view of the harbor faded away and was replaced by the other side of the brick wall. "Okay. We're safe now," she said. "No one can get in here. *Now* you can tell me what all the fuss is about."

"It's a long story," said Septimus.

"It usually is, Sep," said Jenna with a smile, "especially when you're telling it. Come on, then, let's get somewhere warm. And there's someone else who'd like to hear the story too," she added mysteriously.

Jenna set off along the winding Queen's Way, which was quiet and still after the blustery harbor front and carried no sound from outside. She hurried forward and Septimus, Simon and Jim Knee followed in single file, their footfalls quiet on the smooth mosaic. Soon they were around the first bend and another line of candles sprang alight, illuminating the next stretch of the alleyway. This way and that the Queen's

Way took them until they had lost all sense of direction. As they rounded yet another bend Septimus—who was now a little taller than Jenna—could see over her shoulder to a wide wooden door, which formed the end of the alley. From a small window in the middle of the door shone a bright yellow light. The light grew brighter as they approached and soon Jenna was taking a large golden key from her pocket, unlocking the door and holding it open.

"Welcome to my Port Palace," she said.

They stepped inside. A few fat candles on a table lit a wide passageway—which Jenna called the cross passage—with a warm glow. In the dim light Septimus could see that to his left was an ancient screen of dark wood carved with a series of crowns and initials, in the middle of which was an ornate door covered in gold leaf that glowed a deep red gold in the light of the candle flames. To his right was a plainer wooden screen, which had two smaller doors set into it.

Jim Knee put his hand out to touch the right-hand wooden screen, which was warm from the heat of the kitchen behind it—as he knew it would be. The jinnee felt a little strange. He took advantage of his Master being occupied to lean against the warm wood and think. Sometimes the incessant clatter of humans, particularly young ones, was too much for the jinnee and he longed for some stillness. The shadows of the cross passage gave him just that.

Septimus had forgotten about Jim Knee. He and Simon followed Jenna along the passage and watched her turn left, as he expected she would—nowadays Jenna and gold seemed to go together. He saw Jenna lean on the gold-leaf door and give it a shove. The door protested with a creak—as Jim Knee knew it would—and reluctantly opened a little. Jenna put her head around the gap and yelled, "Hey! Guess who I've found!" Then she turned to Septimus. "Come on, Sep. *Push.*"

Together they pushed the complaining door open to reveal an ancient hall, as tall as it was wide, with finely carved oak timbers soaring up into the shadows of the roof. Layers of woodsmoke hung in the air, blurring the light from candles placed in alcoves in the walls and giving the place a mysterious air. A blazing log fire in a wide, low-arched fireplace set into the right-hand wall threw a semicircle of light into the gloom—and standing in the middle of the light was Nicko. Grinning.

Septimus was amazed. "Nik! What are you doing here?" he asked, hurrying across to his brother.

Nicko looked amused. "Same as you both, I should think. Pootling around the Port minding my own business—well, Jannit's business, actually. Bumped into Jenna."

"The Queen's Way from our Journey Palace came out here," said Jenna. "See that cupboard?" She pointed at a small cupboard near the fireplace, with faded gold letters that read UNSTABLE POTIONS AND PARTIKULAR POISONS. "I was expecting to end up at home, or maybe at Aunt Zelda's, so I was really surprised. I had no idea where I was. I had a look around, and eventually I found the way out along that alleyway. I was *so* relieved to find I was in the Port. And then I saw Nik and it was so good to talk to someone *normal* again."

Nicko grinned. "There I was, looking forward to a nice, cold night on the supply boat when I got dragged back to yet another Palace—sheesh, how many do you need—to hear all about *Mama*."

"Aha, *Mama*," Septimus said. "I've not heard about her yet."

"You will," said Nicko with a grin.

"No, you won't," said Jenna sternly. She joined them by the fire and threw herself down on the pile of cushions in front of it. "Not unless you tell me what's going on first. Sit down, Sep. Simon. Spill the beans."

Septimus held his hands out to the fire to warm them. “This is so weird, Jen. I’ve never seen this place before. Where actually *is* it?”

“You know the last of the really old houses on the waterfront? Just before you get to the beach?”

“I think so . . .”

“There’s a boarded-up old warehouse just past them—well, it looks like an old warehouse. But it isn’t. It’s a façade built around this place. Listen. We’re right by the beach; you can hear the waves outside.”

The hall fell silent and they listened. Septimus realized that the background sound he had thought was the hissing of damp logs on the fire was actually the muffled swash of waves on the shore.

“Okay, Sep,” said Jenna. “*Now* tell me what’s going on.”

And so Septimus explained all that had happened since Jenna had left the Palace for her Journey. At the mention of her uncles, Jenna exclaimed, “I’m not surprised. I *thought* there was something weird about them.”

Septimus shook his head. “I think they were just unlucky, Jen. They were in the wrong place at the wrong time. Shamandrigger Saarn and Dramindonnor Naarn were—”

"Shh!" hissed Simon. "Don't say their names."

Septimus laughed. "I didn't know you were superstitious, Simon. That's witchy stuff."

"No, it's . . ." Simon looked around; he could not get rid of a feeling of being unsafe, sitting with his back to the room. "**Darke** stuff too, you know," he whispered. "Names matter. You *know* that, Sep."

Jenna looked surprised at the new familiarity between her brothers.

Septimus remembered his own **Darke** name, Sum. "Yeah. Okay," he admitted.

To the background of an increasingly noisy sea crashing onto the beach outside, Septimus told the whole story of the Two-Faced Ring—apart from one thing. He didn't want to spook Jenna. But she knew.

"But it's not only Merrin who's the bait, is it, Sep?"

"Well . . ."

Jenna got out her little red book and with a practiced ease of one who knew her way around it backward, she flipped to a page titled *Feuds and Enemies* and passed it to Septimus.

It was a long list and Septimus wondered about the confrontational nature of some of the Queens. But he did not have to look far—right at the top of the list were the names of the Ring Wizards. "Ah," he said.

"I know about the Queen shooting them both in the heart, Sep," said Jenna. "I know it was *her* ring they were **Committed** to. I know they swore revenge on her descendants. And, right now, I know that means me."

Everyone looked around uncomfortably. Hearing Jenna say what they all knew made it sound far too real. Jenna lowered her voice. "This place is kind of creepy. I reckon something bad happened here and that's why they closed it up."

Nicko lightened the atmosphere. "Doesn't it say in your Queen instruction manual, Jen?"

"If you are going to be rude, Nicko Heap, I won't tell you about my Journey. Or anything else, for that matter."

"Oh, go on, Jen. You know you want to tell us." Nicko's stomach rumbled loudly. "You know," he said, "the weird thing is I can smell roast potatoes."

Jim Knee had once spent a short but not unpleasant life as a jinnee-cook in a Palace kitchen. As soon as he walked into the cross passage, Jim Knee knew he was back. After getting over his shock, Jim Knee remembered how much he had enjoyed his time there—until the very last ten minutes. And so, when Jenna, Septimus and Simon had gone into the hall, Jim Knee had taken a deep breath and, remembering the motto—*in left, out left*—he had pushed open the little left-hand door and stepped into the kitchen.

A trail of goose bumps swarmed over Jim Knee's skin as he had walked into the room. It smelled the same. It looked the same. It *was* the same. This was where he had spent twenty years of his last life and to Jim Knee's surprise, all was exactly as he had left it.

Because there was a Queen-to-be in residence, the kitchen and all its contents, like the candles in the Queen's Way, had **Magykally** come to life. Jim Knee wandered around, looking at everything he remembered so well, and very soon he was pottering happily. He found a large roast chicken and a pile of cooked potatoes exactly as he had left them, and set about carving the chicken and roasting the potatoes using his high-speed fire method, which worked well and left surprisingly few scorch marks on the wall.

Ten minutes later Jim Knee pushed his way into the hall carrying a huge plate of cold chicken and hot roast potatoes. He paused a moment and studied the smoke-filled room. It was the just the same: the soaring beams, the inefficient fire, the crest on the massive lintel above it. Jim Knee gritted his teeth and inspected the wall behind him. Yes, there it was—low down, carved into the plaster in old-fashioned angular writing:

TALLULA CRUM
HAS A BIG BUM.
IF SHE EATS ANY MORE
SHE'LL GET STUCK IN THE DOOR.

Jim Knee harrumphed quietly to himself. He was surprised to find that it still annoyed him. He remembered the little brat of a Princess who had taken a dislike to her—for Jim Knee had been a *her* in that life. He remembered how the child had very carefully written the graffiti in her best pen and made sure she, Miss Tallula Crum, a cook of generous proportions—and portions—had seen it. And how the Queen had insisted it stay because "children must be allowed to express themselves."

Jim Knee set his plate of chicken and potatoes in front of the fire. He offered it to all, as a jinnee is bound to do, but to his relief there was plenty left for him. And so, to the background swash of the waves outside and Jim Knee's quiet sucking of chicken bones, Jenna began the story of her Journey.

31
Jenna's Journey

"*Well, after she, I mean* my mother, the Queen, nearly had a fight with Mum—yes, Sep, she was really rude to Mum—we went up to the Queen's Room, like I expected, and through the Queen's Way. Only we didn't come out at Aunt Zelda's, we came out into . . ." Jenna shook her head in disbelief. "Oh, it was so *weird*. One minute I was in a tiny dark cupboard with the ghost of my mother; the next I

was standing in a boat."

"A *boat*?"

"Yep. And not just any old boat. It was amazing. Long and narrow with a sweeping-up pointy thingy at the front—all right Nik, a *prow*—covered in gold. The inside of the boat was all shiny and black and there was a big red canopy at the back with lots of tassels hanging down from it. Underneath the canopy were three chairs, just like these . . ." Jenna waved her hand at the line of little red-and-gilt chairs that were set back against the wall.

"Two of the chairs were empty but sitting on the right-hand one was an oldish lady—a Queen—who had spoken to me at the Dragon House. I was really pleased to see her; I felt like I had a friend there.

"My mother took my hand very formally, like we were at a dance or something; she led me to the chairs and we both sat down. It was then I realized something really amazing. She wasn't a ghost anymore—my mother was alive! I didn't know what to say—I kind of wanted to jump up and hug her but she just sat on her chair and smiled at me like I was some kind of visiting aunt or something. But the old lady put her hand on mine and squeezed it and said, 'Hello, Jenna, dear. I am your grandmother and I've been *so* looking forward to this.'

"I must have looked really shocked because she said, 'Do not worry. We've all been on the Journey. It was just as strange for me.' Which was lovely, but my mother still said nothing, which upset me. I've always been disappointed that she had never **Appeared** to me at home but since I read *The Queen Rules*, I knew there was a reason for that. But now there was no excuse for her being so distant with me. My grandmother seemed to understand, though. She kept hold of my hand and squeezed it tight. Oh, Sep, she was *lovely.*

"Anyway, I decided that if my mother was going to be so stuffy with me then I would be the same way with her. So I got into Princess mode and sat on my dinky little chair, looking around me like I did this kind of thing every day. I decided to try and figure out what was going on. The first thing I realized was how *hot* it was. I longed to take off my winter cloak but I was determined not to move a muscle before my mother did. We were definitely at sea because I could smell the salt in the air, but it was weird, because it wasn't like the sea at all. It was so flat that the surface looked like it had a skin over it and it glistened like a mirror. But I couldn't see much more than that because we were surrounded by mist with just a pool of light around our boat. The light came from two big candles, one in a lantern set high on the prow and the other in a lantern behind us set on a smaller prow—yes, Nicko, I *know* it's not a prow at the back, but you know what I mean. Sternpost? Okeydokey, sternpost, then.

"The boat was being rowed by four men—two at the back and two at the front—dressed in black and gold with funny red hats a bit like Mum's gardening hat. They were standing up and had long oars that they kind of twisted into the water. The boat moved very smoothly and I could tell we were making good progress because through the mist I suddenly saw a glow from a flame about six feet off the water. We went past it quite fast and along came another and another, and I realized we were following a line of lights. I felt a bit less scared then, because the boat had felt really flimsy to be out at sea and I was relieved that we must be near land.

"Soon I saw some beautiful buildings a little bit like the Palace, only taller and much thinner, looming out of the mist. They went right down to the water and had big striped posts in front of them that glinted in the sun that was beginning to break through the mist. The oarsmen steered our boat through a line of gold-and-red posts and up to a landing stage in front of a big archway. My mother stood up. She arranged her cloak and spoke to me for the first time since we had arrived."

"What did she say?" asked Septimus.

"'We are here,'" said Jenna, pulling a face.

"Nice," commented Nicko.

"Yeah. The oarsmen helped my grandmother, then my mother, then me, out of the boat and we walked up some wide pink marble steps into a massive hall that smelled of damp stone and seaweed. It was so cool in there and such a relief not to be boiled like a lobster anymore! The hall was totally empty and I guessed it was because the sea often came up into it, because the old stones were shiny with water. But even though it was just a bare space, it looked full because it was made with hundreds of different kinds of marble laid in complicated patterns. The walls had kind of wavy stripes in lots of different colors and the floor was laid with a black-and-white pattern that kept zigzagging in front of my eyes. So we walked through the hall in a kind of weird procession with my grandmother at the head of it, then my mother and then me. We went up an amazing wide staircase, each step a different colored marble but all with wavy black stripes running through them. By the time I got to the top I felt really sick. I must have looked pretty green or something because my grandmother took hold of my arm and said, 'Cerys, Jenna is exhausted. She must rest.'

"My mother looked a little annoyed, I thought, but she nodded and said, 'Very well, Mama, I am sure you know best as always. I shall see you in the morning . . . *Jenna*.' She always said my name like it made a bad taste in her mouth.

"My grandmother took me to a long narrow room that led off from the big upstairs hall. She was really sweet and told me not to worry and that 'everything is just as it should be, Jenna dear.' The bed was cold and lumpy, and when I lay down it smelled damp, but I didn't care. I was *so* tired and I just longed to be back home with Mum and Dad and wake up to find that this was all a dream.

"When I did actually wake up, I thought for a moment that I *was* in a dream. But it smelled so different from home—so damp and old—that I soon remembered. I tried to get back to sleep but I couldn't, so I decided to explore. Someone had lit a candle and left it on a table by the door, so I took it and crept out of the room.

"Once I was out of my stuffy room and in the upstairs hall,

I felt quite excited. It was much nicer being on my own and not feeling upset all the time about my mother. So I decided to look around. It was dark and my candle didn't shed much light but I could see delicate old chairs and tiny sofas, each with a table, set along the walls between the massively tall double doors that opened off. On every table burned a candle so I could see the walls really clearly, especially as they were covered in gold leaf, which shone even though I could tell it was very old. It was a beautiful place."

"*Pa*lace," Nicko said, grinning. "*Another* one."

Jenna stuck her tongue out at her brother. "Yes, Nicko, another Palace. One needs at least *three*. So anyway, rude boy, I decided to head for the huge window at the end of the hall and see what was outside. I tiptoed past beautiful paintings hung all over the wall—all of people who looked a little bit like me, I thought. But they weren't Queens or anything special, just people in all kinds of old-fashioned clothes. And as I went by I felt like they were all looking down at me, kind of saying hello. It was weird, but nice too because I began to feel that I belonged, that somehow I was part of this place just as much as I was part of the Castle back home.

"So I got to the huge window—which had rows of little

circles of glass in it—and I looked out. It was amazing. Outside there was a river, not very wide compared with ours, but totally different. It had houses all along it on both sides and there was no riverbank because all the houses went straight down into the water. And they were really, *really* old. Some were kind of falling into the water, some were wrapped up in what looked like shiny paper and others were just about okay. There were lights on and I could see people moving about inside them; I could look right into their rooms. But no one noticed me and I just watched and watched. A few boats came down the river; some were quite big and made a strange noise. And they moved without sails or oars too. There weren't many because I could tell it was really late, but I could still hear the sounds of people laughing and talking and having fun."

Jenna continued. "So there I was, watching from the window, feeling quite happy, really, when I heard a soft, smothered cough from somewhere way back in the big room behind me. I decided to act like I had known whoever-it-was had been there all the time—which I was suddenly sure they had been. I swung around and stared into the dark. I could see nothing in the middle, just the edge of the room in the low lights of the little candles on the tables and the soft shine of the walls, but I wasn't going to let the watcher know that.

"'Good evening,' I said. 'I don't believe we have been introduced.' My voice sounded weird in the dark and I realized that this was the first time I had spoken in that place.

"'Good evening,' came a reply. The voice surprised me—it was a girl. She had a really weird accent and she sounded a bit like that stupid witch Marissa. So I wasn't about to like her."

"You and Marissa fallen out, have you?" teased Nicko.

"She's a two-faced cow," said Jenna.

"Fair enough."

"Anyway, I told this girl that it was rude to hide away in the shadows and stare. By then I could see better in the dark and I saw that she was sitting on the floor in the middle of the room. I saw her get up and walk toward me. I decided not to move. *She* could come to *me*." Jenna smiled. "I guess I was already picking up some Queen stuff.

"As she came closer I could see that she looked nothing like Marissa at all, so I felt a lot better about her. She turned out to be really nice. She came up and kissed me on both cheeks—that's what they do there to say hello—"

"Sounds fun," Nicko said with a grin.

"Nicko, you have become so *rude* recently," Jenna told him sternly. "You spend too much time in the Port."

Nicko looked sheepish.

"Actually, if you had been there you would never have met any girls at all, because it turned out that girls pretty much weren't allowed out. If they did go somewhere they were never on their own. I wasn't allowed out, that was for sure. If it hadn't been for Julia—that was her name—I wouldn't have seen anything but the inside of that crumbly old Palace and what I could see from the window. All the time that I spent there I was with my mother and grandmother." Jenna sighed. "Gosh, I was *so* bored sometimes. They droned on and on about our family and where they came from, all the things I was expected to do when I got home, blah blah blah."

"So if girls weren't allowed out, how did you and Julia get away with it?" asked Nicko.

"We wore masks. At night anyone could go *anywhere* with a mask on. All you needed was a long cloak and a pair of boy's shoes. As long as you didn't speak, everyone thought you were a boy. It was brilliant. Julia took me to all kinds of places. It was a beautiful city."

Jim Knee finished his last potato. Very quietly he got to

his feet and moved away into the shadows. He felt sick, not because he had eaten nearly two pounds of roast potatoes and half a greasy chicken, but because he had spent thirty years of a life in the place that Jenna described—and fifteen of those had been in a prison just below the waterline that had flooded with every high tide. The dank, nasty smell of it had suddenly washed right over him.

No one noticed Jim Knee get up. Jenna continued her story. "If it hadn't been for Julia I would never have met the Alchemists."

"There were *Alchemists* there?" asked Septimus.

"You bet. I know so much more about Marcellus now. That's where they come from, Sep. The same place as I do—or my family did once, a very, *very* long time ago. They are from an island in the Lagoon."

"The Lagoon?"

"Yep. That's what the whole place was called. It was full of islands. We were on the biggest one, but there was another where the Alchemists lived—where they made a special kind of dark Glass. You know, Sep, like the one that Marcellus made."

"Oh. *That.*" Septimus grimaced. He still had nightmares

about being pulled through Marcellus's Glass.

Jenna looked around and lowered her voice. "There was loads of Castle stuff there, Sep. I wished so much that you could have been there to see it all too. In fact, there was so much I—*what was that*?"

There was a loud *crash* behind them. A hidden door in the paneling sprang open and from it two wild-eyed Heap uncles came screaming into the hall.

32
HEAPS VERSUS HEAPS

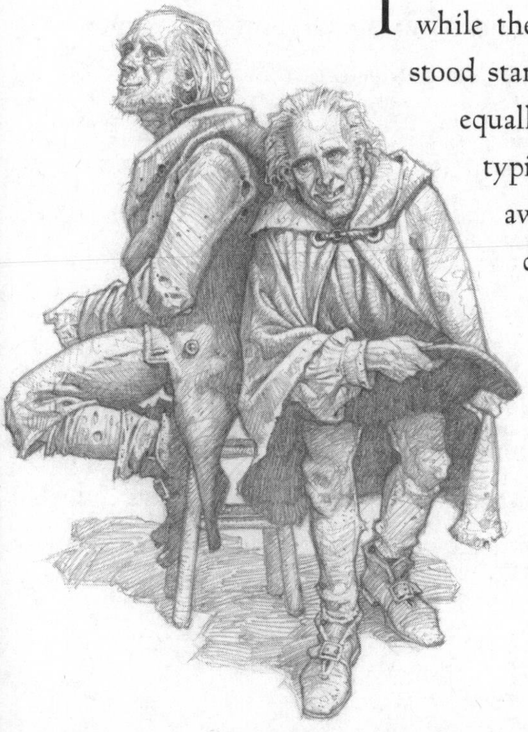

There *was a moment of* stillness while the opposing Heap camps stood staring at each other, both equally shocked. With their typically Heap straw hair awry, their old multi-colored robes hanging from them, wet and filthy with mud, it looked like it was just daft old uncles Edmund and Ernold who had crashed out of the wall. A pang of pity went through the four genuine Heaps at the sight of them. Jenna had to fight back a desire to rush over and ask them to come and sit by the fire. For some moments no one moved. The invaders took stock, their gaze traveling around the hall, eyes like searchlights, alighting on each occupant, noting them and moving on to the next as if checking off a list.

Those on the list stared back, like frozen rabbits. Time slowed; the moment seemed to last forever until—*crash!*—the door in the paneling slammed shut. In a flash Simon threw himself in front of Jenna but Nicko shoved him away. Simon swung around angrily. "I'm not going to hurt her, Nik!"

"I *know* that. But you're needed. You gotta stop them. You and Sep. Use your **Darke** stuff, Si—*anything*!"

Simon grinned—Nicko had called him *Si*. It was all Heaps together now, just like it used to be. Heaps against the world, although right now it still felt like Heaps against Heaps. It was hard not to believe Ernold and Edmund were playing a bizarre practical joke.

Suddenly any lingering doubts evaporated—they spoke. Switching seamlessly from one to another, in voices cold and empty as if they came from the bottom of a deep, dark cave.

"We have."

"Come for."

"The."

"Princess."

Their voices had a bad effect on Jenna. It was as if some ancestral memory had kicked in. Fighting off the urge to run screaming from the room—which she guessed was exactly what the Wizards wanted—Jenna steeled herself to reply. Maybe, she thought, if she answered calmly, they would merely pay their respects and leave. Jenna took a deep breath to steady her voice only to find, to her irritation, that Simon was answering for her.

"She is not here," he said.

The Wizards exchanged knowing smiles.

"*Nomis.*"

Simon flinched at the mention of his **Darke** name.

"You are."

"One."

"Of us."

"No!" said Simon. "I am—"

"Not," Septimus finished for him, deliberately echoing the Wizards.

"You."

"Lie," snarled the Wizards.

"We see."

"The Princess."

"And you *are*."

"One of."

"Usssssss." The last word was hissed like a snake rearing up to strike.

With that, the Heap uncles lurched forward, like a pair of automatons. This odd gait was mainly due to their utter exhaustion, but it was also because there was still just enough of Ernold and Edmund Heap left to resist the **Darke** Wizards' intentions.

Septimus, Nicko, Jenna and Simon backed away toward the door. In the shadows behind the approaching Wizards Septimus could see the nervous wobble of a yellow stack of doughnuts, but he put Jim Knee out of his mind. Right now he needed to focus on one thing. He had to raise a **SafeShield**—something he had never done before.

Deciding to **Shield** only Jenna and Nicko—the less people **Shielded**, the more effective the **Shield**—Septimus put his arm around Simon's shoulders and walked him sideways out of the **Shield** space and then he spun around, clenched his fists and threw them open. To Septimus's relief a bright band of purple light shot out from his raised hands and, to Jenna and Nicko's surprise, dropped over them to form a small, cloudy dome. It was a very basic **SafeShield**, but it did the job. Jenna and Nicko stared out like a couple of mice trapped under a bell jar. The **Darke** Wizards laughed.

"How very."

"Quaint."

There was a sharp *snap* like bones cracking, a flash of light, and suddenly Edmund and Ernold Heap were each holding a gleaming black stave, smooth as glass.

Simon stared at the staves in horror. He had never seen one, but he knew at once what they were: **Volatile Wands**. He knew that within them, concentrated in the tiny silver spine that ran through the length of the **Wand**, lay a distillation of **Darke** power. **Volatile Wands** were powerful, accurate and incredibly dangerous. Simon felt sick—they didn't have a chance.

There was a thunderous *craaaack*. The walls of the hall shook and from the ends of each **Wand** a bullet of light emerged, *zub zub*, heading straight for the **SafeShield**. Jenna and Nicko threw themselves to the ground but the bullets never reached the **Shield**—Simon twisted his cloak up into the air and caught them. His cloak burst into flames and, unperturbed, as though his cloak caught fire on a regular basis, Simon threw it to the floor and stamped on it.

"Come on," he dared the Wizards. "You can do better than that."

Septimus thought Simon was being a little rash. He had no doubt that not only could the Wizards easily do better than that, but they were about to prove it.

Simon, however, knew the game to play. He knew **Darke** Wizards fed off fear and that a scornful disdain was the best defense. He also knew that he had to back it up with a show of strength, and so Simon reneged on his promise to Lucy that he would never again mess with the **Darke**.

Using the last of the flame from his cloak, he Conjured a **FireSnake** and sent it blazing through the air. It hit the Wizards and wrapped itself around them once, twice, three times and began to tighten. But like all things **Darke** it was a two-sided weapon. In a moment Shamandrigger Saarn and Dramindonnor Naarn had turned it to their advantage. Using the flame they sent up a plume of black smoke and **Threw** it over Simon and Septimus, imprisoning them in a circle of burnt-snake fumes.

Then Shamandrigger wound the **FireSnake** around his **Wand** and hurled it into the smoke, where it scorched Septimus's hair and fell writhing to the floor. Simon had the presence of mind to stamp on it, but neither he nor Septimus could find a way out of the choking smoke.

Now the **Darke** Wizards headed across to the **SafeShield**. Holding their **Wands** like javelins, they stabbed them into the shimmering purple dome. It emitted a wounded groan and the purple light began to grow dim.

"Jen, I'll distract them and you make a break for it," whispered Nicko. "Get to the Queen's Way. They can't follow you there."

"Shut up, Nik," said Jenna.

"You *what*?" asked Nicko, not sure he'd heard right.

"Just *be quiet*, will you?" Jenna snapped.

Nicko felt scared. Something odd had happened to Jenna.

With that the **SafeShield** died.

Jenna found herself looking into the eyes of her pitiful, bruised, battered and utterly terrified uncles. But lurking deep within she saw the **Darke** Wizards' malice. Jenna had been scared a few times since the day she had learned she was Princess, but had never felt as frightened as she did now.

Nicko grabbed her hand and squeezed it, and Jenna regained her courage. She squared up to the disheveled, muddy figures and demanded, "What do you want?"

The reply came, filling the hall with fear.

"The end."

"Of your."

"Line."

"As we."

"Promised."

Jenna reached up and took off her gold circlet—the one that so very long ago Hotep-Ra had given to the Queen.

"No, Jen!" whispered Nicko, thinking she was surrendering.

"Yes, Nik," said Jenna. She held the circlet in both hands at arms length as though offering it to the Wizards, while Nicko looked on, shocked and unsure what to do.

Among the many things that Jenna had listened to on her Journey was the story of the Queen's **Committal** of the two **Darke** Wizards to the ring. She had listened to it carefully because it was about something she recognized. But the story had come at the end of a long and tedious day involving many rules and regulations and Jenna had been sleepy. She remembered her grandmother chanting the **Committal** to her as the evening sun came streaming through the tiny round windowpanes. She even remembered dozily chanting it back. Now—hoping that it would come back to her as she spoke—Jenna began the one thing that the Ring Wizards dreaded to hear: "By our Power, at this hour, we do you . . ."

At the onset of the **Committal**, the Wizards shrank back.

From within the **Darke** smoke Septimus and Simon saw a chink of light and threw themselves at it. They burst out, spluttering, to find to their amazement the two Wizards backing away from Jenna. Now was their chance.

Eject? mouthed Septimus to Simon.

Simon nodded and made the sign of two crossed index fingers for the **Darke**.

Septimus gave him the thumbs-up. If ever there was a time to use the **Darke** it was now.

"Tceje!"

Nothing happened. Shamandrigger Saarn and Dramin-donnor Naarn swung around and pointed the **Volatile Wands** at them instead of at Jenna, who was still speaking.

"Not working. Need their **Darke** names," hissed Simon.

Thinking of his own **Darke** name, Sum, Septimus took a

gamble. "**Tceje!**" he yelled. "**Tceje**, Reg and Ron!"

"No!" shouted Jenna as—as if on castors—the **Darke** Wizards shot away from her, exiting backward like all respectful courtiers had done in the past—but at ten times the speed.

At last Jim Knee sprang into action. He opened the door in the paneling, bowed politely as the Wizards shot through it and then slammed it shut. Beaming, the jinnee leaned against it, looking as triumphant as if he himself had **Ejected** the Wizards.

"Good one, Sep!" said Simon.

"Yeah." Septimus grinned.

But Jenna did not agree. "You dumbos!" she said.

"*What?*" Septimus and Simon said in amazement.

"What did you do that for?" Jenna demanded.

"Just trying to save your life, Jen. That's all," said Septimus, looking at Jenna as though she had gone crazy. "Is that a problem?"

"Yes. I mean, no. I mean . . . oh, Sep, you *dillop*. I had just remembered all the words. For the **Committal**. But you and Simon just helped them *escape*."

33
Scorpion

Jim *Knee was shocked. He'd* come very close to jinnee suicide, which is what a jinnee is considered to have committed if he allows his Master to be murdered in his presence. Not only is this fairly disastrous for the Master, it is also pretty bad for the jinnee: he is evaporated on the spot into a convenient receptacle, which more often than not ends up in the hands of the murderer. There is an old jinnee saying, "Murderers do not good Masters make," which is true. However, Jim Knee was not about to impart this information to his Master. It was desirable that his shock appeared to be due to the narrow escape his *Master* had had.

But no one noticed Jim Knee's shock—everyone in the room was in a similar state. They gathered around the little door in the paneling where the Wizards had so recently been **Ejected**.

"What I don't understand is how they got into the cupboard in the first place," Nicko was saying. "And when? Me and Jen were here on our own for ages and they could easily have got us then." He shuddered at the thought. "So why wait until we were all here?"

"It is not a cupboard," said Simon. "It's some kind of old tunnel. You can smell it. We wouldn't have **Ejected** them into a *cupboard*, Nik."

"It is Smugglers' Bolt." Jim Knee's voice gave everyone a surprise. The jinnee had been unusually quiet since he had arrived at the Port Palace.

"Smugglers' Bolt?" asked Jenna. "What's that?"

"I thought you knew, since it's your Palace," said Jim Knee. "It's a tunnel to the Castle."

"All the way to the Castle? All the way from *here*?"

"Indeed. A foul and fetid way, used only by those desperate to escape the law of the Port."

"Or the Castle," said Septimus.

"Quite so, Master."

"But how do you know?" Jenna asked Jim Knee.

Jim Knee was silent. Like all jinn, he was uncomfortable speaking about previous lives.

"Answer the question, Jim Knee," his Master told him a trifle impatiently. "How *do* you know?"

"I've been here before," Jim Knee said. "I was once the Royal cook."

"So you've been down the tunnel?"

"Er, no." A terrifying memory flashed through Jim Knee's mind: a midnight raid. Screams. Pistols firing. Axes hacking at the doors. And—as poor, unloved Tallula Crum—watching everyone escape down the tiny steps, knowing that there was no way she would ever be able to fit. Knowing that this was the end of another life.

"Then how do you know for sure that it goes to the Castle?" asked Jenna.

"I *know* it does. It was used a lot when I was cook. Precious things were taken through it for safety. The Port was wild in those days."

"No change there, then," muttered Nicko.

They all stared at the door, longing to open it and see what lay beyond, and yet not daring. "I think we should check to see if they're really gone," said Jenna.

"They won't hang around here," Septimus pointed out. "Not now they know you know the **Committal**."

"But I want to see for myself," said Jenna.

Nicko put his hand on his knife, which he always kept in a sheath hanging from his belt when he was in the Port. "Yeah," he said. "If we're going to stay here tonight, we have to check. We don't want them sneaking up on us when we're asleep."

"But I **Ejected** them," said Septimus, a little peeved that his **Magyk** was not being taken seriously. "They can't come back."

"They're **Darke** Wizards, Sep," said Nicko. "They can do what they like."

"Nik's right," said Simon. "We should put an **Anti-Darke** on the door at the very least. In fact, I would suggest a **Lock** and **Bar** as well."

"I wasn't going to leave the door unguarded," said Septimus irritably. "That would be stupid. But I need to think carefully about what to do."

"We *all* need to think," said Simon, annoyed at not having his expertise considered.

Jenna was tired of all the discussion. It was her Palace and she wanted to know everything about it. So while the boys were bickering, she pulled open the little door to Smugglers' Bolt.

"Jen!" A chorus of protest greeted her action.

Jenna took no notice. She peered into the dark. A waft of stale, unpleasant air blew into her face. She picked up a nearby candle and pushed it into the darkness beyond the open door. In its light Jenna could see some tiny steps, no more than a foot wide, disappearing downward between two tapering walls of chiseled stone. It was the narrowest tunnel she had ever seen.

The boys were all looking over Jenna's shoulder now. Even Nicko—who loathed confined spaces—wanted to see. To everyone's relief the tunnel was deserted.

"They've gone," whispered Jenna. And then she realized where they had gone. "*Back to the Castle.*" Quietly, Jenna closed the little door. She had heard that sound could travel a long way through a tunnel. She put her finger to her lips and beckoned everyone away to the fire, where she took up her position in front of the huge stone lintel and said, "We have some plans to make. Fast."

Simon, Septimus and Nicko nodded.

"We can't let them loose in the Castle—we absolutely *can't*. So that means I have to do the **Committal** before they get out," said Jenna. "And to do that I have to be ready and waiting for them at the exit from Smugglers' Bolt."

"Jim Knee, how long does it take to go through Smugglers' Bolt to the Castle?" asked Septimus.

"It used to take about nine hours," replied Jim Knee. "It was not a pleasant trip, I was told. But who knows the state it is in now? It could take even longer."

"Where does it come out?" asked Jenna.

"Number Sixty-Seven Wizard Way—in the backyard. Of course it was a secret but my little scullion-boy's mother used to live at Number Sixty-Seven and he told me. He was a brave lad. On his day off he'd run all the way home through that tunnel and be back first thing the next morning. Without fail."

"Where *is* Number Sixty-Seven?" asked Simon—the

numbering system in Wizard Way bore little or no relation to where the building was sited.

Septimus sighed. "It's Larry's place," he said. "Larry's Dead Languages. *Great.*"

Jenna had been thinking. "So . . . I need to be there in nine hours' time. Unless **Darke** Wizards travel faster?"

"They are constrained by the bodies they **InHabit**," said Septimus. "Until they can get their own form back—which they can't until they win the battle with the person they are **InHabiting**. And so far Edmund and Ernold are still hanging on in there. So far . . ."

The full horror of what had happened to her uncles began to dawn on Jenna. "Oh, that is so *horrible*," she whispered. "Poor, poor Uncle Ernold and Uncle Edmund."

"Yes," said Septimus. "There's a book I had to read before my **Darke** Week, called **InHabitees** *Remember*. There aren't many that do remember, of course, but a few have been rescued before they were completely **Consumed**. It's unbelievably awful. There's an entity inside your head, controlling your body, pushing you to exhaustion, trying to get you to give up, to allow them to take you over. And you can't rest, not even for a second . . ."

"I can't bear to think about it," murmured Jenna.

"But our uncles are tough old birds," said Simon. "I think we can be sure that the time the you-know-who take to travel the Bolt will still be limited by the state that Eddie and Ern are in."

"You mean they won't die on the way back?"

Simon looked uneasy. "Um, yes. So I think nine hours minimum to the Castle is right."

Nicko looked worried. "We ought to get going," he said. "The tide's against us now, though with any luck the wind is still in our favor. It will be a bit bumpy but I reckon if we leave now we'll get to the Castle in about five hours."

"But the Port Barge went ages ago," said Jenna.

"I've got Jannit's supply boat, Jen," said Nicko. "That's how I got here."

"Oh! Yes, of course. Okay, we'd better go."

"You've forgotten something," said Simon.

"What?"

"You're assuming that the you-know-whos are going to keep going to the Castle. But there is nothing to stop them turning around. In fact, maybe they aren't heading for the Castle at all."

"Once Merrin is there, they will," said Septimus.

"Even so, we need to make totally sure that that is where they go, *now*. And for all we know there may be branches off the tunnel. Are there, Jim Knee?"

Jim Knee shrugged. "I don't know. No one ever told me there were. But then no one ever told me anything, as I recall." Jim Knee didn't like to remember how lonely he'd been as Tallula Crum. His only friends then had been the homesick little scullion-boy and the sweet pies he used to make at night for comfort. Now that Jim Knee thought about it, he could see that there had probably been something not right about Tallula Crum; she had, he suspected, been a little slow in the head. But when he had actually been Tallula Crum he hadn't understood that. He had just felt puzzled and unhappy. All the time. Jim Knee sighed. Life was much better now.

Unfortunately for Jim Knee that was about to change.

"There *must* be other entrances in the Port," said Nicko. "I can't imagine all the smugglers politely lining up outside the Port Palace to get into the Bolt, can you?"

"You're right," said Septimus. "Jim Knee will have to go after them. Quickly."

"What?" said Jim Knee, hoping he hadn't heard right.

"Well, it's too dangerous for anyone else to go."

"It is too dangerous for me too, Master," said Jim Knee.

"As Jim Knee, yes. But not as a scorpion."

Jim Knee was horrified. "A *scorpion*?"

"A scorpion can survive almost any conditions. They are particularly good in dark tunnels and superb at traveling over bumpy terrain. And with its pincers a scorpion will be perfect for herding two **Darke** Wizards."

"They are also particularly *small*, Master. It will take a scorpion many weeks to scuttle all the way to the Castle. That's if it doesn't get stamped on first."

"So you will **Transform** into a *large* scorpion, Jim Knee. As large as is compatible with scorpion life. Which, if I remember rightly, is about the size that will fit nicely down those steps."

Jim Knee stared at his Master. Sometimes he was too clever for his own good. He was certainly too clever for Jim Knee's good. Jim Knee leaned back against the little door and his yellow hat drooped disconsolately. He thought of the bony exoskeleton, the eight little pointy legs, the clamping pincers, the horrible hairy tail looped up behind him, dangling its sting, and all those *segments*. Jim Knee shivered. He hated segments.

"About ten feet long, plus pincers," said Septimus. "That should give you enough speed to catch up with them."

"And what do I do when I catch up with them, Oh Master?"

"You will herd them toward the Castle end of the tunnel. You will not allow them to turn back. Jenna and I will be waiting there when you arrive."

"Very well, Oh Master," said Jim Knee. "Your wish is my command and all that. Unfortunately."

"Yes, it is," Septimus replied gruffly. He felt bad about Jim Knee. It was tough being a jinnee, he thought. Tough to have all the sensibilities of a human, and yet to be forever at the mercy of another. And it must be especially tough to not even be in control of the form your own body took. But Septimus knew that if he wanted Jim Knee to do his bidding he must not show any weakness. And so, when Jim Knee caught his eye pleadingly, Septimus merely said, **"Transform."**

There was pop of yellow light and a loud clattering. Suddenly a ten-foot-long scorpion stood in Jim Knee's place, waving its yellow-tipped sting at the end of its tail.

"Eew!" gasped Jenna. The scorpion turned toward her and gave her a reproachful stare. "Sorry, Jim Knee. Nothing personal."

In reply the scorpion opened its pincers and shut them with a sharp *snap*. It wanted to say that it didn't get much more personal than this, thank you very much, but its conversational skills were severely limited. It consoled itself with waving its sting angrily at its Master. It could tell from the expression on its Master's face that he wasn't too keen on pointy stings.

Septimus was not at *all* keen on pointy stings. He moved smartly off and opened the door to Smugglers' Bolt. "Jim Knee, it's time to go. *Move*."

Jim Knee's Master had no idea how difficult it was to obey. The scorpion swayed from side to side in utter confusion. There were so many legs. How did you move *eight* of them? And they were so complicated—he had, for goodness' sake, *fifty-six knees*. Which way did they bend? And—oh, no—some of them swiveled too. What should he do—move the front two first and then the back two? Or first one side and then the other? Or was there some weird combination like one-three-five-seven, then two-four-six-eight? And if there was, how did you number your legs? Did you begin at the front or at the back? Left or right?

Septimus returned to the scorpion. "Come on, Jim Knee," he said impatiently. "Get a move on."

The scorpion regarded Septimus accusingly. Clearly its Master had given not a moment's thought to the question of *legs*.

"Command him," said Jenna. "Then he'll have to."

"Jim Knee, I command you to—" He glanced back at the open door to the tunnel and lowered his voice. "Enter Smugglers' Bolt. *Go!*"

The scorpion was thrown into a state of panic: it was commanded; therefore it had to go. It activated its third left leg, the leg shot backward and its pincer feet snagged on the back leg. The back leg, which was more powerful than the others, wiggled to free itself and the scorpion began to wobble. It teetered for a few seconds, its legs splayed out and it landed on its stomach. Its tail drooped and clattered down onto the floor. Ten long feet of glistening black scorpion—plus pincers—was laid out in front of them like a bizarre rug.

"Rats," said Septimus.

"Might be better if he *was* a rat," observed Nicko.

"Rats are notoriously sensitive to the **Darke**, unlike scorpions, which are impervious," said Septimus. "Come on, everyone. Help him get up."

"Right." Nicko gulped.

Jenna kneeled down and pushed her hands under the smooth black carapace. "It's only Jim Knee," she said. "If we all just put our arms underneath we can kind of flip him back on his feet."

The scorpion's pectines waved unhappily. It did not like the sound of "flip."

Septimus, Simon and Nicko joined Jenna. "One, two, three—*flip*!"

The giant insect was surprisingly light. It flew up into the air, legs waving, and landed delicately on its eight little pointy pincer feet. Its tail resumed its curve and the scorpion staggered forward, segments breathing hard, inhaling the damp air that was rolling in from Smugglers' Bolt.

Transformations are slower to take over the mind than the body, but now the scorpionness of Jim Knee's being was seeping into his brain and his legs began to work. He discovered that it was easy—there were just two movements.

Legs-number-one: forward. Legs-number-two: back. Legs-number-three: forward. Legs-number-four: back.

And then: legs-number-one: back. Legs-number-two: forward. Legs-number-three: back. Legs-number-four: forward. It was simple: in the first step the middle two legs acted as a pair. In the second step the front two legs and the back two legs acted as two pairs.

Chanting silently to himself, Two-three-together, two-three-apart, Jim Knee trundled past four tall, blobby things—wondering how they balanced on only two legs—and headed gratefully for the delicious smell of damp and decay that wafted out from the darkness of Smugglers' Bolt.

The four blobby things watched him go, seeing the reflection of the candle flame on his shiny pincers and listening to the rattle of pincers on stone as Jim Knee headed slowly downward. (With fifty-six knees, steps required particular attention.) As the scorpion disappeared into the darkness and all became quiet, Nicko closed the door. "I wouldn't like to hear *that* coming along the tunnel behind me," he said.

Far below in the darkness, Tallula Crum's final wish had been granted: she was running freely through Smugglers' Bolt.

⁜ 34 ⁜
Smugglers' Bolt

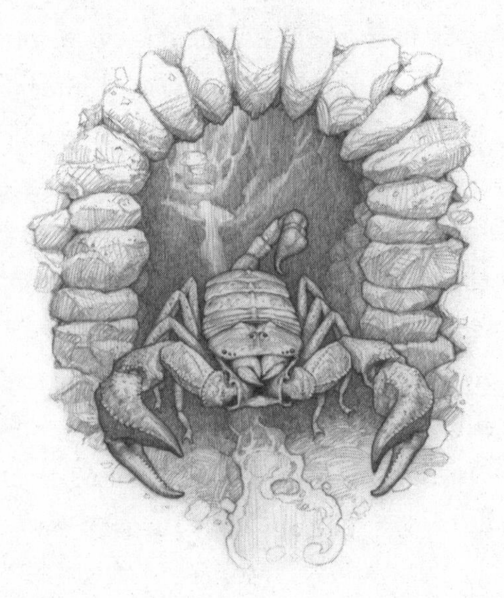

When *a jinnee is* **Transformed**, he or she becomes a strange hybrid. In the very center of the **Transformed** creature, like the stone within the fruit, its old human self remains, observing and guiding from deep within. But it is the outer creature that it has become that floods the jinnee's senses. And so, as Jim Knee scuttled along the rough rock floor of the Smugglers' Bolt, it was scorpion instincts that drove him onward through the dark—which was lucky for Jim Knee, for the Smugglers' Bolt was a place no human would choose to be.

The tunnel was utterly devoid of light but the scorpion felt at home; the darkness was where it belonged. It trundled merrily along, its pincers brushing against the narrow walls, its yellow sting arched high above its head gauging the height of the tunnel, telling it all it needed to know. A wonderful feeling of lightness and agility suffused it as it hurried through the tunneled rock, heading out of the Port, following the tunnel downward as it dipped below the Marram Marshes.

Jim Knee was free—there was no way that his Master could get to him. He could do whatever he chose. Jim Knee's choices were, however, severely limited. He could not turn around, for Smugglers' Bolt was much narrower than he was long, and Jim Knee did not relish the thought of spending eternity as a giant scorpion wedged across a tunnel. Neither could he stop moving, because he had discovered that when he did, his legs had a disconcerting desire to tangle and send him crashing to the ground. And going backward with fifty-six knees to think about was not an option. So, Jim Knee could indeed do whatever he chose—provided that what he chose to do was to move forward along Smugglers' Bolt.

Smugglers' Bolt—or the Bolt, as it had been known to generations of smugglers, brigands and footpads—had been hewn from the great plate of rock through which the river carved its way from the Castle to the Port. Some half a mile out from the Port, the Bolt dipped even more steeply down to dive below the Marshes. The air quality fell and the atmosphere became oppressive. It was this section that had once terrified even the most hardened of Bolters—as regular users of the tunnel were known. Here the more fainthearted would turn and run back, often leaving their contraband behind. But not the scorpion—it scurried along, trundling over the rotten old barrels of ill-gotten gains that lay strewn along the rocky floor of the tunnel. Down, down it went through the darkness, and when it reached the muddy water filling the lowest point of the Bolt it did not panic as many a smuggler had done, but plunged into the brackish gloop and waded on, closing its spiracles, tightening its segments to protect its delicate little book lungs and keeping tabs on its middle legs which, Jim Knee had discovered, were the key to smooth running and had a tendency to get tangled if not concentrated on. And so, like a large mechanical toy, the scorpion clattered on its way—two-three-*together*, two-three-*apart*, two-three-*together*, two-three-*apart*, two-three-*together*, two-three-*apart*—rapidly closing in on the two desperate men staggering through the darkness.

Down in the deepest, foulest part of the Bolt, gasping in the bad air, Edmund and Ernold Heap staggered onward as their **InHabitants** pushed them ruthlessly forward through the tunnel, sending them stumbling through pools of sludge, tripping over fallen rocks, crashing into the rough tunnel walls in the pitch-blackness. The Ring Wizards were utterly careless of the two Heaps, using them up in their drive to reach the final stage of their **Reversion**, when they would be able to take their ancient form once more.

It was here, in the depths below the Marram Marshes, that Jim Knee caught up with his quarry. He heard them first—the sound of their labored breathing and their groans as they tripped, the splash as they fell, and their cries as they were forced to their feet or sent hurtling into yet another rock. Jim Knee slowed his pace—the last thing he wanted was to mow Edmund and Ernold down like a steamroller—and now he kept his distance, matching them step for step. And even though pity had no place in a scorpion brain, in the deep Jim Knee part of its thoughts, pity is what the scorpion felt.

On the far side of Deppen Ditch, the strange procession began the upward climb. The air began to feel fresher and the scorpion noticed that ahead of it, the desperate gasping for breath had eased a little. With its pincers waving in excitement at the change of air, the scorpion scrambled up the now-sandy floor as the tunnel dried out and leveled off below the fields. The going was faster now and the scorpion clattered happily on, pausing only when the two Heaps stopped for a moment to gulp in a downdraft of fresh air, like parched men swallowing water.

Edmund and Ernold had stopped beneath the first farmstead after Deppen Ditch. Named Smugglers' Rest, it was here, clambering up a ladder through a shaft known as the Bail Out, that those who had braved the Bolt would emerge gasping for fresh air and the sight of the wide sky. Even now, air still poured into the tunnel from the ventilation shaft—a large chimney—around which the farmhouse was built.

The Heaps were not allowed long to drink the air, but from Smugglers' Rest onward their path was easier. Smugglers' Bolt now became a shallow tunnel, running no more than six to eight feet below the orchards and fields of the Farmlands. In the past, it had had numerous exit points into farmhouses along its route to the Castle. Most farmers had indulged in a little bit of smuggling when duty on brandy, lace and sweet wine from the Far Countries was astronomically high. In those days it had been well known in the Castle that, if you wanted to buy good wine at a reasonable price, then a lonely farmhouse on the winding road to the Port was your best bet. And if the farmer declared that it was her own homemade wine, you would be well advised not to comment on the surprising lack of a vineyard—or indeed the weather to grow the grapes.

The exits to the farmhouses had also served as ventilation points for the tunnel, and its closeness to the surface had allowed many other ventilation shafts to be driven down through the soil—camouflaged by drinking troughs, sheep shelters, cow barns and all manner of farm equipment. While these were maintained, the tunnel had been so well ventilated that it was said that in springtime you could smell the apple blossom in the Bolt.

But not anymore. Some two hundred years earlier, the Port

duty rate had been drastically reduced and the whole smuggling business had stopped overnight. Smugglers' Bolt quickly fell into disuse. Over the following years many ventilation shafts had filled up with soil, or simply collapsed, but the tunnel—solid as the rock it ran through—had stayed as it was.

And now there was no scent of apple blossom for Edmund and Ernold as they staggered on toward the Castle, just the thick smell of soil and the unkindness of rock.

In Smugglers' Rest, Daisy Pike sat up and nudged her husband awake. "Mooman," she said. "There's someone downstairs. Go and have a look."

"Why me?" asked Mooman.

"Why not?" said Daisy.

Mooman was no good at arguing. He sighed, got out of bed and tiptoed down the stairs, avoiding the creaky one. At the foot of the stairs his legs felt weird and he had to sit down on the bottom step. A magnificent ghost in ExtraOrdinary Wizard robes was pacing to and fro in their front parlor. Mooman had never seen a ghost before—not a ghost of a human, anyway. He had seen plenty of cow ghosts, of course; all his much-loved old cows still grazed in their fields and came to greet him. But he had never seen a human. Until now.

As Mooman stared in amazement, the ghost stopped pacing and appeared to be deciding something. Mooman thought it looked like it was something really important. Then, clearly having made a decision, the ghost hurried across the room to the huge stone chimney that came up through the middle of the farmhouse. It positioned its feet carefully, stood up poker-straight with its arms by its sides and slowly began to sink through the rug. Mooman wondered where the ghost was going—and then he remembered what lay beneath: an old trapdoor that he had hammered shut years ago and covered with a rug after Daisy had complained about "nasty, smelly drafts" coming up from it. Mooman watched until all that was visible of the ghost was his rather distinguished head resting on the rug like a stray football. Then it, too, sank and disappeared.

Mooman shook himself and went back upstairs to find Daisy sitting terrified, bolt upright in bed with the sheets pulled up around her.

"Why were you so long?" she whispered. "I thought something awful had happened. I thought you were dead or something."

Mooman got back into bed and discovered that he was trembling. "N-no," he said. "It's not me what's dead. It's him."

Daisy's eyes widened in horror. "Who?"

"That ancestor of mine. That ExtraOrdinary Wizard. It were his ghost."

"Not *Julius Pike*?" asked Daisy.

"Yeah," said Mooman. "The very same. Amazin' when you think about it. Me bein' descended from him." He grinned at Daisy, showing the gap where his two front teeth should have been. "Maybe I got some **Magyk** in me—eh?"

"No, Mooman, you most definitely do *not*," Daisy told him.

Mooman blew out the candle and settled back under the covers. "I wonder what he was doin' down there. He looked in a right state. Hope he doesn't start playin' up and chucking things around."

Daisy yawned. "He'll be all right. They're good ghosts to have, the old ExtraOrdinaries. Nice and civilized. Now go to sleep, Mooman. It'll be time to milk the cows before you know it."

The ghost of Julius Pike sank down through the Bail Out—an oak-lined shaft with a ladder propped up inside. Smugglers'

Bolt held no terrors for Julius Pike. He had, as a boy, "Run the Bolt" many times, and he remembered it well.

Julius had enjoyed growing up in a farmhouse at the center of so much activity. The farmhouse was isolated—bounded by the Marram Marshes, the river and its extensive lands, which contained orchards, sheep and a small herd of dairy cows (but not a single grapevine), but to the young Julius it had felt like the center of the universe. Julius was the youngest of five much older brothers, who all worked on the farm, and he was a solitary child. He would sit by the big ventilation chimney, reading quietly, but also **Listening** for footsteps—and often the rumble of trolleys—coming along the tunnel not very far below. He would open the trapdoor beside the chimney and wait, hoping that someone interesting would emerge. And usually someone did.

However mad or bad the person was, whatever crime they had committed in the Port or were planning to do in the Castle, they were unfailingly polite and grateful to Julius's mother, Martha Pike. She would sit them down by the kitchen fire and feed them a hot drink and a mutton pie, no questions asked. In return they would give her a little "merchandise" and tell the young Julius stories of their adventures, keeping the inquisitive child amused for hours. It was a Wizard—indulging in a little part-time smuggling—who had first awakened Julius's interest in **Magyk** and who had told him what his mother already knew—that he had a **Magykal** gift. And so, at the age of fourteen, Julius Pike had left the farmhouse for an Apprenticeship at the Wizard Tower and had, for the first time, traveled to the Castle overland. But when he was homesick he would—like Tallula Crum's little scullion-boy—Bolt home to see the orchards and eat a mutton pie.

And now he was back in the Bolt once more. The ghost hurried along, heading toward the Castle. He felt quite disturbed by the trail he was following. It was **Darke** and full of what his mother used to call Bad Intentions.

A ghost can move a great deal faster than two exhausted human beings and it was not long before Julius Pike heard the pitiful moans of Edmund and Ernold. The ghost hung back and **Listened**.

It was then Julius realized that he was not the only one following them. Beneath the malevolence of the Ring Wizards and the despair of the Heaps, he caught a whisper of something else: the presence of an ancient entity. As the ghost wafted along, slowed by the pace of the two failing humans in front of him, Julius pondered what the entity could be. There was a strange sound to it, a rhythmic rattle, which intrigued him. It sounded oddly insectlike and yet there was something old and wise and human about it. It puzzled Julius for some time as he followed the twists and turns of the tunnels and the gasps and groans of the Heaps. It took the ghost a few miles to figure out that the mysterious entity must be a **Transformed** jinnee. Julius felt relieved. Even as a ghost he did not relish the thought of being alone in such close confinement with two evil beings. It was good to have some company.

And so, through the night, not far below the Farmlands, the strange procession made its way slowly and painfully along Smugglers' Bolt, heading toward the next exit—Number Sixty-Seven Wizard Way.

Back at the Port, Jenna, Simon and Nicko stood shivering on the harborside, watching Septimus do his **Transport** back to the Wizard Tower—the sooner Marcia knew what had happened, the better. As the purple fuzz of **Magyk** dispersed into the night air and Septimus was gone, Nicko hurried them off to Workman's Quay, where Jannit's supply boat was moored.

Soon they were heading out into the night. Nicko had been right: it was a bumpy ride. The wind against the tide threw up waves and the boat reared up and down as it crashed its way into the mouth of the river where the tide and current met.

Nicko stood at the helm, smiling broadly. He loved the excitement of sending the boat through the wild water—something that he did not do often enough, now that he was Senior Apprentice at the boatyard and was so often overseeing work and enviously watching the new Apprentice, sad little Eustace Bott, head off on yet another errand to the Port. Nicko's two passengers were less thrilled with the journey. Jenna and Simon sat in the cuddy, wrapped in damp blankets that smelled of tar, and tried to get some sleep.

It was going to be a long night.

35
SPRUNG

At *the top of the* Wizard Tower, Septimus was back safe from his **Transport** and asleep in his bed. Marcia, however, was wide-awake. She had just finished sending out a practice **Alert** to the entire Castle and was now touring her new **LookOuts** checking on the result. Judging by the huge number of candles

that had rapidly appeared in the majority of upstairs windows, the practice had been a great success.

The **Alert** was a new safety measure. Shocked by the casualties caused by the **Darke Domaine**, Marcia had been determined that no Castle inhabitant would ever again be caught unawares by **Darke Magyk**. To this end she had set up an intricate system of **Alerts** in every building. Of course not everyone had accepted the presence of a **Lert** in their home or business—Larry in Number Sixty-Seven Wizard Way being one of those who didn't—but most were only too glad.

Marcia watched the lighted windows grow dark once more and retreated to her kitchen to instruct the coffeepot. While she was waiting for the coffee to brew, she picked up an unopened envelope banded with red and gold. It was, she knew, from Milo. Marcia stared at the envelope while the coffee-pot made its usual happy spluttering sounds. "Huh," she muttered at the envelope. "More pathetic excuses." The coffee began to bubble up; Marcia leaned over to the cooker and set fire to the envelope and whatever lay within.

Marcia had just poured the coffee when she heard a knock at the big purple door. That night, the door was under instructions to admit any senior Wizard Tower Wizard, and Marcia heard it swing open. She braced herself for Jillie Djinn's stare and strode through the sitting room to see who was there.

It was Dandra Draa. Marcia was pleased; she liked Dandra and right then she could do with some company. The Sick Bay Wizard was hovering uncertainly, unsure whether to come in. "I have something important, Madam Marcia," she said.

"Oh, please, just call me Marcia," said Marcia.

To both Marcia and Dandra's shock, the ghost of Jillie Djinn chose that moment to speak for the first time. Her high, wavering voice poured into the room, a brittle stream of noise. "*Call me Marcia . . . oh, please, call me. Oh, Marcia, call me, please.*"

Dandra emitted a small shriek.

"Drat!" said Marcia. "I'd hoped for at least a couple more months' silence."

"*A couple more . . . I'd hoped for . . .*"

Marcia sighed. "Come in, Dandra," she said. "It's very good to see you."

"*To see you . . . too . . . see you . . . see too you too see you.*"

"If she carries on like this I'm going to *kill* her," muttered Marcia.

"Job done, I think," said Dandra with a wry smile.

Marcia smiled grimly in return. She liked Dandra's sense of humor. "Indeed. Come through to the kitchen, Dandra; have some coffee."

"*Have some coffee . . . coffee some. Have . . . the kitchen, Dandra. Come.*"

Marcia thought that she would go crazy if she listened to the ghost's jangled singsong a moment longer. She steered Dandra briskly through the room and closed the door very firmly behind her.

The ghost of Jillie Djinn sank back into the cushions of the sofa. She wore a satisfied smile. Jillie Djinn: one, Marcia Overstrand: nil. And she had nine more months to hone her skills.

As Marcia instructed the coffeepot—*two cups, with sugar, and hot this time*—Dandra placed a mangled band of gold on the kitchen table. "I find this," she said. "It is the ring, I think."

Marcia picked up the fragile gold circle with care, then got out her **Enlarging Glass** and inspected it. "Goodness, I do believe it is," she said. "It shows signs of recent **Darke** activity. And . . . ah, yes . . . here, I can see the imprint of the heads." She looked up and smiled for the first time that evening.

"Dandra, that is wonderful. Wherever did you find it?"

Dandra smiled. "Stuck in a Wizard's shoe."

"*Really?*"

"He come to Sick Bay with sore foot. So first I look at the shoe. And this is stuck in it. There is nothing wrong with his foot." Dandra shook her head. "He is, what you say—fusspot?"

"Yes, that is exactly what we say," said Marcia. She smiled at the forlorn, distorted ring thinking how, according to legend, it had once been treasured by a Queen and yet had spent so long containing such evil beings. Marcia felt sad that it would have to contain them once again, but it was much safer that the Ring Wizards should be **Committed** to their original ring, rather than risk one of the untried **Triple** bowls.

"Thank you so much, Dandra. It's so lucky you found it—and that you knew what it was." Marcia sighed. "Right now I could do with a bit of luck."

Dandra sipped her strong, sweet coffee, made exactly how she liked it. She took her job of being responsible for the health of *all* the Wizards in the Tower seriously and thought that Marcia looked in need of some support. "Your ghost, he not here? I mean nice old ghost with naughty jokes."

"Oh, Alther. No. He's, er, out."

"You alone too much," said Dandra. "Is not good."

Marcia sighed. "It goes with the territory," she said.

Dandra looked puzzled.

"My job. It goes with the job."

"But you need talk. Everyone need talk."

Marcia did not reply. It had been a long time since anyone had been concerned about her in this way and she felt quite emotional.

"You worry about Ring Wizards," said Dandra.

Marcia nodded.

"You know how to get them come to *you*?"

Marcia looked interested. "Do you?" she asked.

"You find person who have last worn ring. Then you take prisoner."

Marcia smiled. She liked Dandra's no-nonsense approach.

"You do this, I think?" asked Dandra.

Normally Marcia would not have confided what she called sensitive information to a new Wizard, but she felt she could trust Dandra. "Yes. In fact, he is on the way here, right now."

Dandra smiled. "Then all will be well. The Ring Wizards return to get him and *you* get them, *yes*?"

"Well, yes. At least, when Jenna—Princess Jenna—gets here."

"Huh. Why wait for Princess?" asked Dandra, whose experience of royalty had not been good, having involved three warring Princesses, all of whom had in turn laid siege to her home village.

"She's the only one who knows the **Committal**," said Marcia.

Dandra looked horrified. "*You* not know?"

"No," admitted Marcia. Knowing that it made her appear incompetent, she hastened to explain. "But you see, Dandra, that's what the Pyramid Library is for. It's like an extra brain for the ExtraOrdinary Wizard. We couldn't possibly remember everything, but what we *do* know is where things are and how to find them." Marcia smiled ruefully. "But even an ExtraOrdinary Wizard can't find what isn't there."

"And the **Committal** *not* there?" asked Dandra.

"Not anymore," said Marcia. "Some ExtraOrdinary Wizard in the past **Removed** an awful lot of stuff. And he or she was none too careful how they did it." Marcia shook her head. "It's disgraceful. And this afternoon I have discovered that the **Remove** has spilled over into the Ancient Arcane section and taken out some of most delicate and precious information."

Dandra was shocked. "You only *just* discovered?"

Marcia could see Dandra's good opinion of her rapidly disappearing. "Well, yes. But we don't open the Ancient Archives unless we absolutely have to—they are extremely fragile. Of course we check the indexes occasionally, and in the Archive Index the **Committal** was listed as present."

"But it *not* present?"

Marcia shook her head miserably. "No. It's gone. Utterly gone. So the only record of it we now have is with Princess Jenna."

"Who not here."

"No. Well, not yet. She is on her way. I . . . just don't know if she is going to get here in time."

Dandra was silent for a while. "I see why you worried," she said.

"Thanks," said Marcia, feeling a whole lot worse.

Silence fell. Marcia stared at the frying-pan clock on the kitchen wall—one of Alther's old treasures. Looking at it usually made her feel better, but tonight it had no effect. All she could think was that she was now drawing two **Darke** Wizards back to the Castle with no means of destroying them once they arrived. And when they did arrive she would have to rely totally on Jenna's version of the **Committal**. It was not a position any ExtraOrdinary Wizard would choose. She was placing everyone in terrible danger. Marcia put her head in her hands—she felt very frightened.

Dandra put her arm around Marcia's shoulders. "It okay. We all here. Together." Marcia nodded. She blinked away tears and saw that the hour hand on the frying-pan clock had crept around to three. "They should be in sight now," she said. "Would you like to come up to the **LookOut** with me?"

Marcia's rooms, which took up the whole of floor twenty of the Wizard Tower, had four new **LookOuts**—one on each face of the Tower. She and Dandra headed for the South **LookOut**, a long, narrow chamber next to Septimus's bedroom, more like a corridor than a room. The chamber was dark but light poured in from a round window at the end, so crystal clear and bright that it seemed to Dandra as though the moon itself was sitting at the end of the room.

Dandra followed Marcia inside and as she closed the door behind her, the atmosphere in the room became hushed and heavy. Marcia hurried to the window at the end and beckoned Dandra to stand next to her. There was only just room.

Dandra was amazed at how clear the view from the window was. The crystal concentrated every detail and showed a huge vista below, extending from the Forest—where Dandra was sure she could see every leaf and branch as they shook in the wind that was howling in and buffeting the Castle—along past the Moat, where a chop of waves was breaking up its dark surface, and away to the cold snake of the river heading down toward the Port.

Marcia was shocked; she hadn't realized it was such a wild night. She raised her hands and held them cupped over the crystal window, focusing on the most distant bend in the river as it emerged from the swath of Forest. It was here she hoped to see Nicko's boat—with Jenna safe inside it. Dandra watched, fascinated, as Marcia squeezed her hands together and then drew them apart so that a small circle of glass was visible between them. Slowly Marcia drew her hands farther away from each other and Dandra saw the view of the river bend enlarge, until it filled the whole window. Marcia let her hands fall and she and Dandra stared into the distance.

"There!" said Marcia. "Look!"

It was no more than a tiny white speck. But as Dandra looked, she could see that it was the sail of a boat, heeled over, leaping through the waves. "Big waves for river," said Dandra.

"It's awful," said Marcia. "I had no idea the weather was so bad." She shivered and enlarged the view again. The image became a little blurred but within the fuzz she could see Jenna and Simon sitting wrapped in blankets, while Nicko stood at the helm, clearly loving every minute of it. Marcia watched the little boat, fascinated by its rapid progress as it danced through the water; the sight of Nicko's breezy confidence made her feel a whole lot better. "They'll be fine," she said. "Nicko will bring them back safely."

"Now is the barge boat," said Dandra. "See, she comes too."

Sure enough, the huge white sail of the night Barge now hove into view. Heavy but steady, the Barge plowed around the bend that Nicko had very nearly flown around. Nicko must have only just overtaken it, thought Marcia. She imagined that he had enjoyed that. Marcia smiled and looked more closely at the Barge. Hovering above she saw a faint glimmer that she knew to be Alther; on the Barge below she saw no more than the flapping canvas cover of the passenger area. But Marcia knew that if Alther was there, then so were Merrin and Nursie.

Marcia turned to Dandra and smiled. "They're all on their way," she said.

"Good. I go now," said Dandra. "You sleep."

"Maybe," said Marcia doubtfully.

But Marcia did sleep. The **Alarm** woke her two hours later and she was up at once. Five minutes later she was shaking Septimus awake. There was no time to lose.

Down in the Great Hall of the Wizard Tower, in the soft blue light of early morning **Magyk**, all was quiet. Marcia and Septimus stepped off the stairs—still slow on Nighttime mode—and walked over to the tall silver doors. As they went, the floor greeted them: GOOD MORNING, EXTRAORDINARY WIZARD. GOOD MORNING, EXTRAORDINARY APPRENTICE. IT IS A BEAUTIFUL MORNING. ALL IS LOOKING GOOD. Marcia grimaced—the floor only became optimistic when things were really bad.

The wind had blown away the rain clouds and the dawn sky was a clear, pale green as Marcia and Septimus emerged from the Wizard Tower. Wizard Way was peaceful and deserted—apart from the lone figure of Beetle, muffled in his dark blue robes, waiting outside the Manuscriptorium. As soon as he saw Marcia and Septimus emerge from the shadows of the Great Arch, he gave a brief wave and hurried to meet them. The three walked quickly down the middle of the Way, moving through the long, sharp shadows that fell across the yellow stone, catching shafts of crisp yellow light as it glanced through the occasional gap. The floor was right; it was indeed a beautiful morning.

The trio stopped outside the rundown façade of Number Sixty-Seven Wizard Way—Larry's Dead Languages Translation Services—and took a collective deep breath. Marcia ran her hand down the edge of the door and Septimus and Beetle heard the rapid clicks of the line of locks unfastening themselves.

So did Larry.

Larry was up early, translating an obscure dialect spoken only by six people who lived beside an oasis in the Hot, Dry Deserts of the East. He was not in the best of moods, having had a disturbed night due to a crowd of what Larry called "yobs" banging on his door half the night. So when Marcia pushed open the door with a hefty shove, Larry was not at his best.

"*Oi!*" he yelled.

To Larry's great irritation Marcia strode in, followed by his ex-employee, Beetle—who had snubbed him the previous day—and the know-it-all ExtraOrdinary Apprentice. Larry grabbed a chair—one of his favorite weapons—and was on his way to meet the intruders. "Out!" he ordered, jabbing the chair at them in the manner of a lion-tamer who was thoroughly sick of lions.

Marcia was not a fan of Larry. "Indeed, Mr. Morologus, that is *exactly* where you are going. Out."

"How dare you?" Larry demanded, advancing with the chair.

Marcia's answer quickly followed in a flash—a small purple one, to be precise. And when the flash disappeared, Larry was sitting on his chair outside his door, looking in.

"Rude man," said Marcia and then, as Larry rattled the door handle, **"Lock!"**

The door obeyed. Marcia raised her voice above the furious banging of Larry's fists on the door. "Now, Beetle, perhaps you would be so kind as to show us the way?"

Beetle led Marcia through the shop and along a maze of narrow corridors, lined with shelves stacked with chaotic mountains of papers. At last Beetle stopped by a cupboard whose door had fallen off, spilling its papers across the floor. He drew back a smelly old curtain, unbolted the collection of nailed planks that Larry called a door and gave it a hefty kick. The door creaked open to reveal a small, damp courtyard stuffed full of Wizards.

"Good morning, everyone," Marcia said perkily.

"Morning, Madam Marcia," came a gloomy chorus from the fourteen Wizards who had been on guard all night. Marcia surveyed the bedraggled group, clustered around a ramshackle wooden hut standing in the middle of the courtyard, typical of one of the old Castle outside lavatories—or privies, as they were known. The Wizards, sodden after the night's rain, stood huddled together like a small herd of blue sheep lost on a lonely, windswept hill. The courtyard was pervaded by the dismal smell of wet wool.

"I take it there is nothing to report?" Marcia said briskly.

"No, Madam Marcia," came the gloomy chorus.

"Can we go now?" came a brave voice from the back. "We're perished."

Others chimed in.

"Frozen."

"Totally, utterly *frozzled*."

"I think my toes have fallen off."

Marcia sighed. Wizards were not what they used to be. She could see they would be no use at all in the state they were in. "Yes. You can go. Thank you all very much. I realize it hasn't been the most interesting night's work."

To a background of mutterings—"You can say that again"; "I've had more fun having my teeth taken out"; "Bloomin' waste of time"—the Ordinary Wizards climbed up the ladder they had fetched after Larry had refused to answer the door for them, and clambered over the wall. The soggy Wizards then trailed back to the Wizard Tower, their job done.

Beetle's job of guiding Marcia through Larry's warren of a house was also done, and there was somewhere else he very much wanted to be. "I think it would be a good idea," he said, "if I went down to the Palace landing stage and met Jenna."

"A *very* good idea," said Marcia. "Bring her straight here."

Beetle clambered up the ladder and over the wall. Then he was gone, hurrying down to the river, feeling more excited about meeting Jenna than he thought he should be.

Marcia rubbed her hands together in the early morning chill of the dark courtyard. "Right, Septimus, let's have a look, shall we?" Gingerly, she opened the door of the rickety old hut and peered inside. "It's clever," she said, her voice muffled by the hut. "You wouldn't think anything of it. Just an empty old privy with a wooden floor. But when you look closer you can see that the entire floor is a trapdoor."

Marcia stepped back to let Septimus see.

"We should make sure it really does lead to Smugglers' Bolt and isn't just a hiding place for contraband," she said. "There are a few of those around, apparently. I suggest you lift the trapdoor and have a look."

Warily, Septimus unfastened the bolts and lifted the trapdoor up a few inches. A smell of damp and mold wafted out. Marcia kneeled down and got out her **FlashLight**. She shone it into the gap and saw a line of narrow steps leading down into darkness. Suddenly she switched off the **FlashLight**.

"Something's coming," she whispered. "*I can feel it.*"

Very carefully, Septimus let the trapdoor down. "That's *way* too fast," he said.

Marcia stood up, brushing the dirt from her robes. "Septimus, I am so sorry. This must mean that Ernold and Edmund have been . . ." She stopped, unable to bring herself to say anything more.

Septimus said it for her. "**Consumed.**"

36
TO THE CASTLE

"We *must prepare ourselves,"* Marcia said. "I doubt that Jenna will get here in time. We need to keep the *you-know-who* at bay until she arrives."

"Encapsulate?" asked Septimus.

"Precisely. It must be done very carefully. We can't risk any fissures forming."

"So not too fast."

"Indeed."

"An even depth."

"Precisely. About three inches all over."

"That's *thick.*"

"There's a lot of power to keep at bay, Septimus. We must be sure."

"Okay. Shall I pace it out?"

"Yes." Marcia got out her pocket sextant and quickly calculated the height of the hut. "Seven point five eight recurring," she said.

"Circumference: thirteen exactly," said Septimus.

"Right. Let's get this as good as we can!" Marcia did some rapid calculations. "Okay. Now, Septimus, I'll need you to—"

"*Got you!*" Larry's angry face appeared at the top of the wall. "How *dare* you throw me out of my house, you interfering old witch!"

Marcia bristled.

Larry was treading on dangerous ground, but he clearly did not care. "Get out of my yard!" he yelled. "Or do I have to come over and drag you out?" Larry—or possibly his ladder—wobbled with indignation.

"If you value your safety," Marcia said icily, "I suggest you do no such thing."

"Are you threatening me?" Larry demanded. "Because if you are I—"

There was a loud crack of splitting wood and Larry was gone.

"Never trust a ladder," said Marcia. "Now, let's get on. I dread to think how close they are."

One hundred and eighty seconds later the old privy hut had taken on a very different appearance. It was covered with a glowing skin of purple light, which was slowly hardening, like a chrysalis. Septimus watched, enthralled—he had never seen a real **Encapsulation**. It was a tough piece of **Magyk** to get right. Septimus had practiced on a few small objects but the **Capsules** either collapsed like a burst balloon or ended up lumpy like an old potato. But Marcia's was perfect. It covered the hut evenly and smoothly, and as it hardened it began to lose its purple sheen and turn a delicate blue. Soon the color would leave it and a transparent glasslike substance would cover the entire structure, forming a barrier so impenetrable that not even a ghost would be able to get through.

But until all color was gone, the **Capsule** could be breached. It was an anxious time. Just in case, Marcia stationed Septimus around the back of the little hut, and she watched the front.

Suddenly a gasp came from behind the hut. "There's something . . . coming through . . ."

A flash of fear shot through Marcia. She raced around

to Septimus in time to see a tall purple ghost pushing itself through the hardening **Capsule**.

Marcia was extremely relieved. "It's an old ExtraOrdinary," she murmured. "How very . . . *extraordinary*."

An elegant figure emerged, his cropped gray hair banded by an old-fashioned ExtraOrdinary Wizard headband, his thin features and sharp, beaky nose giving the impression of a gaunt bird of prey.

"Oh," said Septimus. "It's Julius Pike!"

"That," said Marcia, "is extremely good timing."

As Julius Pike **Composed** himself after the unpleasant **Passing Through** of the back of the hut—wondering why someone had decided to put the door on the other side from where it always had been—the **Capsule** lost its last tint of blue and became completely clear. Marcia smiled. Nothing was going to get out of there now.

Julius bowed to Marcia in the old-fashioned formal style. "ExtraOrdinary," he said. "Forgive my intrusion in your most excellent **Magyk**. I am sorry to have interrupted your tutorial."

"No apologies necessary, I assure you," said Marcia.

It was a tradition among ExtraOrdinary Wizards that whenever they met an ExtraOrdinary Wizard ghost for the first time (**Gatherings** did not count) the Living must introduce themselves and, bizarrely, inquire after the health of the ghost. With the immediate threat lifted, Marcia proceeded to introduce herself and then Septimus.

The ghost of Julius Pike stopped her. "No need, ExtraOrdinary, for Septimus and I have met before. In another Time—my Living Time." The ghost smiled sympathetically at Septimus. "I am very glad to see you safe here, Apprentice. I would like to say that when we met before I was not aware of what had happened to you. I merely assumed you were yet another mildly deranged Alchemie Apprentice." The ghost turned to Marcia. "Marcellus Pye was, at that time, my very good friend, but even then there were things he did that I could not endorse."

"Indeed?" said Marcia.

"Kidnapping a boy from another Time was one of them."

"Quite," said Marcia. Every word the ghost spoke made her like him more. Marcia remembered her manners. "I trust you are well?" she inquired.

Julius gave the standard reply: "As well as any ghost may

be." The ghost continued, "I have come to warn you"—like everyone who spoke of the Ring Wizards, he dropped his voice to a whisper—"that two most **Darke** and foul Wizards are, at this very moment, on their way to the Castle through the Bolt. It is extremely fortuitous that you have chosen this very place for your **Capsule** tutorial."

"It's not one little bit fortuitous," said Marcia. "It is totally deliberate."

"Ah. So you know. So it is *your* scorpion following them?"

"It's mine, actually," said Septimus.

"Well, well." Julius was impressed. He turned to Marcia. "ExtraOrdinary, these **Darke** Wizards are from the Two-Faced Ring, which I know of old. In the early hours of the morning I **Felt** them heading for the Castle. I have come to warn you."

"We know," said Marcia. And then, thinking she had been a little curt, she said, "But thank you. I very much appreciate your concern."

There was something Septimus had to ask. "What did the Wizards look like?"

"It is very sad," said Julius Pike. "They are **InHabiting** two old tramps, probably found them sleeping in a ditch somewhere. **Darke Magyk** is not kind to—"

Marcia cut in. "How long have we got?"

"I overtook them using an old passing place in the Bolt some two hours ago, but the tramps are being pushed forward at a merciless pace. I estimate possibly an hour."

"An hour!" Marcia was horrified. "Septimus, go! As soon as Jenna arrives bring her here. There must be no delay. *None whatsoever.* Hurry, hurry!"

Septimus was halfway up the ladder when he realized that leaving Julius with Marcia was not a good idea. He was pretty sure that Marcia knew that Julius Pike had been the ExtraOrdinary Wizard at the time of the Great Alchemie Disaster. It would not take her long to start asking the ghost a lot of awkward questions—and getting even more awkward answers. Septimus now shared Marcellus's opinion that Marcia would close down the **Fyre**, even at this late stage, if she knew about it. He also knew from Marcellus that it was Julius who had closed it down previously. It was not safe to leave the ghost of Julius Pike alone with Marcia.

Septimus looked down from the ladder. "Um, Marcia," he said. "I wonder if Julius could come with me?"

"Whatever for?" Marcia asked.

Septimus felt bad about what he was going to say, but he told himself it was actually the truth. "I'd just feel happier, that's all. It's hard to explain."

Marcia had never heard Septimus talk like that. It worried her.

"Yes, of course. Now, hurry, *hurry!*" Marcia watched Septimus climb up the wall and drop down the other side, avoiding the broken ladder. He was followed by Julius Pike, who had done the very same thing in his time as an Apprentice. With the backyard to herself, Marcia fretted. She hated waiting but there was nothing else to be done.

Septimus and the ghost of Julius Pike hurried along Wizard Way toward the Palace. The warmth of the sun and the spring tweeting of birds made Septimus's spirits rise: soon all would be back to normal. He had no doubt that the Capsule would hold the Wizards securely until Jenna got there. Then all she had to do was say the **Committal**—which, knowing Jenna, she would have been practicing all night—then the Wizards would be back in the ring and Marcellus could **DeNature** it in the **Fyre**. It could all happen that very day, he thought. And he was really looking forward to seeing the **Fyre** with Marcia.

It would be good to have no more secrets. Septimus pushed to the back of his mind the thought of Ernold and Edmund. Right then he did not want to think about that.

They headed across the Palace lawns toward the Palace landing stage, where Septimus could see Sarah, Silas and Beetle waiting. Beetle and Silas were shading their eyes against the glare of the sun and Sarah was jumping up and down, waving. Septimus knew that Nicko's boat must be in sight. He raced the last hundred yards to the landing stage and saw Jannit Maarten's supply boat speeding toward it, dancing through the sparkling water. Nicko was windswept and smiling at the helm, Jenna and Simon leaning out, waving.

Septimus turned to Julius with relief. "Jenna's back," he said. "It's going to be okay."

Unconcerned about the safety of royalty, the ghost was staring at Beetle. "Why is the Chief Hermetic Scribe not in the Manuscriptorium?" he asked.

Septimus remembered that Julius Pike had a reputation for being picky about protocol. It seemed a little misplaced right then. "A Chief Scribe doesn't have to always be at the Manuscriptorium—does he, Beetle?" Septimus raised his voice to include Beetle in the conversation.

Beetle turned and saw the unfamiliar ExtraOrdinary Wizard ghost approaching. The first-time greeting etiquette applied also to Chief Hermetic Scribes. Beetle bowed politely.

"O. Beetle Beetle, Chief Hermetic Scribe at your service, ExtraOrdinary."

"Julius Pike, at yours," said the ghost impatiently.

"I trust you are well?" asked Beetle.

"As well as a—oh, *for goodness' sake!*" spluttered Julius. "I'm well—which is more than you or anyone here will be if you don't get back to the Manuscriptorium right now."

"*What?*" Beetle looked shocked.

"Chief Scribe. I really don't know what you think you are doing, leaving the main exit from the Bolt unsupervised by yourself at a time like this."

Beetle's jaw dropped. "Main *exit*? In the *Manuscriptorium*?"

"Where else would it be?" snapped Julius.

"I—in the backyard of Number Sixty-Seven," stammered Beetle.

"Does an old privy hut look like a main exit to you?" asked the ghost scathingly.

"No . . . but . . . oh, *sheesh*. Where *is* it? Where in the Manuscriptorium, I mean?"

Shocked, Julius Pike realized that no one knew about the main exit. "There's a trapdoor at the back of the Vaults," he said.

"*Where?*" asked Beetle.

"I will show you," said Julius. "There is no time to lose."

⊹ 37 ⊹
EXITS

A *flustered Foxy peered through* the Manuscriptorium door—the **LockDown** was really spooking him.

Password? he mouthed at Beetle. Beetle spoke into the hidden speaking tube beside the door and the password whispered through the Front Office. Trembling, Foxy **UnLocked** the door and let his Chief in, along with a very disheveled Princess and an unfamiliar ExtraOrdinary Wizard ghost.

"Hi, Foxy," said Jenna. And then, "*Marissa.* What are you doing here?"

Marissa shrugged. "Oh, you know. *Stuff.* Like waiting for Beetle." She giggled. "*Hello*, Beetle."

Jenna was pleased to see that Beetle did not look particularly thrilled to see Marissa.

"Hello, Marissa. Hey, Foxy, is everything okay?" Beetle asked anxiously.

Foxy didn't think anything was okay at all, but he knew what his boss meant. "Um, yeah."

"We missed an entrance," said Beetle, striding past Marissa. "We have to find it right now."

"But we **Locked** all the entrances that were in the book, honest," said Foxy.

"It wasn't in the book," said Beetle. "I didn't know about this one when I wrote the protocol."

"Oops-ee," said Marissa.

Beetle stopped at the door that led from the Front Office into the Manuscriptorium. "Okay, Jenna?" he said. "We better get straight down there."

"Hey, can *I* come?" said Marissa.

"No," said Beetle as he and Jenna hurried into the Manuscriptorium.

"Oh, after *you*," said Foxy as Marissa pushed by him and barged after Beetle.

Beetle set off between the rows of tall desks, trailing Jenna, Marissa, Foxy and the increasingly anxious ghost of Julius Pike.

"Princess, Chief Scribe," said the ghost. "You are putting yourselves in great danger. We *must* wait for the ExtraOrdinary."

"I could go with Beetle instead," said Marissa. "Then Jenna could go home. I could easily do the whatever-it-is. Couldn't I, Beetle?"

"No," Beetle and Jenna said together.

To everyone's surprise, the agitated ghost suddenly took a turn to the right and began to **Pass Through** a row of desks. In Julius's day the desks had been arranged differently and he was forced to tread the old aisles. "Princess," he called as he veered rapidly away from them, "you must wait!"

Beetle, Jenna and Marissa reached the concealed door in the bookcase at the back of the Manuscriptorium and the ghost emerged spluttering from a nearby desk.

"Princess, hear me, I beg you. They gain strength with

every second," said Julius. "Septimus told me you survived one encounter—which was very fortunate—but do not assume you will survive another. This time they are unlikely to just stand there and politely listen to you."

Beetle hesitated. He hadn't thought of that. He looked at Jenna. "Perhaps we *should* wait for Marcia."

"No!" said Jenna. "This is our only chance. If we hurry we can be waiting for them when they come out of the Bolt and we can surprise them. Anyway, I've got a **Protection Charm**." Jenna opened her hand to show a small **Shield Charm** that Marcia had given her a while back. She smiled. "It's worked so far."

Julius Pike snorted derisively. "A speck of ice in a furnace."

Jenna put on what she now thought of as her Queen voice. "Julius, I refuse to discuss this any more. It is my duty to do whatever I can to protect the Castle. Beetle; let's go."

"Yep. Foxo, go to the Front Office. Septimus went to fetch Marcia. When they arrive bring them down to the Vaults. Fast!"

"Okay, Chief."

Marissa watched the concealed door in the bookshelves close with a quiet *click* behind Beetle, Jenna and the ghost. Grumpily, she followed Foxy back to the Front Office, plonked herself down in the big chair by the desk and began doodling rude words in the Day Book. Marissa was very annoyed. She had spent the most boring night *ever* with a load of geeks, only for Beetle to snub her. She hoped Jenna's stupid **Protection Charm** was rubbish. It would serve her right.

Foxy, who was a little scared of Marissa, went to the front door and stared anxiously out into Wizard Way. A group of Printer's Apprentices hurrying along to work saw Foxy's long nose squashed against the glass in the door and made rude faces. Foxy returned the compliment. Everything outside seemed so normal, thought Foxy, and it was such a lovely morning. Surely, he thought, nothing could be really bad when the spring sun was shining so brightly.

But Julius Pike knew better. As Beetle led the way down the steeply sloping passageway that went to the Vaults, the rushlights flickering as he and Jenna ran past, Julius became increasingly upset—the Princess was heading toward certain death and it was *all his fault*. He should have gone back and informed the ExtraOrdinary Wizard of the missed main exit, not blurted it out to a couple of impulsive teenagers, which was what the Princess and the Chief Hermetic Scribe were.

And now the reckless teens were hurtling down the tunnel to the Vaults with apparently no more concern than if they were late for lunch.

Julius did not give up. "Stop, stop!" he urged, rushing along the snaking twists and turns of the tunnel as it headed sharply downward. Jenna and Beetle took no notice. Sometimes, thought Julius, being a ghost was incredibly frustrating. He longed to race ahead, block the tunnel and tell them to act sensibly, but he could do nothing except beg them to stop.

Jenna and Beetle had now reached the long, steep flight of steps that went down to the Vaults. Julius's hopes were raised when he saw that the Chief Scribe had stopped for a moment. Maybe he was, at last, seeing sense. But to Julius's disgust, all he did was to reach out and take the Princess's hand, and then lead her down the steps—to her doom, the ghost was convinced.

The ancient door to the Vaults, with its wide slabs of oak studded with nails, was at the foot of the steps and it was, to Julius's relief, firmly closed. As Jenna and Beetle reached it, Julius made one last plea.

"Princess, leave now, I *beg* you!"

Jenna wheeled around angrily. The ghost was stopping her concentrating on the **Committal**. "Just shut up and *go away*," she hissed.

Julius Pike looked aghast. The manners of the young were shocking. No Princess would have ever spoken to an ExtraOrdinary Wizard like that in his Time—especially not to a ghost. Ghosts were *always* treated with respect. No wonder the Castle was such a mess. He saw the Chief Scribe squeeze the Princess's hand and give her an encouraging glance. Then Jenna pushed open the door to the Vaults.

And screamed.

Standing behind the door, as if waiting for her, were Ernold and Edmund Heap. Wretched, ragged, hollow-eyed, bruised and battered, they stood holding on to each other for support. Who knows what, if anything, the two Heaps were conscious of at that moment. They were now thirty-eight hours into their **InHabitation** and during that time had been forced to run to the Port and back through the most punishing terrain. The very few people who have been rescued from a **Consuming InHabitation**—one that is designed to end with the exhaustion of the body rather than mere continued use—have reported that there is a moment when the mind becomes aware that it is on the verge of total occupation and makes a last, desperate stand against its invader.

And it was this moment that had arrived for Edmund and Ernold. The sight of Jenna once again opening a door to them brought back memories of when they had first seen her at the Palace, and stirred a last-chance rebellion. Now, for a few desperate moments, they found the strength to fight the Ring Wizards.

The ghost of Julius Pike watched, amazed, as Jenna stood her ground in front of the two desperate-looking tramps. He realized now that they were identical twins—two wretched, exhausted men who were bravely surviving against the **Darke** Wizards. The ghost watched Jenna take the gold circlet from her head and offer it out in both hands to the men. Terrified, Julius waited for the **Darke** Wizards to pounce—surely they would not allow this opportunity to destroy the Princess to pass. But no, somehow their victims were still holding out. Julius saw the two men wrap their arms around each other's shoulders and stare at the Princess as if willing her on.

And so, looking deep into the eyes of her uncles, Jenna began the **Committal**.

Julius was impressed; the words flowed easily and fluently, and as Jenna moved through the words, both the ghost and Beetle felt that time itself had slowed down. Neither dared move. They watched as Jenna held herself utterly still, all her concentration poured into the words she was speaking. The Heaps, too, were immobile, each trying to hold on to his mind as he struggled to keep the last glimpse of consciousness that would allow him to stand against the Ring Wizards for a few precious seconds more. But the stillness belied a huge tension of opposing forces, perfectly balanced for that moment, like a tug-of-war rope that is still only because the two teams are evenly matched.

Julius did not know the exact words of the **Committal**, but he knew the pattern that ancient **Incantations** took, and he could tell that Jenna was now heading toward the end. But both he and Beetle could also tell that the Heaps were nearing the end of their strength. Silently they urged Jenna on, Julius waiting for the **Keystone** word that would signal the beginning of the end of the **Committal** and render the Wizards powerless. The ExtraOrdinary Wizard ghost knew all 343 possible **Keystone** words and, increasingly anxiously, he waited for one of them.

Suddenly, Jenna stopped speaking. Julius waited for her to continue—it was dangerous to pause for too long. But Jenna stayed silent and Julius realized with horror that Jenna thought she had finished.

The Heaps' eyes began to roll.

Jenna waited for the **Committal** to work.

The Heaps' fists began to clench.

Julius Pike could stand it no longer. "Run!" he yelled. "For pity's sake—*run!*"

Beetle grabbed Jenna's hand and pulled her away. Jenna looked shocked. It hadn't worked. *It hadn't worked.* Why? She had remembered every word right. She *knew* she had.

To the accompaniment of groans from Edmund and Ernold, Beetle and Jenna tore up the seemingly endless steps. It was like one of Beetle's nightmares. He ran as fast as he could, aware that he and Jenna were in full view of the Wizards, presenting what must have been the easiest target they had ever had. At any moment he expected them to be felled by a **Thunderflash** or worse. Up, up they ran, and suddenly they were at the top, around the corner and leaning breathless against the wall.

"Breath . . . back," panted Jenna, cramming her circlet back on her head.

Beetle nodded, unable to speak. He had the most terrible stitch in his side. As he fought for breath, Jenna peered around the corner. She turned back and grinned, holding her arms out and making pincer movements with her hands.

Down in the doorway, two giant scorpion claws held Edmund and Ernold Heap prisoner; beside them lay two snapped **Volatile Wands**.

Beetle and Jenna crashed into the Manuscriptorium. "Foxy, get everyone out!" Beetle yelled.

Foxy didn't need telling twice. Thirty seconds later Marissa, Partridge, Romilly and Moira Mole were outside. "I'm taking Jenna to the Wizard Tower for her own safety," said Beetle. "I suggest you all come too."

"Forget it," snapped Marissa. "I've got better things to do," and she headed off to Gothyk Grotto.

Beetle headed up Wizard Way, pulling Jenna behind him. "Beetle, *wait*," said Jenna, who had seen Septimus and Marcia hurrying up Wizard Way. "There's Sep and

Marcia. We have to tell them."

"No!" said Beetle. "It's not safe."

"I'll tell them," said Foxy, determined to be brave. "You go on ahead."

"We'll *all* tell them," said Partridge. "Come on, Foxy."

As Jenna and Beetle hurtled through the Great Arch they overtook the ghost of Alther Mella, who was herding Merrin and Nursie across the Courtyard in the manner of a shepherd rounding up two particularly stupid sheep. He watched Jenna and Beetle disappear into the Wizard Tower and heard hurried footsteps behind him. Moments later Marcia and Septimus, along with an assortment of scribes, came pounding through the Great Arch. As soon as they were in, Marcia took off her amulet and pressed it into a small indentation beside the Arch. The pitted old Barricade came rumbling down through the middle of the Great Arch, **Sealing** the Courtyard.

Edmund and Ernold Heap dragged themselves up the long, steep steps from the Vaults. Behind them lay a badly damaged scorpion, its pincers mangled and burned.

The Ring Wizards were becoming angry—their hosts

were putting up much more of a fight than they had expected. What the Wizards had not accounted for was that Edmund and Ernold Heap were identical twins. All through the nightmarish trek along the Bolt, if one weakened the other encouraged him onward; in this way the Heaps had managed to keep going far longer than would have been possible if two unrelated Wizards had been **InHabited**. But the Heap twins had used their very last ounce of energy in protecting Jenna and now, as they fell out of the concealed door and ricocheted through the desks of the Manuscriptorium like two slow-motion pinballs, they were at the end of their endurance—and the Ring Wizards were at the end of their patience. The twins were hurled through the flimsy door that separated the Manuscriptorium from the Front Office, smashed into the stacks of papers piled up by the window and thrown through the front window.

Edmund and Ernold Heap lay crumpled on the pavement in front of the Manuscriptorium, sprinkled with rainbow shards of glass. A few passersby rushed over to help—but they stopped dead when a green mist began to swirl out from the bodies of the Heaps and rise up to form two pillars at least ten feet tall. Recognizing the **Darke Magyk** for what it was, people ran to the Wizard Tower for help only to find, to their dismay, that the Barricade was down. They hurried home and locked their doors.

But two visitors, Vilotta Bott and Tremula Finn, who had just arrived on the night Barge for the ***Magyk** of the Castle* tour, stayed to watch. The tour had not been going well. The Wizard Tower was unaccountably shut; not even the Courtyard was open. In the fabled Wizard Way most of the shops were closing, rather than opening, and now, to cap it all, the tour guide had run off.

"At least someone's putting on a bit of a show," Vilotta whispered to her friend.

Within the striking green pillars Vilotta and Tremula saw the mist circling slowly, purposefully, creating shadows and shapes. They were very impressed when within each one a human form began to solidify—ten feet tall, wearing the ancient carapace armor of a Warrior Wizard and a very odd cloak, which looked dark and sparkly at the same time. Vilotta and Tremula were pleased—this was more like it. They watched in delight as shimmering green particles spun around the two impossibly tall figures like candy floss.

"I suppose they're on stilts," whispered Tremula.

"They're very good; it's really hard to stay still on stilts," replied Vilotta.

As each wandering atom found its place the beings became clearer. The mist began to evaporate, sending sparkling, dancing motes up into the beams of sunlight that glanced off the silver torchpost outside the Manuscriptorium.

"*So* pretty," murmured Tremula.

Suddenly there was a blinding flash of light and four beams of thin red light shot from the beings' brilliant green eyes.

Vilotta and Tremula gasped with excitement.

In unison, Shamandrigger Saarn and Dramindonnor Naarn flung out their arms and two new **Volatile Wands** appeared. They swung around, the pinprick beams from their eyes sweeping along Wizard Way. Vilotta and Tremula offered a shy round of applause.

"It's very realistic, isn't it?" said Tremula, a little nervously.

It was horribly realistic.

Four red rays of light swung back and came to rest on Vilotta and Tremula. "Ooh, that prickles," giggled Vilotta.

"This is a bit scary," whispered Tremula.

"It *hurts*!" Vilotta gasped. "Ouch! Get *off* me." She tried to brush the beams away.

Tremula screamed.

Craaaaack! A **Bolt** of lightning zipped from each **Wand** and Vilotta and Tremula fell to the ground, wisps of green smoke rising from their new trip-to-the-Castle summer dresses.

Shamandrigger Saarn and Dramindonnor Naarn looked at each other, the ghost of a smile playing about their thin lips. Thousands of years spent trapped side by side in the Two-Faced Ring had given them a communication that did not require speech.

Fyre *. . . We smell it . . . In the air . . . The means of . . . Our destruction . . . Must be . . . Destroyed.*

The Ring Wizards spun around and marched down Wizard Way in perfect step. They left behind two brightly colored piles of rags outside Bott's Cloaks, and outside the Manuscriptorium what appeared to be two empty, muddy sacks, strangely sad in the late spring sunshine.

38
DRAGONS AWAY

T*he fat, opalescent* **Searching** *Glass* sat like a crouching spider on its gimbals in the center of **Search** and Rescue. The circular black-walled room was dim with shadows, the only light coming from the **Magykal** Glass that floated mysteriously inside its delicate black frame. Marcia and Hildegarde were staring into its depths in horror.

Hildegarde had her hands clamped over her mouth. "*They've killed them!*" she cried.

"Oh, those poor, *poor* men," Marcia murmured.

"I . . . I can't believe it. It's so *awful*," said Hildegarde. "And those women. Fancy just standing there, *watching*."

Marcia shook her head. "People forget that **Magyk** is a dangerous thing."

The quiet gloom of the **Searching** Room mirrored their somber mood as Marcia and Hildegarde stared at the image of two ten-foot-tall armored figures striding off down Wizard Way, their cloaks streaming behind them, trailing wisps of **Darke** Light. Wizard Way was, Marcia was relieved to see, deserted—the **Alert** was obviously working.

"Where are they *going*?" Marcia muttered anxiously. "Why aren't they coming here for Jenna and Merrin?"

"But they don't know Jenna and Merrin are here, do they?" Hildegarde said.

Marcia was finding Hildegarde irritatingly dense. She wondered if she had made a mistake in allowing her to move from sub-Wizard to a full Ordinary. "Hildegarde, of *course* they **Know**. These Ancient Beings have links to their past like . . ." Marcia sought for a way to explain. "Like *fish*."

"Fish?"

"On a line. A long line. Which you reel in."

"So what are they reeling in now?" asked Hildegarde. "Haddock?"

Marcia glanced sharply at the new Wizard—was she being cheeky? But Hildegarde, who was a mistress of deadpan, looked utterly serious.

Marcia sighed. "Who knows?" she said. "Watch where they go. Keep me informed. Thank you, Hildegarde."

Back in her rooms, the ghost of Jillie Djinn greeted Marcia in her own special way.

"*A fine fish . . . a haddock is . . . reel it in . . . reel it in.*"

Marcia gave a start. Jillie Djinn's powers of speech had progressed a good deal and the ghost now had a disconcerting ability to know what she had just been talking about, which Marcia found extremely creepy. She rushed past and headed up to the Pyramid Library, where another almost equally annoying ghost greeted her.

"You will be pleased to know that we have found the Hotep-Ra **Committal Template**," said Julius Pike.

"You *have*?"

"Here it is," said Septimus. He pointed to a small square of yellowing vellum lying in the middle of the desk around which he, Rose, Beetle and Jenna—who was busy writing—were gathered. Marcia rushed over to inspect it. She took the delicate **Template** between finger and thumb and gazed reverentially at Hotep-Ra's tiny, spidery writing, full of swirls and curlicues.

"*This really is it.* The **Committal Template**." Marcia felt as though she had been given a reprieve. But something, she thought, did not make sense. She looked at Julius sharply. "So where was it?"

"In the **Hidden** Shelf in the Ancient Archives."

Marcia was flummoxed. "But there *is* no **Hidden** Shelf in the Ancient Archives."

Julius looked smug. "Clearly there is."

"So why was this not recorded in the **Hidden** Index?"

The ghost did not reply. He looked, thought Septimus, decidedly shifty.

"It seems to me, Mr. Pike, that in your time as ExtraOrdinary Wizard you **Hid** a good many things without recording them," Marcia observed tartly.

The ghost was evasive. "Like all ExtraOrdinary Wizards, I did what I considered best."

"An ExtraOrdinary Wizard cannot take it upon themselves to decide what future ExtraOrdinaries will or will not need to know. Your behavior is worse than high-handed—it is downright dangerous. Your actions have put us all in great peril."

There was an awkward silence—everyone knew that it was very rude of a current ExtraOrdinary Wizard to criticize previous incumbents—particularly to their face. Septimus decided to smooth things over. "Well, at least we have it now," he said.

Jenna put down her pen and pushed a sheet of paper across to Marcia. "There—that's what I said."

"Thank you, Jenna." Marcia took the paper. She placed it next to Hotep-Ra's writing and compared the words on both. After some minutes she shook her head, puzzled.

"I don't understand. Will you check them please, Septimus?" Painstakingly, Septimus compared what Jenna had written with Hotep-Ra's **Template**—twice—and he, too, shook his head and passed it along to Beetle. Beetle did the same and passed it round to Rose.

"Well?" said Marcia.

"They're the same," all three said. "Identical."

Marcia turned to Jenna, choosing her words with care. "Jenna, when you spoke the **Committal** you were in a terrifying situation. Maybe you didn't say this *exactly*?"

Julius Pike chipped in impatiently. "Marcia, I assure you, the Princess said those very words. The problem is that the words were incomplete." He stabbed a thin, ghostly finger at the vellum **Template**. "As is that. They are *both* missing the **Keystone** word."

"Julius, don't be ridiculous. How can Hotep-Ra's very own **Template** be incomplete?"

Julius Pike spoke very slowly, clearly fighting to keep his temper. "I do not know. But it is. What is written there does not have a **Keystone**."

"Not everything has a **Keystone**," said Marcia, also trying to keep her temper.

"Everything that Hotep-Ra did had a **Keystone**. It is the ancient way."

Marcia stared at the vellum. "Well, not in this one, Julius. *Clearly*." She looked at Jenna. "I think you must have transposed or omitted a word."

"But I *didn't*."

"Jenna, this is no reflection on you. But someone once said—someone I admire very much—that when you have eliminated the impossible, whatever remains, *however improbable*, must be the truth. And it is impossible that Hotep-Ra has not written the **Committal** right."

Jenna stood up angrily. "But this *is* what I said."

Marcia adopted a soothing tone that really annoyed Jenna. "Jenna, you were incredibly brave. It cannot have been easy to remember—"

"There is no need to patronize me as well as disbelieve me, Marcia. Excuse me, everyone." With that Jenna walked out of the library. They heard her rapid, angry footsteps clattering down the stone steps.

"Someone go after her, please," said Marcia wearily. "Thank you, Beetle."

Those left fell silent. Septimus was thinking. "Maybe," he said, "there is more than one improbable truth. You see, when I spoke to Hotep-Ra—"

"When you *what*?" Julius Pike interrupted.

"Spoke to Hotep-Ra," Septimus repeated.

The ghost gazed at him openmouthed.

From his pocket Septimus took a large blue-black pebble with a slight iridescent sheen to it. It nestled in his palm, showing a brilliant gold "Q" set into the stone. He put it on the desk in front of the ghost. "I went on the **Queste**."

Julius Pike went virtually transparent. "The **Queste**?" he whispered.

"Yes."

"And you *returned*?"

Septimus could not resist. He grinned. "Here I am, so I guess I must have."

"*Septimus* . . ." warned Marcia.

Julius Pike looked stunned. "You *came back*. Unlike two of my Apprentices. Oh, my poor, dear Syrah. . . ."

Marcia held her hand up to stop Septimus. She knew what he was going to tell Julius. "This is not the time," she said.

"So you met the ghost of Hotep-Ra on the **Queste**?" asked Julius.

"No. I met Hotep-Ra himself."

"But . . . *how*?"

"It's a long story," said Septimus. "I'll write it down one day." He turned to Marcia. "One of the things Hotep-Ra asked me about was damage to his **Templates**. He was afraid they might have been degraded by the **Darke** stuff that DomDaniel brought to the Tower—degraded just enough so that they still looked okay, but they no longer worked. Of course I didn't know anything about them at the time. But I think this is what must have happened."

"Well, that *is* an explanation," Marcia conceded. "If the **Template** is changed, then all other forms change with it at the very same time—including the spoken form. Which was why Jenna's was identical." She sighed. "So it's hopeless. The **Committal** is lost forever. *Septimus, where are you going?*"

Septimus was already halfway out of the door. "I'm going to see Hotep-Ra," he said.

Marcia leaped to her feet. "Don't be ridiculous!"

"I'm not being ridiculous. I'm going to ask him what the **Committal** is. He must know."

"Septimus, I will *not* allow you to go back to that ghastly House of Foryx. You'll never come out again."

"My **Questing Stone** gives me safe passage," he said. "I can go into the House of Foryx and always come out in my own Time. *Always.*"

Marcia sighed. She thought of the alternative: of the **Darke** Wizards roaming the Castle unhindered, of the never-ending danger to Jenna—to everyone—and she knew she had no choice but to agree. "So . . . how do you propose to get there?"

There was only one way that made sense right then. "By Dragon Boat."

Septimus found Jenna and Beetle down in the Great Hall of the Wizard Tower. Beetle was trying to persuade Jenna to come back upstairs, with little effect.

"Jen," said Septimus. "I'm going to get the original **Committal** and I'd like you to come with me."

"You bet," said Jenna. "Anything to get out of here."

The door of the duty Wizard's cupboard opened a fraction and Milo's head appeared. "Jenna," he whispered. "I *thought* I heard you. I hope you're not going outside."

"Milo! What are *you* doing here?" said Jenna.

Milo sighed. He had been stuck in the cupboard ever since the Barricade had come down. "I do sometimes wonder," he said. "Jenna, please, you *must* stay here. You are in great danger."

"Jenna will be okay," said Septimus. "We're leaving the Castle at once."

"Very sensible. I will escort you."

Jenna was about to protest, but Septimus stepped in. "Thank you," he said. "We're going to Jannit's boatyard."

Milo took a serious-looking dagger from a small scabbard at his waist. Its shiny steel glinted purple, reflecting the lights flickering across the floor. "They won't get past me," he said. "Oh. *Bother.*"

Milo saw Marcia striding purposefully across the Great Hall at the head of a group of seven of the most senior Wizards. "Jenna, here are your guards," she said. "You must allow them to surround you completely until you are safely aboard. *Milo!*"

Milo sighed. "Hello, Marcia."

"You've had a wasted visit, Milo," Marcia said acidly. "Hildegarde is busy at the moment. She has more important things to do."

"Marcia, please, it's not—"

"Of any consequence," Marcia cut in. "Put it away, please, Milo. The Wizard Tower is a weapon-free zone."

Milo sheathed his knife, muttering, "Sorry."

Marcia turned to Septimus and Jenna. "**Search** and Rescue have a fix on Saarn and Naarn. They are heading up Alchemie Way, so you have a clear run to the boatyard. Hurry!"

Jenna looked at Beetle. "Will you come too? *Please?*" she asked.

Very regretfully, Beetle shook his head. "I can't leave the Manuscriptorium at a time like this."

Jenna sounded disappointed. "No, of course you can't. I'm sorry, I didn't think."

"But I'll come with Milo and make sure you get to the boatyard okay," said Beetle.

The great silver doors to the Wizard Tower swung open, and the party set off down the steps and headed across the Courtyard. Septimus, Beetle and Milo led the way, followed by a protective ring of seven Wizards, in the middle of which was Jenna. They **UnLocked** a small side gate and moved stealthily along the snaking pathway that led to the tunnel into Jannit Maarten's boatyard.

The two Ring Wizards marched up Alchemie Way *left-right-left-right-left* covering the ground fast in their five-foot-long strides. At the foot of the Alchemie Chimney they stopped and stared up at it. Some brave watchers from the corner house on Gold Button Drop saw four pencil-thin beams of red light travel up the chimney and linger on the thin line of white smoke that emerged. They saw the ten-foot-tall shining beings turn to each other and agree something between them. Then, to their terror, they saw them swivel on their heels and head toward them. They dived under their bed and did not come out until the next morning.

Spit Fyre was in his usual place beside the Dragon Boat. His presence every night since Jenna had **Revived** her had given the Dragon Boat great strength. She was now fully recovered and her long, dark days covered in ice were no more than a distant memory. Spit Fyre opened an eye and regarded the oncoming party with interest, and at the sight of his Master he thumped his tail down with a bang. The Dragon Boat opened her eyes and bent her neck toward Spit Fyre, who lifted up his head and gently bumped her nose.

Nicko was showing Eustace Bott how to fix a keel bolt, but when he saw Milo, Septimus and Beetle leading a group of Wizards toward the Dragon Boat he put down his tools. Something was going on. "Eustace, I'll be back in a moment," he said.

Nicko headed over to the Dragon House, not quite believing what he was seeing—it looked to him as though Jenna and

Septimus were going off in the Dragon Boat. The Wizards were now gathered inside the Dragon House and above their heads Nicko could see Septimus standing at the tiller, looking as if he was waiting for the wind to change. Jenna was in the prow, leaning down and saying something to Beetle. The dragon's head was held high; a glint of emerald green glanced from her eyes, which were bright with excitement. With a delicate swanlike movement, the dragon lowered her head so that she was looking Jenna in the eye. Nicko saw Beetle jump back rather quickly, then, shocked, he heard Jenna's whisper echo around the Dragon House: "*Take us to Hotep-Ra.*"

Nicko leaped up onto the marble walkway and pushed past the Wizards. "*Are you crazy?*" he demanded.

"Nik, please don't be upset. We *have* to," Jenna said.

"You can't go back to that awful place. *You can't.*"

"I'm really sorry, Nik. We have no choice. We *have* to go."

Nicko knew Jenna well enough not to argue. "In that case," he said, "I am coming with you." And he jumped on board.

Now the purpose of the marble walkway that ran around the inside of the Dragon House became clear. It needed every one of the seven Wizards—plus Milo and Beetle—to push the Dragon Boat out from her berth. She was a heavy boat and moved slowly at first, but as the first ray of sun touched her nose, the dragon stretched her long neck out of the shadows of the Dragon House to feel the warmth. Now she began to glide easily out of the dim blue light, neck and tail arching up to greet the sun, her iridescent green scales shimmering in the sunlight.

Beetle, Milo and the Wizards walked the Dragon Boat along the narrow confines of the Cut and guided her out into the Moat. Jenna, Nicko and Septimus looked at one another, remembering the night—so long ago now—that they had brought her there, wounded and dying.

"I never thought we'd all be here again. Like this," said Nicko.

"I did," said Jenna. "I knew we would. One day."

While the Wizard escort made their way out of the boatyard, the Dragon Boat floated out into the middle of the Moat. She was watched in awe not only by Beetle, Milo and Eustace Bott, but also by a small boy in an attic window above the Castle Wall. Even Jannit Maarten looked mildly impressed as the dragon's magnificent wings—neatly folded along the hull—began to move slowly upward and unfurl until they were spread so wide the wing tips touched both banks of the Moat.

"Ready?" Septimus called down to his crew.

"Aye," said Nicko, lapsing into sailor-speak.

"Ready!" called Jenna.

"Septimus! Septimus!" a shout came from the boatyard.

"Wait," said Septimus. "There's Rose."

Breathless, Rose reached the edge of the Cut. "I've"—*puff, puff*—"got something for you. From Marcia. Here!" She waved her arm.

"Chuck it over, then," said Nicko.

Rose shook her head. "I'm a really bad shot," she called. "It might fall in the water."

"I can row you out," Eustace offered. "I got my boat." He pointed to a small rowboat tied up to the bank.

"Oh Eustace, you're a star!" said Rose.

Eustace blushed. No one had ever called him a star before. A few minutes later Rose was standing on tiptoe, leaning against the smooth, burnished gold of the Dragon Boat's hull, and Septimus was stretching down to take a small velvet **Charm** bag, in which he knew was the **Flyte Charm.**

"She's such a beautiful boat," said Rose shyly. "Does she really fly too?"

"Like a bird," said Septimus.

"Wow . . ." Rose breathed. "That is just so . . . wow."

"Are we going or what?" demanded Nicko.

"Oh, sorry, I'll get out of your way," said Rose.

"You're not in our way," said Septimus, reluctant to see Rose go.

"Oh, but I am. Good luck. I'll be thinking of you."

"Yeah. Me too."

"Oh, for goodness' sake," said Nicko. "Get the girl on board and stop fussing."

"Gosh!" said Rose. "I *wish*. But . . ."

"Marcia would have a fit," Septimus finished for her.

"Yes, she would." Rose smiled. "Well, safe journey."

The Dragon Boat got ready for takeoff. She pushed down the tip of her tail and stretched out her neck as though reaching for something far away, and then with a loud *thwoosh* her wings came down, sending water splashing onto the banks and Eustace Bott's boat rocking. She began to move down the long, straight section of the Moat in front of the boatyard, slow at first but soon picking up speed. Seven wingbeats later Nicko felt the *thrum* of the water running below the hull disappear and he suddenly remembered how disturbing it felt to be in a boat that flew.

Septimus, however, felt utterly at home. He was surprised how much flying the Dragon Boat felt like flying Spit Fyre. Confidently, he pushed the tiller away from him, wheeling the creature up above the Castle walls. A continuing gentle pressure on the tiller brought the Dragon Boat around once more above the boatyard where Beetle, Milo and Eustace Bott waved. Jannit, however, stood impassive, arms folded, not at all pleased to see her Senior Apprentice going absent without leave—although she was more than pleased to see that *that wretched dragon* was going too.

As the Dragon Boat flew high up above the Castle, Spit Fyre—like the dutiful son he was—followed her. But Septimus had yet to realize that Spit Fyre was coming too. All the Dragon Boat's passengers had eyes for was what they could see far below: the Wizard escort now gathered outside the Manuscriptorium around the bodies of Ernold and Edmund Heap.

⁺⁺39⁺⁺
INTRUDERS

Simon *was home for an* early lunch when he and Lucy—like the rest of the Castle—had received the **Alert**. Every house that had accepted the **Alert** system now possessed a small luminescent box beside their front door, which normally glowed a dull green. When this was **Activated** by the Wizard Tower, the box turned a brilliant red (or yellow for practice drills). The door of the box then flew open and released the

Lert—which looked like a large red hornet—which proceeded to buzz noisily through the house and **Alert** everyone there. Lucy hated the **Lert**.

"Argh, get it off me!" she yelled, batting it away as it circled her head.

"Just keep still, Lu," said Simon. "It will go away in a minute and look for someone else." Sure enough, the **Lert** suddenly switched its attentions to Simon, sending him running back to the door to thump the **Alert Off** button. The **Lert** zoomed back into its box, Simon clicked the little door shut and raced back to the kitchen.

"It's a bit much doing another drill so soon after last night," Lucy grumbled as she fished two boiled eggs out of a pan. Then she noticed Simon's expression. "Si . . . what's the matter?"

"Lu, it's not a drill."

"It's *not*?"

"Nope. The panel isn't yellow—it's red."

Lucy jumped to her feet. "What's going on?"

"I dunno, Lu. But I have to go and warn Marcellus. He won't know a thing about this."

Lucy was horrified. "Simon, no!"

"I'll be fine. I'm quite good at looking after myself, you know."

Lucy sighed. One look at Simon told her she could not stop him. "Oh, Si, be careful."

Simon took a heavy gold **SafeCharm** from his pocket—the strongest one he possessed. "Lu, keep hold of this *all the time.* I will put a **Bar** on the house when I go. Love you." Simon gave Lucy a quick kiss and hurried off before she could make him change his mind.

Marcellus was blissfully untroubled by any **Lerts**. Now that the **Fyre** was at full strength, he was terrified that it might reveal a new weakness in the Cauldron so, in addition to his regular tapping, he had begun to do visual inspections. In the old days his Drummins had done this, running across the Cauldron like lizards on a hot rock, their suckered fingers and toes taking them wherever they wanted to go, their sharp eyes seeing every detail. But Marcellus had to do it the slow, human way—with spectacles, a ladder and a **Fyre** Globe.

This morning, Marcellus had dispensed with the ladder and was inspecting underneath the Cauldron. Spectacles firmly clamped onto his nose, he looked up at the circle of light that the **Fyre** Globe cast onto the Cauldron's smooth iron surface. Suddenly something caught his eye—a small, lighter-colored circle of metal from which a starburst of skillfully repaired cracks radiated out. Marcellus peered through his **Enlarging Glass** at the tiny circle. He smiled; it was a typical Drummin repair: a little plug of iron surrounded by a ring of brass solder that glinted red in the light. He ran his fingers lightly over its surface but felt nothing—it was smoothed flat, blended in perfectly with the surrounding darker metal. It was a beautiful piece of craftsmanship. But Marcellus was puzzled. He peered again at the little circle at the center of its web, wondering what could have caused it. It looked almost like a bullet hole, he thought. It was very odd. And then it struck Marcellus—*this* was the damage that had caused the Great Alchemie Disaster. The sudden certainty took his breath away, and a thousand questions raced through his mind with no hope of an answer. How he would love to be able to ask old Duglius Drummin what had happened. A great wave of sadness washed over Marcellus and he leaned against the rock, taken aback by how very alone he felt without the Drummins.

Suddenly, Marcellus heard the *claaaang* of the lower **Fyre** hatch closing and the distinct sound of *two* sets of heavy footsteps on the top platform. Marcellus was not particularly sensitive to atmosphere, but in his **Fyre** Chamber his instincts were heightened. And right then his instincts were telling him *keep out of the way.* Marcellus shrank back into the shadows beneath the Cauldron, wondering *who was it?* He supposed it was possible that in some kind of emergency Simon had brought Septimus with him. Or even Marcia. But there was something about the footsteps that did not sound like Simon or Septimus—and they certainly did not sound like Marcia. Marcellus realized that for the first time in his life he actually *wanted* to hear the tippy-tappy sound of Marcia Overstrand's pointy purple pythons. Things, he thought, must be bad.

Marcellus listened to the protesting squeaks of the ladder as the intruders began to climb down. After what felt like an eternity listening to each step getting closer, a clang reverberating above his head told Marcellus that the intruders had reached the Viewing Station.

Marcellus decided to risk a quick look. Silently, he slipped out from the protection of the Cauldron and looked up. Some thirty feet above, silhouetted against the red light, Marcellus saw a nightmare—two impossibly tall figures wearing cloaks of what he could only describe as dark light, moving and shifting, so that it was impossible to see any boundaries in their form. And beneath the cloaks Marcellus caught a glimpse of iridescent green armor, segmented like the carapace of a giant insect. Like two passengers on a ship, gazing at the sunset, the figures stared down at the brilliant circle of **Fyre**.

Marcellus experienced another Time Slip. Back to a time a few weeks before the Great Alchemie Disaster, when Julius Pike had brought a visiting Wizard to see the **Fyre** without asking his permission, and he had spotted them from pretty much where he was standing now. It was such a strong feeling that Marcellus was on the verge of yelling, *Julius—what do you think you are doing*, just as he had done before, when one of the figures stepped back and Marcellus saw the green glow of his face and the searing glance of his brilliant green eyes.

The Time Slip vanished.

Up until that moment, Marcellus had not believed in evil. During his long life he had come across many variations of being bad: lies, treachery, deceit, violence and just plain nastiness, and he would be the first to admit that he had probably been guilty of a few himself. But "evil" had undertones of the supernatural that Marcellus found hard to accept. But no longer. He *knew* he was in the presence of evil. And he knew why—*these were the Ring Wizards.*

Marcellus sank to the ground, and there he sat on the dusty earth, trying to figure out what had happened, while all kinds of terrible thoughts went through his mind. Marcellus put his head in his hands. It was all over now. Everything he had worked for was finished. He slumped down in despair and *something tapped him on the top of his head.*

How Marcellus managed not to scream was a mystery to him. Maybe, he thought later, he had recognized the soft, slightly apologetic touch. Whatever the reason, Marcellus leaped up and swung around to find himself face-to-face—with Duglius Drummin.

⇸40⇷
KEEPERS

Head held high, the Dragon Boat flew quickly away from the Castle, the gilding on her hull shimmering in the sunlight. As her huge, leathery wings beat slowly *up-and-down-and-up-and-down,* creaking a little with the unaccustomed effort, she took a direct path out across the river and over the orchards of the lower Farmlands, pink with late apple blossoms. She was followed by a smaller, greener, leaner dragon who was flying his fastest to keep pace with her.

"Spit Fyre, go home!" Septimus yelled.

Keeping his hand on the tiller, Septimus looked back, past the great scaly tail of the Dragon Boat and its golden tip to his dragon, who followed like a faithful dog.

"Spit Fyre coming too?" asked Nicko.

"No," said Septimus. "He's not."

"That's not what *he* seems to think," Nicko observed.

Septimus was not pleased. "Spit Fyre! *Go home!*" he shouted again.

But Spit Fyre appeared to hear nothing—although Septimus suspected he heard perfectly well. His dragon wore the smug look that showed that he knew had gotten the better of his Master.

"Bother," said Septimus. "He can't come with us. He won't be able to keep up."

Jenna had not noticed Spit Fyre. She sat in the prow of the Dragon Boat, looking back at the Castle—a perfect golden circle surrounded by blue and green—and tried to shake off the feeling that she was deserting the Castle just when it needed her.

Septimus caught Jenna's eye and smiled encouragingly. He

remembered the last time they had flown together, when they were being pursued by Simon, and he thought of how different everything was now—and yet not completely different. The Two-Faced Ring was the last link of the chain of **Darkenesse** that led back to DomDaniel, and Septimus was determined to break it. Jenna returned Septimus's smile and leaned against the Dragon Boat's neck. The sunlight glinted off her gold circlet and her long dark hair streamed out behind her. Septimus had a sudden sense that he would remember this moment forever.

Nicko, however, was less inclined to remember the moment. To his embarrassment, he was feeling sick. He couldn't believe it—he was never seasick. But there was something very unsettling about the constant *up-and-down-and-up-and-down* motion of the Dragon Boat that bore no relation to anything sensible like waves. Queasily, Nicko stared over the side and concentrated on the world in miniature as it passed far below, hoping that would make the sickness go. Soon he saw the fine silver line of Deppen Ditch and the hazy green flatness of the Marram Marshes beyond, peppered with little round islets rising out of the mist.

Jenna made her way along the deck toward Septimus.

"Sep . . . you know . . . Uncle Eddie and Uncle Ern . . ."

"Yes," Septimus said quietly.

"Well, do you remember how Aunt Zelda got Merrin back from being **Consumed**?"

"Pity she ever did," growled Nicko.

"Yes . . . well, maybe she could do the same for them."

"Maybe." Septimus looked down at the Marshes below. Somewhere among the mist lay Aunt Zelda's island—but where?

"The Dragon Boat knows how to find Aunt Zelda," said Jenna. "It wouldn't take long. *And it's their only chance.*"

"You're right," said Septimus. He looked back at Spit Fyre. "Besides, I have a package to drop off. A great big green one."

Wolf Boy was standing by a large and very gloopy patch of mud, trying to persuade the Boggart to collect some Marsh Bane.

"I don't go out fer Marsh Bane in the day," the Boggart was saying. "Not anymore. If yer so set on it, you can come back an' ask at midnight."

"But you're never here at midnight," Wolf Boy was saying.

"I *is*."

"Not when *I* come to see *you*, you're not—*hey!*"

"No need ter shout," complained the Boggart—but to thin air.

Wolf Boy was running back to the cottage, yelling, "Zelda! Zelda! The Dragon Boat—*the Dragon Boat is coming!*"

Aunt Zelda came to the door, her face flushed from boiling a mixture of eels and a fresh crop of Bogle Bugs. Stunned, she watched the Dragon Boat and her faithful follower cruise low over the island, circle twice and swoop in to land on the Mott—the wide Marsh ditch that encircled the cottage.

Aunt Zelda was so shocked that she could do no more than shake her head in disbelief and stare at the great plumes of muddy water that arched into the air as the Dragon Boat hit the Mott. When Aunt Zelda wiped the spray from her eyes, she saw her beautiful Dragon Boat furl her wings and settle into the Mott, and it seemed to her as though the Dragon Boat had never been away. There was a sudden flash of red against the gold of the hull, and Aunt Zelda saw Jenna leap down and run up the path toward her.

"Aunt Zelda!" yelled Jenna.

"Hmm?" said Aunt Zelda, still transfixed by the sight of the Dragon Boat.

"Aunt Zelda," Jenna said urgently, grabbing both of Aunt Zelda's somewhat sticky hands. "Please, listen. *Please.* This is *very* important."

Aunt Zelda did not react.

"Give Zelda a moment," said Wolf Boy. "She's had a shock."

Jenna waited impatiently while Aunt Zelda, her eyes full of tears, gazed at the Dragon Boat. Suddenly Aunt Zelda shook her head, wiped her hands on her dress and turned to look at Jenna. "Yes, dear?"

Quickly, Jenna launched into her story before Aunt Zelda's attention wandered. She made it fast and simple and soon came to the end. "So you see, Aunt Zelda, your nephews, Ern and Eddie. They *so* need your help."

Aunt Zelda said nothing.

Wolf Boy prompted her, "You'll need Drastic Drops, Urgent Unguent and your modified Vigour Volts. Won't you, Zelda?"

Aunt Zelda sighed.

Jenna was beginning to despair when suddenly Aunt Zelda looked at her with the old, wise gaze that Jenna had missed so much. "Jenna dear. My memory is going. My powers are weakening. I know that I would not be able to bring my very silly but—by the sound of it—brave nephews back to this world."

"Aunt Zelda, you can. *Please.*"

Aunt Zelda shook her head. "I can't." She turned to Wolf Boy. "But I know someone who can."

It was Wolf Boy's turn to shake his head. "No, Zelda. That's a Keeper's skill."

"It is indeed a Keeper's skill. Which is why, Wolf Boy—or I think I should call you Marwick now—I am giving you this." From her pocket, Aunt Zelda took a small silver chain, made with delicate triple links. "It's the Keeper's chain. It got a little tight for me last year and I took it off. I knew then that my Keeping Time was drawing to a close. But it will fit you perfectly, Marwick dear."

Wolf Boy was shocked. "No, Zelda!"

"*Yes,* Marwick. Soon I will forget where the Keeper's chain is and then I will forget even what it is. You must take the chain now, while I still understand what it is I am giving you." Aunt Zelda smiled at Septimus and Nicko, who had come up the path to join them, leaving Spit Fyre sitting beside the Dragon Boat. "You see, now we have everyone we need for a handover. We have the Queen—well, as near as makes no difference—and the representative of the ExtraOrdinary Wizard as witnesses. All I need now is the permission of the Queen."

Jenna knew what to say. "Keeper, I give it."

"Your Grace, I also give it," Aunt Zelda replied. She handed the chain to Jenna, who had to stand on tiptoe to fasten it around Wolf Boy's rather grubby neck.

"Gosh," said Wolf Boy. He touched the delicate chain and the echoes of all those who had worn it before ran through his fingers.

From another pocket, deep in her faded patchwork dress, Aunt Zelda took a bunch of keys, all different shapes and sizes, and handed it to Wolf Boy. "You will be a good Keeper, Marwick," she said.

"Thank you, Zelda," said Wolf Boy. He looked around at his friends and shook his head in disbelief. "Wow. Hey. Well, I'd better get on. Got work to do. Uncles to fix. *And fast.*"

Aunt Zelda hugged Wolf Boy hard. "And you will do it, Marwick. I know you will . . ." Her voice trembled for a moment, then she swallowed hard and said brightly, "Well, now. You don't want me hanging around getting in the way. I shall go and talk to the Dragon Boat."

Wolf Boy, Jenna, Nicko and Septimus watched Aunt Zelda walk away down the path to the Mott.

"Oh, dear," said Jenna. She took out a red silk handkerchief and blew her nose.

"Yeah . . ." said Wolf Boy. He looked at his friends. "I'll do my best, I promise. I'd better go now. Get there as quick as I can."

"Good luck, Marwick!" Jenna called out.

Wolf Boy raised his hand in acknowledgment and disappeared into the shadows of the cottage.

Jenna, Septimus and Nicko walked slowly down the path. The Dragon Boat lay still and majestic in the water, her head dipped down to Aunt Zelda, who was stroking the dragon's soft, velvety nose. Spit Fyre watched. He looked, thought Septimus, a trifle jealous.

Aunt Zelda gave the dragon a last affectionate pat and stepped away. "Well, dears, you had better be off. I must say the Dragon Boat looks beautiful. You have cared for her very well."

Jenna looked at Septimus as if to check something out with him. He nodded.

"Aunt Zelda," Jenna said. "Would you like to come with us in the Dragon Boat?"

Aunt Zelda shook her head sadly. "I can't leave the cottage empty. We have an awful Marsh Brownie problem at the moment. They'll be in as soon as I'm gone. They'll eat *everything.*" She looked regretfully at the Dragon Boat. "Oh, but I would have *so* loved to."

Five minutes later a reluctant Spit Fyre was outside Keeper's Cottage. "Spit Fyre, I declare you official Dragon Guardian of Keeper's Cottage," Septimus told him. "Do not let a Marsh Brownie—or any other Marsh creature—within ten yards of Keeper's Cottage until Aunt Zelda returns. Understood?"

Spit Fyre thumped his tail crossly. He understood all right—he had been outmaneuvered. He began his first Dragon Guardian circuit of the cottage and wondered what Marsh Brownies tasted like. He intended to eat as many as he could.

In a great spray of muddy Marsh water, the Dragon Boat took off from the Mott. Septimus wheeled the Dragon Boat around the cottage to check up on Spit Fyre and then they flew out across the Marshes, heading for the dunes and the sparkling sea beyond. Aunt Zelda sat up at the prow with Jenna, her hand resting on the smooth scales of the dragon's neck. She smiled contentedly, gazing out into a distant future that only she could see.

41
DEEP TROUBLE

Down in the Deeps, behind the Cauldron, Marcellus was squashed into a Drummin burrow. The rock face of the Fyre Chamber was peppered with entrances that led to a hidden city—a complex system of chambers and branching tunnels shaped like a hollowed-out tree within the rock. The main trunk was a wide, winding thoroughfare, big enough for even a human to clamber up, and from this branched many smaller tunnels. These were the Drummin public spaces, lit by GloGrubs, with the larger chambers lit by tiny Globes of Everlasting Fyre. The smaller tunnels led to groups of private chambers (which the Drummins called nests) where they slept. These were arranged in clusters branching off a central passage, and although Drummins preferred not to share a nest, the clusters were sociable affairs and often occupied by groups of friends who had grown up together.

Marcellus was in the largest public chamber of all, one that he could actually sit up in. Beside him squatted the compact figure of Duglius Drummin. Like all Drummins, Duglius was hard to spot unless you knew he was there. Drummins had a look of the earth about them. Their long hair was plaited and knotted into thick ropes, which were smeared with earth. Their chalk-white skin, which had never seen daylight, was covered with a fine dust from the rock, and their broad fingers and toes—which ended in fat, squashy suckers that allowed them to swarm across both rock and Cauldron alike—were grimy with dirt. If there was one word that could be used to describe a Drummin, it was "grubby." But from the grime and dirt two big, round black eyes, bright and questioning, took in every detail of Marcellus Pye. From the moment he had tapped his old Master on the shoulder, Duglius Drummin had not stopped smiling—so broadly that Marcellus could see the Drummin's tiny yellow teeth.

Marcellus and Duglius were conversing in the sign language the Drummins preferred to use. Duglius was telling Marcellus, *Julius Pike, he did drag you away so roughly that we thought he would do away with you. Most sorrowful were we as we made all safe and repaired the breach that caused the* **Fyre** *and then did set all ready for when the* **Fyre** *might begin once more. Ah, Alchemist, it were terrible cold by then and we was horrible slow. But we got back to our nests in time for to catch the last bit of rock warmth—enough to make our cocoons.*"

Cocoons? signed Marcellus.

Aye. To sleep the long sleep.

I did not know.

Duglius winked at Marcellus. *We Drummins must have our secrets too, Alchemist,* he signed. *The cold is our lullaby, the warmth of the* **Fyre** *our morning sun.*

Marcellus had forgotten the lyrical lilt of Drummin talk, which spilled over into their signing so that their hands seemed to dance as the words tumbled out. He relaxed, forgetting the danger for a moment. He was back home with his family and together they could work something out.

A little later Marcellus was not so optimistic. He had crawled out of the burrow only to be confronted by a frighteningly bright red glow filling the cavern. The light sparkled off the ancient twisted metal embedded in the rock so that the vaulted roof of the cavern seemed to be covered in the shining silvery web of a giant crazed spider. The air seemed to crackle and spark as Marcellus breathed it in, and it left the taste of metal on the tip of his tongue. Suddenly another Time Slip took him back to the very beginning of the Great Alchemie Disaster. *This was how the air tasted then.*

Fighting back panic, Marcellus dropped down into the shadows below the Cauldron. The heat was oppressive; already the sweat was pouring down his brow and his woolen robes hung heavy and hot. Marcellus crept stealthily under the round belly of the Cauldron. Tortoiselike and purposeful, he moved out from the protection of the Cauldron until he saw the massive shadows of Shamandrigger Saarn and Dramindonnor Naarn cast onto the opposite wall of the cavern. Marcellus watched them for some minutes, but they were motionless and gave no clue as to what they were doing. A slight movement behind him caught his eye and Marcellus's heart raced with fear. Very slowly he turned around only to see a line of Drummins looking up at him, their black eyes wide in the darkness, seeing far more than he could ever see. Marcellus smiled—he had forgotten the Drummins' habit of following him around. He signaled that they should stay where they were and, determined to see what was happening, he began to move slowly out from the protection of the Cauldron.

And then Marcellus saw them—high above on the Inspection Walkway, directing pencil-thin beams of red light onto the top of the **Fyre**, the intruders were walking slowly around the Cauldron, as though they were stirring a huge pot of broth. Marcellus saw the Alchemical blue flames leaping up to meet them, like fish jumping for bugs, and he knew what was happening—slowly but surely, the **Fyre** was being **Accelerated**.

Alchemical **Fyre** has many contradictions—one of these being that, unlike normal fire, the addition of coal will calm and contain it. Like a lion rendered drowsy by devouring a small antelope, Alchemical **Fyre** will be soothed by a blanket of coal.

Marcellus knew he must act fast. Hidden in the roof of the **Fyre** Chamber was a huge hopper of cannel coal, but the levers to release it were in the control room—and the only way for him to get there was in full view of the Wizards. He decided to make a run for it—but to give himself a chance first he needed to take off his shoes.

The movement caught the eye of Shamandrigger Saarn. Rapier blades of red light left the **Fyre** and swung down across the floor, searching. Marcellus froze, balancing on one leg like a stork. Methodically, the rays swept across the floor, back and forth, back and forth, getting ever closer to Marcellus. He closed his eyes and waited for the inevitable.

Therunnk. The sound of the **Fyre** hatch opening echoed through the cavern. The red beams swung upward. Marcellus opened his eyes. He saw Simon drop down, stop, and then shoot back up the ladder like a rat up a drainpipe. Simon was very nearly through the hatch when one of the beams caught his rapidly exiting boot and sliced into it. Marcellus heard a scream and then the *claaaang* of the **Fyre** hatch slamming shut.

Marcellus sank back into the shadows, shocked. *Had Simon gotten out?* More to the point, had *all* of Simon gotten out? Or was his foot still lying on the Upper Platform? No, Marcellus told himself sternly, he must not think like that. He must believe that not only had Simon gotten out, but that he was on his way to Marcia to warn her what was happening. Because now, after Duglius had told him the truth of what caused the Great Alchemie Disaster, Marcellus wanted Marcia to know *everything.*

Simon's experience at the hands of the Ring Wizards had made Marcellus realize that he had no chance of getting to the Control Room alive. But the Drummins just might.

Back in the Drummin burrow, Marcellus sat with Duglius and his deputy, Perius.

Duglius, Marcellus signed. *I am going to get help.*

Duglius looked doubtful. He didn't see what help Marcellus could get. But it was not his job to question the Alchemist. He merely signed: *What can we do, Alchemist?*

Marcellus had it planned. *One set*—this was what working parties of Drummins called themselves—*to go to the control room, where they must let down the coal to protect the* **Fyre** *rods. One set each to the water inlet and to the outlet to keep the water flowing. All sets on call to replace any sets, er . . .*

Destroyed, signed Duglius, matter-of-factly.

Yes. Unfortunately that will be necessary, signed Marcellus. "And now, Duglius, I shall take the Drummin way out."

Duglius looked at his Master critically. "You won't fit," he said.

"I will have to fit," said Marcellus.

Like a blindworm, Marcellus crawled up through the main Drummin way—the large burrow that ran up inside the rock like the hollowed-out trunk of a tree. There was not much space for a six-foot-tall Alchemist who had recently been eating too many potatoes.

Marcellus saw the way winding ahead, speckled with tiny wriggling lights, the GloGrubs that had colonized the burrows thousands of years in the past. The trunk went up at a slope that was gentle for a Drummin but fiendishly steep for a human. It was hot and horribly stuffy and, like a Drummin, was coated with a fine dust. The dust made the climb even more difficult—it caused Marcellus to slip and slide and it got into his lungs, making him wheeze and gasp for breath.

But anger drove Marcellus on. Anger at what Duglius Drummin told him he had found beneath the Cauldron after Julius had shut down the **Fyre**. Anger at how he had been misled. But most of all, Marcellus was angry that, because of the deceits of Julius Pike, the Castle had once more been put at risk. And so he scrabbled and scraped his way up through the main burrow, past the tiny branching burrows that led to Drummin nests that until only a few hours ago had been filled with Drummin cocoons.

As he climbed painfully upward, Marcellus noticed that the rock was becoming cooler and he guessed that he was now moving out of the cavern, away from the **Fyre**. The branches leading to the Drummin nests had ceased, and to Marcellus's relief the escape burrow had actually widened. The gradient had also eased and the burrow settled into a series of loops like a huge corkscrew along which Marcellus was now able to crawl rather than climb. Spirits rising by the minute, Marcellus crawled fast, no longer caring about skinning his knees or scraping his fingers or the fact that, with the GloGrubs growing sparse, he was crawling in semidarkness. He was, he was sure, very nearly at the escape hatch that would take him into the lower Ice Tunnel beneath the Great Chamber of Alchemie.

And then disaster struck. As he rounded another turn of the corkscrew, Marcellus crawled at some speed into a rockfall. With the hollow thud of a coconut hitting the ground, Marcellus's head made contact with the rock. A shower of stars exploded in his eyes, he reeled back and collapsed into the dust. And there he lay, eyes closed, blood trickling from a spreading bruise on his forehead.

Far below in the Chamber of **Fyre**, a Drummin set—the third to try—at last reached the Control Room. They swarmed up the wall and swung the first of the bank of levers down. Seconds later, with a thunderous roar, a cascade of coal tumbled down the chute in the roof and fell through the air into the Cauldron. As the rain of soft coal hit the flames, a tremendous *hisssss* filled the Deeps and a great cloud of black dust rose into the air, covering the Ring Wizards and turning their green carapaces a dusty black. Buzzing with anger, like two wasps emerging from hibernating in the ashes of the grate, the Wizards wheeled around searching for victims but found none—a Drummin in a dusty cloud is very nearly invisible. Thwarted, the Wizards swung their red light beams across the blanket of coal that now rested on top of the **Fyre**. With a great *whooomph*, the coal ignited and a sheet of flame leaped into the air. The Wizards were jubilant.

Far below in the sooty dust, the Drummins, too, were happy. As long as the coal burned, the **Fyre** was safe.

Slowly, slowly, the flames from the coal fire began to creep beneath the Castle. They spread through the Vents that Marcellus had so recently opened, warming the rock above and the floors of the older houses. People threw open their windows, complaining of the late afternoon heat, and when the evening clouds came in from the Port, the rain sizzled as it hit the pavement.

Up in **Search** and Rescue, Hildegarde saw the first flame as it licked up through the pavement in front of Terry Tarsal's shop. She raced down to the Great Hall, where Marcia had set up what she called her "command post."

"Fire!" yelled Hildegarde. "Fire, fire, *fire!*"

42
FORYX

While Marcellus lay unconscious in the dark, the Dragon Boat flew into the night—across the sea, over the Isles of Syren where the CattRokk Light shone bright, and on toward the Land of the House of Foryx. Septimus, Nicko and Jenna took turns at the tiller—not to guide the dragon, who knew where she was going, but to keep her company

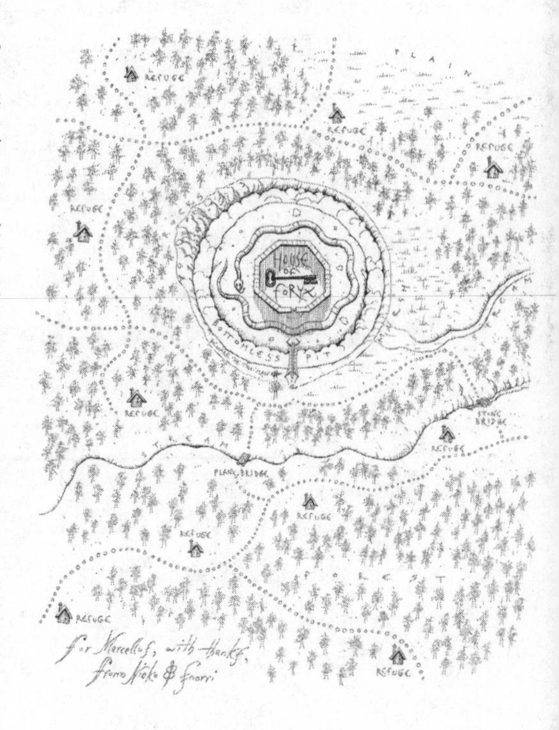

on her journey. The night was calm and clear and the stars glittered like ice crystals spilled across the sky. Lulled by the *up-and-down-and-up-and-down* of the Dragon Boat, Nicko lay on his back staring up at the night until he began to believe he was back at sea, rolling through a storm swell riding in from the ocean.

In the small hours of the morning Septimus saw landfall and took the Dragon Boat down low to see where they were. As they flew over a long sandspit dotted with fishermen's shacks on stilts, Septimus caught sight of a little girl gazing out of a lighted attic window. He waved and the child waved back. She watched the Dragon Boat go on her way, then fell asleep and dreamed of dragons.

The Dragon Boat flew on, above the Trading Post where a necklace of lights showed its line of harbors, across the inlet on which they lay and then over a maze of sandbanks that gave way to marshes, then miles of flatness of drained farmlands. They were now in the Land of the House of Foryx.

While it was still dark back at the Castle—and darker still where Marcellus lay—for those on the Dragon Boat the night began to slip away. Aunt Zelda, who was sitting in the prow with Jenna, who was sleeping curled up under a quilt, saw a thin band of pale green appear on the horizon above the darkness of the nighttime fields.

"We are flying into the sun," Aunt Zelda whispered.

Steadily, *up-and-down-and-up-and-down*, the Dragon Boat flew on. Wrapped in another of Aunt Zelda's quilts, Nicko dozed, while Septimus drowsily held the tiller and watched the land passing below. In the encroaching dawn he saw the shapes of scattered farmhouses dark against the land and the glow of the occasional lonely light as people began to wake and go about their early-morning tasks.

The band of pale green spread slowly across the sky and washed into a dull yellow. Far below the shining band of a river wound through a patchwork of fields dusted with snow. Jenna woke and yawned. She felt stiff and cold but the sight of the lightening sky ahead, which was now taking on a delicate pink hue, revived her. She became aware of Nicko moving around the deck and turned to blearily say good morning.

Nicko was advancing with two mugs in one hand, holding on to the gunwales with the other. "Morning, sleepyhead," he said. "Drinkies."

He passed Jenna and Aunt Zelda mugs of hot chocolate.

"Wow, Nik, thanks."

"You can thank Sep. He's got some new gizmo in that bag of his."

"A *hot*-chocolate Charm?" Jenna smiled.

"Yep. Each in its own mug. Neat, hey?"

"Thanks, Sep," Jenna called down the boat.

"S'okay, Jen. Hey, I can see the forest now!"

Jenna looked down and saw that the landscape was changing fast. The dusting of snow had become a continuous blanket of white that showed dark lines of tracks winding through large expanses of trees. As she watched, the treetops grew closer and closer together and the tracks disappeared, hidden beneath the canopy of white.

Like the forest beneath them, the Dragon Boat's crew fell silent. The steady *swoosh-whoosh* of the wingbeats was the only sound as the dragon flew onward until all that could be seen below was a featureless sea of snowy treetops stretching out to the wide horizon. On and on they flew, gazing down at the trees, until they lost their sense of direction and even Septimus began to wonder if the Dragon Boat was flying around in circles.

All traces of pink were gone from the sky when the crew sensed a change in the Dragon Boat's flight. The wings began to slow to a *swoosh-oooosh-whoosh*, the dragon's neck dipped and Jenna saw her emerald eyes scanning ahead.

A sudden flash of sunlight from a gap in the clouds lit up a fragile silver arc strung high above the trees, making it sparkle like a giant, dew-drizzled spiderweb—and the bridge to the House of Foryx was revealed. Even Septimus, who had terrifying memories of crossing the bridge, was taken aback by how beautiful it looked. A few seconds later the sun slipped behind the clouds and the bridge was gone, blending once more into the white skies. The Dragon Boat leaned sharply into a turn and headed downward.

And then, suddenly, the House of Foryx was there. Stark-black against the snow, a great fortress of granite, it sat in solitary splendor on a pillar of rock encircled by a deep and dark abyss. Its four huge octagonal towers, which surrounded an even larger octagonal core, reared up into the white sky, and above them wheeled a murder of crows, cawing at the morning.

"Oh, dear," whispered Aunt Zelda.

Nicko slid along the deck and came to sit next to Aunt Zelda. She put her arm around him and wrapped him in her quilt. Nicko, who did not like to be "fussed," as he called it, did not resist. Together he, Aunt Zelda and Jenna watched the House of Foryx draw closer.

Nicko shivered. What really spooked him was not the building—it was the knowledge that inside the fortress below, where Time did not exist, there were so many people, their lives suspended while they waited to go back out once more to their own Times. Just as he and Snorri had once waited . . . and waited . . . and waited. Nicko looked down at the blind windows, covered with a shifting film like oil on water, and wondered which one it was that he and Snorri had spent what had felt like an eternity gazing out from. Suddenly he got up and made his way up the sloping deck to Septimus.

"Sep. Don't go back in there. *Please.*"

"Hey, Nik, it's okay," said Septimus. He pulled the **Questing Stone** out of his pocket and turned it upside down to show Hotep-Ra's hieroglyph underneath it, gold against the black. "See, this is my pass. It means I can come and go as I please. I can always return to my Time. It really *is* okay this time."

Nicko shook his head. "I don't believe it."

"Nik, even if you don't believe the pass will work, it is *still* okay. You and Jenna are here. Aunt Zelda is here. In our Time. If I don't come out, you can ring the bell and ask for me, and then I can walk back out into our Time. You *know* that."

Nicko shook his head again. "You can't trust them."

Septimus knew there was nothing he could say to win Nicko over. He renewed his grip on the tiller and began to guide the Dragon Boat low across the House of Foryx, toward a glass dome in the very center, invisible from below. Unlike the dead windows in the rest of the House of Foryx, a soft yellow light spread up from the dome and glowed in the gray morning air.

Hotep-Ra had become a creature of habit. In a place where Time did not exist, the ancient Wizard had created his own rhythm of time. Every day, to the second, he did the same thing, and often he even thought the same thoughts. The last time his routine had changed had been when a young Apprentice named Septimus Heap had come to see him at the end of his **Queste**. How long ago that had been, Hotep-Ra had no idea. It could have been the previous day. It could have been hundreds of years in the past. In the House of Foryx it made no difference.

That morning, Hotep-Ra's routine and thoughts traveled their usual tracks: he lit a candle, lay back in his chair beneath the dome, gazed up into the white-snow sky and thought about his Dragon Boat. So when Hotep-Ra actually saw the brilliant gold and green of the Dragon Boat fly overhead, he was not at first surprised. It was only after her second pass that Hotep-Ra realized that his Dragon Boat actually *was* outside. In what Time she was, he did not know. But she had come for him, as he had known one day she would.

Hotep-Ra got out of his chair and said to his Apprentice, Talmar Ray Bell, "I am just going outside. I may be some time."

Talmar looked horrified. "Don't say that!"

Hotep-Ra smiled at his Apprentice. "Why ever not?"

"It's bad luck," she said. "Someone said it once and never came back."

"I'll be back," said Hotep-Ra.

"Someone said *that* once too."

The Dragon Boat was coming in to land. She knew where she was heading, but her crew did not. Septimus felt the tiller move beneath his hand as the Dragon Boat tipped forward in a steep dive. With her wings outstretched and her tail down like a brake, she dropped down toward the wide, flat marble terrace at the front of the House of Foryx.

"Sep, she can't land there!" Jenna yelled.

All, except for Aunt Zelda, closed their eyes. And so it was only Aunt Zelda who saw a ripple pass across the surface of the marble like wind over silk, and the marble become a lake of milk-white water. The Dragon Boat glided in with practiced ease—for she had landed there many times before. Then she folded her wings and settled down in front of the House of Foryx like a bird on its nest.

Septimus peered over the side—the marble looked solid once more. "It's **Thixotropic**," he said.

"It's *what*?" said Nicko.

"Solid. But goes liquid under pressure."

"Don't we all," said Nicko gloomily.

"Actually, Nik, we *don't*," said Jenna. "And you in particular do not. Don't let this place get to you. You forget that without it you wouldn't be here with us at all."

Nicko nodded. "Yeah. I know. I just want to keep it that way."

"We *all* want to keep it that way, Nik. And we will."

"Time to go," said Septimus. He dropped the gold-and-azure boarding ladder over the side of the boat, and climbed down. Nicko followed. A minute later they were standing on the steps of the House of Foryx, where five hundred years in the past Nicko had once waited with Snorri, and not quite so long ago Septimus had stood with the **Questing Stone** in his hand. Then it had glowed a brilliant red; now it was a deep blue-black with Hotep-Ra's shining gold hieroglyph giving him safe passage back to his own Time. He hoped.

The door to the House of Foryx towered above them. It was a forbidding sight—huge planks of ebony held together with iron bars and massive rivets. The grotesque monsters and bizarre creatures carved into the doorframe stared down at Septimus and Nicko as if daring them to ring the bellpull, which emerged from the mouth of an iron dragon that thrust its head through the granite wall.

Septimus did dare. The sound of the bell clanged distantly and some minutes later, as he expected, a small batlike man wrenched the door open.

"*Yeeeeeeeeeeeeeeeees?*" said the man.

Septimus knew how argumentative the little man could be and he got in fast. "I have come to see Hotep-Ra. I have a pass." He showed the man the **Questing Stone**, hieroglyph side up. The doorman peered at the stone and Septimus braced himself, expecting trouble—which he got.

"I have never seen one of these before," said the doorman suspiciously.

"You won't have," said Septimus. "This is the only one."

"*Weally?* You will have to show it to the Guardian." The little man looked at Nicko. "I suppose you want to come in too," he said, sounding annoyed.

"No *way*," Nicko replied.

The shortsighted doorman peered at Nicko more closely and a flicker of recognition passed over his face. Suddenly his little wiry arm shot out and grasped Nicko around the wrist. "I wecognise you! You have Time to serve!" And with a strength unnatural for his size, he pulled Nicko across the threshold.

In the Dragon Boat, Jenna watched, horrified, as Nicko disappeared into the shadows of the House of Foryx. She saw Septimus dive in after him and the door slam. They were gone.

Jenna knew she had to get Nicko out. "Aunt Zelda," she said, "I'm going after them."

"Be careful, dear," said Aunt Zelda. "It doesn't look very nice in there."

"It's not. Now, Aunt Zelda, this is really, *really* important.

If I get pulled in too you have to come and ring the bell. But you must *not* come inside. Just keep ringing the bell until we come out. Okay?"

Aunt Zelda looked confused. "All right, dear. But why don't I go in?"

"It's dangerous, Aunt Zelda. You mustn't."

"It doesn't seem right, dear, me staying outside when it's dangerous in there. You might need help."

"No, we won't need help—well, not like that. The only help we need is for you to stay outside. Here. In this Time."

Aunt Zelda frowned, trying to work it out. "All right, dear, I'll wait. This time."

With a horrible feeling she had made Aunt Zelda even more confused, Jenna climbed out of the Dragon Boat, walked across the expanse of white and went up the steps to the door. Then she took a deep breath and tugged on the bellpull.

The door opened.

To her great relief, there stood Nicko with Septimus, holding out his **Questing Stone** with a big smile. "See, it worked, Jen. It will always bring me out in my own Time. And it set Nicko free too."

Nicko grimaced. The **Questing Stone** had indeed set him

free, but not before he had been imprisoned—for how long he did not know. He quickly stepped into his own Time and enveloped Jenna in a hug.

Jenna was so shocked by Nicko's haunted look that she did not notice the tall old man who stood in the shadows behind him. But when he stepped out of the House of Foryx—for the first time in many thousands of years—and Jenna saw the ancient ExtraOrdinary Wizard robes embroidered with **Magykal** symbols and the formal ExtraOrdinary Wizard headband around his long white hair, she knew who he was.

"Hotep-Ra!"

"Princess," he replied in a surprisingly deep voice—and a very odd accent—and bowed his head. A few snowflakes drifted down and settled on his white hair; Hotep-Ra looked up, as if surprised by the touch of the snow. It was then that he saw the Dragon Boat waiting for him. He caught his breath and then set off across the white marble terrace, his long purple staff clicking as he went.

Jenna, Nicko and Septimus followed at a respectful distance.

"Been waiting long?" Nicko asked Jenna nonchalantly, as though she had been hanging around for the Port barge.

"Five minutes maybe," said Jenna.

Septimus and Nicko exchanged glances. "See," said Septimus. "I told you so."

They stood quietly by, not wishing to disturb the reunion. They saw the dragon turn to look at her old Master and arch her neck down to greet him. They saw Hotep-Ra put his hand on the dragon's velvety nose and a silver streak ran down from the dragon's eye. It dropped onto the ground and rolled toward Jenna. She picked it up and held it in the palm of her hand: a dragon tear of pure silver.

There was something that Septimus knew he must do. He took off his Dragon Ring and offered it to Hotep-Ra. "This belongs to you," he said.

Solemnly, Hotep-Ra took the Dragon Ring. "Thank you," he said. "But it shall be yours again before very long, I promise you." Septimus felt strange as he watched Hotep-Ra place the ring on his right index finger and he saw the emerald eye of the ring dragon glow and the ring adjust itself to fit its old Master's finger.

Hotep-Ra climbed aboard and fussed about—as someone who has not been aboard their boat for a few thousand years will do. He invited Aunt Zelda to sit beside him at the tiller and called to Jenna.

"Princess, I believe we have a **Committal** to look at."

Jenna climbed aboard. She took out her tattered copy of *The Queen Rules* and passed it to Hotep-Ra, open at the page where she had written the **Committal**.

Hotep-Ra looked shocked. "This book was beautiful once," he said.

Jenna felt responsible. "I'm really sorry."

Hotep-Ra got out his **Enlarging Glass** and peered at Jenna's handwriting. "The **Keystone** is missing," he said. "This can never work."

Jenna got her best pen out of her pocket. "If you tell me the **Keystone**, I'll write it down," she said.

"Princess," said Hotep-Ra, "let me explain. I was not one of those lazy Wizards who always used the same **Keystone**. I had a different one for every one of my twenty-one major **Incantations**." He sighed. "Unfortunately it is a long, long time ago and I cannot remember which one I used."

Jenna was aghast. "Don't you have it written down?"

"Apprentice, please explain," Hotep-Ra said to Septimus. "We must go."

While Hotep-Ra took the Dragon Boat up into the sky,

Septimus told Jenna, "You see, Jen, Hotep-Ra inscribed his **Incantations** into the pyramid on top of the Wizard Tower. He wanted them to last forever and it was a way of making them incorruptible."

"But Sep, you told me that those hieroglyphs are—what was it? Gobbledygook, you said."

"They are," said Septimus. "That is the whole point—they are a blind. To call up the real ones we need to use the **Keye**."

"*What key?*"

"Well . . ."

Jenna sighed. "I suppose we don't have that, either."

"Um, not right now, no. The **Keye** is actually the very tip of the pyramid. When your ancestor was busy shooting those Ring Wizards, they got so mad that they sliced off the top of the pyramid and **Shrank** it."

"Why would they do that?" asked Jenna, thinking that sometimes she did not understand Wizard behavior at all.

"Well, actually it was meant to happen to Hotep-Ra but he outwitted them."

"So where is this top bit key-thingy?"

"Hotep-Ra gave it to the Queen."

"So, what did *she* do with it?"

Septimus looked to Hotep-Ra for help.

"She said she would put it somewhere safe," said Hotep-Ra.

"Oh, *no.*" Jenna groaned. Whenever Sarah lost anything it was always when she had put it "somewhere safe."

"Princess," said Hotep-Ra. "You must go back to the Palace and find the **Keye**."

"But I've never even *seen* it."

"Well, it must be somewhere," said Hotep-Ra.

Jenna had heard that from Sarah too. It did not inspire confidence.

"For speed, I suggest you take the direct route back. Hold tight." With that, Hotep-Ra wheeled his Dragon Boat around and dived into the abyss.

43
ROCKY TIMES

Marcellus opened his eyes and saw nothing. He tried to sit up and hit his head. Marcellus groaned. *Where was he?*

And then he remembered. He remembered the Ring Wizards down in his precious Fyre Chamber, trying to destroy his delicate, beautiful **Fyre**. He remembered his long, painful climb up through the escape burrow, and he remembered that he *had* to get to Marcia and warn her what was happening. But most of all he remembered how angry he was—and why. Spurred on by his fury, Marcellus attacked the rockfall that was blocking his way. His hands found a gap and methodically he began removing each stone and sending it rolling down the burrow behind him.

Down in the Chamber of **Fyre**, with a wall of flames roaring above and the dizzying drop below, Duglius Drummin was drumming the narrow rim of the Cauldron and keeping an anxious watch. The brilliant orange flames from the coal were shooting high into the air, dancing and whirling as they were sucked up into the Vents, feeding on the gases that were drawn up with them. Duglius wore a grim smile. He did not like to see the flames, but he knew that they were a necessary evil. As long as the coal burned on top, the delicate blue flame of the Alchemie **Fyre** below was protected. And in the vast hoppers inside the cavern roof, Duglius knew there was still a large store of coal left.

Duglius continued along the rim—his suckered feet protected by their heat pads—drumming the metal as he went. The Cauldron was still intact but there was a duller sound to the ring of the hammer, which worried him. Something was changing. As Duglius listened yet again to the *cling* of his hammer, out of the heat haze he saw the fearful shapes of the Ring Wizards coming toward him along the Inspection Walkway. Steadfastly, the old Drummin carried on drumming. As he drew near and saw the Ring Wizards' green armor shimmering in the glare, their dark cloaks flying out in the updraft of the flames and their wild eyes shining with excitement, Duglius could not help but hold his breath in fear; but he kept going and passed by with no harm. The Ring Wizards, like all Wizards, treated Drummins as vermin and paid them no attention—although this had not stopped them from destroying two Drummin sets heading for the Control Room for the fun of it. This time, to Duglius's relief, they paid him no attention and he continued safely on his way.

Duglius found his second-in-command, Perius Drummin, waiting for him on the Viewing Station.

There's rockfall a-coming down the escape burrow, Duglius Drummin, Perius signed. *Wish you I do go to see what is to see?*

I shall go to see, Perius Drummin. You will please take over from me.

I will take over from you, Duglius Drummin.

Thank you, Perius Drummin. Please open the Cauldron Heat

Vents to the Ice Tunnels. It is time.

It is time, Duglius Drummin, Perius agreed.

Duglius's climb up the escape burrow was considerably faster than Marcellus's, but it was made more difficult by the rocks that came hurtling down. It was a slightly bruised Duglius who reached Marcellus just as he was clearing the very last rock away. A soft touch on his foot told Marcellus that Duglius was there.

While Duglius was climbing up, the Dragon Boat was flying down—into the abyss. Around and around she went, spiraling down into the depths of the canyon that encircled the House of Foryx. Hotep-Ra stood at the tiller, concentrating hard on keeping the wing tips of his Dragon Boat safely away from the sheer rock of the canyon walls. It would have been a testing task for any pilot, but for one who had not flown for many thousands of years, it was a huge challenge.

No one wanted to distract Hotep-Ra. Jenna, Nicko, Septimus and Aunt Zelda had no choice but to stare silently into the mist, notice how cold it got as they went ever deeper and listen to the screams of whatever-it-was that haunted the abyss. They hoped that Hotep-Ra had a good reason for what he was doing.

At last the Dragon Boat landed with a *swooooosh* and a plume of ice-cold water sprayed into the boat. She settled into the pool of dank water that lay on the floor of the abyss, folded her wings and fastidiously arched her tail out of the water. The emerald green of the dragon's eyes shone through the dusky gloom as she turned her head and looked at Hotep-Ra as if to ask what he thought he was doing coming to such a forsaken place.

Hotep-Ra enlightened neither his dragon nor his crew. He took a pinch of **Sprite Sand** from his pocket and held it in his fist. Then, as though sowing seed, he threw his arm out and a cluster of tiny lights flew up from his hand. The **Sprites** swirled into the air and gathered around Hotep-Ra like a swarm of bees, bathing him in a bright light. Septimus was entranced. He had read about ancient **Lighting Sprites**, whose **Magyk** had been lost long ago. He had thought what a lovely idea they were—little personal spheres of light that followed you around, and he had heard that some **Guiding Sprites** even showed you the way.

Hotep-Ra bowed to Aunt Zelda. "Madam Keeper," he said,

waving away Aunt Zelda's protests that she was no longer Keeper. "Excuse me for a few minutes while I assist these young travelers in their return to the Castle. I trust that you and I will then have a more pleasant journey in the Dragon Boat."

Septimus, Nicko and Jenna frowned at one another. This didn't sound good. Aunt Zelda looked concerned. "But how are they getting to the Castle?" she asked.

"I will explain when I return. I will not be long."

Aunt Zelda gave Jenna, Septimus and Nicko a worried wave as they followed Hotep-Ra and his **Sprites** down the embarking ladder and away into the darkness. The light from the **Sprites** and the splash of their footsteps soon faded and Aunt Zelda was left alone in the gloom. She eased herself up from beside the tiller and felt her way along to the prow. The dragon lowered her head to greet her and Aunt Zelda sat, stroking the dragon's velvety nose, whispering calming sounds—as much for her benefit as the Dragon Boat's.

Out of sight of Aunt Zelda, the **Guiding Sprites** led the way, dancing through the mist. Hotep-Ra and his crew followed them, stumbling through puddles and over the uneven ground. The floor of the abyss was not a pleasant place to be. The mist swirled around, cold and clammy, and when Septimus turned to look back at the Dragon Boat he could no longer see her; a pall of gloom hung between them. They struggled on, following the **Sprites**, and soon the dark rock face reared up in front of them and Septimus saw that Hotep-Ra was heading for a small, rusty iron door set deep in the rock.

Suddenly Septimus felt a cold grip fasten around his neck and the livid face of the Toll Man whom he had once pushed into the abyss materialized in front of him, its eyes glittering with hate. A malevolent voice hissed in his ear. "See, now I have my revenge."

"**BeGone**, fiend!" Hotep-Ra's staff came down between the Toll Man and Septimus and the wraith disappeared.

"Thank you," Septimus muttered with relief.

Hotep-Ra smiled. "I too have enemies in the abyss," he said. "And in the abyss is where they stay. Aha, here we are!" He tapped his staff on the iron door, it swung open and the **Sprites** flew inside like an excited swarm of bees.

Septimus followed Jenna, Nicko and Hotep-Ra into an ice-cold chamber hollowed from the rock. The **Sprites** led them across to another door, which Hotep-Ra opened to reveal something that they had all seen before.

Cradled between two metal lattice platforms lay a purple-colored tube with rounded ends, about fifteen feet long. There were four hatches ranged in a line along the roof, the front one being the larger. Along the side of the tube was a line of tiny green glass windows and below it were runners that rested on two parallel metal rails, which sloped steeply down into the dark mouth of a tunnel.

"It's the *Red Tube*!" gasped Septimus.

"Only purple," said Jenna.

Hotep-Ra looked very surprised. "It is indeed a *Tube*. But I did not expect you to recognize it."

"Once I helped to get one just like that back to CattRokk Light," said Septimus, smiling at the memory. He had loved piloting the *Tube* under the sea, seeing the fish swimming by and the feeling of being in another world.

"So you understand how it works?"

"Sort of. I wasn't in it for long."

Hotep-Ra smiled. "Even so, this is good news. You will be off to the Castle in no time."

"In *that*?"

"Of course."

"But how? There is no water here."

"But there is ice. Ice or water, it is all the same to a *Tube*."

Nicko shivered. He'd refused a ride in the *Tube* before, and the thought of having to go into its coffinlike space now was terrifying.

Hotep-Ra pushed the end of his staff onto a rubbery black button in front of the oval hatch. With a faint whirr, the hatch flipped open, a dull purple light switched on inside the *Tube* and a smell of old leather and iron wafted out. Nicko felt sick.

Septimus peered down. Inside he saw the high-backed bench seat for the pilot, a simple set of dials and the thick green windshield that wrapped around the front of the *Tube*. It was even more cramped inside than he remembered. He knew Nicko would hate it.

"Okay, Nik?" he said.

Nicko did not answer.

Jenna decided it was time to be a bit Princessy. She turned to Hotep-Ra and said, "Hotep-Ra, Septimus and I will go in the *Tube*, but I would like Nicko to help with the Dragon Boat. It's a long way to the Castle and some of your journey will be through the night."

To Jenna's surprise it wasn't only Nicko who looked

relieved. Hotep-Ra did too. Jenna guessed that the frail old Wizard had not been looking forward to the long flight on the Dragon Boat with only Aunt Zelda as crew.

Nicko flashed Jenna a thank-you smile and watched anxiously as she and Septimus dropped down through the front hatch into the red glow below. He saw the tops of their heads, fair hair and dark, as they both settled into the pilot seat. Hotep-Ra peered down.

"Do you remember the controls?" he asked.

"I think so," Septimus replied.

Hotep-Ra ran through the controls and then described what he called the "launch protocol" ending with, "and the power pedal is at your right foot, the brake at your left. Steer with the little wheel, although you will hardly need to; it is a straight run from here to the Castle."

Nicko looked amazed. He thought of the long journey that he and Snorri had once taken across the sea, marshland and frozen forest to get there, when all the time there was what Hotep-Ra called a straight run. Hotep-Ra saw Nicko's bemused expression and smiled at him. "This is why, Nickolas Heap, I built my House of Foryx here. But like you I have a fear of enclosed spaces. I have only traveled that way once—and once was enough, believe me." He turned back to the *Purple Tube*. "Ready?" he called down.

"Um. Yes. Ready." Jenna and Septimus's voices echoed hollowly up through the open hatch.

Nicko noticed that Hotep-Ra looked as nervous as the voices below sounded.

"When you release the *Tube*," said Hotep-Ra, "you will drop steeply down the approach tunnel and enter the Ice Tunnel. You understand?"

Jenna and Septimus exchanged glances. "Yes," they replied.

"Now, please put your seat belts on."

Nervously, Jenna and Septimus fumbled with the stiff old leather belts and managed to clip the buckles tight.

"Good luck," said Hotep-Ra. "Now you may begin the launch sequence."

Along the curved metal dashboard were seven numbered brass dials. Jenna now turned the first one until it clicked into position. The top hatch closed above them with a *hisssss* and all went dark.

"This is *scary*," Jenna whispered. Septimus swallowed. His mouth felt dry. Jenna's fingers found the second dial, she turned it to the click and a line of tiny red lights lit the dashboard. The third made the headrest move down to fit them; the fourth dial sent a whoosh of air, which smelled of the sea, rushing into the capsule. Now Septimus took over. He turned the fifth dial, which switched on a brilliant white headlight and lit the way in front of them. This was not particularly encouraging—it showed a pair of glistening silver rails plunging down a steep drop into the circular black mouth of a tunnel. The sixth loosened a tether. Before he turned the seventh dial, Septimus looked at Jenna, his face eerily purple in the light.

"Okay?" he asked.

Jenna nodded. "Okay."

They both guessed what would happen when Septimus turned the last dial. They were right: as the dial clicked into place, the *Tube* tipped forward and the next moment they were hurtling down the rails toward the gaping black O.

Nicko watched the *Purple Tube* shoot into the circle of darkness—and then it was gone. It felt to him like it was gone forever.

⟻ 44 ⟼
SOMEWHERE

F*ar below the snowy Forest,* the *Purple Tube* hurtled along the longest, straightest Ice Tunnel that Septimus had ever seen. Its runners glided smoothly over the ice and its headlight picked out the glittering frost that swept past them in a blur of white.

"This is *fast*!" Jenna gasped.

Septimus stared out of the thick glass of the windscreen, transfixed by the black circle of darkness that always stayed the same distance ahead. "Don't you think it feels like *we're* staying still and the tunnel is moving?" he said.

"Sep—don't say that!" Jenna put her hands over her eyes. "That is too weird." She peered through a gap between her fingers. "Now that's what *I* see—the *tunnel* moving."

"Sorry, Jen."

They fell silent for a while, listening to the constant rumble of the runners of the *Tube* traveling over the ice. After a while Septimus said, "I wonder where we are now—I mean I wonder what's above us right now?"

Jenna shivered. "I don't want to even think about all the stuff above us, thanks very much."

"Oh. Sorry."

"That's all right. Just remind me not to travel in one of these with you again. Or at all, actually." She smiled at him. "Horrible boy."

Septimus stuck his tongue out at Jenna and carried on staring at the white blur outside the window. It was mesmerizing.

The *Tube* sped on and they lost track of time. It was about an hour after they had started when Jenna, sounding worried, said, "Sep. It's gone kind of wobbly. Do you think something's broken?"

Septimus had noticed too. The smooth run had changed

to an unpleasant shake that came up from the runners and was giving a bone-jarring ride. The low background rumble had become so loud that Septimus had to raise his voice to be heard.

"Perhaps we had better slow down," he said. "If something is wrong and we crash at this speed . . ."

"I'm going to put the brake on," said Jenna, moving her left foot across to the broad plate that came up from the floor on her side.

"Yep. Good idea."

Cautiously, Jenna pressed her foot down on the brake. The *Tube* slowed to a crawl, but the shaking became even more pronounced.

"Something's wrong!" said Jenna, snatching her foot off the brake.

Suddenly, Septimus realized what it was. "It's the jinn, Jen!"

"Oh, do stop saying silly rhymes, Sep. This is not nice. Oh!" The *Tube* gave a particularly big lurch and Jenna fell sideways.

Septimus caught her. "It's okay, Jen. I know where we are. And I know what's happened. It's the ice. It's really churned up—look, you can see it in the headlight. This must be where the warrior jinn marched to the Castle, which means that we must be under the Isles of Syren now."

Jenna peered through the glass. "Hey—you're right!"

"No need to sound so surprised," said Septimus, grinning.

Jenna thought about what Septimus had said. "So we are under the sea now, right?"

"Yes. I suppose we are."

Jenna shivered. "All that water above us, Sep. It's so . . . *scary*."

Septimus didn't want to think about it. "I'll speed up and get us out of here."

"Not too fast, okay?"

Septimus pressed the pedal on his side of the floor; the *Tube* picked up speed and settled into a gentle bumping along the rutted ice.

After some minutes Jenna said, "Is there an Ice Tunnel hatch below the Palace, Sep?"

"I suppose there must be. I've never seen it though."

Jenna sighed. "I wish Beetle were here. He'd know." She turned to Septimus. "Everything feels kind of right when Beetle's around, don't you think?"

"Perhaps you ought to tell him that sometime," said

Septimus, giving Jenna what Sarah Heap would have called a meaningful look.

Jenna went pink. "Shut up, Sep," she said.

"Okeydokey. Now I've been thinking. There's a sign to the Wizard Tower in the Ice Tunnel below, so I bet there's a sign to the Palace too."

"So how near do you think we are?" Jenna asked.

"We can't be too far," said Septimus. "It didn't take very long from the House of Foryx to the Isles of Syren, did it? And the Castle is much closer."

"Perhaps we ought to slow down," said Jenna anxiously. "We don't want to miss the sign and get lost under the Castle." The *Tube* hit a particularly deep rut and shook alarmingly. "*Slowly*, Sep!"

"Don't panic, Jen."

"I am *not* panicking. You are going way too fast."

Irritated, Septimus slowed the *Tube* to an uncomfortable bump while Jenna stared out of the thick green glass screen, searching for a sign to the Palace.

After some minutes, Jenna said, "How big did Hotep-Ra say this pyramid was? I mean, is it like head-size or more kind of nose-size?"

"Nose-size," said Septimus. "He said it would sit comfortably on your hand."

"That's really small," said Jenna gloomily.

"And the Palace is really big," Septimus said equally gloomily.

"The only thing I can hope for is that my mother, the Queen, will tell me where it is."

Septimus looked at Jenna. "Do you think she will?"

"No," said Jenna. "*Sep, look out!*"

Septimus snatched his foot off the power pedal. "Jen—brake, brake, *brake!*"

In the bright beam of light of the *Tube*, Jenna and Septimus saw the most bizarre sight. Poking up from the floor of the Ice Tunnel were the head and shoulders of a man. He was staring at the oncoming *Tube* in utter horror. Jenna slammed her foot on the brake and the *Purple Tube* skidded to a halt just in time. The head-and-shoulders stayed where it was and continued to stare, its mouth opening and closing like a goldfish thrown out of its bowl.

"Jeez. It's *Marcellus.*" Septimus reached over to the hatch dial and clicked it up, the pilot hatch swung open and in seconds he was up and out into the chill of the Ice Tunnel, clambering down the ladder and running and sliding across the ice toward Marcellus, closely followed by Jenna.

Blinded by the headlight, Marcellus was convinced that he was about to be run down. He heard Septimus's voice but thought he was imagining it. It was only when Septimus shook his shoulder that Marcellus realized he was not—just then, anyway—going to die.

Jenna slid to a halt beside them, shocked at what she saw. Marcellus was in a terrible state. He was covered in dirt and streaked with dried blood that ran down from a huge bump on his forehead. "Marcellus!" she gasped. "Your head! *What has happened?*"

It was too much for Marcellus to explain right then. "Stuck," he replied.

"Okay. Let's get you out," said Septimus.

Jenna grasped one shoulder and Septimus the other. "One, two, three—*pull!*"

"Ouch!" Marcellus yelled as he was wrenched from the tiny escape hatch and pulled out onto the ice—which felt, Septimus thought, unusually soft. As Marcellus lay groaning on the ice, Septimus briefly caught sight of a small, dusty face with squashy, broad features and a pair of large, round, black eyes staring at them from the ice. But before he could say anything, the little eyes were gone.

"Marcia . . ." Marcellus said feebly. "See Marcia. Got to tell her."

Septimus was beyond being surprised by anything—if Marcellus suddenly wanted to tell all to Marcia, that was fine by him. "Okay. Now, Marcellus, can you stand?"

Marcellus nodded and then groaned once more. His head hurt badly. He allowed Jenna and Septimus to help him to his feet and walked unsteadily between them to the *Purple Tube*.

Unseen, Duglius popped his head out of the hatch once more to make sure his Master was safe. He saw Marcellus being helped to climb up the rungs on the side of the *Tube* and deposited with some difficulty through the hatch. He saw the Apprentice and the Princess clamber in after him and when the *Tube* hatch hissed closed, Duglius dropped back down the Drummin burrow escape hatch and pulled it shut too. Then he took a shiny mat—known as a slider—from a stack just below the hatch and sat down. With one push Duglius was away, hurtling down the escape burrow, GloGrubs jumping out of his way, dust kicking up into his face. It was something he had not done since he was a young Drummin, so very, very long ago, and once again Duglius felt the sheer joy of being alive. And as he headed down, Duglius was determined that he, his Drummins and his **Fyre** were going to stay that way.

Inside the *Purple Tube*, Marcellus was slumped on the bench seat behind the pilot's. Jenna sat with him. "Marcellus," she said, "we have to get to the Palace Ice Hatch. It's really important. Can you tell us the way?"

"Not Palace," mumbled Marcellus. "Marcia."

"Palace first, then Marcia," said Septimus firmly. Marcellus's eyes were beginning to close. "Jen, keep him awake."

"Marcellus—*Marcellus!*" Jenna gently patted Marcellus's bloodstained cheeks to keep him awake. "Please. *Marcellus.* This is very important. We have to get to the Palace Hatch. *Marcellus.* The Palace Ice Hatch. *Which way?*"

The urgency in Jenna's voice at last got through and Marcellus dragged himself back from the comforting sleep that beckoned to him. Marcellus knew every inch of the Ice Tunnels and even in his confused state he was able to direct them to a signpost that read TO THE PALACE.

Septimus took the turn and coasted to a halt beneath the Palace Ice Hatch. He took his Alchemie **Keye**—a round gold disc—from around his neck and handed it to Jenna, saying,

"Press it into the dip in the middle."

Septimus opened the passenger hatch and Jenna scrambled out. Water dripped on her head as she stood on top of the *Tube* and pressed the gold **Keye** into the indentation in the silver hatch above. "It's open!" she called down. "I'll be as quick as I can!" With that she was gone.

Septimus stared through the greenish glass at the ice outside. Something was wrong; the ice looked different. And then he realized what it was—it had lost the frosty sparkle that he had always loved. Septimus opened the pilot hatch. "Marcellus, I'll be back in a minute," he said, and swung himself up and out of the hatch and down onto the ice. Septimus was shocked. It was *slush*.

He looked up at the curved roof of the tunnel high above and a splat of water landed on his face. Rubbing his eyes, Septimus clambered back into the *Tube*. Now he knew for sure—*the Ice Tunnels were melting*.

Jenna pushed open the trapdoor at the top of the flight of steps that led up from the Ice Tunnel. She threw aside a heavy (and horribly dusty) rug and found herself in the coat cupboard just off the Palace entrance hall. Coughing and sneezing, she threw open the door, rushed out and ran straight into Sam.

"Jen!" Sam gasped.

"Sam. No time to explain. Small gold pyramid. Very, very important. We have to find it. It's somewhere in the Palace."

"Where in the Palace?"

"Sam, if I knew that I wouldn't be looking for it, would I?"

Sam looked at his little sister. "It's really important, isn't it?" he said.

The enormity of the search almost overwhelmed Jenna. "Oh, Sam . . . yes, it is. I don't know how I'm going to find it. I really don't."

"I'll get the boys. We'll find it."

"I gotta go and check somewhere out first, Sam. I'll be back here in ten minutes, okay?" Jenna rushed off.

In the Queen's Room Jenna and the ghost of her mother had another confrontation.

"Ah, the little gold pyramid. So heavy for something so small," said Queen Cerys.

"Where is it?" Jenna asked.

"Where is it *what*?"

Jenna took a deep breath and counted to ten. "Where is it, *please.*"

"Where is it, please *what*?"

Another count to ten. "Where is it please, *Mama.*"

"Daughter, you cannot have everything at once. This mystical treasure is for Queens only. You must wait until you are crowned."

With great difficulty Jenna subdued the urge to jump up and down screaming.

"Mama. This is not for me. It is for the Castle. If we do not have it now, then there may not *be* a Castle by the time I am crowned."

"Daughter, do not exaggerate."

Jenna took yet another very deep breath and said in a barely controlled voice, "I am not exaggerating. Mama. Please. Do you know where the little gold pyramid is?"

"I know where I left it," said Queen Cerys. "But given the *disgusting* mess, I could not say where it is now."

"So where did you leave it?" asked Jenna.

"I shall tell you where when you are Queen. And not before."

Desperately, Jenna tried another tack. "Is Grandmamma here?"

"No, she is not. You will have your little pyramid when you are crowned and I shall say no more on the subject until then. Now, daughter, go and calm yourself."

Jenna gave up the struggle. "*Aaaaaaaargh!*" she yelled at the top of her voice and rushed, screaming, out through the wall.

Sam had rounded up Sarah and the boys, and they were waiting for Jenna in the entrance hall.

"No luck?" Sam asked, although Jenna's face already told him the answer.

"Nope."

"Oh, dear," said Sarah. "If Queen Cerys doesn't know where it is, I don't know what we can do. It could be anywhere."

Jenna sighed. "It could be anywhere" was another of Sarah's phrases when she was looking for something—but a much less hopeful one than "it must be somewhere."

"Oh, but she *does* know where it is," Jenna said angrily.

Sarah brightened. "Well, that's wonderful."

"But she wouldn't tell me."

"*She wouldn't tell you?*"

"Not until I'm Queen."

Sarah was appalled. "Even though you told her how important it was?"

"Yup. She said that she knows where *she* left it, but given the disgusting mess everywhere, she could not say where it is now."

"Well, that's it!" said Sam. "She's told you where it is."

"What do you mean?" asked Jenna.

"Think about it—where is the one place that Cerys has seen that is a disgusting mess?"

"Oh, wow! Sam you are just brilliant! It must be in—"

"Mum's room!" chorused Jenna, Sam, Edd, Erik and Jo-Jo.

Sarah Heap looked offended. "I know it's a bit lived-in, but I think calling my little sitting room a disgusting mess is going too far."

Some minutes later, Sarah's little sitting room was even more of a disgusting mess. The efforts of four heavy-footed Forest Heaps plus a frantic Jenna and an embarrassed Sarah (who was trying to clear up little dried mounds of duck poo as they went) had reduced what fragile order there had been to a massive pile of what Jenna called "stuff" in the middle of the room. And on top of the stuff sat Ethel the duck, roosting like a wild turkey on its nest.

Jenna looked around the unusually empty room in despair. "It's not here," she said. "Mum, are you *sure* you've never seen it?"

"Never," declared Sarah. "And I know I would have remembered a little golden pyramid. It sounds so cute."

"Maybe my mother didn't mean this room after all," said Jenna disconsolately. "After all, the whole Palace is a mess, really."

"But the Queen hasn't seen the rest of the Palace," said Sam. He kicked the fluffy rabbit doorstop in frustration.

"Hey," said Jenna. "It didn't move."

"It's a doorstop," said Sam. "That's the whole point."

In a flash, Jenna was on the floor trying to pick up the rabbit. "It's so *heavy*!" she gasped. "Mum—scissors!"

Sarah looked at the pile of stuff in panic. "They must be somewhere . . ."

Suddenly four sharp Forest knives were unsheathed.

"No!" cried Sarah. "Not Pookie!" But it was too late—the fluffy pink rabbit lay eviscerated on the floor and a small pyramid-shaped lump of leather fell out from its stuffing with a *clunk*.

"Poor Pookie," said Sarah, picking up the limp rabbit.

Sam retrieved the leather pyramid and held it up triumphantly.

"That old thing?" said Sarah dismissively. "Very dull. I found it on the shelf when we moved in. It was nice and heavy, so I sewed it into Pookie to make a doorstop."

"Sam's right, Mum," said Jenna. "I reckon this is it."

"I *know* it is," Sam said, excited. He sat down on the unusually empty sofa and, biting his lip in concentration, Sam carefully cut through the tightly stitched thread. As the seams opened out, Jenna was thrilled to see the shine of gold beneath. A few moments later, a small gold pyramid tumbled out onto Sam's lap and fell onto the floor with a heavy *thud*. Sam picked it up and held it out to Jenna. "There you are, Jens. Just for you."

"I've got it!" yelled Jenna, triumphant. Clutching the pink rabbit—which had seemed the safest place to keep the slippery and remarkably heavy little pyramid—Jenna jumped into the

Purple Tube and took her seat next to Septimus. "Let's go!"

"Why have you got Pookie?" asked Septimus as Jenna plonked the eviscerated rabbit—which Sarah had quickly stitched closed—down between them.

"Pyramid," said Jenna, still breathless. "Pyramid in Pookie."

"Oh. Right." Septimus shook his head in bemusement.

Guided by Marcellus, Jenna and Septimus piloted the *Tube* through the Ice Tunnels, heading toward the Wizard Tower. The *Tube*'s runners bumped along the slush, scraping the brick below, and the thuds of chunks of ice falling from the roof and hitting the metal *Tube* reverberated inside. The headlight illuminated the brick-lined walls of the old Ice Tunnels and the pools of water that gathered in the dips of the tunnels. More than once they had to take the *Tube* down into water-filled dips of the tunnels, some of which Septimus remembered sledding through with Beetle not so very long ago.

Jenna and Septimus glanced anxiously at each other but Marcellus was surprisingly jolly. "Back to normal, at last," he said.

Septimus said nothing. Marcellus had always been disapproving about the Ice Tunnels and he didn't want to get into an argument right then. But he knew how thick the ice was in some of the narrower tunnels and Septimus could not help but ask himself, *Where was it going to go?*

Some minutes later, Jenna said sharply, "Did you hear that?"

Septimus nodded. He could hear a deep rumble behind them. Automatically he glanced back over his shoulder, forgetting that the *Tube* had no back window. All he saw was Marcellus sitting bolt upright, and, despite the bruise spreading across his right eye, looking very perky indeed. Smug, even, thought Septimus.

The *Tube* began to shake and behind them they heard a thunderous roar as though an army of horses was galloping toward them.

Jenna gasped. "Something's coming," she said. She, too, swung around in her seat, forgetting there was no back window. Marcellus no longer looked smug.

Suddenly the roar enveloped them. A wall of water picked up the *Tube* and at once they too became part of the noise, the rush, the dust, the grit, and the surge of the flood that was rushing through the now ex–Ice Tunnels. Terrifyingly fast and out of control, they were swept along with the flood. Septimus struggled to keep hold of the wheel that steered the

Tube while Jenna stared wide-eyed through the swash of the water, desperate not to miss the turn to the Wizard Tower. At last through the spray, Jenna picked out the initials "WT," with a large purple hand painted onto the wall that pointed to a wide tunnel branching off to the left.

"Left!" she yelled. "*Left!*" Together she and Septimus fought the wheel around to the left and felt the *Tube* reluctantly turn. The nose stuck briefly in the mouth of the tunnel, but then it was swung around by the floodwater and sent hurtling on past the turn, buffeted from side to side, crashing along with the flood.

"It's a circuit!" yelled Septimus. "We'll go around and try again!"

"Okay, Sep! We can do it!"

On the backseat Marcellus looked green. He was beginning to think that maybe the Ice Tunnels weren't such a bad idea, all things considered.

⁜ 45 ⁜
FLOOD

Marcia **UnLocked** *the door to* the Stranger Chamber and peered inside. Alther greeted her wearily. Although ghosts do not tire physically, they can still become mentally tired, and after spending more than twenty-four hours in close proximity to Nursie and Merrin, Alther was feeling like a wet rag. Nursie was snoring in the Stranger Chair, while Merrin was sprawled on the sofa kicking the table legs and watching the water jug wobble.

"Good morning, Merrin," said Marcia.

Merrin stared at Marcia. "Morning," he said suspiciously.

Nursie opened her eyes. At the sight of the ExtraOrdinary Wizard, Nursie came straight to the point. "You keeping us prisoner?" she asked.

"Midwife Meredith, as I am sure Mr. Mella has explained, you and your son are here for your own safety."

"Leave that lever alone!" shouted Alther.

Merrin had begun aiming desultory kicks at the lever beside the fire. "I didn't touch it," he said sulkily.

"I would advise you *not* to," said Alther. "Marcia, a word, please."

"Quickly, Alther," said Marcia.

"Do I *have* to stay in here?" whispered Alther. "They are, as Septimus would say, doing my head in."

"I'm sorry, Alther, but there's no one else around right now who is Stranger Chamber–trained. Or, frankly, who I can trust not to throttle Merrin."

"That boy is a total nightmare," said Alther.

"Exactly. And only you can handle it, Alther. Now, I really

must go." With that Marcia closed the door, leaving Alther alone with his charges.

Unable to bear the ghost of Jillie Djinn, who had taken to shouting "Fire, fire!" every few seconds, Marcia had set up her headquarters in the Great Hall. A large round table had been taken from the canteen, which Marcia had **Primed** and then **Projected** onto it a permanent map of the Castle. The watchers in the **LookOuts** were sending down messengers every fifteen minutes with reports on the spread of the fires, which were now springing up all over the Castle. It was Rose's job to indicate these on the table by placing a **Fire Tablet** where the reported fire was. If it hadn't been for what the **Fire Tablets** represented, Rose would have really enjoyed her work. She had a leather bag of thick red discs that, when pressed down onto the **Primed** table, burst into flame and kept burning until **Quenched**. So far Marcia had not **Quenched** any and, after a message from the West **LookOut**, Rose had just placed a line of four more **Fire Tablets** in a particularly old part of the Castle. The fires were now spreading from house to house.

On a separate table safely away from the **Fire Tablets** lay *The*

Live Plan of What Lies Beneath, which Simon—with a heavily bandaged foot propped up on a chair—was watching intently, reporting on a strange shadow that he had first picked up hovering above the Chamber of **Fyre**. Simon had then tracked it to the Palace, where it had stopped for some time. Both he and Marcia were convinced that this was the Ring Wizards. The shadow was now moving through the tunnels toward the Wizard Tower and causing Marcia some concern.

The doors to the Wizard Tower swung open and Beetle hurried in. One glance at his expression told Marcia it was yet more bad news.

"The Ice Tunnels are in flood," said Beetle.

A collective gasp came from everyone in the Hall. Marcia stared at Beetle in disbelief. "They can't be," she said.

"They are. The tunnel below the Manuscriptorium is a torrent of water. How Romilly got out I do not know."

"Romilly was down there?"

"She was monitoring the melt," said Beetle. "She was quite a way into the system when she noticed that it was suddenly speeding up—chunks of ice were falling from the roof and the runners of the sled were hitting brick. She headed back but as she got to the long straight below the Manuscriptorium she heard a roar. Poor Romilly, she knew exactly what it was. A wall of water picked the sled up and she was carried along—she only escaped by grabbing on to the rung just below the Ice Hatch."

"But she's all right?" asked Marcia.

"Shocked. Bruised. But okay."

Julius Pike wafted over from the table where he had been staring at the fires. "ExtraOrdinary, you must act now. You cannot allow the **Fyre** to rage out of control."

"Thank you, Julius," Marcia snapped. "However, I am not prepared to risk anyone's life until we have a chance of success. We shall wait for the **Committal**."

"I hope you will not wait in vain," said the ghost.

"I have faith in my Apprentice," said Marcia.

"Marcia!" Simon called out. "The shadow—it's just turned into the Tower tunnel. The Ring Wizards—they're heading this way!"

The *Tube* was indeed heading that way—although with some difficulty. Jenna and Septimus had just fought to stop it from sweeping off down a wide tunnel that Septimus knew led to Beetle's once-favorite sledding slope and they were now careering down the tunnel that led to the Wizard Tower. The *Tube* pitched from side to side as it rocketed along, banging against the walls. The dark, swirling water came almost to the top of the thick green glass of the cockpit window, and what was left of the window was spattered with spray. Septimus peered through, wondering how they were going to be able to see the little archway that led to the Wizard Tower.

"Coming up!" Jenna yelled.

In the light of the headlamp Septimus saw the rapidly approaching sign: TO THE WIZARD TOWER.

"Stop!" shouted Jenna.

"It won't!" yelled Septimus. "The brake doesn't work in water!"

"Anchor out!" Jenna yelled.

"What anchor?"

"There!" Jenna pressed a red button on Septimus's side of the cockpit. They felt something shoot out from beneath the *Tube* and it slewed to a jarring halt. The nose of the *Tube* banged violently against the wall and sent them sprawling.

"Phew," Septimus breathed. "That was close."

"Very close," said Jenna. "Right by the steps, in fact."

The *Purple Tube* had stopped beside the small archway that

led to the Wizard Tower steps. Septimus opened the hatches and looked out. The roar from the water shocked him and a rush of spray hit him in the face and splashed down through the open hatches.

"Aargh!" came a yell from Jenna, inside. "Cold!"

The steps leading up to the Wizard Tower were above water, but between the *Tube* and the safety of the bottom step rushed a narrow but turbulent stream of water. "We're going to have to jump for it!" Septimus shouted.

"Marcellus, time to get out," said Jenna.

Getting out seemed like a very good idea to Marcellus. With Septimus and Jenna's help, he pulled himself up through the hatch, slithered down the side of the *Tube* and made a remarkably agile leap across the flood onto the step.

"Pookie!" yelled Septimus.

"Like I'd forget!" Jenna shouted, grabbing the pink rabbit from the seat and clutching it firmly around its middle. Inside she could feel the sharp corners of the pyramid digging through the fabric.

The ice-cold spray and the roar of the water had brought Marcellus to his senses. He held out his hands to Jenna and Septimus and they leaped over the gap and grasped hold.

Marcellus pulled them up and together they hurried up the steps to a shining purple door on the left-hand side at the top.

Septimus stared at the purple in dismay. "It's **Sealed**," he said.

"But you can **UnSeal** it, can't you, Sep?"

Septimus shook his head. "Not from this side. It is **Sealed** against us."

On the other side of the **Seal**, Marcia said to Beetle, "I've **Armed** the **Seal**." She sighed. "I've never done that before. It's unethical, in my opinion. But needs must."

"Unethical—why?" Beetle asked.

"The **Arming** can kill anyone who touches it, but there is no apparent difference to the layperson from a normal **Seal**. Most Wizards will notice it, of course, although there are some that probably wouldn't." She sighed. "But it should keep the most powerful of **Darke** Wizards at bay for a while. Let's hope it lasts until Jenna gets back."

Beetle did not reply. The thought of Jenna at the House of Foryx upset him; he wished now that he had gone with her when she had asked him.

* * *

Only a few inches away from Beetle, Jenna put out her hand to touch the **Seal**. Septimus grabbed her hand and pulled it away. "Don't touch!" he whispered. "It's **Armed**."

"**Armed?**"

"*Shh.* Yes, can you hear it buzzing?"

"Why are you whispering?" hissed Jenna.

"Because Marcia doesn't use **Armed Seals**. She thinks they are wrong."

Jenna looked at Septimus, scared. "You don't think the Ring Wizards are . . . *in there*, do you?"

"I can guarantee they are not," Marcellus said. "Duglius would not allow it."

"*Duglius?*" Jenna and Septimus exchanged worried glances. Marcellus's mind was clearly wandering.

"My head Drummin," said Marcellus.

"I'm not surprised your head hurts, Marcellus," said Jenna soothingly. "You have a huge lump on it." A wave splashed up and she looked down to see that the water was now covering the lower two steps. "*Sep,*" she whispered, "*the water's rising.*"

As Jenna was speaking, a huge surge of water ran through the tunnel, sending the *Purple Tube* bucking like a frightened horse. The anchor broke free and the *Tube* was dragged into the current—and then it was gone, merrily bouncing and banging along the roof of the tunnel.

Jenna, Septimus and Marcellus watched the light from the headlamp rapidly fade, plunging them into darkness. Septimus waited for his Dragon Ring to begin to glow, until he remembered that it was now back on Hotep-Ra's finger.

They were on their own.

They stood in the dark, feeling the chill of the water lapping around their ankles. Something bumped up against Septimus's boot and he looked down. It was his beautiful Wizard Tower sledge that he had left tied there after his last run through the Ice Tunnels with Beetle to celebrate him becoming Chief Hermetic Scribe. Septimus untied the sled's azure-blue rope and, feeling as though he had found a friend, held on to it tightly.

Meanwhile, Jenna clutched the sodden and increasingly heavy pink rabbit to her. She was beginning to wonder if all they had gone through to get the **Committal** was going to come to nothing.

A wave swashed over them, taking the water up to their

knees. "Apprentice," said Marcellus, "you could try the old-fashioned way of finding out who is on the other side. You could shout."

Another wave, which washed water up to their waists, convinced Septimus that he had nothing to lose. "Marcia!" he called out, his voice echoing in the domed, watery space. "It's me—Septimus!"

There was no reply.

On the other side of the **Armed Seal**, a whispered conference was in progress.

"It is a trick," said Julius. "Your Apprentice cannot possibly be back yet."

"It is not a trick," said Marcia. "It is Septimus. I can **Feel** it."

Milo joined Marcia. "You should go with what you feel," he said.

"Feelings!" said Julius. "Huh! That old mumbo jumbo."

A wave pushed the water up to their chests. Marcellus raised his arm to check how much headroom they had left. Enough for two more waves, he reckoned. That was all.

"Let your rabbit go," he told Jenna. "You will need both hands soon."

"But it's got the *pyramid* in it," said Jenna. And then, seeing Marcellus's puzzled look, she said, "It has the **Keye** to the **Committal** in it—the words that will put the Wizards back in the ring."

Marcellus remembered. "Then give it to me. I will not let go of it, I promise you."

Jenna gave the heavy, sodden pink rabbit to Marcellus. He took it by the ears and very nearly dropped it in surprise at its weight. But Marcellus was no stranger to carrying lumps of gold and he quickly stuffed it into the large leather pouch that he wore hidden under his cloak, where Pookie the rabbit joined a collection of gold coins and nuggets.

Released from her burden, Jenna put all her energy into yelling, "Marcia! Let us in!"

On the other side of the **Shield**, Milo gasped. "I can hear Jenna!"

"So can I," said Beetle.

"It's an old **Darke** trick," the ghost of Julius Pike told them. "You hear the people you long for. That's how a **Darke Domaine** begins."

Beetle hesitated. The ghost was right—he knew that well enough.

Marcia also faltered. She looked at Milo. "He's right," she said.

"No, he's not," said Milo. "That's my Jenna out there. And your Septimus. Let them in."

Another surge of water had left Marcellus the one only able to stand and keep his head above water. Septimus had regretfully let go of his sled and now both he and Jenna were clinging to Marcellus, their heads bumping up and down against the brick roof of the stairwell. They knew the next wave would be their last.

"*Mar . . . ceeee . . . aaaaaah!*" they yelled.

Jenna's and Septimus's cries echoed out of the little broom cupboard and into the Great Hall of the Wizard Tower. A crowd of concerned Wizards gathered at the cupboard door.

"Marcia's not there," said Septimus despairingly. "She would let us in if she was. It must be the Ring Wizards."

Another—mercifully small—wave washed up to their

mouths and set them coughing and spluttering.

"Marcia! Let us in, for pity's sake!" yelled Marcellus. "*We are drowning!*"

"That settles it," said Julius. "It *is* the Ring Wizards. They have Marcellus hostage."

Jenna, Septimus and Marcellus clutched one another. In a moment they would be gone—washed down the Ice Tunnels to begin an endless circuit in the currents like three Ice Wraiths.

Jenna gave one last desperate scream. "*Heeeeeelp!*"

"Marcia," said Milo. "That was Jenna. I know my child."

"And I know mine," said Marcia. "I mean—I know Septimus. Be *quiet*, Julius." With that she **UnSealed** the door.

A great wave of freezing water swept through the **Seal**, bringing with it three half-drowned people and Septimus's Wizard Tower sledge, which **Passed Through** the ghost of Julius Pike like a blade of cold steel. The wave surged out of the broom cupboard and deposited Jenna, Septimus and Marcellus like stranded fish on the floor of the Great Hall. On and on the water came, until the combined efforts of Marcia and as many Wizards who could fit into the broom cupboard managed to **Stop** it. Then, while the water lay gently swashing to and fro, a dripping wet Marcia rapidly repaired the **Seal**.

Shattered, Septimus, Jenna and Marcellus could do nothing more than collapse onto the padded bench outside the Stranger Chamber and watch the Wizards **Sweep** the water out from the Great Hall, sending it cascading down the marble steps into the Courtyard, where it slowly drained away.

Dripping wet, wringing her cloak out as she splashed across the Wizard Tower floor, Marcia came hurrying toward them, relief that they were safe written across her face. She kneeled down beside Jenna and Septimus and grasped their hands, shocked how icy cold they were. "You did your best," she said, consolingly. "And that is all you can do."

Septimus knew that Marcia thought they had never made it to Hotep-Ra, but neither he nor Jenna had the energy to explain. Septimus nudged Marcellus. "Rabbit," he said.

Too exhausted to speak, Marcellus nodded. He pulled the dripping pink rabbit from his pouch and wordlessly he handed it to Marcia.

46
SHOWDOWN

Dark columns of smoke were rising into the sky, each one a family's home or livelihood going up in flames. In the very center stood the Alchemie Chimney with a massive plume of black smoke belching from it, like a Witch Mother on a midnight moot conducting her acolytes as they danced around her.

The breeze blowing at the top of the Wizard Tower brought with it the acrid smell of smoke but up there, Septimus had other things on his mind. With the **Flyte Charm** clutched tightly in one hand and the **Reduced** top of the pyramid in the other, he was lying facedown, hovering at arm's length above the flat silver platform of the pyramid roof, on which the decoy hieroglyphs were incised. He must not—Hotep-Ra had impressed this upon him—make contact with the silver. If he did, the **Keye** would not work.

Hotep-Ra had told Septimus that he had stored his twenty-one **Incantations** inside the pyramid roof of the Wizard Tower. They were filed in order of use, with—he thought—the most recently used one at the top, so the **Committal** should be the very first one to **Appear**. If it didn't, then that meant he had stored them back to front and it would be the very last to **Appear**. Septimus must then scroll through by lifting the little pyramid **Keye** off its indentation and replacing it. Every time he did this, another **Incantation** would **Appear**.

Very carefully, Septimus dropped the little gold pyramid into the **Lock**—the square indentation in the center of the hieroglyphs that had puzzled him and so many generations of Wizards and Apprentices before him. The little pyramid fitted the **Lock** exactly—just as a **Keye** should. Immediately, a symbol appeared on the blank silver square on top of the **Keye**, and Septimus felt heat rising from the silver platform.

As he backed away, Septimus watched in awe as the meaningless hieroglyphs below began to dissolve and become words that he could understand: *A **Riddance** for the Smell of Pig.*

Septimus read the words and his heart sank—the **Incantations** were in reverse order. Pushing to one side the question as to why the first **Incantation** Hotep-Ra ever did in the Castle was for getting rid of pig smells, Septimus lifted up the pyramid **Keye**. The jumbled hieroglyphs returned and the top of the **Keye** became blank once more. He dropped the **Keye** back into the **Lock** and up came another symbol on its top and on the platform, the next **Incantation**: *A **Healing** for the Young.*

With the heat from the intense **Magyk** blazing in his face and the wind that always blew at the top of the Wizard Tower buffeting him to and fro, Septimus laboriously counted his way through the **Incantations**, dropping and picking up the **Keye**, until at last he reached the twenty-first. Holding his breath in suspense, Septimus dropped the **Keye** into the **Lock** for what he desperately hoped was the last time. A symbol appeared on top of the **Keye** that Septimus recognized: *Hathor.* And for the twenty-first time, the hieroglyphs dissolved into words. This time they read: *A* ***Committal*** *to Gold.*

"Yay!" yelled Septimus. Taking great care not to make contact with the silver platform (he could not bear the thought of having to scroll through everything again), Septimus took out his stylus and recording **Tablet** and meticulously wrote down the words to the **Committal**. He checked them three times—stopped himself from checking a fourth because he *knew* he had copied them right—took the **Keye** from the **Lock** and watched the words change into meaningless hieroglyphs once again.

Septimus put his **Tablet** safely into his secure pocket, stood up and stretched out his aching arms. He looked down to where Rose was watching anxiously from the little library hatch below and his happy wave told Rose all she needed to know.

"Hooray!" she called up. And then, "Are you coming down now?"

There was nothing Septimus wanted to do more. Even with the security of the **Flyte Charm**, heights still made him feel hollow inside. With the **Keye** safely joining the **Tablet** in his pocket, he slowly descended through the smoky air.

* * *

In the Wizard Tower below, Marcellus Pye saw the ghostly figure of Julius Pike sidling toward the spiral stairs. Marcellus thought he was seeing things. He closed his eyes but when he opened them, Julius was still there.

"Can you see that ExtraOrdinary Wizard ghost?" Marcellus whispered to Jenna.

"Yes," said Jenna. "He's a pain in the neck."

"So it *is* him." Marcellus got to his feet and wobbled.

"Marcellus, sit down," said Marcia sternly. "You ought to be in the Sick Bay."

"Huh!" said Marcellus. "Excuse me, Marcia, Princess, there is something I have to do." He gave an old-fashioned bow and headed off unsteadily.

The ghost of Julius Pike watched Marcellus approaching with dismay. The Alchemist—hair plastered to his head, a livid bruise spreading around his right eye, his robes tattered and torn—looked as though he had been in a fight and was wanting another.

Marcellus stepped in front of the ghost. "Julius."

"Marcellus," said Julius, sounding somewhat unenthusiastic. "Um, how are you?"

Marcellus smiled. "Alive," he said tersely.

A group of nearby Wizards who were cleaning up gasped at Marcellus's rudeness. It was extremely bad manners to draw attention to one's Living status when talking to a ghost. However, right then, manners were the last thing on Marcellus's mind.

"Julius, you *snake*. It has taken me nearly five hundred years to figure this out, but now at last I know what caused the Great Alchemie Disaster."

"Jolly good," said Julius somewhat impatiently.

"Indeed, I know not only *what* caused it, but *who*—you!"

"*Me?*" Julius sounded shocked.

"Yes, *you*, you lying toad. You arrogant old f—"

"Marcellus!" Marcia had hurried over to intervene. "I realize you have had a severe blow to the head, but I must ask you to abide by the Wizard Tower code of conduct. ExtraOrdinary Wizard ghosts are our guests and are to be treated with courtesy and respect."

"I am sorry, Marcia," said Marcellus, seething. "But I must have my say. I have waited long enough."

"You may have your say, Marcellus, but you may not insult our guest."

"Thank you, ExtraOrdinary," said Julius. "I must be off now."

"Not so fast, Julius!" said Marcellus. "Perhaps you will do me the courtesy of hearing what I have to say."

"It is late, Marcellus. Some other time. Excuse me."

"I will *not* excuse you. And neither would Marcia if she knew the truth about what you did."

"Marcellus, what is this about?" asked Marcia.

Marcellus spoke slowly, all the while looking Julius Pike in the eye. "*This* is about how a man—who for years I counted as my best friend and my confidant—how he destroyed my life's work, and the work of all the Alchemists who went before me. And, as if that were not enough for him, how he then deliberately destroyed my reputation."

"How so, Marcellus?" asked Marcia.

"How so? I will tell you how so. This"—Marcellus made a huge effort to control himself—"*person* here, in order to impress some tin-pot Wizard from I-don't-know-where, not only invaded my Chamber of **Fyre**—*yes, Marcia, as you have already guessed, it does exist and I apologize for keeping it from you*—he then deceitfully, deviously and recklessly threw the most dangerous thing possible into the **Fyre** Cauldron—the Two-Faced Ring!"

Marcia looked confused. "What is wrong with that? Surely, that is what *we* are going to do after the **Committal**."

Julius Pike sensed an ally. "Quite, ExtraOrdinary. This is purely a fuss about protocol. I admit I did not ask your permission, Marcellus, for which I apologize. But this has nothing to do with the Great Alchemie Disaster, which happened *weeks* later."

"Julius, it had *everything* to do with it. If you want to **DeNature** something in the **Fyre** you don't just chuck it in like an old candy wrapper. The **Fyre** Cauldron is not a dustbin. **DeNaturing** by **Fyre** is a delicate task. You must keep the object suspended in the very center of the **Fyre** for many days and whatever you do, *you must not let it touch the side of the Cauldron*."

Julius Pike began to **Disappear**. This did not go down well with Marcia.

"Mr. Pike. Pray do us the courtesy of remaining visible."

"Thank you, Marcia," said Marcellus. "So, Julius, when you threw the Two-Faced Ring into the **Fyre** it sank down through the **Fyre** rods and sat on the bottom of the Cauldron where, over the next three weeks, it **Migrated**. And the moment it made the hole, the Cauldron cracked, the water rushed out and the **Fyre** rods began to heat up, which they do when they lose water suddenly. My Drummins contained the **Fyre** by dousing it with our special cannel coal, as they are doing at this very moment—do not interrupt, Julius; this is the Alchemie Way and it *works*. But you, Julius, would not trust us to do our job. You would not listen to me when I explained. You panicked. You shut off our water. You shut off our air and just to make sure, you forced me to ice up our beautiful cooling system that kept the whole Castle warm in the winter. It was *you*, Julius, who caused the Great Alchemie Disaster."

"Rubbish!" spluttered the ghost.

"Julius, it is the truth. I know this because after you **Sealed** my **Fyre** Chamber, my Drummins found the Two-Faced Ring on the ground. They knew what it was and they threw it into the drainage system to get rid of it. But they could not tell me, because by then you had dragged me away, and had left my faithful Drummins—more loyal to me than *you* ever were—to die."

"Drummins?" asked Marcia.

"False creations," said Julius Pike. "Alchemical abominations."

"They are living, breathing, sentient beings, however they may have been created," retorted Marcellus. "But leaving the Drummins to die was not enough for you. You had to make sure that Alchemie died too."

"For the good of the Castle, Marcellus," Julius protested. "Which Alchemie had so very nearly destroyed."

"No, Julius. Which *you* had so very nearly destroyed, by your deceit. And it did not stop there, did it? You falsified records, you obliterated ancient knowledge and you instilled a deep suspicion of Alchemie into all Wizards, so much so that to this day all new Wizards swear to 'abjure all things Alchemical,' do they not? And yet in the past, Wizards and Alchemists did great things together. They worked as one. And in order to finally rid ourselves of this ring, we shall have to do so again. There is no other way."

Marcellus became aware that a large crowd of Ordinary Wizards had gathered and were listening in shocked silence. When they realized that he had finally finished all he had to say, a few began to clap in approval. The ripple spread and soon the Great Hall was ringing with the sound of applause.

* * *

Rose and Septimus were spinning down through the floors on Emergency setting when they heard the sound of the ovation rising to meet them.

"They know you've done it, Septimus," said Rose. They jumped off the stairs to find it was not they who were the center of attention but Marcia and Marcellus, arm in arm.

"Crumbs," Rose whispered to Septimus. "It looks like they're going to get married or something."

"No *way*!" said Septimus.

Marcia caught sight of Septimus. She saw the horrified expression on his face and her heart sank. "It didn't work, did it?"

"Yes, it did. Perfectly. I've got the **Committal** here."

A huge smile spread across Marcia's weary features and her green eyes sparkled for the first time in days. "Septimus, that is wonderful. I should have known it would be you who would finally **DeCypher** the top of the Pyramid. Congratulations! I think I can safely say that you have passed your **DeCyphering** module with distinction. And then some."

Septimus looked at Marcia and Marcellus, who were still

arm in arm. "So, um . . . do I need to congratulate *you*?" he asked.

"You can if you like," said Marcia. "From today we have a new partnership!"

"Oh."

"Septimus, I am surprised you are not more excited. A partnership between Alchemie and **Magyk** is what you have wanted for a long time. No more secrets."

"So you're going to move in together?"

Marcia looked at Septimus uncomprehendingly for some seconds. Then a flash of understanding, swiftly followed by dismay, crossed her face and she dropped Marcellus's arm like a hot potato. "Goodness, no! Oh, horrors. Perish the thought. This is a *business* relationship."

Erk Erk Erk . . . Erk Erk Erk . . . !

The Stranger Chamber **Alarm** chose that moment to save Marcia from any more embarrassment. With almost a feeling of relief, Marcia raced over and threw open the blue door. Inside she met a very agitated ghost.

"He pulled the lever!" yelled Alther. "Stupid, *stupid* boy!"

Marcia stared at the gaping hole in the floor where the

Stranger Chair should have been. A damp and not very pleasant smell drifted up from it.

"Which setting?" she asked anxiously.

"Moat. It's on Moat."

Marcia felt relieved. At least it was possible to get people out of the Moat. "Idiot!" she said.

"I know. Marcia, I am *so* sorry. I took my eye off him for *one* second. That was all, I promise you—"

"Oh, Alther, I didn't mean *you* were the idiot. I meant Merrin. *You've* been wonderful. Don't worry, we'll get some Wizards down to the Moat right away. Merrin must come straight back here. I do *not* want those Ring Wizards being drawn out into the Castle."

As Marcia hurried off, something occurred to her. "Alther, who was sitting on the Chair?"

"Oh, Nursie, of course."

"So how come Merrin's gone too?"

"He jumped in after her. He actually seemed very upset; I don't think he meant to do it." Alther shook his head. "He's a funny lad. You can't help but feel sorry for him."

Marcia nodded. "You know, Alther, I think this is the first time that Merrin has cared about anyone but himself. Maybe there's hope for him yet."

"Maybe. I'll take some Wizards down to the Moat, pronto."

"Thank you, Alther."

"Oh, anytime. Well, no, *not* anytime. Actually, to be frank, *never again*."

Marcia smiled ruefully. "Indeed, Alther. Never again."

47
Fyre

The little pyramid **Keye** was on the map table, sitting on the footprint of the Wizard Tower—which it fitted perfectly. Watched by Milo, Marcia, Septimus and Marcellus, Jenna was sitting at Marcia's command table writing the complete **Committal** into *The Queen Rules* in her most careful handwriting.

"Septimus, would you fetch Julius, please," said Marcia. "I would like him to check this before we go."

Septimus found Julius with

some difficulty—the ghost had become very nearly transparent. But as requested, and with great care, Julius checked through the **Committal**. "Yes . . . yes, I believe it to be correct. Hathor, see there, is the **Keystone**," he said, his long finger pointing to a bird symbol in a square.

"Thank you, Julius," said Marcia. "We do value your knowledge."

"You are very welcome," the ghost replied somewhat stiffly.

"Julius," Marcia continued.

"Yes?"

"Do you not have something to say to Marcellus?"

"Oh!" Julius made an odd, ghostly coughing sound. "Marcellus. I am. Um. Sorry. I . . . I apologize."

"It is those who lost their lives in the disaster to whom you should apologize," said Marcellus.

"Yes. I . . . I realize that."

"Not to mention all succeeding ExtraOrdinary Wizards who were denied essential knowledge of the Castle. And access to the skills of Alchemie for nearly five hundred years."

"Yes . . . well."

"And to my Drummins, whom you knowingly left to die."

"Apologize to *Drummins*?" Julius was aghast.

"I leave it you to consider your actions, Julius. I can say no more." With that Marcellus turned on his heel and walked away.

Jenna watched Marcellus go with a good deal of sympathy. She closed *The Queen Rules* and got to her feet. "Okay," she said. "I'm ready to do the **Committal**."

"Not on your own," said Milo. "I am coming with you."

"Jenna will not be going alone," said Marcia. "You can be sure of that, Milo." She got to her feet. "Excuse me a moment."

Marcia quickly returned with Marcellus. "Our Castle Alchemist has a suggestion," she said.

Marcellus smiled happily. He knew what it meant for Marcia to freely use his old title. "It is extremely dangerous approaching from the **Fyre** hatch," he said, "as Simon here will attest." Simon nodded. "I suggest we go to the **Fyre** Chamber through the Covert Way."

"Covert Way? *Another* secret, Marcellus?" Marcia asked with a wry smile.

This was still a sensitive subject for Marcellus. "It is not *my* secret, Marcia," he retorted.

"It is mine, ExtraOrdinary," admitted Julius. "The Covert Way is the direct connection between here and the **Fyre**

Chamber and emerges on the Chamber floor, behind the Cauldron. I **Concealed** it after the Great Alchemie Disaster. It lies beneath the spiral stairs. I will show you."

In the cramped and dusty inspection space beneath the spiral stairs, Milo, Marcia, Septimus, Jenna, Beetle, Marcellus and the ghost of Julius Pike were gathered, looking at a roughly plastered, blank wall.

"There is an ExtraOrdinary **Conceal** here."

"*Not* noted in the **Concealed** Register," said Marcia tartly.

"No," admitted Julius.

ExtraOrdinary **Conceals** were undetectable and used only by ExtraOrdinary Wizards within the confines of the Wizard Tower. A condition of their use was that they should be entered in the **Concealed** Register so that every ExtraOrdinary Wizard would know what was **Concealed** where in the Wizard Tower.

"So what have you been **Concealing** here, Mr. Pike?" asked Marcia.

"A moving chamber that will take us to the Chamber of **Fyre**."

"Really? Well, I suggest you **Reveal** it right away." Septimus could tell that Marcia was furious.

Julius obeyed and a smooth and shiny black door in the wall was **Revealed**: Marcia gave Septimus and Marcellus a quizzical look. "*That* looks familiar."

"Yes, I know," Septimus said guiltily.

"Was that what you were doing on that terrible day—traveling to the **Fyre** Chamber?" Marcia asked.

Septimus felt really bad. "Yes, it was."

"Goodness!" said Marcia, shaking her head.

"I *so* wanted to tell you," said Septimus. "But I had promised not to."

"A promise very reluctantly given," said Marcellus. "But it was necessary, Marcia. I needed his help. You do understand?"

"I do understand," she said. "And it will never be necessary again." She turned to Julius. "Is this safe?" she asked.

"Yes. When I **Concealed** it I left it **Charging**," said Julius. "I always believed that maintenance of the moving chamber was important. Unlike the Alchemists who left theirs to look after itself."

"Huh," harrumphed Marcellus.

Up until then Septimus had found little to agree upon with

Julius Pike, but he had to admit that the ghost had a point about maintenance.

"Very well, Julius," said Marcia. "Take us through the Covert Way."

Julius Pike placed the palm of his ghostly hand onto a worn patch to the right-hand side of the door—then snatched it away. "I forget that I am a ghost," he said despairingly. "It must have a Living hand."

Septimus considered that he had some experience in the matter. "I'll do it," he offered.

The ghost shook his head. "It will not recognize you," he said. "This Covert Way would open only for the **Identity** palm prints of the then-ExtraOrdinary Wizard—who was myself—my Senior Apprentice and the Castle Alchemist."

"Well then, Marcellus can do it," said Marcia.

"It will not recognize me," said Marcellus. "Julius removed my **Identity** from everything."

"I could smash it open," Milo offered eagerly.

"It doesn't work like that," said Marcellus snappily.

"Then I shall just have to climb through the hatch like everyone else," said Jenna. "It will be all right."

"No," said Marcellus. "It will *not* be all right."

"Syrah!" said Septimus suddenly. "Julius, she was your Senior Apprentice! Will it recognize her palm?"

Julius heaved a hollow ghostly sigh that gave everyone goose bumps. "If she were alive, indeed it would," he said mournfully. "After Syrah vanished on the **Queste**, I did not have the heart to remove her **Identity**. However, Apprentice, she is *not* alive. I do not know why you say such foolish things."

"I thought you were going to tell him," Septimus said to Marcia.

Marcia looked tetchy. "It's been just a little bit busy here, Septimus. I've had more important things to think about."

"Yes, of course. Sorry. So, shall I take Mr. Pike up to the Sick Bay?" asked Septimus.

"Yes," said Marcia. "Don't be long, will you?"

Ten minutes later, a wobbly, emotional Syrah Syara, supported by Rose—who had been nominated as nurse by Dandra Draa—and an equally wobbly Julius Pike joined the party beneath the Wizard Tower spiral stairs. Still trembling from the shock of having just met the ghost of her much-loved Julius, Syrah placed her thin, translucently pale hand onto the smooth black material of the entrance to the Covert Way.

Septimus watched, trying not to remember his last experience in the identical moving chamber on Alchemie Quay. But unlike him, Syrah did not have to push all her weight against the concealed opening plate. The lightest touch of her palm caused a bright green light to shine beneath. Then the oval door slid noiselessly open and the blue light inside the chamber came on.

Jenna, Marcellus, Milo and Marcia looked at one another in surprise—they had never seen anything like it.

"What *is* this?" asked Marcia, peering into the featureless chamber. "I can't feel any **Magyk** here."

"It depends what you call **Magyk**," said Marcellus obscurely.

With some trepidation, Septimus followed Marcellus, Marcia, Milo, Jenna, Beetle, Syrah—supported by Rose—and Julius into the chamber. It was a tight squash. Syrah now placed her hand on the inside wall and a bright red light glowed beneath it. The door closed silently. No one said a word. The blue light gave everyone an unearthly pallor and made the whites of their eyes oddly prominent. Septimus noticed that Marcia was trying hard not to look scared—and not entirely succeeding. Milo, who was used to confined quarters in ships, was more robust. He grasped Marcia's hand encouragingly, and to Septimus's surprise Marcia did not object.

A small orange arrow now appeared beside the door. It pointed, Septimus was interested to see, not vertically downward, but diagonally. Syrah swiped her hand across the arrow and everyone—even Septimus and Marcellus, who were expecting it—gasped. They felt the stomach-churning sensation of the chamber falling, but with the added strangeness of it taking a diagonal path. Jenna, who was stuck in the middle, began to feel queasy.

The journey took less than a minute, but by the time the chamber finally shuddered to a halt, Jenna felt sick. She suspected it was not because of the ride but the thought of what awaited her outside. Everyone exchanged nervous glances in the blue light. Milo put his arm around Jenna. "We'll be with you every step of the way," he said.

Jenna nodded. Then, putting on her best Princess voice, she said, "Syrah. Would you open the door, please?"

The door opened and heat and a tremendous roar, as if from a huge waterfall, hit them. One by one, they stepped out into the shadows, shocked by the fierce red glow and the great curved wall of the black Cauldron that rose in front of them.

The exit from the moving chamber was a few steps up from the earthen floor of the cavern, behind one of the thick, riveted legs that supported the Cauldron. There was no view of the **Fyre** Chamber at all from the exit and in the old times this had annoyed Marcellus, particularly when he had visitors from the Wizard Tower whom he wanted to impress. But now he was thankful for the cover. Marcellus checked all was safe, then beckoned to everyone to follow. Jenna went to step down and then stopped.

"Oh!" she gasped. *The floor was alive.*

A sea of small, squashy, dusty faces were gazing up at her, their dark eyes shining. Jenna looked down at their unblinking gaze and for a moment she knew what it was like to be a Queen in front of a vast crowd.

"What *are* they?" Jenna whispered to Marcellus.

"Drummins," said Marcellus. "Do not worry; they will make a path for you. Drummins do not like to be trodden on. Ah, here is Duglius."

Duglius scrambled up the wall like a lizard and offered Jenna his hand—warm, callused and gritty with dust. Jenna took it and his suckered fingertips stuck delicately to her hand. "Welcome, Princess, to the Chamber of **Fyre**."

"Thank you," said Jenna. She felt the little suckers unstick themselves and very carefully she stepped down into the shadows.

Marcia turned to Syrah, who was leaning against the wall of the chamber, deathly pale against the shiny black surface. "Syrah, you must remain here," she said.

Syrah swayed dizzily and Rose helped her down to the floor. "You'll be okay," Rose said. "I'll stay with you."

"So shall I," said Julius, glad of an excuse not to venture into the Chamber of **Fyre**.

"Thank you, Rose," said Marcia. She looked out into the unknown that lay in front of her. "Rose. If anything, er . . . happens, you must close the door immediately and take the chamber back to the Wizard Tower. Get a Senior Wizard to put an anti-**Darke** on it *at once*. You understand?"

Rose nodded somberly. "Yes," she said. "I understand."

Marcia took a deep breath and stepped out into the Chamber of **Fyre**.

"Welcome, ExtraOrdinary Wizard with snakes upon her feet," said Duglius. "Welcome to the Chamber of **Fyre**."

Marcia smiled graciously and with the words "Thank you,

Duglius Drummin. It is an honor to be here," she wiped away the lingering mistrust between Drummin and Wizard.

When Marcellus, Milo, Septimus, and Beetle had left the moving chamber, Duglius jumped down from the wall. "Follow me," he said. "We will make a path for you."

And they did. The Drummin crowd parted like water as, in single file, they followed Duglius beneath the round belly of the Cauldron. Beetle was last. He looked back and saw the path closing behind him and a multitude of little dark eyes staring up at him. He quickly turned around and followed Septimus through the crowd.

Jenna and Marcia were the first to emerge from beneath the Cauldron. They stopped, amazed at the sudden, searing brilliance of the light and the soaring height of the Chamber of **Fyre**—the glitter of the webs of silver shining in the roof far, far above and the massive black roundness of the Cauldron bellying out above them. They waited while everyone gathered together, silent and subdued. What struck every single person was the sense of the presence of evil.

"Where are they?" Jenna whispered to Marcellus.

Marcellus pointed up to the Inspection Circle around the top of the Cauldron, some thirty feet above their heads. Jenna squinted upward but could see nothing—the glare of the flames dazzled her; it was like looking at the sun. Duglius led them around the base of the Cauldron, heading toward the metal steps that would take them up to the Viewing Station and onto the Inspection Circle. As they drew near, two shadows fell across them—everyone froze. They waited for the Ring Wizards to pass overhead like a dark storm cloud, then set off once more until they came within sight of the steps and the Viewing Station above.

Duglius held up his hand and the party stopped. "Here is safe to wait," he said.

"Thank you, Duglius," said Marcia. "I will go first, then Jenna."

"Then me." Beetle and Milo spoke together.

"And me," said Septimus.

"No," said Marcia. "The more of us who go, the more dangerous it becomes."

"Marcia. I am coming with Jen," said Septimus. "Whatever you say."

"We are *all* coming," said Marcellus. "We cannot leave you to do this alone."

Jenna remembered what her grandmother had said one evening as they had sat watching the water. "Sometimes, dear, you just have to be what I call *Queeny*. It may seem strange at first but it always works."

And so that is what Jenna did. "*I* am doing the **Committal**; I shall choose. The fewer people who are in danger, the better. Marcia and I will go. No one else." She looked at Marcia. "And *I* shall go first."

Marcia bowed her head. "Very well," she said.

From her ExtraOrdinary Wizard belt, Marcia drew out what remained of the Two-Faced Ring and handed it to Jenna. Jenna noticed that Marcia's hand was shaking—and Marcia noticed the Jenna's hand was shaking. Neither said a word while Jenna looked down at the twisted band of gold, which lay in her palm so lightly that she could hardly feel it. It was time to go—but before she went, there was something Jenna wanted to say.

"Beetle," she said.

"Yes." Beetle gulped.

"I just wanted to say that I am really sorry that when you were in the **Sealed** Hermetic Chamber . . . you know . . . after the **Darke Domaine** . . . that I didn't stay to see if you were all right. Well, not properly all right. I *so* wish I had. I did really care about how you were, even though I know it didn't look like it."

It took Beetle some seconds to reply. "Oh. Gosh. Well, thank you." He reached out for Jenna's hand and took it. "Be careful up there, hey?"

Jenna nodded and held Beetle's hand tightly.

"Time to go," said Marcia briskly.

Marcia and Jenna walked toward the foot of the steps, Marcia spoke urgently in a low voice. "Jenna. Remember I will be right behind you all the time. When we near the top I will put a **SafeShield** around us. When we are close enough to"—she glanced upward—"*them* . . . and you are ready, tell me. I will let the **Shield** go. You must then begin the **Committal** at once. I will protect you. You must not concern yourself about *anything else*. Concentrate only on the words of the **Committal**. When you say the **Keystone** word, there will be a flash of light. Throw the ring into the light but do not stop speaking. Be sure to finish."

Jenna and Marcia reached the steps. They glanced upward at the flimsy metal lattice that would its way up around the black belly of the Cauldron into the searing light far above, and exchanged nervous smiles. Then Jenna put her foot on the first step and Marcia followed. Slowly, stealthily, they began the long and lonely climb up out of the protection of the shadows and into the glare and heat of the fire.

As they disappeared from sight, Milo put his arm around Beetle's shoulders. "All right?" he asked.

"No. Not really," said Beetle.

"Me neither," said Milo.

Jenna and Marcia headed up toward the heat and the roar of the fire. As they neared the top of the steps Marcia tapped Jenna on the shoulder. **Shield** *now*, she mouthed. Jenna nodded. An opalescent blanket of **Magyk** fell around Jenna and Marcia, cutting the roar of the fire to a distant murmur, turning the scorching heat down to merely hot and making the Ring Wizards—who were so very near—feel oddly distant. With the sensation of walking underwater Jenna stepped up onto the Viewing Station. Despite the raging fire in front of her, the loudest sound she heard was the *tip-tap* of pointy python shoes as Marcia followed her.

Inside the **Shield** Marcia's voice rang clear. "They are on the Inspection Circle going counterclockwise. I can see the **Darkenesse** behind the flames. To give us the advantage of surprise, I suggest we creep up from behind. If we get onto the Circle now, they won't even see us."

Jenna had planned very carefully what to do, but no amount of planning could prepare her for how scared she now felt. "Okay," she said, "let's go." She stepped down onto the surprisingly shaky walkway and felt Marcia follow. They set off in a counterclockwise direction. Unnerved by not being able to grab hold of the handrails because of the **Shield**, but insulated from the horror of the wall of fire on her left and the dizzying drop to her right, Jenna moved along the Inspection Circle as carefully as any **FootFollowing** witch.

There was a sudden intake of breath from Marcia, and Jenna stopped dead. Two figures, too tall to be human, clothed in **Darke** light, their long, straggly hair streaming in the rush of air that was swirling in to fuel the flames, were no more than a few feet in front of them.

"That's them," said Marcia—rather unnecessarily, Jenna thought. "Tell me when you're ready."

All Jenna wanted was to get it over with. "Now," she said.

"Sure?"

"Yes. I'm sure. Take the **Shield** away."

Marcia let go of the **Shield**. "We're out!" It was like stepping into an oven where a thunderstorm was raging. The Ring Wizards swung around and at once Marcia threw on a **Restrain**, but not before the red rays of light from their eyes had seared across Jenna's cloak, sending up wisps of smoke.

Clutching the ring in her hand, Jenna began to speak the **Committal**. "By our Power, at this hour, we do you . . ."

The Wizards sprang forward, their hands like the claws of a pouncing tiger, their long curved nails heading for Jenna's neck, pushing with all their strength against the **Restrain**. But Jenna remembered what Hotep-Ra had told her. *Stand firm. Look them in the eye. Say the words.*

And so she did.

Steadily, Jenna made her way through the **Committal**, determined not to rush and to speak each word clearly. As she stood defiantly on the walkway, the almost unbearable heat from the fire scorching her cloak, Jenna was unaware that behind her Marcia was struggling. Marcia didn't know if it was the terrible heat, or the combined power of the Wizards, but the **Restrain** kept slipping and every time it did, the Ring Wizards moved a little closer.

But Jenna did not flinch.

Desperately, Marcia listened for the **Keystone**. She watched, powerless, as the ten-foot-tall beings pushed against her **Magyk**, inching toward Jenna. And then, at last, there came a soft word, almost drowned by the roar of the flames: *Hathor.* There was a flash of dazzling purple light, and Jenna threw the ring into it. There was a scream and the Ring Wizards began to melt like candlewax. Concentrating hard, Jenna moved smoothly through the last seven words, and at the final word, **"Commit,"** darkness fell.

Within the Chamber of **Fyre**, Time was suspended.

Now, from deep inside the void of Time, the Ring Wizards finally understood what their fate was to be. Two blood-chilling howls of fury and despair filled the Chamber of **Fyre** and set everyone's hairs on the back of their necks tingling. Seven timeless seconds passed while the Ring Wizards were **Subsumed** into the gold of the ring and as Time kicked back in, a vortex of wind swirled through the Chamber of **Fyre**, throwing everyone to the ground.

Jenna and Marcia clung to the guardrail of the Inspection Circle as the whirlwind spun above the Cauldron, taking the flames with it, spiraling them up through the Alchemie

Chimney and sending them bursting out into the evening sky.

A shocked silence fell in the Chamber of **Fyre**. No one moved. All that could be heard was the soft *fuff-fuff-fuff* of the tiny blue flames of the Alchemical **Fyre** and a *cling* as a gold ring with two screaming green faces imprisoned in it hit the lattice walkway and dropped through one of the holes.

"The ring!" yelled Marcia. "*Get the ring!*"

Milo caught it.

48
A Queen

Marcellus *was smiling from ear* to ear as he slowly lowered the Two-Faced Ring, suspended on a golden chain, toward the beautiful, blue Alchemical **Fyre**. Marcia very nearly told him to get a move on. But she didn't. Marcellus was, she thought, allowed to savor the moment. He deserved it.

Marcellus was as happy as he could remember being for a very long time. He was back in his **Fyre** Chamber by right and about to **DeNature** the very thing that had destroyed his life so very long ago. He watched the faces of those he had gathered around him for this moment, transfixed by the ring as it dangled above the tiny blue flames that flickered gently across the top of the **Fyre** Cauldron. Here were people that Marcellus had grown to care about—the ExtraOrdinary Wizard, the Chief Hermetic Scribe and the Queen-to-be, not to mention his old Apprentice, Septimus, and his new Apprentice, Simon, who had come along with the accomplished chimney architect, Lucy Heap. There was Alther Mella, and also the very first ExtraOrdinary Wizard, Hotep-Ra, of whom Marcellus was quite in awe. And as the ghost of Julius Pike, escorted by Duglius Drummin, joined them, Marcellus felt rather outnumbered by ExtraOrdinary Wizards.

The Two-Faced Ring was now dangling just a few feet above the **Fyre**, and the tips of the delicate Alchemie flames leaped up to meet it, like fish jumping for insects on the surface of a stream. The pure light of the **Fyre** illuminated the evil green faces trapped in the ring for the very last time. They flashed in anger and as Marcellus lowered them into the **Fyre**, clapping and cheering erupted from the assembled watchers.

Marcellus turned to his audience. "It is done," he said. "The Two-Faced Ring will stay in the center of the **Fyre** for twenty-one days. Then the ExtraOrdinary Wizard—I mean Madam

Marcia Overstrand, although naturally, all ExtraOrdinary Wizards here are welcome to attend—and I will retrieve the ring, which by then will be no more than a lead band. As we transmute lead to gold, so we transmute gold to lead. It is the Alchemie way."

Marcia had bitten her tongue for long enough. "Oh, give it a rest, Marcellus," she said. "Come and have some lunch."

Three weeks later, all the Drummins had gathered beneath the Cauldron. Duglius glared at the late arrivals—young teens who rarely emerged from their burrows before midday.

"We are all here, we are?" Duglius inquired.

A singsong murmur of assent spread through the dusty crowd.

"Good Drummins. There is a ghostly person who has a thing to say to all of us all."

A murmuring spread through the crowd as the ghost of Julius Pike **Appeared**, glowing bright in the gloom.

"Drummins," Julius began nervously. "I, um, have come to apologize. Many hundred years ago I did all Drummins a great wrong. I did not listen to your wisdom. I left you all to die. I did not care. For this I am truly, truly sorry."

A murmur of surprise spread through the Drummins. Duglius signed for them to be quiet. "Do we Drummins all accept this sorry, do we?" he asked.

Another murmur began and this time Duglius did not interrupt. It continued for so long that Julius was beginning to think they would not accept his "sorry." He felt sad at the thought. Over the previous weeks, the ghost had, at Marcia's suggestion, accompanied her on a series of visits to the Drummins in order to get to know and understand them. Like Marcia, Julius had grown to like and respect them. He was surprised to find how much it now mattered to him that the Drummins felt the same about him. Julius waited anxiously while the Drummin crowd was clearly discussing him, illustrating their discussion by pointing their suckered fingers at him.

At last the discussion subsided and Duglius signed to the crowd. They made a sign back to him, which looked to Julius like a refusal. Duglius turned to the ghost and Julius felt nervous.

"We, Drummins," said Duglius. He paused. "We do accept your sorry, we do."

"Oh!" Julius sounded surprised and pleased. "Thank you,

Duglius. And thank you, Drummins, all." He bowed and floated up the ladder to join the group on the Viewing Station above.

Julius was just in time to see Marcellus present Marcia with the **DeNatured** ring. "It is done," said Marcellus.

Marcia looked at the plain lead band resting on her palm. "It is done," she agreed. "Thank you."

Marcellus bowed. "It was, I can truly say, my pleasure."

Marcia smiled and handed the lead band to Hotep-Ra, who inspected it closely. He sighed. "It is for the best. But who would have thought that it was once a beautiful gold ring," he said, giving it back to Marcia.

Marcia had an idea. "Can you turn this back to gold?" she asked Marcellus. "To how it was when Hotep-Ra gave it to the Queen?"

"Indeed I can," said Marcellus. "And I shall do so with great pleasure."

Preparations now began for Jenna to be crowned Queen.

Hotep-Ra decided to stay for the Coronation and he continued as the honored guest of the Wizard Tower. Everyone, even Marcia, was a little overawed to have the founding

ExtraOrdinary Wizard take up residence in the Tower, but Hotep-Ra was used to a quiet life in the House of Foryx and preferred to spend most of his time in the Pyramid Library with Septimus and Rose. One morning, during a visit to the Sick Bay to see Jim Knee and Edmund and Ernold Heap, Marcia confided in Dandra Draa that she was worried that Hotep-Ra did not like her.

"It not *you* he not like, Marcia. It that nasty little ghost on your sofa."

Marcia felt relieved, but she made her way back to her rooms with a heavy heart. How she would love to have cozy evenings sitting by the fire with Hotep-Ra, Septimus and Rose discussing **Magyk**. Trust the wretched Jillie Djinn to ruin a once-in-a-lifetime opportunity. She opened the door and Jillie Djinn welcomed her with what had become her usual greeting: "Fire!"

Marcia stomped up to the Library, where Hotep-Ra was sitting at the table, explaining an Arcane **Transformation** to an enthralled Septimus and Rose. "Excuse me for interrupting," she said apologetically.

Hotep-Ra smiled. "Come in, Marcia, my dear. It is always good to see you." Encouraged, Marcia joined them. "Hotep-Ra,

I have a question," she said.

"Yes?"

"Is there any way of removing a ghost from their place of entering ghosthood during the first year and a day?"

Hotep-Ra shook his head. "Generally, it is not possible. But if, like your friend on the sofa downstairs—"

"My *friend*!" Marcia was shocked.

"Is she not?"

"No! No, no, *no*! I can't stand the woman—I mean the ghost. That is why I am asking. Is there any way of getting rid of her?"

Hotep-Ra smiled. "Ah. I see. Well, you are fortunate. She has short legs, does she not?"

Marcia was bemused. "Yes, she does. Short, fat little legs, actually."

Hotep-Ra smiled. "Then it is an easy matter."

That evening Marcia **Lit** the fire in her sitting room and sat around it with Hotep-Ra, Septimus, Rose, Simon, Lucy and Marcellus talking quietly about **Magyk** and Alchemie. A feeling of contentment stole over her—this was how it was meant to be.

Outside, in the wide corridor that led to the stairs, sat the sofa. And on the sofa sat the ghost of Jillie Djinn. Her little legs had never touched the ground.

MidSummer Day—the traditional day for a Coronation—drew near. Jenna decided, despite Queen Cerys's disapproval, that she wanted it to take place beside the river.

Sarah Heap began to panic. "What if it rains?" she said.

"It won't," declared Jenna.

Jenna's grandmother thought it was a wonderful idea. "I wanted to have mine outside too, dear," she said, "but I let my mother talk me out of it. Remember, today you can do what you want and, take it from me, it won't always be like that. I would make the most of it."

And so preparations went ahead, and the Palace and its gardens once more became the busy hub of the Castle. The four Forest Heaps stayed to help Sarah and Silas get things ready, and everyone lent a hand—except for Milo, who once again had disappeared.

On Coronation Morning Marcia was up early. Milo, to Marcia's annoyance, had insisted on a 7:00 A.M. appointment at the Palace to "check everything is tiketty-boo, if that's all right with you, Marcia." Marcia arrived as the Clockmaker's clock was striking seven. She knocked on the Palace doors and yawned. She would be glad when the Coronation was over and Hotep-Ra—lovely though he was—had gone home, so that she and Septimus could get back to normal.

The doors were flung open. "Good morning, Marcia," said Milo chirpily.

Embarrassed, Marcia stopped in midyawn. "Oh! Morning, Milo."

"Good morning, Madam Marcia." A familiar voice came from behind Milo.

"Hildegarde!" said Marcia.

Milo turned and clasped Hildegarde's hands in both of his. "Thank you so much, Hildegarde," he said. "It's been a long night. You have been wonderful."

Hildegarde blushed. "It was my pleasure," she said as she squeezed out of the door past Marcia.

Marcia watched Hildegarde hurry off down the Palace drive. "*Well!*" she said.

It was a distinctly frosty Marcia whom Milo escorted through the Palace entrance hall. At the entrance to the Long

Walk, Milo stopped. "Close your eyes," he said.

"Milo, I do not have time to play silly games," Marcia snapped.

"Please," Milo said. He gave Marcia the slightly lopsided smile that she had liked so much, so very long ago.

Marcia sighed. "Oh, all right."

Milo took Marcia's hand and led her into the Long Walk—she knew where she was by the chill of the old stone passageway. "You can open your eyes now," said Milo with a smile in his voice.

Marcia was lost for words. After some moments she managed, "It's *beautiful!*"

Stretching as far as Marcia could see down the Long Walk, the ancient Palace gold candleholders were back in their places. Tall and elegant, in each burned a fat beeswax candle, filling the normally musty Walk with the subtle scent of honey. The light from the candles illuminated treasures that Marcia dimly remembered from before the Bad Old Days: Ancient portraits of the Queens, beautiful painted statues settled back into their niches, polished wooden chests, little gilded tables and chairs, and, covering the old threadbare carpet, intricately patterned rugs in soft blues and reds.

Milo began to speak. "When I first came back to the Palace and saw what DomDaniel's thugs had taken, I swore that by the time my Jenna was Queen I would have returned everything to its rightful place. But it was not until I met Hildegarde that I was able to do this."

Marcia said nothing. But she was beginning to understand.

Hildegarde had once been part of the Sales Force who had, under instructions from DomDaniel, sold off all the Palace treasures—mainly to fund DomDaniel's lavish banquets. Hildegarde had joined the Wizard Tower as part of Marcia's Second-Chance Scheme and had always wanted to make amends for her part in ransacking the Palace. And so when Milo asked her to help him track down as many of the old treasures as possible, Hildegarde had jumped at the chance. She had kept a note of every sale and with her help, Milo was able to buy back most of the long-lost treasures. He had spent the last weeks touring the Farmlands with a cart, picking up the more distant finds and hiding them in the locked rooms at the end of the Long Walk. On Coronation Eve, Milo and Hildegarde worked through the night, and by the morning the Long Walk was transformed into the wonderful place that Marcia now saw.

"So why didn't you tell me?" asked Marcia.

"Well, at first I thought you would object to me using the valuable time of a Wizard for non-**Magykal** purposes. But after those unfortunate misunderstandings, I did try to tell you. But you wouldn't listen. So I wrote you a letter explaining."

"Oh," said Marcia a little sheepishly.

"Which I could tell you hadn't read," said Milo. He smiled. "I reckoned you were still in such a temper that you probably threw it in the fire or something. So I figured the only way was to show you."

"It's wonderful," said Marcia. "A new start for the Palace. Has Jenna seen it?"

"No," said Milo. "I wanted it to be a surprise for her Coronation Day. I am about to show her. But I wanted to show you first."

It was a most **Magykal** day. The sun shone—as Jenna had known it would—and the entire Castle turned out to see her.

In the morning, accompanied by Sir Hereward, Milo showed Jenna the Long Walk. Buzzing with excitement,

Jenna wandered through the Palace gardens, glad of some time to be alone and think about what her future might hold. The gardens were decorated with the multitude of Coronation offerings that had caused Sarah Heap so much trouble. Metallic red and gold Coronation Bunting hung from the trees and glittered in the sunlight, the lawns were strewn with the huge assortment of Coronation Rugs, and Coronation Cushions were scattered underneath the brightly colored Coronation Sunshades. Jenna thought they looked wonderful. As she wandered down toward the river, Jenna came to a sudden halt. Running the length of the lawn was the longest table (the Coronation Table) covered with the longest, whitest cloth (the Coronation Cloth) that she had ever seen. The table gave her a strange feeling when she saw it. At first she was not sure why—and then she remembered. It was a much, *much* bigger version of the table that Sarah had once laid ready for breakfast on her tenth birthday—the day when her life had changed and she had discovered that one day she would be the Castle Queen.

In the afternoon the Palace Gates were thrown open and the Castle inhabitants began to drift in and enjoy the gardens and the Coronation Tea, which was now laid out on the long table. The table was piled high with the Coronation Plates, Coronation Candelabra, Coronation Biscuit Tins, Coronation Cups and Coronation Cutlery that had been brought to the Palace. To the plinky-plonky sounds of the Coronation Pianola, 1,006 Coronation Cupcakes, 2,027 Coronation Biscuits and 7,063 Coronation Sandwiches were consumed that afternoon. Along with—inadvertently—twenty-three caterpillars, fourteen slugs and a baby spider.

By the end of the afternoon, Jenna was convinced that she had talked to absolutely everyone who lived in the Castle at least twice. As the daylight began to fade, a respectful silence fell and Jenna began to feel a little nervous. Beetle, Septimus, Milo, Marcia, Sarah and Silas joined her as she walked down toward the riverbank, where she had decided the Coronation itself would take place.

And as Jenna stood on the threadbare Coronation Carpet surrounded by Sarah and Silas Heap and her seven brothers, the ghost of Queen Cerys looked at the Heaps with undisguised horror. Like Theodora Gringe, she wished they would just *keep to the back*. But another ghost, Queen Matthilda, stood chatting happily to Alther Mella and his partner, Alice Nettles. She was smiling broadly. Queen Matthilda thought the Heaps were "a breath of fresh air," she told Alther with a smile.

As the light of the setting sun turned the river a deep orange and sent glints of green glancing off the Dragon Boat, which lay bobbing quietly beside the landing stage, Hotep-Ra picked up the simple, True Crown that he remembered so well, and placed it on Jenna's head, saying, "Jenna. I name you Queen. All will be well in the best of all possible worlds. So be it."

A ripple of polite applause ran through the crowd—Castle people did not believe in making a great fuss of their Queens. But as the new Queen wandered around the Palace lawns, she was surprised and touched to find how popular she was. People flocked to her to offer their congratulations and tiny gifts—tiny because tradition dictated that a Coronation gift must be able to be held in one hand. (This was something that had passed Milo by.)

Marcia gave Jenna the **Transmuted** ring that had once belonged to Hotep-Ra's Queen. Hotep-Ra **Magykally** rebound *The Queen Rules* in soft red leather with an imprint of the Dragon Boat stamped upon the front, and furnished it with a pure gold clasp and corners—the first to be made in the

Fyre—courtesy of Marcellus. Wolf Boy—who now called himself Marwick—had come with Aunt Zelda and arrived only just in time. Aunt Zelda had not only gotten stuck in the cupboard door coming out of the Queen's Way, but she had insisted on bringing the rather large Storm Petrel with her, which she had told Marwick had followed her home on the Dragon Boat. Relieved to see Jenna at last, Marwick thrust a grubby leather drawstring bag into her hand and smiled.

"Ooh, pebbles!" said Jenna, opening the bag excitedly. By then she had been given so much gold and so many jewels that she was genuinely happy to see a bag of perfectly round, plain pebbles.

"Yeah. But not all the time," said Marwick cryptically.

Jenna took out the largest pebble and held it in the palm of her hand. It felt oddly familiar.

Suddenly, Jenna felt the pebble move. A small head emerged and then four short, stumpy legs. "Petroc Trelawney!" she cried. The pebble paid no attention; it raised itself up on its little legs and walked a few steps over to where a small cupcake crumb was stuck on Jenna's finger.

"He's got kids," said Marwick. "They're *everywhere*. We wondered why we kept finding pebbles in the kitchen until

Zelda saw them walk in one morning."

"So she remembered?" asked Jenna.

Marwick smiled. "Yeah. She figured out who it was at once."

Jenna loved having Petroc Trelawney back, but the gift she treasured most was the one Beetle gave her: a small gold heart with the True Crown engraved on it. "I found it in the Saturday market," he said. "It's really old. I think it belonged to a Queen a long time ago. I hope you don't mind. That it's a heart, I mean."

Jenna smiled. "Oh, Beetle, I don't mind at all."

⁜ 49 ⁜

AN EXTRAORDINARY WIZARD

A*fter the Coronation, Hotep-Ra decided* to return to the House of Foryx. Very early, one warm morning in early July, Jenna, Beetle and Septimus stood on the Palace landing stage beside the Dragon Boat, which glinted with brilliant flashes of gold and azure blue in the early-morning sun. Standing at the tiller of the Dragon Boat was Hotep-Ra.

It reminded

Hotep-Ra so much of the time long ago when another Queen had said a tearful farewell, that he looked around to check there was not a pair of **Darke** Wizards swooping down upon them. Hotep-Ra smiled. Of course there wasn't. At last the two evil beings that had destroyed his own family, his wife and children, and then pursued him three times around the world were gone forever.

Hotep-Ra regarded Jenna pensively. She looked so much like his own dear Queen from long ago, with her gold circlet shining in the sunlight, her long, dark hair blowing in the breeze and concern in her eyes. She would be a good Queen, thought Hotep-Ra—not one of the crazy ones, not one of the silly ones and definitely not one of the nasty ones, although she might possibly be one of the more determined ones.

Jenna was clutching her beautiful new binding of *The Queen Rules*. "Thank you," she said. "Thank you for *everything*."

Hotep-Ra bowed. "I merely showed you how. *You* were brave enough to actually do it."

"Bye, Jen. See you later," said Septimus, as casually as if he were just going down the road.

Jenna sighed. She hated the thought of Septimus going back

to the House of Foryx. "Bye, Sep. Come back soon. Promise?"

Septimus jumped onboard and joined Hotep-Ra at the tiller. "I promise, Jen. Bye, Beetle. See you."

"Safe journey, Sep."

"Thanks. Time to go. *Byeeeeee.*"

Jenna and Beetle watched the Dragon Boat sail out into the middle of the river and turn so that she was facing into the wind. Septimus took down the sail and the mast. Then the Dragon Boat raised her green wings high and brought them down with a *swoosh*, sending waves rippling out, splashing up against the landing stage. They watched her take off, rise up into the sky and fly out across the Farmlands, heading for the open sea beyond the Port. They waited until the Dragon Boat was no more than a little speck in the sky and then turned and walked slowly back together toward the Palace.

It was midnight when the Dragon Boat landed in her usual place outside the House of Foryx. Hotep-Ra insisted that Septimus spend the night there. "You cannot fly back tired, Apprentice. It is dangerous. Sleep here and return tomorrow." And so, trusting his **Questing Stone** to bring him out into his own Time, as it had done before, Septimus went into the House of Foryx once more. But before he did, just to be certain that he was back in his own Time when he came out, he wrote the date in the snow: 4TH JULY, 12,004.

It was the next morning—or so Septimus hoped—and Hotep-Ra was escorting him down from his rooms, when something very strange happened. They had reached the balustraded landing, which looked out over the huge entrance hall, and Septimus stopped for a moment to look down at the crowded scene below, misty with candle smoke. Suddenly, the doors to the outside lobby flew open and a young man strode in. He was wearing ExtraOrdinary Wizard robes.

"Simon!" gasped Septimus. "It's *Simon!*" He turned to Hotep-Ra in panic. "Something has happened to Marcia! And not Simon, *no*—he can't be ExtraOrdinary Wizard. He *can't*."

Hotep-Ra smiled. "Well that settles a little bet I had with your Alchemist," he said. "Your heart is with **Magyk**." Septimus did not reply—he was staring in utter dismay at the young ExtraOrdinary Wizard, who was now pushing his way through the crowd and glancing nervously up at the landing.

"Which is a good thing," Hotep-Ra continued, "because that young ExtraOrdinary Wizard is not Simon Heap. He is Septimus Heap."

"*Me?*" gasped Septimus. Dumbstruck, he watched himself coming up the stairs.

"Good-bye, Apprentice." Hotep-Ra held out his hand and Septimus shook it, aware that *he* was getting nearer. "We will meet again," said Hotep-Ra. "As you can see."

Septimus managed a strangled "G'bye" and turned to go. Two steps down he met himself coming up. He looked at his older self, who put his hands up as if to stop him. "Whoa, don't speak. Bit dangerous, Timewise, apparently. I wondered when we'd meet—if it might be this time."

Septimus didn't think he could speak if he tried.

"Marcia's fine," said his older self. "And that is all you want to know right now."

It was true; that was all Septimus wanted to know.

Outside the House of Foryx, Septimus stared at the Dragon Ring that was now safely back on his finger, and shook his head in amazement. Then he checked that he was indeed back in his own Time—sure enough there was the date, still fresh, scrawled in the snow. Dazed, Septimus and the Dragon Boat headed off home, back to the Castle where one day he would be its 777th ExtraOrdinary Wizard.

Which, he now knew, was exactly what he wanted to be—Septimus Heap, ExtraOrdinary Wizard.

Arthur C. Clarke's Third Law:
Any sufficiently advanced technology
is indistinguishable from ***Magyk****.*

Endings

Sick Bay Bulletin:

Posted by Dr. Dandra Draa

Mr. Jim Knee

Mr. Knee has regained enough strength to **TransForm** to his current jinnee status. We are treating the injuries to his hands and we hope for a good recovery.

Scribe Barnaby Ewe

Doing well.

Messrs. Ernold and Edmund Heap

In deep **DisEnchantment**. Critical.

Miss Syrah Syara

Is now in the convalescent room. She is making good progress but please note that visitors are not permitted to stay for longer than *half an hour.*

Matron Midwife Meredith and Merrin Meredith

Discharged. Good riddance.

QUEEN JENNA

Jenna took her job as Queen very seriously. She opened up the Throne Room and held informal meetings there once a week for any Castle inhabitants who wished to discuss a problem. Jenna soon found herself acting as judge in various petty disputes and this led her to set up an informal court system that was, unusually, run by a ghost—Alice Nettles.

Jenna was helped in day-to-day affairs by the ghost of her grandmother, Queen Matthilda. Her mother, Queen Cerys, occasionally ventured out from the Queen's Room, but it was unfortunate that every time she did so, she bumped into Sarah Heap and the terrifying duck-with-the-prickles that had once **Passed Through** her. Jenna found her mother's disapproval a big disappointment, but it did bring her closer to Milo.

BEETLE

Beetle was soon considered by all in the Castle—and Marcia in particular—to be the best Chief Hermetic Scribe there had ever been. The only downside was that Beetle's mother became extremely boring about her son—"He's the Chief Hermetic Scribe, you know"—and lost a good few friends on account of this. But everything else for Beetle was good, and when Jenna invited him to dinner one night at the Palace, things got even better.

MARCIA

The next few years were comparatively uneventful for Marcia in contrast to the early years of Septimus's Apprenticeship. But Marcia liked a challenge, and she did begin to find things a little tame after a while. After a surprise visit from Sam Heap and Marwick, she began researching the Ancient Ways. It was a fascinating study, and a feeling of restlessness at being fixed in the Wizard Tower slowly crept up on her. But Marcia had her priorities right. She stayed put and guided Septimus steadily through the last years of his Apprenticeship—and occasionally consented to go to the Little Theatre in the Ramblings with Milo Banda.

AUNT ZELDA

On her journey back from the House of Foryx with Hotep-Ra, the Dragon Boat had encountered the tail end of a storm—and a large Storm Petrel. Aunt Zelda and the bird recognized each other at once. The Storm Petrel was none other than Aunt Zelda's brother, Theo Heap. Theo had Shape-Shifted into a Storm Petrel many years earlier, and Aunt Zelda had always known that one day a storm would blow him back to her. And now it had.

The arrival of Theo told Aunt Zelda that her Time Had Come. After Jenna's Coronation, she asked Theo to take her into the Forest where their brother, Benjamin Heap, also a Shape-Shifter, now lived as a tree. Theo had been in the habit of visiting Benjamin Heap and knew where to find him. Silas begged to come with them—he longed to see his father once again but because of a **Forget Spell** cast by Morwenna Mould, he could not remember how to find him. Sam was concerned about Silas finding his way home again and offered to come too.

The four Heaps set off on one of those bright Forest mornings when the sunlight filtered down through the leaves and danced across the Forest floor like reflections on water. The Storm Petrel sat on Aunt Zelda's shoulder and directed her ever deeper into the Forest until they reached the quiet, green dimness of the Hidden Glades. There, Theo left Aunt Zelda,

Silas and Sam beneath the spreading branches of Benjamin Heap and flew up to the very top of the tree, where he quietly told Benjamin that their sister had come to the Hidden Glades in order to enter ghosthood. Benjamin Heap's leaves rustled as he nodded slowly. He understood—his sister was old now and it was Time.

As the sun began to sink in the sky, Silas and Sam said a tearful farewell to Aunt Zelda. Their last glimpse was of her leaning quietly against Benjamin Heap, surrounded by a pool of sunlight. Aunt Zelda smiled at them and then she seemed to fade away, her worn old patchwork dress blending into the dappled shadows of the glade.

MAXIE

When the Forest Heaps came to the Castle for Simon's wedding, they had—at Sarah's insistence—stayed with Sarah and Silas in their old room in the Ramblings. On their first night there, Jenna, Nicko, Septimus and Simon came over and everyone spent a wonderful evening together. It was past midnight when Maxie lay down beside the fire with the Heap boys, just as he used to do. He was, Nicko remarked, wearing a typical Maxie smile as he fell asleep. The old wolfhound never woke up: he died surrounded by all the people who loved him.

MARWICK

As soon as Wolf Boy became Keeper he knew he had outgrown his old name. Now he truly was Marwick. His first act as Keeper was to successfully use Aunt Zelda's potion, and all she had taught him, to bring Edmund and Ernold back from the brink of death. From then on, all his doubts about whether he had the skills to be Keeper were stilled.

After Jenna's Coronation, Marwick returned alone to Keeper's Cottage. Although he missed Aunt Zelda very much, he enjoyed his own company and was content with only the Boggart and Bert for company—plus a few pet rocks that had evaded capture. However, with the Dragon Boat now permanently based at the Castle, Marwick did begin to wonder what the purpose of being Keeper was. It was not until much later when a visit from Sam—a visit that surprised not only Marwick but Sam, too—made him understand that he was also Keeper of one of the most Ancient Ways. After that Marwick embarked on an incredible voyage of discovery. The entire world, he realized, was at his feet.

MERRIN AND NURSIE

Merrin and Nursie were successfully fished out of the Moat, but both were very shocked and bruised, and Nursie had a broken arm. They spent some time in the Sick Bay recovering, then returned to the Doll House and resumed their chaotic lives. But things were subtly improved. Their neighbors, the Port Witch Coven, now treated them with respect, and all the petty **Spells** and **Bothers** that had regularly come flying over the backyard fence stopped, and Nursie relaxed.

To Merrin's surprise, Nursie never reproached him for pulling the lever and sending her hurtling down the terrifying dark slide into the Moat, and for the first time in his life, Merrin actually felt remorse for something he had done. He began to understand that his mother really did care for him no matter what he did, and he, too, began to relax.

Merrin made a big effort to be nice to his mother—he was not always successful—but Nursie appreciated the effort. Merrin's first genuine smile was a big occasion for Nursie. She knew then that one day her Merrin would be a good boy—with any luck.

SYRAH SYARA

Syrah remained weak and confused for many months after she woke. Marcia gave Julius Pike leave to stay in the Wizard Tower, and the ghost spent much of the time talking to Syrah about the old days. Eventually Dandra Draa decided that this was not doing Syrah any good and suggested that Julius go back to his old haunts. To Marcia's surprise, Syrah seemed relieved to see Julius leave, and from then on she began to grow stronger.

Syrah moved to some rooms at the top of the Ramblings and spent most of her time tending her rooftop garden. She remembered little **Magyk** and had no recollection of her time on the Isles of Syren, although seeing Septimus always made her feel uneasy.

THE FOREST HEAPS

SAM

Sam seriously considered taking up Silas's suggestion of an Ordinary Apprenticeship at the Wizard Tower, but after his walk into the Forest with Silas and Aunt Zelda, things changed for Sam. He realized that he belonged outdoors—the inside world of the Wizard Tower was not for him. And so, after telling a disappointed Silas that he had decided against an Apprenticeship, Sam accompanied Marwick back to Draggen Island and helped him get settled.

In the autumn Sam returned to Camp Heap in the Forest and was shocked to discover that it was now occupied by a wolverine pack. He narrowly escaped attack and spent an uncomfortable Big Freeze up in the trees with Galen the Physik woman. By the time of the Big Thaw, Sam had had enough. He returned to the Castle, and it did not take much persuading to get the other three Forest Heaps to head out to the Marshes with him that summer. (Luckily for Edd and Erik, Marcia had decreed that all Apprentices were now allowed a month's vacation.) The Forest Heaps spent a happy month in the sunshine of the Marram Marshes and the company of Marwick, reliving their Camp Heap times together. Summer in the Marram Marshes became a fixture for the Forest Heaps for many years to come.

EDD AND ERIK

It was Edd and Erik who eventually took up Apprenticeships at the Wizard Tower, so once again the Wizard Tower was host to twin Heaps—but this time it was a much more successful relationship. Edd and Erik joined the Apprentice Rotation Scheme and settled in happily, living in the Apprentice Dorm in the old Sick Bay on the first floor of the Wizard Tower. They learned fast and were, as Silas said to Sarah many times, a credit to the Heap name.

JO-JO

To Sarah's dismay, Jo-Jo Heap moved out of the Palace into a small room at the less-scary end of Dagger Dan's Dive and got a job in Gothyk Grotto in order to be close to his ex-girlfriend, Marissa. With Matt and Marcus Marwick already working there, this did not make for a harmonious atmosphere in "the Grot," as it was known to its fans. There were many occasions when Igor, the owner of Gothyk Grotto, was tempted to fire the entire staff and begin again, but the truth was that the four teens were a charismatic bunch and brought in a lot of customs. Jo-Jo in particular—being the son of a Wizard and fluent in basic **Magyk**—was a great asset. So Igor retreated to his room at the back of the shop, learned some new riffs on his nose flute and left them to it.

OTHER HEAPS

NICKO

Nicko finished his Apprenticeship with Jannit and became a partner at the boatyard, allowing Jannit to take six months off each year and do hibernation in a big way. Two summers later, a letter from Snorri mentioning a tall, young fisherman unsettled Nicko more than he had expected, and he began to make plans. Wisely he decided not to mention them to his mother. Not just yet.

SIMON AND LUCY

Simon continued as Apprentice to Marcellus. He enjoyed most aspects of the job—apart from the guided tours of the Great Chamber of Alchemie and Physik. But Simon had learned enough about life to understand that nothing is perfect, and when Marcia asked him to be the liaison between the Great Chamber and the Wizard Tower, Simon accepted with great pleasure. Now at last he had a reason to come and go as he pleased at the Wizard Tower—something that he had never thought possible.

After the completion of the Alchemie Chimney, a craze for fancy turrets swept the Castle and Lucy found that she was much in demand. She quickly had many projects under way—which was good because the knitted-curtains business never quite took off. And soon Lucy's comments to Simon about baby feet made perfect sense—Sarah was thrilled to discover that the first Heap grandchild was expected on MidWinter Feast Day.

SILAS AND SARAH

Silas went back to working at the Wizard Tower, where he kept an anxious watch on Ernold and Edmund and a proud eye on Edd and Erik. Silas was very touched when Marcia, apologizing for doubting him and keeping him in the Stranger Chamber, gave him the Counter-Feet **Charm** that she had discovered in the Pyramid Library during her reinstatement of the Alchemie files. Silas immediately began creating new Counter-Feet sets and arranging a tournament. Sarah settled into a happy round of spending time with Jenna at the Palace, checking up on Jo-Jo (and really annoying him) and visiting Edd and Erik (and, at times, annoying them, too). Lucy also saw more of her mother-in-law than she would have liked but she appreciated Sarah's attempts to help her get the house sorted out in time for the new arrival.

SEPTIMUS

Now that Septimus knew in his heart that **Magyk** was what he truly wanted to do, his Apprenticeship settled into an uneventful course. Both he and Marcia enjoyed the last years of his Apprenticeship—the first not to be blighted by the specter of the **Draw** for the **Queste** hanging over it. Septimus and Rose spent more and more time together, much to Marcia's disapproval, but that is another story.

THE LITTLE GIRL IN THE FISHERMAN'S SHACK

Alice TodHunter Moon was the name of the little girl who waved to Septimus the night he flew the Dragon Boat to the House of Foryx. Alice—who answered only to the name of Tod—never forgot her sight of the Dragon Boat that night. It sustained her through many difficult times. She knew that one day she, too, would fly in the Dragon Boat and meet the great Wizard who waved to her from the stars. Alice was right, and her story is soon to be told in the TodHunter Moon series.

Thank You

There are some special people I really want to thank for being part of Septimus, without whom the series would not be the same—or quite possibly would not have happened at all.

So . . . a big, big thank-you to my agent and friend, Eunice McMullen, who was the first to see the beginning of *Magyk* and love it. Eunice, thanks for all your support over the years and for making sure that Septimus & Co. got a great home with HarperCollins in the USA and then with Bloomsbury in the UK.

An equally massive thank-you to my editor and friend at HarperCollins, Katherine Tegen, from whom I have learned so much about writing and without whom I know the Septimus Heap series would not have grown to be what it is.

And to Mark Zug, whose beautiful and atmospheric

pictures for Septimus Heap never fail to amaze and delight and are always *so* just right. I don't know how Mark does it, but he seems to have a direct line to what Septimus is about. Thank you, Mark.

Thank you to my husband, Rhodri, who has patiently read each book many times in their various drafts and still insists that he really *does* enjoy them—and who listens with great attention while I try to explain the myriad twists of plot and get my thoughts straight for the umpteenth time. *And* does the VAT.

To my lovely Laurie, whose quick-fire ideas have been an inspiration and such *fun*.

To my equally lovely Lois, who once had to read the first four chapters of the initial draft of *Magyk* before she was allowed any pizza—and then tell me what she thought.

To Dave Johnson, without whom Nicko would not have had an attack of the giggles at the Wendron Witch Summer Circle.

To Karen and Peter Collins, who helped us keep going when times got tough when I was writing *Physik*.

To all the copy editors, particularly Brenna, who so patiently and graciously read through the final drafts of all the books and from whom I have learned a whole ton of stuff about writing nitty-gritty—particularly echo and repetition and repetition and echo.

And thank you to all the translators who do such amazing work in **Transcribing** the Septimus Heap series into other languages, and especially to the ones—hello, Merlin—who ask the most amazingly detailed questions in order to make sure everything is as good as it can be.

Thank you, too, to all the wonderful foreign publishers who have put so much into the series, particularly to the great people I have met over the years: Albin Michel in France, Hanser in Germany, Querido in Holland, Wahlströms/Forma Books in Sweden, WSOY in Finland, Pegasus in Estonia, Ursula at the British Council in Tallinn, and g'day to all at Allen & Unwin in Sydney.

And last but definitely not least, thank you to all at Bloomsbury Publishing here in the UK, especially my editor, Ele Fountain.

You've all been **Magyk**!